W9-BUP-376

The Magdalena Curse

Also by F. G. Cottam

The House of Lost Souls

Dark Echo

The Magdalena Curse

F. G. Cottam

Thomas Dunne Books
St. Martin's Press
New York

This is a work of fiction. All of the characters, organizations, and events portrayed in this novel are either products of the author's imagination or are used fictitiously.

THOMAS DUNNE BOOKS.
An imprint of St. Martin's Press.

THE MAGDALENA CURSE. Copyright © 2009 by F. G. Cottam. All rights reserved. Printed in the United States of America. For information, address St. Martin's Press, 175 Fifth Avenue, New York, N.Y. 10010.

www.thomasdunnebooks.com
www.stmartins.com

Library of Congress Cataloging-in-Publication Data

ISBN 978-0-312-64325-6

First published in Great Britain by Hodder & Stoughton, an Hachette UK company

First U.S. Edition: August 2011

10 9 8 7 6 5 4 3 2 1

A12005 724187

For Haydn, Alison, Emmeline and Joseph. With love.

I would like to thank John and his staff at the Riverside Cafe on Queen's Promenade for alleviating writerly solitude with their unfailing warmth and good cheer. Not to mention world class cappuccino.

The Magdalena Curse

Chapter One

In his bedroom on the floor above her, she heard the boy shift in his sleep and murmur or sigh to himself. She looked up at the thick beams and rough plaster of the low sitting-room ceiling. The boy's room, small and once a cosy refuge for him, was over to the right. She had become very alert to sound in the night. The boy's torment had made her so. She looked at her watch and saw that it was close to one in the morning. She got up and poked at the embers of the dying fire, then returned to the armchair and made a shawl again of her blanket, around her shoulders. She made a pillow of the cushion at her back. There was no more noise from above. She could hear the sound of wood greying into ash in the hearth before which she sat. It was a trickle, infinitely faint. She could hear her own heart. That was a steady, rhythmic thump. She could hear the wind soft on the slope of heather outside, harsher through the branches of the yew tree beyond the kitchen door. So sensitive to noise had she become, that she could no longer bear to light the room at night with the scented candles she had packed before coming here. The hiss of wax and the guttering of wicks were sounds she could no longer comfortably endure.

She smiled to herself, huddling under her blanket. She was probably as alert to sound as all his military training had made the owner of this house. He was away, had left two days ago, pursuing the most urgent mission of his life. He was retired now. He had retired a full colonel but had done so early. He was still relatively young, still fit, a formidable man.

I

But she did not think that any of his dangerous skills would help him very much in trying to save the son he loved. She very much hoped, in this, that she was wrong.

She looked at the little table next to where she sat. Her laptop lay open on the table. She left it there, she thought sometimes, simply to remind herself of who and what she was. There were two lines of italics centred on the screen. They emerged white out of the blackness surrounding them. *This computer is the property of Dr Elizabeth Bancroft.* That much, she knew. That much, she was certain of. But the last few days, lived in this high and remote place, had left her sure about very little else.

She thought about picking the laptop up and searching the internet again to establish what more she could about the symptoms manifested by the poor child upstairs whose father had entrusted him to her care. But after the most recent episode, she knew she would merely be going through the motions. That event, witnessing it, had finally put paid to all her high-flown theories. There had been various theories. They had ranged from food intolerance, to delayed shock and deferred grief, to the effect of over-exposure to violent video games. She had entertained all of them to varying degrees. And in their way, in their elegance and plausibility, they had entertained her. But they had proven to be nothing to do with what was happening to the boy.

It was what doctors did, wasn't it? It was not dissembling and it wasn't avoidance. It was diagnostic discipline. Without an effective diagnosis, you could not treat illness effectively and therefore you were useless to your patient. She had looked for a rational explanation as to what was wrong with the child, compelled by instinct and professional habit, and if she was really honest also by professional pride. But now her instinct was strongly at odds with her discipline. It had been since the events in the boy's bedroom, the night that provoked his father's departure. Since then, for two days, she had been in turmoil over it. She realised how deluded and complaisant she had been before. She was not complaisant now. She wanted to call the boy's father, ask him what progress he was making. But he might answer, hoping for comfort from home, for encouraging news. And she could offer none. Remote from the last person left in the world whom he loved, Elizabeth did not want to make matters any worse for him.

She looked around the room. It was lit by a desk lamp sharing the table with her laptop and a standard lamp over against the wall next to the door that led to the stairs. There was no noticeable light from her feeble log fire. The walls were of exposed brick between supporting beams and the floor was flagged in stone. The windows were uneven in size and latticed with lead and looked gratifyingly sturdy. The house had been here since the fifteenth century and the room reflected the fact. There were rugs on the floor. The furniture was old and plain and of a piece with the building that housed it. They had brought no artefacts with them, Mark Hunter and his ten-year-old boy, Adam. They had brought no pictures or keepsakes to remind them of Mark's dead wife and daughter, the mother and sister lost to his son. There was nothing on display, anyway. She assumed it was all locked away in their hearts.

'Call me Mark,' he had said, extending his hand on her first visit here, after the early episodes of Adam's affliction. She had arrived in the morning, at 7 a.m., at the beginning of her working day. She was aware of course of the concern he felt for his son. That had been obvious from his tone of voice when he reached her at the surgery. But meeting him, she had seen something else. She did not think of herself as an intuitive woman. Here, she did not need to be. She was familiar with the story. Everyone in the locality had heard about the tragedy. And when she met him, she saw more than worry over the nightmares afflicting the boy. Her first impression was of how handsome a man Mark Hunter was. But grief marked him. He wore his loss as starkly as a shadow cast in strong sunlight.

Adam was asleep when first she saw him. He was lying on his back. His head rested on his pillow and his face was raised to the milky morning light. It was unlined of course and framed by wavy blond hair worn long. She knew that children were often seductive little creatures in repose, their features innocent of mischief while they slept. But he was not merely cute. Adam Hunter was extraordinary. There was no other word adequate to describe him than the one that came into her mind. He was neither cute nor angelic nor exotic. He was simply the most beautiful boy Elizabeth had ever seen.

'Fine-featured,' Mark Hunter said, from behind her, reading her thoughts. 'He's fortunate in that he takes after his mother in his looks. But he's been a tormented little soul these past couple of weeks.' He edged past her and reached for his son, brushing the hair away from Adam's forehead where the damp of perspiration had stuck it in strands. He did this tenderly. And then he stooped and kissed his son there.

Elizabeth had put her doctor's bag on the bed. She opened it with a click that was Mark Hunter's cue to leave her with her patient. He took the hint. 'I'll see you downstairs, doctor,' he said.

'Please call me Elizabeth. He's sleeping deeply. I won't wake him just to ask questions. If he wakes of his own accord, I'll interrogate very gently.'

'Do what you must.'

'I'll examine him. I'll take his temperature and gauge his

blood pressure. I will need to speak to the child. We may require a referral and can't refer without a thorough examination, which means an assessment of his emotional state.'

'I'm gratified you have the time.'

Elizabeth looked at her watch. She lifted Adam's wrist, feeling for his pulse. She smiled at his father. 'I don't,' she said.

Adam's room had a view through its single window of the heather descending in green and purple swathes down the hill. At the bottom of the hill, the stream glimmered in the morning mist she had climbed out of on the drive up there. She looked around the room, impressed by how much his father had done in making it a den for his boy. She supposed he had been mostly away at his various clandestine wars until the deaths of his wife and daughter. She guessed it had been pretty much his wife's job entirely to carry out the domestic commitments. But it was his now, and in the fabric and furnishings of the child's room, in its posters and shelves of books and toys, it had been thoughtfully accomplished.

After the examination, while she waited for the child to wake, he made her tea.

'How long have you been keeping him out of school?'

'Just for these last few days. It's caught up with him. He hasn't the concentration.' He looked at his watch. 'You must have other house calls to make.'

'Let's give him twenty minutes. If he doesn't stir in that time I'll come back tomorrow.'

'How does he seem to you?'

'He's slightly underweight. He's perhaps very slightly anaemic. His pulse is rapid for a sleeping ten-year-old. But generally he is healthy.'

Mark Hunter looked at her. His hair was greying. He had blue eyes. Their pale clarity belied the things she supposed they must have seen in a bloody career.

'When did it start?'

'The nightmares began about three weeks ago. At least, that's when he started to complain about them, to fear his room and his bed. It would get to eight o'clock and the approach of bedtime and I'd see the trepidation on his face. But it began before then. I'd heard him mumbling before that, Adam talking to himself.'

'It's normal for children to talk to themselves.'

'Not to argue with themselves it isn't, doctor. Not to indulge in ferocious debate.'

She thought it interesting that he reverted to the formality of her title when he felt his judgement challenged. 'He has a computer in his room.'

'Equipped with a firewall and all the other safeguards you'd expect. You've seen the pictures stuck up on his walls. He likes Manchester United and listens to Girls Aloud.'

'No monsters, then.'

'No monsters.'

'At least, no monsters to your knowledge.'

Hunter frowned. He sipped tea.

'After the accident, did Adam sleep with you?'

'For a while he did, yes. And it was as much for my comfort as for his. But crying one another to sleep each night was not healthy for either of us. That stopped when we moved here.'

'Abruptly?'

'You will not think this a case of separation anxiety when my son wakes, doctor,' he said.

She framed another question in her mind. She felt she was gaining valuable insights. But the question never got asked. There was a keening cry from above. It was a sound of such abject terror that it caused the hairs to rise and prickle coldly on the back of Elizabeth's neck.

Mark Hunter was on his feet. 'I'll introduce you and then

6

leave you with him. The dreams scare him but he wakes from them lucid and with only a vague conscious memory of what he dreamed of. But they leave something for a few hours. They leave a residue.'

'They leave a what?'

'You will see.'

'Dad?' The voice from above them was plaintive.

Mark hesitated.

'What?' Elizabeth asked.

He looked at her and the look was hard. 'Please remember your promise to question my son gently.'

It was cold when he left her with Adam. The boy sat up in his striped pyjamas, pale and alert. It felt so cold to her in his room that she was surprised she could not see his breath when he exhaled. She extended a hand to the radiator. The metal was hot under her fingers. And the window was open only a fraction. Outside, it was a mild November morning. It was warmer out than in and that made no sense. She smiled at Adam and he tried to smile back as she poured him a glass of water from the carafe on his bedside table. She looked at the posters on the walls. His team posed confident and grinning for their formal start-of-season photograph, various players grinning and triumphant, parading trophies in grainier, blown-up shots placed around it.

'Is Rooney your favourite player?'

'Paul Scholes,' he said. His voice was shaky. He tried to smile again. He could not will away the desperation in his face.

'What did you dream about, Adam?'

He raised his glass between both hands and drank. 'I don't remember. It was a cold place, I think. I think there was snow and ice. I think there were big icicles there, pointed in the cold. But there were no people or buildings or cars or anything.'

7

'Was it scary?'

He looked down at the glass in his hands. 'It's always scary,' he said.

She opened her bag, reached for her thermometer. He had not been running a fever before the dream. But in the chilly room, in its aftermath, she would have bet money he was running a fever now.

She was with Adam for twenty minutes. It was long enough with a ten-year-old child. She did not want to exhaust him. He was getting a lot of sleep, but little apparent rest. When she had said goodbye to him, his father walked her across the gravel spread outside his house to the stand of conifers where she had parked her car on the bony, hilltop earth.

'He speaks fluent Russian, Mark. I'm impressed. It's an unusual accomplishment in a child. He must be very bright. How long has he been studying the language?'

Mark bit his lip and looked at the ground. 'He doesn't speak a word of Russian, Elizabeth. In a few hours, he won't remember a single syllable.'

'I don't understand.'

'It's what I told you about. It's the residue the dreams leave. After a few hours, it vanishes like dew.'

'How can that be?'

'The dreams belong to someone else. My son is possessed by them.'

'Does he know what you did in the military?'

'No.'

'You were in the SAS.'

'Was I?'

'You were involved in covert operations. You were awarded medals for gallantry.'

'Was I?'

'It was in the paper, Mark. When you came here and bought this place, it was in the *Chronicle*.'

'If it was in the *Chronicle*, then it must be true.'

'You must be open with me if I am to help your son.'

'And I shall be, doctor. But you asked me about what Adam knows. Being open to you is not the same as bragging to my son about the men I've killed.'

Elizabeth got into her car. She was gifted at languages. She spoke only a smattering of Russian from a voluntary stint a few years earlier gained during the second Chechen conflict. She had not had the time to learn the complex subtleties of the Russian tongue. Events had intervened. Adam had spoken it with much profanity in a strong Siberian dialect.

The dreams belonged to someone else.

She had made a fool of herself in front of Mark Hunter. She was not sure of very much about the morning's events, but she was certain of that. Driving away from him, she did not think she had ever felt more foolish in her adult life.

He called her that afternoon. She had given him her mobile number in case of emergency. Her practice was largely rural, far flung. Isolation itself was a problem, a cause of anxiety, for some of her elderly patients in particular. Giving them the mobile number could allay that. What it cost her in privacy she thought a worthy sacrifice to their peace of mind. Healing was a vocation to Elizabeth Bancroft. She thought that being a general practitioner was a sometimes rewarding, sometimes difficult, profession. But her compulsion to do it was a deep and instinctive desire.

'I've rung to apologise,' he said. 'I was high-handed, arrogant with you.'

'And I was the village busybody gossiping at the parish pump,' she said.

He laughed.

'How is Adam?'

'No longer bilingual. Okay. Subdued. This morning you mentioned the possibility of a referral?'

'I don't think the need is acute. But we should not discuss his case over the phone. I'll call in tomorrow evening, on my way home. I can chat to Adam before he goes to bed and then outline my thoughts afterwards with you.'

'You work long hours.'

'Yes, Mark. I do.'

She felt relieved that he had called. She was concerned about Adam's case. She wanted no unnecessary obstacles to bringing a happy conclusion to his ordeal. Thankfully, that appeared to be his father's only priority too. It was why he had phoned her. He was pretty desperate, she thought, under the English, officer-class poise he affected. His son was all he had and Colonel Mark Hunter MC, GC loved the boy very much. She did not think it was the first time he had needed to apologise for his arrogance. It was an inclination in his character he had to struggle to overcome. That was as clear to her as it must be to him. But she was still ashamed of reciting hearsay gleaned from the local free-sheet. That remark she had made about the shrew at the parish pump had come from the heart. Her own family had been victims of cruel gossip down the years. At times it had amounted to persecution. On a couple of occasions it had provoked actual violence. On one occasion, a long time ago, the violence had been terrible. She believed rumour to be pernicious. The way to establish what Adam Hunter knew about his father was to ask Mark, who would tell her truthfully. He had admitted to being a killer to her. But the killing was contingent, had been done in the cause of Queen and Country. Anyway, Elizabeth did not believe his father's dubious exploits the cause of Adam's nightmares. She had seen the way the boy looked at his father. The look was open, adoring. 'Dad' had been the first word on his lips when he woke from his dream, seeking refuge from the fears that haunted his sleep.

She wondered how much Mark knew about the history of his house. All old houses had some pain or tragedy attached to them in this part of the world, she thought. The Highlands had endured some bloody periods down the centuries. Nowhere around here had been immune. Mark's house had been home to a witch finder sent from Westminster by order of Parliament in the time of Oliver Cromwell. Cromwell's imperialist adventures in Ireland were well chronicled. But he had been just as harsh in Scotland. The witch finder had been one more symbol of the brutal oppression England could inflict, on a whim, on its self-styled Commonwealth. He had come and he had found his witches. Of course he had. He had probably been given a quota to meet back in London. He had conducted his trials and got his confessions using the iron heated in the forge and the drowning bucket and the thumbscrews. And he had inflicted his burnings on his poor innocent culprits. And he had been cursed savagely for it all. And he had lived in that very house until felled by the stroke that killed him. It was said that the smell of singed flesh clung to the hills for decades after. But Elizabeth believed only the factual part of the story. And she did not think Judge Josiah Jerusalem Smith, or the curse under which he laboured, responsible for the dreams afflicting Adam Hunter now. Puritans frowned even at Latin. Men like Cromwell's witch finders did not generally inspire anyone to speak Russian.

Her journey to the Hunters' house was slow and difficult the following night. Fog was common in the Highlands in the autumn. But it clung most tenaciously to the gullies and vales and stream banks, and to the forested land. Generally it thinned as you ascended in altitude. But it did not do so on this night. Darkness came very early, conjured prematurely by the mist. Elizabeth was not that familiar with the road. Mist wrapped the car in pale tendrils, an opaque blanket of grey smothering her windscreen as her headlights failed to pick out landmarks and she was filled with the weird impression that the car was no longer anchored beneath her to the earth. She crawled in a kind of limbo along the road for a while, aware of the steep banks descending sharply to either side only when the car canted and the tyres juddered and she corrected her steering. She had hoped to arrive at 7.30. But it was past 8 p.m. when she finally made out the light above her, climbing the hill towards it.

Hunter met her by the door, where he must have been listening out for the approaching noise of her engine.

'There's been a development,' he said, ushering her in, before she could apologise for her lateness. He looked worried. He looked tormented.

She unbuttoned her coat and he took it from her and hung it on a peg beside the door.

'What kind of development?'

'Things have escalated. It has got worse. He's talking now in his sleep. I tried to keep him awake for you. We were playing chess. But he fell asleep over the board, poor little fellow. He's exhausted. I'd carried him up and was tucking him in when the muttering started. I don't know whether to rouse him or leave him. It's gone beyond the conventions of nightmare. He's living the dreams. He's whispering in languages that were dead a thousand years ago.'

Elizabeth put a hand on Hunter's arm. She squeezed. He was close to tears, almost unmanned by what was happening upstairs to his son.

'Have you anything strong to drink?'

'I've whisky.'

'Pour two inches into a glass and swallow it down.'

He tried to smile. 'That's your prescription?'

'Do it. I'll go up,' she said.

Adam was lying peacefully on his back. His breathing seemed regular but slow. His mouth was slightly open and there was a bluish tinge to his complexion that Elizabeth did not like very much. Once again it felt bitterly cold in the room despite a radiator too hot for her to touch for more than a couple of seconds. He was talking. But it wasn't in his own clear, piping tone. There were separate voices. It was like some skilled act of ventriloquism. The voices emanated from his chest and their words were articulated without the boy moving his lips even a fraction. It was uncanny, like a radio broadcast of stories recounted in biblical times, and the very remoteness of the tongues made her shiver in the chill of the room.

Elizabeth had an involuntary memory then, recalling with perfect clarity seeing a ventriloquist perform in a variety show broadcast on television when she had been a little girl of about four or five. The dummy sitting on its master's lap had sung a song while the ventriloquist himself had very deliberately drunk a tall glass of milk empty. She remembered the song. It was, 'I Belong to Glasgow'. She had been puzzled, wondering how it was done. Now, more than a quarter of a century on, she puzzled again, wondering how this squall of dead voices was emerging from the mouth of the sleeping boy.

Some of it was in Latin. Some of it was Classical Greek. She thought some of it was from St Luke's Gospel, recited in Hebrew. She recognised quite a long passage from Milton's *Paradise Lost*, sonorously intoned in an English dialect she had never heard spoken. The really unnerving thing was when two voices spoke at the same time. One rising babble of voices almost forced her to flee from where she stood. There was anger and mockery there in the chill room and she could equate none of it with Adam. She lifted one of his eyelids and then measured his pulse. His heart rate was regular and his sleep deep, even if it wasn't restful. The voices subsided for a moment and she crept out in the charged silence. They were no more alive, the voices, she thought, than had been the ventriloquist's doll. If they had been, they would have addressed her. She did not think she could have endured that. This was bad. But she thought there was some explanation that the science of her calling could accommodate. Had the voices addressed her, had they acknowledged her presence, she would have been staring at the void.

Hunter was seated in one of two armchairs angled to face the hearth when she descended the stairs. She could smell the peaty aroma of whisky. An open bottle and two glasses occupied a small table placed between the chairs. She would not join him in a drink. The unfamiliar road would require total sobriety even if the fog had lifted. Elizabeth had seen the carnage caused by vodka-fuelled driving in her time in Russia. She had seen the victims thrown through windscreens on arctic nights, pasted by their innards and then welded by them, frozen to the bark of the conifers their cars had collided with. Such sights offered no encouragement to drink and drive. A decade on, the gory images of accidental death still stayed with her.

'I think he is undergoing some kind of nervous trauma,' she said. She sat down. 'I think he has downloaded something, some game involving magic or possession or demonology or a stew of those things. It's overwhelmed him. We should check if any of his schoolmates are similarly afflicted.'

'They're not. You would know. They would be your patients. And you know it isn't that.'

'You should have his computer's hard drive examined and find out what is on it. And find out what he's deleted from it. It isn't just download sites. Check your credit and debit card bills. See if he has bought something on eBay, some hardcore Death Metal-inspired thing, some game involving the Apocalypse. Or one of the occult series shown on television in America and available here as a box set of DVDs. Some of those shows are heavy stuff.'

'You think my son was reduced to this by watching episodes of *Buffy*?'

'Check whether he's subscribed to an online fraternity. The Goth subculture can be very dark.'

'It isn't that. You know bloody well it isn't.'

It was quiet, now. The murmurs from above had ceased. Adam lay quietly and apparently still in his bed. She heard something large caper by outside. It brushed the wall of the house with a coarse flank. A deer, she thought, befuddled, made clumsy by the mist.

'There's something I didn't tell you, Mark.'

Hunter drained his glass. 'I'm just going to have a look at him. Make sure he's okay.'

He came back down half a minute later. There was relief on his face, which was slightly flushed by the whisky.

'There's something I need to tell you,' she said again.

'And there's something I need to tell you. But by all means, ladies first.'

She paused. And then she began. 'I told you Adam spoke yesterday morning in fluent Russian.'

'In a strong Siberian accent.'

'And in the persona of a man who recited his name. I did not tell you that part. He was speaking in character.'

'He told you who he was?'

'He stated who he was. He did not engage with me at all. It was not a conversation. It was a speech, a recitation. His voice was raised no louder when I turned my back on him to discover whether it would be. It was not communication. It was impersonation.'

'It was possession. What was the name he gave?'

Again, Elizabeth paused. 'He stated that his name was Grigori Yefimovich Novy. Does that mean anything to you?'

'Yes. Novy was born in Pokrovskoye, in Siberia. The date of his birth was probably 1869. The world knew him better as Grigori Rasputin.'

'Don't you see, Mark? You can just picture some Californian cyber-geek game designer namechecking Rasputin for level three of his warlocks and wizards conspiracy fest. And it has affected a boy, too young to play the game, in the traumatic way we see upstairs. Adam needs psychiatric help, Mark. He has downloaded and been exposed to something he shouldn't have and has frightened himself out of his wits. You are right that the condition has worsened. I know a really good man in Edinburgh. He's expensive, but he will prioritise a case as unusual as this. And he's a kind man with kids of his own.'

Hunter poured himself an inch of whisky. It was the single malt, Oban, she saw from the label, paler than any blend Elizabeth was familiar with, even in the firelight in front of which they sat. She was not a whisky drinker herself. But she had once been very close to someone who was. He raised the glass. The liquor had an oily sheen and moved with an almost viscous laziness as he swirled it in front of his face. She could smell the whisky and she could smell the resin from the pine logs burning in the grate. And there was something else, some rather more esoteric scent she could not place. Perhaps Mark Hunter wore cologne. Military men could be as vain as peacocks. It would not require premeditation to dab on a bit of scent. Quite the opposite, if it was his general habit.

'A psychiatrist.'

'A brilliant man. A compassionate man, also.'

Hunter nodded. He downed his drink. He stood and went

across to an oak chest positioned against the far wall and took some items from a drawer there. They chinked when he put them on the top of the chest. Then he scooped them up and brought them back and they fell from his hands on to their little shared table. She saw his Military Cross and his George Cross on their crisp coloured ribbons. So it was true. He was a hero. There was a medal with the citation scored in French. There was another with an American eagle impressed on the polished bronze. He sat heavily back in his chair and gestured at the decorations.

'Baubles,' he said.

She wondered, was it the whisky talking? She did not think it was. A man with his background would have a good head for the stuff. Discretion had been the basic pre-requisite of his entire military career. Drink might have made him more open to her, less inhibited. But the margin would be slight.

'I have lost my wife and daughter. If I lose my son, my life amounts to the trinkets on that table. Do you know the line from Eliot, Elizabeth?'

She believed she did. It came from *The Waste Land*. It was the famous line about shoring fragments against one's ruins in a bleak attempt at some sort of consolation. She quoted it. Hunter listened as she did so and then sighed.

'Well. These fragments are not enough. I want my boy to have his chance at life. He is my legacy and my gift to the world and my gift to him is his chance at living. I will not willingly have him denied it. Do you understand?'

He was crying. He was doing so silently. But the tears tracked glistening down his face in the orange cast of the firelight.

'You said you had something to tell me.'

He sniffed. 'Adam is possessed. He is the victim of a curse. I incurred it twelve years ago in Bolivia. It was pledged that my progeny would commune with the dead. The hag who cursed me was doubly right, in the event. But I don't think she was thinking of my wife and daughter. I think she was referring to this. And of course it has come to pass.'

Whatever large beast capered outside, it had not left the vicinity of the house. Elizabeth heard the rough smear of its hide on stone again, the scrape of horn on the leaded window glass. There was a snort, or whinny. There was the drag and clatter of heavy hooves.

'Do you think there is anything you can do?'

'There was white as well as black magic in that place. A kind of conflict was being waged there.'

'You actually believe this?'

'I saw it. There was a white witch. She was old and very powerful. She could help me. She could help Adam, if I could find her.'

'Twelve years, Mark. She was old then. She could be dead.'

'No,' he said. 'If she was dead, this wouldn't be happening. This is her ordeal, her test. That was how it was always meant to be played out. I see that now. And if I'm to save my son I have to find her.'

Elizabeth looked at the medals on the little table between them. They shared space with the bottle of Oban and the two glasses, one used, one still free of whisky's happy contamination. The medals looked like nothing in the dull light of the fire. But she had seen combat and its aftermath. She knew something of the courage and selflessness they must have taken to earn. Fuck it, she said to herself. She poured an inch and drank it down in a gulp. 'Would you not consider the psychiatrist, Mark? At my sincere request? Would you not have someone qualified examine the boy's computer files?'

He smiled, but not at her. The thing outside blundered against the door. Hinges strained and the mortise clacked loudly, but Mark ignored it. Elizabeth decided that she would too. She suspected that Mark Hunter had a large gun somewhere for use against threats like the one perhaps posed by whatever was lurking in his grounds. The metal hoard on the table told her he would use his gun coolly and well. Whatever the thing outside was, it posed no threat to Hunter and his son. Whatever slouched out there was too big and too solid a target.

'Why are you smiling?'

'Do you not wonder what that smell is, Elizabeth?'

The scent she had detected earlier had grown much stronger and more prevalent. It drowned the odour of the whisky and the fire. It was not the vain colonel's cologne, unless he had spilled a bottle of the stuff.

'It's frankincense,' Hunter said. 'It smells of fresh pine and lemons, does it not?'

Elizabeth nodded. It did. Richly and intensely so.

'It comes from the country in Africa we now call Somalia. It was popular in the Eastern world at the time of the birth of Christ. It was brought back to Europe by the Templars, after the First Crusade. Western Christians waited a thousand years to smell the stuff brought as a gift to the Nazareth stable by one of the three attendant kings. I believe its source in my house tonight is the room occupied by my son. And I can promise you, its presence here has nothing to do with the hard drive of his computer.'

She stayed the night. The mist did not dissipate and she was too unnerved to risk the road. The spare bedroom was warm and comfortable and the rest of the night passed without incident. The smell of incense was weakening even as she brushed her teeth and in the morning was entirely gone. So was the fog. She enjoyed a stroke of luck when she saw the message light on her phone flashing and discovered her first appointment of the day, a meeting with a pharmaceuticals company rep, had been cancelled. It gave her the opportunity to have a chat with her patient before she was obliged to leave the house.

She found him at the table in the sitting room, still in his pyjamas. He had his elbows on the table and his head rested in his hands. He was frowning, staring at the pieces on the chessboard left from the unfinished game of the previous night. His father was in the kitchen preparing breakfast. He was humming something tunelessly. It occurred to her that once upon a time, Mark Hunter had probably been a happy sort of man. She pulled out a chair and sat beside Adam.

'Do you ever beat him?'

'Occasionally. When he lets me.'

'When he's in a good mood?'

'When he thinks I need the encouragement of a win to keep on playing. But I can tell he's losing on purpose, even when he pretends he's struggling. My dad's a really crappy actor.'

She laughed.

He smiled at her. 'Sorry. I'm not supposed to say crappy. I meant to say Dad's a really lousy actor.'

'Tea or coffee?' Hunter shouted from the kitchen.

'Coffee, please.'

'A Coke for me, Dad.'

'In your dreams.'

Adam turned to her. 'What is wrong with me, doctor? My dad doesn't seem to know and he usually knows everything.'

She paused before replying. 'Did you dream last night? Do you remember your dream?'

He frowned. 'I dreamed something was trying to get into our house in the darkness. It was a wild animal. It was a wolf, I think. But it was massive, the size of a horse.'

'That was the only dream?'

'It was the only one I remember.'

'If I say the word "sleep" to you, what does that make you think of?'

The frown had not lifted from his face. 'Dust,' he said. 'Darkness.'

'I will do everything I can to make you well, Adam. I promise you that.'

The frown lifted. He nodded and smiled at her. But she was aware that she had not answered the question he had asked her. And she could see that he was too.

As soon as she got into the surgery, she emailed the Edinburgh man. She outlined the principal details of the case. He called her back within half an hour. It was Wednesday. He agreed to come and see Adam the following Tuesday. She called Mark Hunter to tell him. He did not seem thrilled by the development. She thought that was natural. In resorting to a succession of strangers to tend to his son, it must seem to him as though Adam and his problems were becoming remote from him. In a loving father, that would not be a pleasant notion. But he was intelligent and had been disciplined all his professional life. He needed to be objective if his son was to be helped. As their short conversation drew to its conclusion, a thought occurred to her.

'When was the last time you went out, Mark?'

'I took Adam to see the military tattoo in Edinburgh.'

'That was months ago. When was the last time you went out as a grown-up?'

He laughed. 'I can't remember.'

'Make plans for Friday night. I'll babysit. Go and have an adult conversation in the pub. Grumble about the weather with someone gnarled and local. Have a few beers. It will do you the world of good.'

'What about your plans for Friday night?'

'They're already sorted. I'm babysitting.' She hung up.

If nothing happens to Adam between now and then.

That had been the unspoken proviso, the precondition that neither of them alluded to, the possibility she knew both of them feared. She prayed that all would remain as it was until Tuesday and the psychiatrist. She felt that once he saw Adam, once he made his sane and fastidious suggestions concerning treatment, all would start to become well. Everything would begin to return to normal. An episode prior to that could be disastrous. It could send Hunter off on his desperate quest to find an ancient witch. What would happen to Adam in his absence? He would be obliged to take the boy with him. But Adam needed calm and comfort and routine, not the chaos of a futile search for some sorceress crone through the empty regions of Latin America.

She thought again about the house. They had lived in a village in Sussex. Then one wintry morning the previous January, the accident had occurred. Lillian Hunter was walking her eight-year-old daughter Kate the half mile to the church hall where her weekly ballet class was held. The car that hit them was being driven too fast on an icy road by a local youth of seventeen who had passed his test only two weeks earlier. The collision happened after his car hit a patch of black ice and went out of control. Lillian and Kate were killed instantly. It was the sort of mundane catastrophe you read about and sighed and shook your head over in the papers in the winter months. And as a consequence, Hunter had left the army and sold up and headed north with his son to escape the past and start afresh without the reminders that would hinder their recovery.

There was nothing wrong with the house. It was isolated, but it was not of itself a sinister or morbid place. It was handsome, picturesque. And in the spring and summer its surrounding countryside was spectacular. Buying it, relocating, was probably the right thing for Hunter in distracting him from his loss. But for Adam? Elizabeth couldn't help wondering at the emotional cost of taking him away from everything familiar to him at such a distressing time. That was a parental dilemma, though, wasn't it? Who was she to judge? She did not have any children of her own. At thirty-four she was certainly young enough. But the calendar was not the whole story. She did not think it likely to happen now. She picked up her pen and scribbled a note to herself to talk to the headmistress at Adam's school. She was Mrs Blyth's GP. It would be easy enough to do. Bullying should have occurred to her as a possible cause of Adam's problems much sooner than this. But at least she could establish whether there had been any bullying before Tuesday's consultation.

The first two hours of her Friday evening child-minding stint passed uneventfully. Then she heard a rumple of sound from above as though Adam had shifted and woken. She stood to go and check on him, alert to further sound, but there was none. A feeling of dread overcame her then. There was nothing obvious to provoke it. But her skin pricked into gooseflesh and her scalp itched coldly, and it took all the willpower and resolution she possessed to make her legs climb the stairs to Adam's snug little room.

She pushed open the door. Moonlight bathed the scene. It was monochromatic, bleeding the brightness from the pictures on the wall, making a drab shroud of the duvet cover on the bed, turning the water in his bedside carafe a gloomy tainted colour.

He was seated upright on the bed. His mouth was stretched in a pantomimic leer. His long hair had been twisted into two careful plaits and there was a look of cunning and wariness in his eyes so dismaying on the face of a ten-year-old child that her own hand rose to cover her open mouth at the shock of it.

He laughed. It was a snigger, vindictive, high-pitched. 'Hello,' he said.

He had addressed her.

She swallowed. She did not reply.

His head jerked to one side as though in some mad impulse of sympathy. 'Are you still angry with me, pretty doctor?'

The voice coming out of the child spoke English, heavily accented. 'Boom,' it said. It paused. 'The rifle I used was a Barrett Light. A Barrett Light is a sniper's weapon. It is British. And it is the best in the world.' Adam's arms jerked up like someone aiming a gun and one of his eyes closed as he looked along an imaginary sight. His tongue protruded in concentration and was then slowly withdrawn as the smile returned. A finger squeezed a phantom trigger. 'Boom,' the voice said. 'That was all it took, pretty doctor. The range was eight hundred metres. No distance for a Barrett Light. A routine shot. And your boyfriend's head exploded like a pumpkin under a hammer blow.'

'Adam?'

'Busy,' the voice said. 'Unavailable.' The child's face contrived a lascivious wink and the body reclined on the bed and the sniper closed his eyes and rested.

Later, when she was sure the boy slept, Elizabeth came back to the room and unravelled the plaits in his hair and combed it out. She did not want Mark Hunter to see the physical interference inflicted on his son. Then she went back downstairs and, goaded by her memories and the grief rekindled, she wept. She was still struggling for composure when she heard Hunter's key in the lock, a few minutes after midnight.

He took off his suit coat and unfastened his tie, then came and sat down in the chair facing hers. He had noticed straight away that something was wrong. He was sober and she was glad of the fact. Probably he had drunk reluctantly, glancing often at his wristwatch, impatient for the time when he could respectably go home. She remembered that she'd felt a stab of pity for him, putting on his tie to go to the local pub. It was a few hours and a lifetime ago. The world had shifted since then. Her sympathies now were engaged with bigger things.

'Should I go up?'

'No. He's sleeping now. He needs a long sleep, I think, or he will wake exhausted.'

'Something happened?'

'Another escalation.' It was ironic, using the terminology of war to describe what had occurred. 'How many men have you killed, Mark?'

He looked at her for a long moment. 'Some would argue there's a philosophical distinction between the deaths you inflict with your own hands and those you delegate. I would not. The answer to your question is too many.'

'And now you're being punished for it, through your son.'

'Except you don't believe that, doctor.'

'Shortly after I qualified, I volunteered with my boyfriend, also just qualified, to do a stint with the Red Cross. We were sent to Chechnya.'

'Christ.'

'Where, as you know, things escalated. We were at the siege of Grozny. All was chaos and butchery. We could do nothing. My boyfriend was killed by a sniper bullet. They got me out in the end lashed to a pallet aboard a cargo plane. Tonight, in Adam's room, I listened as his killer bragged about murdering Peter.'

'Only the dead can speak through Adam,' Hunter said quietly. 'If that is any consolation.'

'It isn't.' She laughed, incredulous at the truth she had witnessed. 'Your son is possessed.'

'I'd wondered why someone who looks like you do is single.'

She stared hard at him.

'It's my training. I was taught to watch out for the unusual, for anomalies. The hours that you work, the absence of a ring on your finger and the fact that you were available to child-mind on a Friday evening are at odds with how you look, Elizabeth. That's all.'

'What did you do, in Bolivia, to incur the wrath of this black magician?'

'We blundered into something. It was a very confused situation, not something we were prepared for. Not something anyone could be prepared for, I don't think. But I did something wrong. Not just wrong. I did something bad.'

'And the white witch? She didn't feel inclined to lift the curse there and then?'

'I'll tell you about it. I'll tell you everything. I've never spoken of it to anyone in all the years since. But you will have to know.'

'Why did you call me in the first place, Mark, if you thought my skills redundant?'

He looked at her. 'I hoped I was wrong. The situation has deteriorated with such awful speed.'

'But it has become clearer. After what I saw tonight, I can explain it in no other way. Something unwelcome and strange has occupied your son, some malevolent force. Adam really is possessed.'

'I know he is, Elizabeth. And it will get much worse than this. And I must find that old woman and persuade her to come back with me and use her power if I'm to have a chance of saving him.'

'You had better tell me about what provoked this,' she said. 'You had better tell me and tell me truthfully.'

Chapter Two

Everything about the deployment in Bolivia was wrong. But before discussing the flawed reasoning behind the mission, Mark thought it important to impress upon Elizabeth just how strange and unknown a place Bolivia had been twelve years ago. It was still exotic now, of course. It was a place of outlandish beliefs and customs. It was high and remote. There was still a primitive poverty in parts of the country that shocked affluent Europeans. But the fact was that those Europeans were there now in increasing tourist numbers to be shocked. Bolivia had become a backpacker destination of choice. The most dangerous road in the world, which Bolivia could rightfully boast, had become the thrill-seekers' weblog cliché. The prison in La Paz had been forced to end its Newgate Gaol traditions under the scrutiny of a curious world. The place where Butch Cassidy and the Sundance Kid had apparently met their bleak deaths was practically a theme park dedicated to the myth of the American outlaws. The shrinking of the world had domesticated aspects and even regions of Bolivia. When Mark had been deployed there as an army captain, not many weeks married, that had yet to become the case.

Any mission was routinely described as business, in the regiment. The more business there was, the better, was the prevailing philosophy. Business meant survival. The lack of it meant perceived obsolescence and inevitable Whitehall-decreed cutbacks in manpower and hardware. Fears entertained by the senior officers had filtered down to the non-coms. Peace was a likely prospect in Northern Ireland, where most of their business was done. Trade was lacklustre in the Province, the market almost exhausted. There was a bit going on in the former Yugoslavia, of course. But it did not add up to much. It was peripheral. The days of their champion, Margaret Thatcher, ecstatic at some piece of stun grenade theatre staged in Hereford, were long gone. Prime Minister John Major was more sanguine about the military and its costs. He might be a patriot. But he had the soul of a Chancellor of the Exchequer, which he had once been.

The Bolivia incursion was a Whitehall initiative. Mark discovered that at a meeting with his own commander, when he attempted to extricate himself from it. He had endured a gruelling training attachment in Belize prior to his wedding only three weeks before this summons. He was supposed to have earned thirty days of leave. They had allowed him twenty-one. He had been summoned by phone at the newly bought home in Devon that he shared with his new wife. They were in bed when the call woke them. He could see no justification for it. There were plenty of other men as good as he was on active duty and with none of his resentment at having to go.

'I can think of three,' Colonel Baxter said over steepled fingers.

'You flatter me.'

'No. I don't.'

Mark wondered who the three were. It didn't matter. Evidently they were already engaged on other missions. Outside, he could hear the punishing thud of percussion grenades, the adrenaline urgency of screamed commands. It was very hot on the base, in their breeze-block hut. It was July. They had opted for a summer wedding. The reception had been held on an island on the Thames at Kingston, where

Lillian was originally from. The water had shimmered on their short crossing to the island under the blue sky of a perfect English day. Rose petals had been strewn on the still surface of the river.

'Dragging one of our best and brightest from the marital bed is not something I do with any relish, Mark. May I call you Mark?'

Hunter was twisting his beret in his hands. He could feel pinned to it the stubborn sharpness of the badge he had been so proud to earn. 'You can call me what you like, Sir. You're my commanding officer.'

'Please don't be petulant,' Colonel Baxter said. His eyes dipped to a document on the desk in front of him. He studied it, biting at his grey moustache with the bottom row of his teeth.

'I'm sorry, Sir.'

'And so you fucking well should be.' Baxter's eyes rose and met his. 'It is a great privilege to be called to arms under the standard of this regiment. Never forget that. Infant children have been deprived of fathers who died valiantly serving our colours with nothing but pride.'

There was no arguing with this. It was military fact, the regiment a family, its sacrifices familiar to and painfully borne by every member. 'I'm sorry, Sir. I am truly and humbly sorry.'

'Good. Your truculence is forgotten.' Baxter picked the document up from his desk again. He did not wear glasses. He did not hold the slim stack of papers away from his face to find a range at which their words would come into focus for an ageing man. He must have been fifty, Mark supposed, but his vision was unimpaired. The colonel enjoyed the reputation of a superb rifleman. He could down a moving target at better than half a mile. As he read the short sheaf of papers in front of him, his hands were unnaturally still.

Mark was impressed but not surprised. You became accustomed to such accomplishments at Hereford.

A cocaine cartel had established a presence in the north of Bolivia, near the town of Magdalena only a few miles from the border with Brazil. This territory was the Amazon, river tributaries and thick rain forest, a region which did not share the high altitude characteristic of much of the country. But it possessed challenges of its own. It was hot, swampy terrain, difficult to travel through, innately hostile to man. Trained at length in Belize, a man from the regiment would find it all very familiar, Mark thought. He would almost be at home. He did not much like the parasitic insects that burrowed under a man's skin. But then he did not greatly care for winter nights concealed in a culvert observing a Republican farm building in the freezing bogs of South Armagh. Join the army and see the world. But do so uncomfortably.

Baxter slid a satellite photograph across the desk. Dense forestation was a black blur covering the whole of the print. Rivers and streams were silvery snakes gleaming, uncoiled. A route through the forest was just the faintest of lines, given away by its straightness. Geometrical precision was alien to this wilderness. There should have been no straight lines. Yet there it was. A route, ruler straight, headed north. Mark followed the trail with his finger. It was too faint to record the rampaging progress of loggers, altogether too neat. And it was too delicate to represent a metalled road. Effort had been made to minimise the path, to keep it as narrow and well concealed as its existence allowed.

'Either they're environmentally sensitive, or they're hiding something,' Mark said.

Colonel Baxter did not answer him.

Faintly, from one of the sets of wooden buildings in the sunshine beyond the hut, Mark heard the cagey, staccato rhythms of a live-fire exercise. They would be rehearsing an ambush in one of the blinds built by the base carpenters, or rescuing hostages from a confusing warren of wooden rooms. His hands were moist in the heat and his tracing forefinger smudged the point where the road ended, the smudge giving more substance to a settlement there than the picture had originally possessed. But it was a settlement, man-made before an attempt at camouflaging it. Again, the geometry gave it away. The small cluster of buildings formed a pattern of rectangles.

'It doesn't look much, Sir.'

'That picture is almost two weeks old. The place could be twice the size by now, heavily fortified and fully operational. You won't know until you get there.'

'I'm assuming a Stealth aircraft took this picture. I'm assuming this is an American initiative.'

'That's essentially correct.'

'They've got some pretty good special forces operatives of their own. I've done joint exercises with them in Germany. You must have done the same in the past, Sir. They're more than capable of dealing with a jungle stockade full of marching powder and a dozen armed thugs from the cartel guarding it. This is a milk-run for their covert chaps.'

Baxter frowned and stood up. He went over to his window. Mark did not think the view especially compelling. Baxter was concealing something. But that was his prerogative, given his rank. 'The special relationship has taken a few hits of late, Mark. There are some bruising personality clashes at a level too high for anyone to be comfortable with them. This mission is seen by the PM as one more symbolic means of cementing our long-standing position with our longest-standing allies.'

'Technically, Sir, our longest-standing allies are the Portuguese.'

'Your co-leader on this mission is of Portuguese origin,

actually. He's a Major Rodriguez. Rodriguez serves of course in the army and under the flag of the United States. I believe he's a linguistic specialist.'

'You mean, a man trained in interrogation techniques.'

Baxter shrugged. 'I don't think Major Rodriguez could be described as a common torturer. He's fluent in seven languages and one of those is Ancient Greek.'

Hunter nodded. He did not think classical scholastic skills likely to be of any use against cartel members. But Rodriguez would have other, deadlier proficiencies. He was confident of that.

'You will join the Americans and a Canadian when you hit the ground. We need to do this, Mark.'

'We need the business.'

'Oh, we always need the business.' Baxter turned. 'And on this occasion we need to get the right business outcome.'

They were there, waiting for him in the darkness as Hunter gathered his parachute at the rendezvous point. Rodriguez and the Canadian, Captain Peterson, were the officers. He was immediately aware of the damp, rain-forest warmth and the rich, almost overpowering smell of the ferns and vines and wildflowers and shrubs surrounding them. There was the furtive rustle around him of large insects and the screeches from above of night birds. Hunter borrowed a folding spade from one of the American non-coms and buried his parachute, counting the men in the darkness as he dug. This task of attempting an accurate estimate of their company strength successfully alleviated the tedium of digging. He had not heard a word spoken by his new comrades in arms. But Hunter supposed that most of them would be from the rural southern states, from Mississippi and Tennessee. They were country boys, he thought, men comfortable with the habit of stealth. They had spent their boyhoods pursuing prey through the swamps for the dinner table. You didn't kill in such circumstances, and you didn't eat. It was a harsh fact of poor rural life. Not for the first time, he envied the American soldiers their easy intimacy with the weapons they carried. These men had cradled rifles and shotguns almost from the moment they left their own cradles as infant boys. And it showed. Around him they formed a watchful, silent perimeter. There were eight of them, he thought. He had counted only five, but the Americans liked even numbers. Rodriguez commanded eight men for this operation. He did not command Peterson. He did not command Hunter, either. There would likely be no departure from consensus. Expertise in the matter of fighting and killing generally bred cooperation.

He finished the job of consigning his parachute to its tomb and cleaned the blade of the spade with a moist handful of undergrowth, giving it back to its owner with a nod of appreciation. There was enough starlight to see by. There was no moon. But a landing in foliage of this density in total darkness would have risked serious injury. There was suffi-cient ambient light, and his eyes were fully adjusting to it. Rodriguez, ethnically distinct from the men he commanded, dark where they were pale, came forward and murmured a greeting and flashed a white smile. He was whipcord lean and his handshake was firm. Hunter liked him instantly. He felt a paddle-sized hand judder jovially against his shoulder blade and turned, and he knew it was the Canadian, Peterson. The grinning Canuck was built like a championship-class light-heavyweight about to step on to the scales. Hunter felt relief settle through him, forcing out the acid corrosion of adrenaline, slowing his heart, obliging him to smile back at his new companions. He would be all right with these two. They were good men. Something solid settled in him and he suspected it was nothing more really than honest relief.

He had never experienced combat as a married man prior to this. He did not wish to make a widow, he realised, of his new wife.

'That was a nice landing,' Rodriguez murmured in his ear. You did not whisper. The sibilant hiss of a whisper carried.

Peterson chuckled, but it was a very discreet expression of mirth.

'You know how hard a night drop can be on the knees,' Hunter said. His pack and personal weapons and their ammunition added fifty kilos to his weight. The knees could only take so much.

'Not to mention the balls, if you have the bad luck to land straddling a tree branch,' Peterson said. 'And I speak from bitter personal experience.'

Hunter squatted beside his pack, on the ground where he had placed it before beginning to dig. From a side pocket, he took a clip for the assault rifle strapped across his chest. He did not insert the clip, because the sound would carry. Instead, he put the clip in the webbing on his pack straps before levering the pack on to his back. It would be handy enough there in a firefight. In the webbing on the strap to the right of his chest, the clip was only inches from his reaching fingers.

Rodriguez made a hand signal to his men. Hunter sensed rather than saw them change formation, a concentration of craft and menace spreading to his front and rear and flanking him. They began to move towards their target, two miles away, a mile or so in the thick forestation that spread almost impenetrably north from the small and isolated settlement of Magdalena. The terrain was very similar to Belize and Hunter's recent training assignment there. But the climate was cooler and less humid, the air slightly thinner. And something else was different. Belize had been an exercise. You could never rid an exercise of its staged and somehow futile atmosphere of dress rehearsal. An exercise, however exotic the location, was essentially a chore. This was real. And the contrast could not have been greater. It was there in the silent, purposeful progress of the men as they fanned out and edged forward towards whatever challenge awaited their formidable fighting skills. There would come a day when Mark Hunter would no longer enjoy this, he knew. There would come a day. He had seen men burned out and unmanned, their nerves broken and their will to fight exhausted. But it had not happened to him. And at that confident moment, he could never imagine that it ever would.

They stopped about a mile north of the settlement that was their target. They gathered in the cover of a deep, steep-sided gully. Vines and creepers grew thick and verdant on the vertical banks of stone, insulating sound. The men took out ration packs and ate breakfast. Because what slight wind there was blew gently from the south, they were able to risk brewing coffee. The coffee was hot and strong and Rodriguez briefed Hunter as they squatted on the ground and drank.

'We've got a cluster of tin-roofed buildings made of wood,' he said. 'They are located like the points of a star around a circular construction at their centre.'

Hunter frowned. 'It doesn't sound much like a processing facility.'

'I don't think it is,' Rodriguez said.

'Why do you say construction, and not building?'

Peterson had walked across to them. He dropped to his haunches and sipped coffee from a steel mug. 'We think it is canvas,' he said. He looked at Rodriguez, who nodded. 'There are dogs, Rottweiler attack dogs, so we haven't been able to get too close. But we think the central structure is a marquee of some kind. It's a rigid construction, framed but not permanent.'

'Unusual for cartel activity,' Hunter said. 'You sure the circus hasn't come to town, Major?'

'They have guns as well as dogs,' Rodriguez said. 'They've strung a fenced perimeter with razor wire. It could be a parley. It could be a conference of some kind.'

'It could be innocent,' Hunter said. 'Relatively speaking, I mean. For all your scant intelligence, they might be environmental activists planning their next attempt to save the planet.'

Peterson chuckled. 'Three weeks ago a party of four eco-tourists went missing in this region. They just disappeared, Captain.'

'Such tragedies can occur naturally of course,' Rodriguez said. 'This is hostile country. But these people were not beginners in the terrain. They were experienced, hardy. And they had with them a professional guide with excellent jungle skills and plenty of experience.'

'No distress call?'

'Nothing,' Peterson said. 'They just vanished off the face of the earth.'

'Have you theorised?'

Rodriguez looked at Peterson and then turned back to Hunter. 'We hit the ground about ten hours before you did. One of my guys is good around dogs. I asked him to volunteer to get in as close as he could on a one-man scouting patrol. He's a boy from the boondocks, like all of them, a kid from the swamps of North Carolina. He got close enough to one of their people to see the garrotte looped around his belt. There was a heavy calibre automatic holstered to his belt and a machine pistol over his shoulder. My boy saw the hilt of a fighting knife protruding from the top of one of his boots. These goons are equipped for a war. Whatever we're dealing with here, it's nothing the American or Bolivian governments know anything about. It's covert, criminal and we have compelling reason to believe it has cost the lives of four blameless people. We need to go in. We need to find out who these criminals are and what they are doing. And we need to neutralise them.'

'Hallelujah,' Peterson said.

Hunter nodded. He was not there to argue. But he was beginning to think that cocaine and processing chemicals were the last thing they might find under the black canvas once past the firepower and the dogs.

'Where do you stand on drugs, Captain?' This question came from Rodriguez. Dawn was breaking. The light was improving. Rodriguez was a finely featured man with brush-cut hair and a trimmed moustache, and his expression was a compelling mix of hardness and delicacy. Hunter would not have wanted this man for his enemy. Even less his interrogator.

'I don't take them, if that's what you mean.'

'It isn't. You know perfectly well it isn't.'

'I've no very strong opinion on the matter. I've been spared their corrosive damage in my own life. I've heard the lectures, seen the films. Essentially, I'm a soldier. I follow orders. I hope the people I am obliged to kill are more bad than good. But the justification for the fight is made much higher up the chain of command than me.'

Rodriguez swirled the dregs of his coffee. He emptied the grounds out on to the foliage under their feet. 'I've seen the films too. It's an epidemic in the States. There are CEOs with five gram a day habits.'

'You mean in Hollywood?'

'I mean in Detroit as much as in Hollywood, Captain. I mean in Boston and Chicago too, in the banking and the industrial worlds. I mean on trading floors and in office suites and hairdressing salons and at country clubs and in the more exclusive sorts of bars.'

'So it's a crusade?'

Rodriguez grimaced. 'You see, Captain, I'm conflicted on this. I believe in freedom of choice. If a General Motors executive pulling in half a million dollars a year wants to spend some of his hard-earned on nose candy, I've got no real argument with that. It's his decision. But the suppliers at source, the cartels, are another matter entirely. They're what the world has now instead of Al Capone. They're bad people and bad news for every region they infest. They undermine national economies and defy elected governments. Them, I'm happy to go after.'

The silence from Peterson during this exchange had seemed uncharacteristic. Hunter turned to the big Canadian. He looked subdued, sad even. He seemed a man far removed now from his habitual chuckle.

'Care to share your philosophy on this?' Hunter said.

Rodriguez rose to his feet and walked away from them.

'I don't have a philosophical standpoint,' Peterson said. 'You used the word crusade. The Major said epidemic. My brother had a stroke at seventeen, provoked by an overdose of the shit we're talking about. You know what a stroke is?'

'An insult to the brain,' Hunter said. That was the literal definition.

'Yeah, well. My brother was called Jimmy. The insult to Jimmy's brain was massive, fatal. I'd kill every pusher I could find, given the time and the ammunition.'

'I'm not even sure we're dealing here with cartel activity,' Hunter said.

Peterson grinned at him. 'We're dealing with bad people, Captain. I'm fucking sure of that. And so are you, I can see your instinct written all over your face.' He gestured with his head in the direction of the guarded settlement a mile to the south of them. 'It's all very simple. It doesn't require philosophical debate. We mop 'em up, we lighten the load of badness in the world.'

Hunter smiled back and nodded. Something conciliatory seemed pragmatic in the light of Peterson's indignant fury.

'What is it you British Army guys say? Home in time for tea and medals. That's us, Captain Hunter, when this little task is completed. We take out the scum and we'll be home in time for tea and medals.'

'Amen,' Hunter said. He got to his feet. His knees were sore from the jump. The coffee had had a diuretic effect. He looked around the gully they were in for somewhere he could pee in relative seclusion in what was now full daylight. Then he wanted to talk to the phantom from North Carolina who had ghosted into the hostile settlement without being detected. The boy had been debriefed already by the other two, no doubt. But Hunter liked his intelligence delivered first-hand, where possible. He did not like to run the risk of having anything lost in translation. They had a full twelve hours before night fell again and they would not move against their enemy until it did. They had ample time in which to map out a strategy. He would start with the Carolina ghost. Crucial elements of his own contribution to their plan of attack might well depend on what Hunter learned from him.

'Mind?' the boy asked, taking out a damp pad of chewing tobacco.

The soldier seated on the ground in front of him was Private Abel Gaul. Given the wind direction and Gaul's proven instinct for elusiveness, Hunter could think of no objection. He shook his head. Gaul smiled and tore off a wad with his fingers and inserted it between his teeth and his cheek. He grinned, his teeth strong and even and discoloured from the habit.

'Ask away, Sir.'

'The sentry you saw?'

'Smelled him before I saw him, Captain. Smelled him even afore I heard him.'

'Body odour?'

'You might say.'

'Describe the smell, Private.'

'Rotten.' Gaul spat tobacco juice.

'Rotten how?'

Gaul was blond and freckled across his nose, open faced and broad shouldered. But he was lithe and his battle fatigues draped loosely over his narrow hips and long limbs. He looked at the ground between them. He stroked his chin. He struggled to find the word. Hunter did not mind the delay in his responding. He was grateful the boy from the Carolinas was taking this so seriously.

'Corrupt,' Gaul said, eventually.

'Was that not more likely to have been the dog? Could the dog not have had paw rot or distemper, or something?'

'Nope,' Gaul said. 'Dog was healthy.'

'What exactly do you mean by corrupt, Private?'

'Rotten.'

Hunter felt somewhat lost. 'Like something dead?'

'Worse than dead, Sir.'

'Worse?'

Gaul nodded. 'Like something gone real bad,' he said. 'Like some dead thing neglected for a long time.'

Hunter shifted position and looked over to where Rodriguez and two other men were field stripping three heavy calibre machine guns. In common with all American operations in Hunter's experience, lightly armed meant armed to the teeth. They possessed enough fire power to mount a successful assault on a fortress. He flicked sweat from his eyebrows. It was hot despite the altitude. Gaul spat his greenish black, tobacco juice spit. Sitting there, cross-legged on the ground, he looked serene. Maybe, Hunter thought, it was just stupidity.

'What did this sentry look like?'

'He was white. He was as white as you and me. Bigger, though. Maybe running to three hundred pounds, and six-two or three, I'd reckon. Shaven-headed.'

'Sounds like a biker.'

'Nope.' Gaul sounded emphatic. 'Definitely wasn't no biker.'

'Or a wrestler.'

'Nope. Weren't no wrestler neither, Sir. Tatts were all wrong for either breed.'

'He was tattooed?'

'Heavily. Across the face and neck. Elsewhere his skin was concealed by his clothing. I couldn't catch clear sight of his hands. Fist holding the dog leash could have been inked too, but I couldn't be sure. Could have been leaf dapple from the starlight on his knuckles. Couldn't rightly be certain.'

The South American criminal gangs wore facial tattoos, Hunter knew.

Gaul spat again. 'Know what you're thinking, Sir. Seen those guys for myself up close in LA. Wasn't gang ink.'

'What then, Private? Ethnic? Tribal?'

'Seen something similar a couple of years ago, Sir. We were mountain training, skiing in New Zealand with some of the Anzac grunts. Got a forty-eight-hour furlough and saw ink similar on the faces of the Maori guys in some of the bars. Only similar, mind. Not quite the same.'

Hunter took this in. 'Anything else, Private? Any other detail that particularly struck you?'

Gaul laughed softly. 'The dog scented me. It cocked his head to where I was laid up, but didn't make any sound. I don't think it could. I think its cords had been cut.'

'Jesus,' Hunter said.

'You're a man comfortable with words, Sir,' Gaul said. 'Give me a real good one for red.'

'Scarlet?'

'Nope. Not bright enough. Want something real bloody.'

'Crimson.'

Gaul went to flick his fingers in what was clearly a gesture of habit, before remembering where they were and the prevailing need for quiet. His hand descended. 'That's the one, Captain Hunter. When the dog turned its stare on me, I'd swear its eyes were crimson.'

The soldier rose to go. But Hunter had one final question. 'Vehicles?'

'One troop carrier. Kind of the old-fashioned sort, with canvas rigged over a square frame in back of the cab.'

'Anything else?'

'A couple of limousines were parked up, Captain. You're an educated man. You ever been to my part of the world?'

'To the Carolinas? No.'

Too bad. Know what a Palmetto bug looks like?'

'It's a giant cockroach.'

'That's what those limos looked like,' Gaul said. 'Black and glossy and I swear to you as ugly as the Palmetto bugs we have back home.'

Hunter joined Rodriguez and Peterson for lunch before they formulated their plan of attack. They pooled their food, as was the custom. This was a ritual that always delivered two things. The first was a chance to share the excellent field rations enjoyed by the Americans and Canadians. The second, less appetising, was the ridicule his own piss-poor British Army rations always attracted when offered in exchange.

A fragment of poetry kept repeating in Hunter's mind the way a catchy song lyric will. He thought it must have been prompted by Peterson's earlier jibe about tea and medals. He assumed this because it was Rupert Brooke and it was a couplet from the poem about the Old Vicarage at

Grantchester. But it wasn't the obvious lines, the famous ones that ended the work on a note of English pastoral wistfulness. Instead, it was:

> The stream mysterious glides beneath,
> Green as a dream and deep as death.

It was odd. Brooke was not a poet Hunter had ever enjoyed. He could not remember last having read him. But the lines were his and there was something sinister about their rhythmic insistence as they reverberated in his head.

Rodriguez tore open a foil pack with his teeth, tipped the contents dubiously into a mug of hot water and began slowly to stir. Hunter recognised the familiar, largely chemical smell of what was optimistically termed lamb casserole. Rodriguez watched it bubble and churn in his mug. Then he looked up at Hunter. 'How did you fare with Gaul?'

'Okay. He was informative enough. Don't think he'd want me as his point man.'

'Oh?'

'He made a comment about my vocabulary. I think he's got me down as a bullshit artist. It could be counter-productive when we go in if your men all think that way.'

'I speak nine languages,' Rodriguez said.

'I was told seven.'

'Then your intelligence is out of date, Captain. My point is simply that this accomplishment doesn't undermine me in the minds of the men.'

'I'm skilled at crochet,' Peterson said. He belched. 'Very skilled. Doesn't necessarily mean I interfere with little girls.'

'I don't know how you eat this shit, Hunter,' Rodriguez said, slopping out his libellously labelled lamb casserole. He reached for the satchel of charts and maps on the ground beside him. 'Let's get down to business, gentlemen. We attack at 2100 hours. Full darkness will have been on us for an hour. We will brief the men at 1700 hours. We need to know what we are about.'

The three men stood and walked the short distance to the small camouflage-covered tent erected as a command centre. In there, over an improvised table, they would iron out every exact permutation.

Hunter did not know why he had allowed himself to become preoccupied by such extraneous details as cult tattoos, the odour of decay and the silent attack dog. All of them had been trained to subdue dogs. And the nature and calibre of the weapons they carried and their physical numbers were far more important considerations than the physical charac-teristics of the men guarding their objective. Still, he felt a growing sense of strangeness. Still, the Brooke couplet echoed and sang maddeningly in his head. He snatched at a sinew of orchid vine trailing down the side of the ravine, crushed it between his hands and sniffed his sticky palms as though the sharp, savage odour of the plant sap could clear his mind and exorcise his thoughts.

After the briefing, on full bellies, Rodriguez and Peterson did what all the men not on sentry patrol were doing and went off to enjoy a couple of hours' sleep. Hunter unpacked his sleeping bag, unrolled his foam undersheet and found a fairly flat spot intent on doing the same. But he could not sleep. The Brooke couplet had receded, finally, in his mind. But his mind could discover no rest. Instead, it was filled with thoughts of Lillian, his new wife. He did not think about or speculate upon their future together. On the eve of combat, he was too superstitious a soldier for that. He did not believe in throwing down the gauntlet to fate. Instead, as the men from Louisiana and Arkansas snored cradling their rifles around him, as exotic birds shrieked in the forest canopy on remote tree limbs above, Mark Hunter thought about what he regarded as the miracle of his marriage to the beautiful woman he loved.

He had met her one evening fourteen months earlier at an event staged at Hatchard's bookshop on Piccadilly. The Irish poet Seamus Heaney had been there to give a reading. He had queued patiently to exchange a word with the great man and have his hardback first edition signed. He was leaning against a wall, grinning at the signature with the book opened in front of him, when she turned among the press of people and spoke to him clear of the surrounding chatter.

'You're a lover of poetry?'

'Yes. I wouldn't be here otherwise.'

She had green, feline eyes and straight, light-brown hair that buckled and splashed heavily around her shoulders. She was very composed, with her wine glass held high in front of her. He thought it the composure that gave her such strong physical impact, though she was very slender and not particularly tall.

'You don't look like a poetry fan.'

'Oh? What do they look like? Generally.'

'Not like a soldier of fortune. Not like someone involved in espionage. Not carrying an intriguing facial scar. In short, not at all like you.' She raised an eyebrow and sipped from her drink. 'Look around.'

They were lit by hot lights above them, surrounded by the spangle of book spines on heaving shelves. The shop was very crowded and most of the men there were red-faced, tweedy, bucolic. The scar under his cheekbone was a shrapnel graze. He thought that perhaps she was here from the publishing company, or the company that owned the bookshop, to look after their star guest. If so, she seemed a very svelte and polished sort of security presence. Lucky old Seamus Heaney.

'Look, I'm not a crank or anything,' Hunter said. 'I like poetry. I can even quote it, should the need for proof arise.'

She appraised him some more. He could not read her expression at all. She wore a red wool coat, unbuttoned. It was early spring outside on the street but very hot in the crowded space they shared. The heat seemed of no concern to her. She cocked her head and looked at the book in his hands and then plucked it from his grip. '*Beowulf*,' she said. 'This isn't Heaney's poetry.'

'It's his translation.'

'It's the story of a monster. My name is Lillian.'

'It's the story of the quest to kill a monster. Three monsters. I'm Mark.' An incredulous thought occurred to him. 'Are you chatting me up?'

She handed him back his copy of *Beowulf* and sipped more wine. 'You are the most attractive man in the room. You might be the most attractive man I've ever met. That will depend. Tell me about yourself, Mark. Don't lie. I will know straight away if you do.'

Afterwards they went for a drink in Covent Garden, where she had a flat. She worked in publishing. But she had been at the Heaney reading purely as a fan. Her book had been signed also. It was the *Collected Poems*. It had been safely tucked back in her shoulder bag by the time of their Hatchard's confrontation.

'What kind of poetry do you like?'

'Modern,' he said. 'Anything I really like is from Manley Hopkins on.'

She laughed. 'You seem entirely too good to be true.'

'I can assure you I'm not.'

'You must think me very brazen. I'm not usually like that. I've wasted the past two years on a relationship that wasn't worth my time. This was a discovery made only a few days ago. It's left me feeling somewhat angry and aggressive.

I'm not usually quite so forthright. And I'm not so pathetic as to think relationships with men define a woman. But I saw you and I saw that you were alone and I didn't want you just to slip away.'

'I'm glad.'

'What do you do?'

Their table in the pub seated only two and they occupied an isolated corner. Mindful of her earlier warning, he told her. She listened. Once again, he found that he could not read her expression. He thought that she was very beautiful. She was the more so the more he studied her. It was not an effect of make-up or of style. It was uncontrived and she seemed hardly conscious of it, though he knew she must be. When he had finished telling her about his life, she smiled and finished her drink and asked him to walk her home. On her doorstep, he kissed her. She dropped a hand on to his shoulder and the touch of her thrilled through him with a force that was almost convulsive.

'What would you like to do now?'

'Take you to bed?'

'I mean, would you like us to see one another again?'

'Oh, God. That was so crass. I'm so sorry, Lillian.'

She fished for her keys in her bag. 'Don't be,' she said. 'There's no harm in optimism. The glass half full and all that.'

He laughed with relief. 'What would you like me to do?'

She had found her keys. She lifted her eyes from them to him. She flicked the veils of heavy hair away from her face, revealing her expression fully. 'I'd like you to court me, Mark. I would like that very much.'

He walked down Catherine Street to the north side of Waterloo Bridge and took the turn of descending steps to the Embankment. He looked along the gentle sweep to the right of the Thames towards the Houses of Parliament.

He would walk the route back to the barracks and his hard mattress and coarse woollen blanket and sleep. There was a light spring fog over the river and the lamps strung along the Embankment were pearly in the rising mist. He was billeted at Chelsea Barracks for a two-day session of seminars. He had seen the details of the Heaney reading in a London free-sheet left by someone on the table he chose at random for lunch in the officers' canteen. He had set down his tray and seen the listing. He had gone to Hatchard's really on a whim. Already he regarded his having met his future wife as a sort of miracle. Nothing up to the point of his deployment in Bolivia would shake Mark Hunter's faith in that grateful conviction.

Now, sleepless in the ravine, he went to get his pack and took from it some paper and a pen. There was an unfamiliar duty he had forgotten to perform and he needed to carry out. He had to write a letter to Lillian that might be his last. It was a new responsibility and it was onerous but he had no choice. She had the right to final words from him should he not survive the coming encounter. He would keep the tone light. He had misgivings about this operation, an uneasiness he could not have articulated to himself, let alone to her. He would not be dishonest in what he wrote. One discovered lie and he believed he would lose her. That was her promise. That was the standard she set. He would not truly have dared to lie to her. She was too precious a prize for him to think of risking the loss. But there was enough honest comedy in the circumstances to allow him some cheer in the writing. And he did not believe he was going to be killed or injured in the contact to come. No soldier really ever does. It's always what happens in a fight to someone else. Hunter wrote with brevity and good cheer, signed his note with a kiss and folded the paper into an envelope he licked shut and put back into his pack. Much had recently changed in his life and the change was greatly for the better. But he was experienced at what he was about to do and he entertained no false modesty concerning his formidable ability to do it.

There was only so much information the men could absorb about their mission. The boys of the South were soldiers steeled for action. They were not repositories of words. They were not lovers of rhetoric. There were only so many times a weapon could be stripped and cleaned and loaded. There were only so many equipment checks a man could make on the tools on which he depended in action for survival. Fifteen minutes before their moment of departure, Hunter, Rodriguez and Peterson gathered in their little canvas command post with nothing else physically to do before setting off on the mile-long route to combat. Rodriguez took out a metal flask, unscrewed the stopper and poured them each an inch of something potent. Hunter sniffed the liquor. It was tequila. They raised their glasses and drained them.

'I'm wondering about you, Hunter,' Rodriguez said. 'I like to know the men I fight alongside. When you're not doing what you're ordered to, what do you choose to do? What's the passion in your other life?'

Hunter wiped his lips with the back of his hand. He was silent for a moment. 'Back at home, my wife and I light a log fire in the evening.'

'It's summer,' Peterson said. 'Even in England, it's summer now.'

'You don't live in the West Country, Captain. We light a fire. And the logs take. And the room fills with the warm scent of pine resin. And I brush my wife's hair as she sits between my knees on the rug in front of me. And I greatly cherish that ritual.'

Rodriguez smiled and nodded.

'That's fucking tragic,' Peterson said. 'It's my understanding you've only been married a few weeks.'

'Not tragic,' Rodriguez said. He shrugged. 'Though somewhat English, perhaps.'

Hunter looked at Peterson. 'And you don't know what it is that makes my wife's hair require the brushing.' He turned to Rodriguez. 'You, Major?'

'I'm teaching my daughter piano,' Rodriguez said. 'I treasure that time we spend together, side by side on our stools at the keyboard. She has a real and precious gift.'

'Jesus,' Peterson said to Rodriguez. 'Is there no end to what you can do?'

Rodriguez smiled. He looked apprehensive, even sad, though such feelings were relative, Hunter told himself. 'What about you, Peterson?'

'I like to read,' Peterson said. 'When I'm not behind the butt of an assault rifle, drawing a bead on anything with a pulse, believe it or not, I like to read. I like to walk in open country. And I like to paint. No country on God's earth like mine for a watercolour painter.'

'What kind of stuff do you read?' the major asked. He sounded genuinely interested.

'Melville. Conrad. I like stories about the sea.'

'And the crocheting?' Hunter said.

'I lied about the crocheting,' Peterson said. 'I'm not the Renaissance man I claim to be.'

Under canvas, in darkness, Rodriguez and Hunter laughed. Peterson laughed with them. When the laughter stopped, the three soldiers embraced one another.

'This is a stroll in the park, gentlemen,' Rodriguez said.

But in that, the major was wrong.

Chapter Three

They breached the compound perimeter at two opposing points and fanned out rapidly, making for the building at the centre, eagerly intent on killing anyone they confronted. Momentum was all with strike troops and every man of them knew it. You went forward. You did not ever take a backward step. Your progress was relentless and murderous and it did not falter until the target was seized and secured. Your very survival depended upon this impetus. The smell of cordite quickly filled the air. Rounds were fired in short, disciplined, staccato bursts by the troops to Hunter's left and right. The return fire it provoked was wild and uncontrolled, promiscuous as the compound's defenders spent a magazine with every burst they triggered. Hunter was aware of bullets zipping by him in the darkness, of their deadly weight and wasted velocity. He heard a mag clatter to the ground forty feet beyond where he progressed in a crouch and aimed a burst of fire in that direction, hitting something solid and provoking a grunt of surprise or pain. He was hit himself then, a hundred and forty pounds of attack dog slamming into him, putting him on the ground, winding him and attempting to bite out his throat. He raised his forearm and the dog clamped a jaw of bristling teeth around the limb and began to toss its head and tear. It made no sound. Its eyes were a dull, sightless crimson. The arm it held was Hunter's left. He took his fighting knife from its scabbard on his right thigh and plunged it to the hilt into the neck of the dog. The animal merely tightened the clench of its jaw on Hunter's arm and he felt the skin puncture deeply and heard his own tendons start to strain and rip. There was a volley of automatic rifle fire, incredibly loud, right over him. The dog slumped and Hunter squirmed from underneath it. Gaul had been wrong. The animal stank like death itself. The blast of its breath in Hunter's face had been the reek of a charnel house.

Peterson was over him, helping him to his feet. 'None of this is right,' he said.

'What do you mean?'

Peterson was panting, sweaty. Over the cam cream it was smeared with his face was already filthy from the smoke of stun grenades and powder burn. 'They're taking rounds,' he said. 'But they're not dying, Captain.'

As if to prove the point, on the ground, the dead Rottweiler twitched and shuddered like a beast stirred and summoned. Its guts lay glistening, spread where Peterson's heavy calibre shot had spilled them. Hunter stared, incredulous and revolted. The twitching animal began to pull itself free of its own gore. Its eyes opened with a ruby glimmer.

'Come on,' Peterson said.

They approached the marquee. It was canvas, black and oily and taut. And it was the vaunting size, Hunter saw, of a cathedral. Guidelines as thick as tow ropes tethered it to metal stanchions pulverised deep into the ground but still proud above the earth to about the height of a man. They could discover no entrance. The firefight all around them was chaotic now. The resistance was impossibly stubborn. Momentum had been lost and, with it, the pattern of attack. There was no knowing enemy from friend. Behind him, as he looked in horror and something like awe at the massive structure in front of him, Hunter could tell from the grunts and screams that the conflict had descended into close-quarter duels fought hand to hand.

They had commanded eight men. They had possessed company strength in total of eleven. It was nowhere near enough. He wondered how many now were left alive. He judged they were no more than three or four minutes into their disastrously misconceived assault.

Peterson took out his knife and tore a long rent with it in the fabric in front of them. He pulled open the rip and gestured for Hunter to step beyond him inside. Hunter looked and saw that the tear revealed a blackness even inkier than the fabric that surrounded it. It was as though the interior of the canvas cathedral absorbed and swallowed light. He swallowed, wondering what they had blundered into, knowing he had no choice but to keep going on. He could smell the sour secretion of fear on the sweating Peterson. He could smell its sharpness on himself. But there was a pervasive odour, gathering in strength all around the compound. It was the corrupt stench of decomposition. It brought to his mind images of defiled and looted crypts and midnight resurrection men. He felt momentarily less like a soldier than someone colluding in desecration.

'Go on,' Peterson said, from behind him. There was raw urgency in the Canadian's voice. They struggled through the tear in the fabric of their new, dark world.

Silence replaced the sound of martial carnage outside. It was completely quiet in the narrow, fabric corridor in which the two men found themselves groping. Orientation was almost impossible and as their eyes adjusted to the gloom, by the pinprick beam of Peterson's tiny flashlight, all they could logically do was aim for the centre of the structure they had breached. It was very difficult. A maze of cloth corridors had been stitched into the marquee. They were narrow and claustrophobic. But their walls were taut, which was a mercy. Hunter imagined them slackening, their black canvas closing in and collapsing, the oily burden becoming flaccid and descending upon them with its silent, suffocating weight. He was not generally prey to such thoughts. Fear and defeatism were strangers to him and he had never known a moment's panic in his life. It was as though these feelings were a contagion he was picking up from the very fabric of the place he was in. He could not see the face of his comrade in arms. But he would have bet Peterson was prey to feelings at that moment identical to his. You had to fight the infection, he thought. It could unman you and leave you helpless without a strong and sustained effort of will.

They emerged eventually into a central chamber. It seemed vast, after the confinement of their maze of cloth corridors. Peterson chambered a round. It was an encouraging sound, a reminder of the Canadian's bravery and belligerence and Hunter was glad of it. The man had saved his life, he realised then. But the thought was brief as what lay in front of them clarified in Hunter's sight and mind.

The scene was candlelit. The light in the chamber was feeble and haphazard, the candle flames seeming to struggle to find the necessary air to feed their flickering life. Pools of illumination dabbed and spat at a figure at the centre of things. She was middle-aged and enormously fat. She was floridly dressed and heavily bejewelled. The light, from a distance, was not strong enough to see her clearly by. It was as though she waxed and waned in the light with the flickering life of the candle flames. She sat at a card table, Hunter saw, as he and Peterson approached. The cards on the table were dull tablets of colour. The game had been set for two players. There was a second chair, more accurately a throne, opposite the one the fat woman occupied. But it was empty.

Spacious tapestries were draped on hanging frames above the place at which the woman sat. Some of these showed figures. Some showed geometric shapes. The figures were neither human nor animal but at some subtle and unnerving stage in between. They had uneasy expressions. To Hunter's eyes, their features combined the cunning found in humankind with the primal malevolence of predatory beasts. The abstract tapestries were more disconcerting, he thought. It was as though in them, geometry, its laws and logic, was somehow undermined. They described sly, anarchic angles and structures. They mocked reason. They defied proof. He thought that you might go mad in their intricate study. Above them, remote on the black concave ceiling of the chamber, a constellation had been painted. But it was a constellation true to no night vista from the Earth. It was alienating, this strange nightscape. It made him feel abject light years away from home and what he knew and understood.

The seated woman turned her head towards Hunter. She wore a green satin turban shaped in complex folds. He knew with certainty that beneath it, she was bald. She opened her mouth abruptly, as if in a yawn so sudden it had surprised no one more than its originator. 'There is something singularly charming about the river at that particular point, Captain,' she said. She spoke in a high, clear voice and her accent was English and refined. 'I can quite see why you chose it, with the curve and shimmer of the water towards the pale arches of the bridge. There is the verdant green of the island. There is the promise of the fun to come under elegant tents in the splash of the summer sun. It's a lovely spot. There might be no lovelier along the entire length of the Thames. It's a wonderful location for a sacrament and celebration. Magical, one might say. I know you agree.' Her mouth snapped abruptly shut. Then she smiled. And the smile was the terrible invitation to share some secret joke.

'What's the old bitch talking about, Captain?' Peterson said. He kept his voice deliberately low. 'Sounds like a fucking travelogue.'

'She's just described the place where my wedding reception

was held a month ago,' Hunter said. He was aware of being so dry-mouthed that his own voice sounded shrill, like one belonging to someone else entirely.

'Oh, Jesus,' Peterson said.

The woman turned to Peterson. Hunter thought it had grown darker in there, the light even further diminished. The painted constellation above them grew remote, as though they orbited through space away from it. The figures on the tapestries were reduced to shadowy spectres. There was a glow to the old woman's eyes that the candlelight could not explain or justify. This glimmer looked to Hunter like the external manifestation of some dark internal energy. He thought the vapid green glow in her eyes was generated by thought. She was a woman, if she was a woman, capable of willing things. Hunter had an instinct for danger honed over years of exposure to the risk of violent death. His hand was greasy with fear when he placed his palm over the butt of his sidearm. The metal felt cold and gnarled and familiar and not at all comforting. On the table, the cards in front of the woman began to curl and then to smoke and smoulder with a harsh stink.

'You should not have interrupted our game,' the woman said.

Peterson said, 'Who are you?'

'I am Miss Hall. That's immaterial. But you have gravely offended my hostess, Mrs Mallory. And that is not immaterial at all. Goodness me, no. It is something you will greatly regret.'

On the other side of the chamber, beyond where Miss Hall sat enthroned, there was a whimper of noise. Hunter pulled his pistol free and released the safety. With the weapon in both hands, and giving Miss Hall a wide and cautious berth, he jogged towards the source of the sound. It was a prone figure in battle fatigues. It was Rodriguez. Blood was smeared around the lower half of his face. Gore congealed in his moustache. He was unconscious and he was missing his hands. His hands had been severed raggedly at the wrists. His wristwatch, the strap still buckled, lay beside him on the floor.

'Get over here,' Hunter screamed at Peterson. 'Morphine, field dressings. Do you have anything we can use to bind his wrists, stop the bleeding?'

'Oh no,' Peterson said. He dropped to his knees, spilled items of medical kit from the pouches on his belt. 'What happened to him?'

'One of the dogs,' Hunter said. 'A pack of them, maybe.' He had cut a length from one of his bootlaces and was using it as a tourniquet, binding one of the Major's wrists.

'Not a dog,' Miss Hall said, from her throne beside the card table away behind them. 'Mrs Mallory was most put out when your commander interrupted our game. I've never seen her so angry. She said he would never play the piano with his daughter again. And nor will he. That was his chastisement. She made him eat his hands.'

'Fuck this,' Peterson said. He got to his feet picking his rifle from the floor where he'd put it to tend to Rodriguez. He turned and aimed it at the woman who termed herself Miss Hall. Hunter remembered he already had a round in the barrel.

'No,' he said. He reached and pushed the point of the weapon towards the floor.

'How the fuck can she know that stuff about the major and his daughter?' Peterson said. He was wide-eyed, hyperventilating, on the point of losing control completely. 'How can she possibly know?'

'Same way she knows about my wedding,' Hunter said. 'Let's all try to live through this, Peterson.'

'Point that weapon at me again, young man, and I will

have you turn it on yourself,' Miss Hall said to Peterson. Her eyes switched between them. 'The fault lies entirely with you. You have come here without invitation. You arrived with hostile intent. You have sabotaged something it took me years to arrange. Be thankful you were not here to experience Mrs Mallory and her wrath. I am sorry about your commander. But his chastisement was not my doing. Leave before I change my mind about allowing you to do so.'

Hunter said, 'Where is Mrs Mallory now?'

Miss Hall grinned at him. Her teeth were large and yellow and too plentiful for her mouth. With a meaty shuffle of enormous thighs, she settled deeper into her seat. 'You would not wish to encounter Mrs Mallory,' she said. 'Not with your marriage bed barely slept in, you wouldn't, young man.'

Hunter had bound both of Rodriguez' wrists, tightly, with his makeshift bootlace tourniquets. Either the ties or shock had staunched the bleeding. Bone protruded white in candlelight from the Major's ragged wounds. He was deeply unconscious. Peterson had pumped two ampoules of morphine into him. Now, the big Canadian put Rodriguez over his shoulder. He handed Hunter his rifle. Hunter had lost his own rifle when the dog had felled him outside. Rearmed, he began to look around for an exit, for an escape route out of the waking nightmare they had blundered into.

From the centre of the room, Miss Hall exhaled a sigh of exasperation. 'You are quite safe. Mrs Mallory left hours ago. Her retinue and their canine charges are long gone.'

'Hours ago?' Peterson frowned. He hefted the burden of Rodriguez on his shoulder. 'That can't be right.'

'You were in the canvas labyrinth for longer than you suppose, Captain. That was Mrs Mallory's doing. She wanted to take her time over the chastisement of your commander. You are quite safe to go outside and return to your camp. The immediate danger has passed.'

Hunter saw that there was a sort of door over in the remote wall of the marquee to the rear of where Miss Hall was sitting. Narrow chinks of daylight defined it subtly in a tall rectangle in the pervading gloom. Out there, dawn had come. He pointed the exit out to Peterson without a word and, cautiously, they began to edge towards it. Miss Hall indulged her exasperated sigh again.

'Come here, Captain Hunter,' she said.

Even with Peterson's assault rifle in his right hand, he thought it wise to obey her. As he got close to her, he began to smell the odour she gave off. It was sour and sharp, like rancid butter, he thought. The closer he got, the stronger it became. It was not like rancid butter. It was worse. It was like some rich, buttery cake spoiled by the intensity of heat and damp. It was all he could do not to retch. He had to overcome revulsion to get close.

'No, Captain,' she said with a yellow smile. 'You are right. I was never pretty. Take off your tunic.'

It was only when he did so that he realised his left arm was hanging, throbbing at his side. The adrenaline that had enabled him to help dress the Major's wounds was entirely spent. He struggled out of his battle dress and saw that his arm, from elbow to wrist, was a suppurating mess of swelling and puncture wounds. The flesh was yellow and puffy and the pain from the bite intensifying all the time. He did not think they had any penicillin back at their makeshift camp. They had no antibiotics. The bite, he knew, was infectious.

There were scarves of silk and satin coiled under Miss Hall's whey-coloured double chin. She unwound one of these. 'Give me your arm.'

With effort, Hunter did so. He was very close to her. She wrapped the lower half of his extended limb in satin. She muttered something in a language he knew he had never heard spoken before. She closed her eyes and opened them again and expelled a plump, fetid breath. 'There,' she said. She let the scarf slip, sticky with blood and puss, to the floor. 'You have proof that I am more good than bad, Captain Hunter. My scarf is ruined. But your arm will be fully re-covered in an hour or so.'

He examined his arm. The limb looked ripe for amputation and the pain had not receded in the slightest. 'A whole hour?' he said.

Her expression became petulant. 'Yes. I cannot work miracles.'

Hunter looked back towards where Peterson patiently bore the weight of their commander.

'I can do nothing for Major Rodriguez. Even if I could, I would not dare undo what Mrs Mallory has done. She is much more bad than good, you see. I would not wish to cross her.'

'Then thank you. I'm grateful for what you have done.'

Hunter made to leave and then hesitated.

'Yes?'

'There were some tourists in this region a few weeks ago.'

'So?'

'They vanished.'

Miss Hall shifted on her throne. 'Your travellers were food for her dogs. No more. As I have told you, Mrs Mallory is much more bad than good.'

There was no sign of their men in the compound grounds in the daylight beyond the marquee. There was no sign of them either when they got back to their camp in the ravine two miles to the north. They made the most comfortable bed they could for Rodriguez in the tent that had been their command post. Hunter thought about their plan of attack. He thought about their shared embrace of comradeship. It wasn't twenty-four hours since their airy philosophising about cocaine cartels and their impact in the world, and the moral implications of armed forces opposing them. As Peterson busied himself brewing coffee, Hunter thought about the letter he had written his new wife in the event that he might not return from battle. The more he thought it over, the less anything of what he had just experienced had to do with soldiering. He had known tenacious enemies in the field, but he had never before fought men who could not be killed. Of all things, it reminded him of *Beowulf*, of the sorcery of the epic poem he'd read in translation, of the contents of the slim volume signed by Seamus Heaney occupying a treasured spot on his bookshelf back at home. His arm had stopped hurting, he realised. He rubbed it, knowing it had healed and that the power used to heal it confounded nature.

'What happened to us?' he said to Peterson, when Peterson proffered a mug of coffee from the pot he'd just brewed.

'I don't know,' Peterson said, on the ground, on his haunches, staring at nothing. He was like that for so long that Hunter thought he would offer nothing more. Then he said, 'Hypnotic suggestion might have been a part of it.'

Hunter glanced briefly towards the little tent. 'What hypnotist possesses the power to make you consume your own hands?'

Peterson grimaced and he turned and looked Hunter full in the face. 'I'm as clueless as you are, pal. I've had guys I've rated very seriously tell me they've been up close and personal with UFOs.'

'We all have,' Hunter said.

'Unless we were set up, unless it was some kind of Pentagon-inspired behavioural experiment, then I honestly haven't a fucking clue.'

Hunter blinked up towards the blue sky. The birds were very loud. It was a vivid day, even beautiful, depending on your frame of mind. 'Rodriguez is going to die, isn't he?'

'We haven't the drugs to treat him even if we had the know-how,' Peterson said. 'This is an operation so covert we don't have any comms equipment at all. The plan is to walk back to a base over the border in Brazil. It's fifty miles, give or take. He's running a high fever. I checked on him just now. Both wounds are infected, unsurprisingly, given how they were inflicted. We don't even know how much blood he lost. I'd estimate more than he could afford to. So, yeah, I'd say the Major's chances of survival are slim.'

'Unless we carry him down to Magdalena,' Hunter said, 'which is what we should have done in the first place.'

It meant blowing their non-existent cover. It meant compromising themselves completely and exposing their failed mission to an always curious world. But what Peterson thought of the suggestion, Hunter never discovered, because at that moment, Major Rodriguez emerged from unconsciousness and cried out aloud to them.

The air in the small tent was suffocating, gangrenous. Rodriguez was sweating and shivering and porcelain pale. They had cleaned the blood from his face. They had bound his wrists to his thighs for fear that he might raise them and, unprepared for it, see the damage done.

'Gentlemen,' he said, when they entered the tent and squatted at his side. 'I cannot feel my hands. I cannot feel them at all.'

'What do you remember, Sir?' Peterson said, gently. He trickled water into the Major's mouth from the bottle taken from his belt.

Rodriguez swallowed water and laughed. 'A dream,' he said. 'An hallucination. I happened on two witches conferring and one of them cursed me. She cursed us all. She did so in a Coptic dialect so ancient I only half understood it. But most of it I got.'

'I'd be disappointed if you hadn't,' Hunter said. 'With languages, Sir, you have a prodigious gift.'

'I can't feel my hands, Captain Hunter. Why is that?'

'It's just the morphine, Major. It's numbness only. Tell us about the curse.'

Rodriguez frowned, recollecting. His breath was coming only in shallow gasps. It was an effort for him. He was not wholly aware. That was a blessing. He was unaware in the cramped tent of the rising stink of his own corruption. 'She said I would not sit at the piano and help teach my daughter to play again. She said you, Peterson, would avoid the sea or pay for the pleasure it gives you with your life.'

'And me?'

'That was most curious of all, Captain Hunter. She said that your progeny would commune with the dead. And your progeny would be afflicted with the gift of prophecy.'

'Afflicted with a gift?'

'Her words, Captain,' Rodriguez said. He smiled. The effort was enormous. 'Not my clumsy translation, I assure you. I merely repeat the contradictory riddle of the sorceress.'

'Thank you.'

'And just a dream,' Rodriguez said. 'Just a bad dream I had.' The smile vanished from his face. 'I was safe when the current was strong,' he cried out. 'I was safe!' He closed his eyes and the breath left him. A moment later, he died.

'I'm going into Magdalena,' Hunter said, over the corpse. 'I'm going to kill the bitch responsible for this abomination.'

'You don't know she's there,' Peterson said.

'Oh, she's there,' Hunter said. 'She's the hostess, remember? And I'm sure she resides in some comfort.'

'First, we bury our dead comrade,' Peterson said. 'We do it properly, with full decorum. It's the least he deserves.'

Hunter put a hand on Peterson's shoulder and squeezed.

He felt ashamed. His haste was undignified. 'Of course it is,' he said. 'Of course it is. Forgive me. I forgot myself.'

They buried the Major deep in soft ground above and away from the ravine. Peterson erected a rough cross and they fired a volley over him. They observed a respectful silence and then returned to the camp. There were plentiful rations, now everyone but the two officers was dead. There were, too, plentiful arms and spare ammunition sufficient to defy a besieging army. But there was only one task that Hunter felt required urgent accomplishment. He looked at his watch. But his watch had stopped – he supposed in the black maze of the marquee, in an experience he could now barely credit. He asked Peterson the time. But Peterson's watch had stopped too. He suspected both instruments had ceased to function at the same moment. No matter. He looked at the sky. He reckoned on four hours before sunset. In some ways, it had already been an industrious day. Before it ended, he intended to give it further, far greater significance. Before setting out, he asked Peterson would he await his return. The Canadian nodded. Until nightfall, he said, maybe a little beyond. And Hunter nodded back. He did not honestly think you could say fairer than that.

It was after dark when he returned. The camp was struck, everything combustible burned, everything else buried. They marched the distance over two days through dense forest to the departure point in Brazil with barely a word spoken between them. They crossed the border without acknowledgement. There was nothing much to say. Each man had to deal with his own rationale regarding their shared experience. They were greeted at the base in Brazil with indifference. No one there knew about the specifics of their mission and no one seemed to care. This was a blessing where Hunter was concerned, he knew. A large part of him wanted to scream and bellow about the ordeal he had undergone. Despite all the thorough and sometimes brutal training he had endured, he had no context for it. But he remained composed. He avoided Peterson altogether. And he suspected Peterson avoided him.

He thought sanity might return with the eventual touching down of the Hercules he was aboard at Brize Norton in Oxfordshire a week later. He watched the pattern of green English fields and hedgerows and sought comfort from their familiarity. He watched the shadow of the aircraft undulate over the familiar ground. He saw the silver sparkle of a stream meander gently through sunlit pasture. And none of it brought a shred of consolation.

He broke down at the debrief with Colonel Baxter. Baxter seemed to interpret this as a delayed show of grief for his dead comrades. Peterson, evidently, had been more composed and cleverer, giving his own account, a few days earlier. Baxter had it on his desk. They had stumbled into a compound run not by a cartel, but by members of a religious cult. Its members had been territorial, hostile and very heavily armed. Their mission had fallen victim to faulty intelligence (that part at least was true, Hunter thought). Their manpower was totally inadequate to the circumstances. The odds had been overwhelming. They would have needed armoured vehicles and at least another two full-strength companies of infantry support to have won the fight. In Washington and London and in Ottawa, the main aim now was to keep the whole matter out of public scrutiny. In a curious way, Baxter said, its failure had cemented the success of the mission. Intelligence was being pooled on cult activity on a global basis, something the Americans had been pushing for since their own embarrassing failure with the Branch Davidian in Texas.

'It's something they've actually been lobbying for since the

Jonestown Massacre twenty-odd years ago,' Baxter said, 'so they're pleased about that. And it's precisely this sort of cooperation involved in covering up mistakes like the one just made in Bolivia that makes the special relationship seem so very special. You've been through an ordeal, Captain. But if it's any consolation to you, it was worth the end result.'

Irony might have been beyond the British Army. But Hunter discovered it was an organisation capable of tact and compassion. At some level, there was an unspoken appreciation of the trauma he had suffered. He was given a month's leave. Then he was given a six-month secondment to a training establishment on the North Devon coast only a forty-minute commute by car from where he and Lillian had set up home. Human beings are resilient creatures and Mark Hunter was a particularly resilient example of the breed. He began to recover from what had happened to him. Denial was never a part of his strategy for coping. But gradually, because the events had been so removed from his normality, he began to perceive them almost as experiences that had been undergone by somebody else. This diminished them in his mind. The events themselves became vague and dreamlike. He could recall them only through an effort of will he was either unable, or profoundly unwilling, to indulge. And that pretty much amounted to the same thing.

He told Lillian of course. He told her in their sitting room, in front of their pine-scented fire, on the evening of the day he returned home to her. He told her everything. She listened in silence, wearing the by now familiar expression he could never read. When he had finished, she stroked his cheek and glanced towards the shelf where he kept his favourite books. 'Quests to slay monsters are best left to mythology, Mark,' she said. She hugged his head to her chest and stroked his hair. And she never made mention of the Bolivian incursion again as long as she lived.

Peterson's suicide jolted him. He was ambushed by the obituary, glancing through a newspaper in the staff room at the college where he taught. It was five months after the mission. It was late November and a sunset flushing the room through its picture window had turned the pages of newsprint pink in his hands. Hunter rose and closed the blinds to rid the room of its hue. He switched on a reading lamp and sat back down again. Details of Daniel Patrick Peterson's distinguished military career were necessarily vague. The obituary devoted far more space to his qualities as a painter. He had exhibited and sold as Daniel Patrick and had been a watercolourist of great critical regard and commercial success. Hunter himself had heard of Patrick. But he had never made the connection. One of his paintings was reproduced alongside the obituary. It showed the ice-bound St Lawrence River, filigrees of frost and icicles delicately rendered in the rigging of trapped sailing boats, their canvas sagging, weighted with ice. Even on newsprint, the quality of the brushwork was obvious. But Peterson had been a man habitually modest about his accomplishments. Hunter had come to appreciate that even in the brief time he had known him. He had been thirty-four when he took his own life.

The morbid detail came to him via military gossip a few weeks after. But it was gossip experience had given him reason to trust. Peterson had hanged himself at home in his study. He had taken the decision so suddenly to end his life that a book still lay open, half read, on his desk. It was Herman Melville's novella, *Billy Budd*. He had disobeyed the witch's command to steer clear of the sea. Of course he had. He would never have obeyed it. He had not been that sort of man. He had defied his curse and paid with his life for doing so.

After six months, Hunter was itching to return to action.

It came. And it was sometimes chaotic and always bloody and often inconclusive. But it confined itself to a reality with which he was comfortable. It gave him no nightmares. He performed his duty with courage and flair. There came the engagement in which he gained the citation that earned him his Military Cross. He won promotion. And after a year, Lillian fell pregnant. And he felt no hint of trepidation, only unconfined joy at the thought of extending their family, of becoming a father. As Lillian's term progressed, he felt happier than he thought he had ever done in his entire life.

Adam was born, healthy and beautiful. Lillian, who had been nervous about motherhood, found that she enjoyed caring for the baby more than she could have imagined she would. She had feared post-natal resentment. A professional woman, someone who set great store by her own independence, she was the classic candidate for it. But her fears were groundless. She loved her infant child, knew that he depended upon her for his health and happiness and was proud of the responsibility of motherhood. And this was just as well. Mark's service took him away for weeks at a time. Adam, a bright child, like most bright children, needed little sleep. He was demanding of attention and stimulation.

Mark, jet-lagged after returning from a mission in the Gulf, drove to the Boots branch in the village four miles away and bought the boy a dummy, exasperated by his general restlessness. Adam settled his lips around the plug.

'There,' Mark said. He sat down and picked up the TV remote. Lillian observed this male duel from the sofa, from under arched eyebrows. Adam stared at his father, his eyes growing large. He sucked, experimentally. He spat the dummy out.

'He isn't the sort of child who can be fobbed off with a dummy,' Lillian said, unable to keep the pride out of her voice.

'Then what the bloody hell does he want?'

'Announcements,' Lillian said. 'He wants announcements.'

And announcements he got. He showed no interest in television, however baby-friendly the fare. He liked building blocks and his simple Lego set. But he enjoyed, above all else, being read to. Mark, when he was there, read to Adam for hours, the boy on his lap never tiring, it seemed, of the stream of stories related in his father's gentle voice. He was almost three when his sister Kate was born and by then had taught himself the alphabet. By the time of his third birthday, he was reading fluently. Mark and Lillian thought little of it. They had no prior experience of children and didn't think Adam's accomplishment unusual. It took the reactions of other people to show them that Adam was remarkable.

He was in the park with his father. It had snowed and there was a hill in the park and they had taken a sled. But they had been there for over an hour and Adam's nose had turned red and his mittens soggy and Mark wanted to get him home and warm him up before the building of the snowman in their garden. It did not seem to snow in winter like it had when he had been a boy, Mark thought, and you had to take full advantage when it did.

Adam was at a stage where he read everything out loud. His reading was a redundant skill, to Mark's mind, because he understood so little of what he read. The pronunciation was eerily perfect. But he did not appreciate the sense of anything without it having to be explained to him at sometimes tedious length. They came upon a park bench. Snow sat on it and lay heaped on its flat arms and the top of its slatted wooden back. Adam pointed a wet, woolly finger at the brass plaque screwed into it. 'In loving memory of Margaret Agnes Crosby,' he said, in his piping, toddler tone. 'Gone but never forgotten in our treasured memories.'

A passing woman paused sharply. She was middle-aged

and grim in tweed with zippered boots and headscarf. She pointed. 'How old is that child?'

'He's three.'

The woman shook her head. Her face soured further. She crossed herself quickly and moved on.

Adam, who'd had his back to her, was oblivious. 'What does it mean, Dad? What does it mean?'

'It means that someone died, son. And someone who loved them is very sorry that they did and misses them very much.'

There was a pause of no more than half a second while Adam's infant mind absorbed this information and its melancholy implications. Then he began to bawl. And he would not be comforted.

Mark slung the sled across his back. He unbuttoned his coat and bent and picked Adam up and enveloped his little body in its folds, in his warmth and strength. And he carried his crying son home consumed by guilt. Adam had not possessed the emotional maturity to process such a poignant sentiment so starkly expressed. His young mind had been overwhelmed by pity and grief. He was three, for Christ's sake. Coping with a bright child was challenging. It got easier as the child got older. But Mark did not ever let himself forget the stricken look on Adam's face on that bleak winter day and the lesson it taught him about the sensitivity and tact required in his relationship with his son.

The years after that went by in a happy blur. Once Kate reached the age of three and began to attend nursery five mornings a week, Lillian turned her hand to writing children's stories. Adam's insatiable appetite for tales was probably the inspiration. She had discovered a talent in herself for improvising stories. She found that she could develop them. Characterisation came to her as easily as plots. Once she had assembled a manuscript, she used her old publishing contacts to get the stuff in front of people able to make editorial decisions. But her children's stories were published on merit. And no amount of string-pulling could have manipulated her sales, which were encouraging right from the appearance of the first book.

Had Mark known how finite things were, how contingent their happiness, how brutally short-lived the lives of his wife and daughter, he would have resigned his commission long before he did. Afterwards he castigated himself for his self-ishness. He had deprived his family of his physical presence to pursue career ambitions in the military. But that wasn't really the case, he later came to realise. He had been as much deprived as they had. He had provided for them, made them financially secure. All jobs involved some sort of sacrifice, and he was probably a better husband and father for the contentment given him by his successful career.

And then Lillian and Kate had been killed. Their deaths were a tragic accident. Nothing could bring them back, or change what had taken place before their departure. On the whole it had been a very happy life. It was gone now. He could only do his best for the child who was all he had left.

In Scotland, in the here and now, Mark Hunter stared into the fading embers of the fire and sank into silence. 'There, Elizabeth,' he said to the doctor summoned to tend to his troubled son. 'There. I've told you everything.'

'Not quite,' she said. 'You haven't told me what happened when you went into Magdalena on the trail of Mrs Mallory.'

Hunter rubbed his face with his hand. 'I'm weary,' he said, 'sick of the sound of my own voice.'

'You need to tell me,' Elizabeth said. 'I need to know all of it.'

It was raining when he walked into Magdalena. A summer storm had gathered in clouds as purple and livid as great bruises in the sky. They had swollen and spread and lightning had whitened them in staccato flashes and the thunder had boomed and the cloud had lowered, and with a chill amid capering gusts of wind, the rain had started to fall. The streets were quiet. The town was a cluster of flat-roofed, adobe dwellings with their shutters drawn, and shops and occasional bars with dripping awnings and blinds pulled down against the downpour. The more prosperous buildings clustered higher and were better appointed than the rest, when he saw them. They were on the eastern slope of the little town. And Mrs Mallory's cockroach of a limousine glimmered wetly in the lightning flashes at the bottom of a high set of steps outside one of them. He kicked in a head-lamp and palmed a shard of the glass that tinkled out of its chrome socket on to the road.

Her door was not locked. She was seated between the windows, in a chair against the far wall of a large, stone-flagged room. Light in the room was sullen and spare under the low cloud cover outside. No lamps were lit to brighten it. There was a grand piano, supporting a bronze bust. There were many photographs on the walls. There were vases of flowers, all dried, all atrophied. Mrs Mallory was as slender as Miss Hall had been obese. She was dressed in an ivory satin dress that concealed her body from her throat to her calves and was cut to show her figure. She wore a tailored jacket draped over her shoulders and her face was concealed by the blue gauze veil of a hat. She lifted the veil carefully and took a silver cigarette case from the inside pocket of her jacket. She tapped a cigarette against the case and lit it with a Zippo lighter. The Zippo seemed incongruously masculine. This was because every-thing else about her seemed almost vampishly feminine. Hunter wondered whether the anger Miss Hall had spoken of had by now subsided. She snapped the Zippo shut and slipped it into a pocket. She exhaled smoke through her nose and it hung in a mist in front of her. 'Come here,' she said.

Hunter was most wary of her eyes. He thought auto-suggestion a strong part of their armoury. He thought she would be far less potent in daylight, away from the swagger of her tapestry battle standards, outside her black, cathedral domain. But this was still her territory. She had long nails that had been shaped and lacquered green. Her jaw was firm and her mouth full and sensuous under a gloss of crimson lipstick. He thought that she was probably about thirty-five years of age. Her cigarette was filter-less and the smoke harsh. When he got close, he saw that nicotine had given the fingers holding it, over time, an ebony stain. Perhaps she was older than she looked.

'What do you want, Captain Hunter?'

'I want you to lift your curse.'

'I won't.'

'Why won't you?'

'I won't because my curse makes the world, to me, a more interesting place.'

Hunter nodded. He was drenched, dripping on to the flag-stones, cold in the chill of the room. He could feel the pull of her gaze. It was very strong. He looked around the room to avoid it. One of the pictures on the wall to her rear showed Butch Cassidy, seated in an ornately carved chair with claws for feet. He wore a three-piece suit and a bowler. It was a detail from the famous Wild Bunch group portrait taken at Fort Worth in Texas in 1901, seven years before the shoot-out in San Vicente in Bolivia that killed him.

'Did you come here merely to look at my things?'

'I've told you, Mrs Mallory. I came here to ask you to lift your curse on the child I have not yet fathered.'

She pulled heavily on her cigarette. Its tip glowed fiercely and faded in the gloom. 'Then look at me.'

He looked instead over to the piano. The bust was of Rupert Brooke.

'I knew him.'

'That's impossible.' Hunter needed to be careful. He had almost met her eye in his surprise at this outlandish claim.

'I met him in Berlin in 1912.'

'You couldn't have.'

'I'm not a liar.'

And he did not want to provoke her. 'What was he like?'

'He was talented and beautiful and very full of himself.'

'And he died young.'

'So he did. But with no assistance from me.' Mrs Mallory chuckled, throatily. It was a coarse sound. It frightened Hunter. He sensed that the veneer of her was very thin indeed. He did not wish to see what it was that lay beneath it.

'I comforted him,' she said. 'He had recently broken up with his sweetheart.'

'Katherine Cox,' Hunter said. He could not imagine this woman giving comfort to anyone.

'You would know, of course. You are a lover of poetry.'

The invitation to look into Mrs Mallory's eyes was really compelling. The curiosity to see their colour and shape and judge their expression and mood was almost overwhelming in its strength. He heard her grind out her cigarette.

'I'm no lover of Brooke's poetry,' he said.

'Frances Cornford famously summed up Brooke in a couplet I'm sure you have heard. She said that he was magnificently unprepared for the long littleness of life. The syntax is very elegant, is it not? But Brooke did not endure a long life, Captain Hunter. And neither will your son.'

He looked at her. And the trap sprung, she smiled. And it was a very familiar smile to Mark Hunter. For Mrs Mallory wore Lillian's face. She cocked her head in a mannerism wholly familiar. 'Come here,' she said, in Lillian's voice. 'Come here and kiss me, Mark.'

He found his feet moving him forward on the smooth

flags. He clenched his fist tighter around the shard of glass concealed in his left hand and felt the grinding bite of pain as its edges pierced his flesh. But the sensation did not unlock his gaze. Of course it didn't. The ruse was wholly inadequate. This creature's will had been strong enough to compel the slow agony Rodriguez inflicted on himself. Pain did not break her spell.

Her features changed as he got closer. She became more herself. She took off the hat and shook out her hair and it was black in sinuous tresses against the alabaster of her facial skin. The bones under the skin sharpened to give her a sculpted look. Her eyes became a cool, appraising grey in her cruel, beautiful face. And still he could not look away from her as she grinned and the talons her fingers had become reached out for him.

'No!'

Her gaze flicked past him and that did break the spell. Hunter lifted his shirt and pulled his pistol from where he had thrust it in his belt and cocked the hammer.

'No!'

He put a bullet in her right eye and when she slid to the floor he put another in her left temple and saw her head jerk as the round hit the floor and ricocheted off it back into her skull. Two shots, double tap. It was the classic drumbeat of SAS execution. Some habits he would never break. He straightened and levelled the pistol at Miss Hall, who had closed the distance very quickly from where he had first heard the shout behind him at the entrance to the room. She must be one of those nimble fat people who were implausibly light on their feet, he thought. And she had said no, and he had disobeyed her. He saw that her lips were pulled back from her big yellow teeth now in a gargoyle snarl. She had claimed to be more good than bad. She did not at that moment very much look it.

75

'I have six bullets left in the magazine of this weapon. A blind man could hit you from here. Take another step and I swear to Christ I'll empty my gun into you.'

He thought she flinched at the mention of a Christian God. But it could have been his imagination. He felt tired and overwrought and angry. It was a severe effort of will not to pull the trigger, not to have the whole grotesque experience he had endured end neatly and conclusively. Miss Hall stood there in a black oilskin, an enormous shape, dripping rain on to the umber flagstones where it gathered and pooled underneath her, the colour of blood.

'Have you the remotest idea of what you have done?'

'I've put an end to something evil. I have got rid of something bad. I've ended it.' He meant the curse.

Miss Hall shook her head. 'On the contrary, you have started something,' she said. 'Because of you, it now begins.'

He half sensed he heard the Rottweiler stir of life in the corpse to his rear. But when he turned she was dead, a thin, lifeless thing, her mesmeric eyes dim behind their closed lids. She had not shown the stubborn reluctance to die of her acolytes at the compound. But he had no time to wonder about that now. He kept his gun on Miss Hall until he had skirted warily around her and reached the door.

'What an ingrate you are,' she said, spat after him. 'And what a fool you are too.'

Outside, the storm vented its fury on the pale little settlement of Magdalena. Hunter opened the palm of his left hand and pried free the glass embedded there in his flesh. He held his hand out palm up and let the deluge rinse it clean. Lastly, he looked up, drawn by a light Miss Hall must have switched on in the spacious drawing room for which Mrs Mallory would never again have a need. He saw her bulky silhouette framed by one of the windows. She seemed to be swaying rhythmically from side to side. He wondered, was this some ritual of grief for her dead adversary in their incomprehensible game? He did not really care to know. It was his ardent wish never to encounter the woman again. He turned and walked on the way out of the town, towards the forest and the camp and to the border and then, blessedly, to home.

Elizabeth Bancroft had her head in her hands. 'Mark?'

'Yes?'

'Why do you think your execution of Mrs Mallory unimportant?'

He was silent before answering. 'Because it has not lifted the curse,' he said.

'Have you ever regretted that you felt obliged to kill a woman?'

'What makes you think she's the only woman I've killed?'

'I think she is. Have you ever regretted her execution?'

'Not for a single moment, Elizabeth. And nor would you have, had you observed the manner of Major Rodriguez's death.'

Elizabeth sat back in her chair. 'I use the term execution. I could equally say murder.'

'You can play all the semantic games with me you want, Doctor Bancroft. I've no objection, so long as you fulfil your duty of care to my son.'

She groaned to herself. He was as stubborn as she was. But locking horns was no way to progress. 'Okay. When exactly did you become aware that this supposedly moribund curse was a live danger to your son?'

He did not answer. Instead, he got up and went out of the room. She waited. She poked in a desultory way at the enfeebled fire. She stopped, only fearing that she was accelerating its death. The night was not warm and they might be up yet a while in it. He returned. He had something flat and rectangular wrapped in tissue paper in his hands. He sat and handed it to her and she revealed the item. It was a framed watercolour. It depicted skaters on a frozen pond. The ice of the pond had been rendered in a way that made it dance and shimmer with winter cold and the blue weals of the skaters' blades upon its surface.

'It's exquisite,' Elizabeth said. She looked for a signature, but could see none.

'He signed them on the reverse side,' Mark said. 'He was a self-deprecating man. At least, he was except in battle. In battle, he was bold.'

Elizabeth flicked the picture over in her hands. 'He sent you this?'

'No. Peterson was long dead by the time it was sent. I've no idea who sent it. I received it a week or so before Adam's dreams began.'

'Is it valuable?'

'That's hardly the point.'

'Is it?'

'Dead painters are not prolific. They're collectible. Daniel Patrick is very collectible. It's probably worth thirty or forty thousand pounds.'

Elizabeth sighed. 'This is way beyond me, Mark.'

'Just help my son.'

She paused. The telephone rang. Hunter made no movement to answer it.

'Aren't you going to get that?'

'No. I'm not. You can get it for me if you wish.'

She plucked the old-fashioned receiver from its cradle on the table between them. 'Hello?' She listened. And then she held out the white ivory of the instrument to Mark Hunter.

He shook his head. 'I'm taking no calls tonight,' he said.

'You might want to take this one, Mark,' Elizabeth said. 'It's a man, wishing to speak to you. He says his name is Mr Mallory.'

Chapter Four

He took the phone from her. She got up and went to check on Adam. It required nerve to do so after the ordeal of her last audience with the boy. But she did not feel she could eavesdrop on Mark's conversation with the cold caller. He had confided much in her but had done so through choice, not circumstance. He deserved his necessary privacy now. And he needed no distractions. The call, unexpected, might be vital. The stakes, she knew, were very high. She had believed that after her ordeal earlier in the night in Adam's bedroom. What Mark had told her only reinforced the conviction. And she had a duty of care to her patient. His father had been right to remind her of that. Mark Hunter was an attractive man and his mystery compelling. But he was not really the point. The boy was the point. He was tormented and she wanted and needed to do everything she could to ease his torment and then rid him of it for good. So she climbed the stairs, filled with trepidation that became a sort of dread as she ascended and the strength and safety of Mark's orbit, the mundane sanity of the sitting room, the fading comfort of the fire, all receded further from her. She stopped outside Adam's door. She could hear nothing from within. She extended her fingers towards the door handle. It was iron and tarnished with age and felt icy to the touch. She was not sure if that was just the chill of the fear she felt. She was not sure of very much at all, just then. Downstairs, she could hear Mark's raised voice as he made some emphatic point to his caller. The substance of the call was genuine. He would have hung up straight away on a crank. And Elizabeth was certain he had mentioned the name of Mallory to no one since his confession to his dead wife on his return from Bolivia a decade ago. That was the only certainty in her mind, as Elizabeth pushed the iron door handle down and entered Adam's bedroom.

He slept soundly with his duvet pulled up around the knuckles of the small fist he held to his face. His expression looked untroubled. The temperature in the room seemed normal. It was cold, but no colder than it should have been in Scotland in the late autumn in an old stone house high on a remote hill. By the light on the landing, through the open bedroom door, she looked at his things on their shelves; at his collection of Alex Ryder novels, his jigsaws and assembled Airfix kits, a scale model tank that worked by remote control, and his Eye Witness series picture books on the *Titanic* and the Victorians and the Glory of Ancient Rome. There was a jar of marbles and some AAA batteries and half a tube of Maynards Wine Gums. It was the innocent paraphernalia of a ten-year-old boy. And she thought that Mrs Mallory, whoever or whatever she was, must be a creature of infinite cruelty and spite. And she wondered, was the caller on the phone downstairs claiming to be a widowed husband or a motherless son? She did not think he would claim to be Mrs Mallory's father. Mark had put the woman's age at about thirty-five. But listening to his description of her, Elizabeth had suspected she was a great deal longer in the tooth than he supposed.

She thought his powers of description extraordinary for a common soldier. But then he had not really been a soldier of the common sort. None of them had – not him nor Rodriguez nor Peterson. Special Forces required special men and they had all clearly been remarkable in their way. And the experience he had survived, and they had not, had been extraordinary. It had been, too, an awful ordeal, she thought. Looking at the sleeping boy she wondered, what dawning horror had compelled a man with Captain Peterson's store of cynical courage to take his own life with such bleak haste?

Elizabeth felt relieved that Adam slept with such serenity. But she also felt a growing sense of anxiety at a detail Mark had related in his account. He had described something. And it had brought to mind a thing both fearful and familiar to her. His description left her feeling the need to travel to somewhere she knew very well and study the thing afresh. She did not want to confront it. It was a thing that had stirred uneasiness in her all her life. But she felt she had to. She could not practically do so of course until tomorrow. But as soon as she could tomorrow, she resolved, she would. She became aware the conversation downstairs had stopped. She took a last look at her patient, at his beautiful head serene on the pillow. She smiled and whispered a brief blessing over him and turned and left the room.

'Husband or son?' she asked Mark as she entered the sitting room.

'How is Adam?'

'He's sleeping peacefully. Well?'

'Whoever he was, he did not persist with the pretence, once he knew he had my attention. He was a messenger. He called himself an emissary, but he was just a messenger with an appetite for pomp.'

'Emissaries usually represent people of great importance, don't they?'

'Or people of great self-importance,' Hunter said.

'Well, Mark. Are you going to tell me?'

'Is it too late, do you think, for a drink?'

She smiled at him. 'In this country you will learn, if you stay, to think that a redundant question.'

Her emissary had claimed to speak on behalf of Miss Hall. She was in Switzerland, and she wanted urgently to see him.

'Our encounter took place over a decade ago. And she speaks of urgency?' Hunter had said to the self-styled emissary.

'She knows what is happening to your son, Colonel Hunter.'

'Then she will know how reluctant I am to leave him.'

They had kept up. They knew about his elevation in rank. But then, somehow they knew the unlisted phone number too.

'She is dying, Colonel Hunter. That is why it is so urgent that you come. And I am instructed to promise you this. Your son will not dream in your absence in Switzerland.'

'She can stop it?'

There was a pause. 'She can delay it. She can defer it, Colonel Hunter. And you will come. We both know you have no choice.'

'Don't I?'

'You love your son. You love him very much. And he is all you have left.'

The fire had pretty much died. Elizabeth shivered and sipped at her whisky. 'What time will you leave?'

He looked at his watch. Friday had gone. It was just after 2 a.m. on Saturday now. 'She has requested I attend an audience arranged for Monday evening. I can get a flight from Edinburgh to Geneva on Monday morning. If I take an early flight I'll have plenty of time. But first I will have to arrange care for Adam. I cannot possibly take him with me. I have seen what these people are capable of. Miss Hall might well be dying. The man on the phone might well be her emissary, and she may be gravely ill as he says. But even if that is true, I cannot take Adam with me. These people possess great and malevolent powers and

I don't want him exposed to the risk of the terrible things they can do.'

'He's already a victim of what they can do,' she said.

'At a remove, yes, he is. But I don't want him anywhere near them physically.'

Elizabeth thought. 'I can't stay with him in the day, Mark. I have a practice to run, patients to attend to. A disproportionate number of them are elderly and isolated. And it would take me a few days at least to organise a locum. But I do know of two very good agency child minders. One of them could prepare his meals and get him to school and back and launder his clothes. One of them at least is likely to be available. If you are prepared to pay for her services, I will stay here with Adam at night until your return.'

'You'll really do that?'

'As you said yourself, I have a duty of care.'

'A duty you would be exceeding, Elizabeth, and by some distance.'

She smiled. 'As you've also said, I have no social life to speak of. It isn't as though I'd have to rearrange my diary.'

'I should not have commented on that,' he said. 'It was very tactless of me.'

'But accurate,' she said. 'You should be content to take advantage of the fact. Anyway, if I'm honest I'm very pleased to be able to help. He is a sweet boy and if I can comfort and reassure him in your absence I'll do it gladly.'

He linked his hands and looked down at his glass on the table between them and blinked.

'You'll pay for a child minder?'

He nodded. It had been a stupid question. But that was not what had silenced his voice. She realised he was too overwhelmed by gratitude and relief to say anything. He had invested hope in this Switzerland trip. For a moment, she glimpsed the depth of the agonies he was suffering on behalf of his troubled son. She stood and walked round the table that separated them. She lowered her hand to where he sat and cupped the back of his head and stroked downward to his collar. She knelt in front of him and took his linked hands in hers and pulled them gently apart and held them. His hands were warm. She could feel their strength. She could feel the circular ridge of scarring on his left palm where he had pressed a shard of headlamp glass into the flesh, spellbound a decade ago.

'It's all right, Mark,' she said. 'But you are very tired. You need to go to bed now and get some rest.'

He looked up at her and smiled. He looked down at his hands, linked in hers. He pulled gently free of her grip and rose and walked out of the room.

It was the first time they had touched since their initial handshake of mutual introduction and greeting. Her instinct had told her it was, at that moment, the thing he most needed. She knew her reaching out to him as she just had, had not been wholly an act of compassion. Neither had it been entirely a signal of her desire. It had been somewhere between the two, dictated by strong and instinctive impulses. And she felt no embarrassment or regret or guilt at having done it. It was what he needed. It had been what she needed too.

She would stay the night. The spare room was prepared. Adam did not seem to have any qualms over the sight of her at breakfast. She had drunk too much with Mark following the phone call from the man claiming to be Miss Hall's emissary to drive the long and tricky route home in darkness. There, the remoteness of this house was an advantage. No busybody would see her car parked outside all night and draw malicious conclusions to spread as equally malicious gossip. She could not scandalise the neighbourhood if there was not a neighbourhood to scandalise. And she was relieved about that. Events in her family history had left her raw where speculation on lax morality was concerned. Minds could be as narrow in these parts as vistas were broad. Prejudices thrived and could endure even down the centuries.

That reminded her. She yawned. She was glad the following day was a Saturday. She would sort out the child minder for Monday first thing. Then, she would go and see if she could dispel the anxiety a part of Mark's account had inflicted upon her. It would mean going back to the family home, to see her mother. Generally, Elizabeth gained nothing but pleasure from visiting her mum. She would buy flowers and a nice cake from the bakery and motor the twenty familiar miles to her mother's door. Those things, she always did. But this visit would be different in the carrying out of a singular task she hoped and prayed would prove of no significance. The anxiety provoked by that one troubling detail in Mark's vivid account could easily blossom into fear. It was why she could not wait beyond tomorrow to have the issue resolved in her mind.

Adam was already seated at the kitchen table when she came down the following morning. Mark had his back to her at the stove. He was whisking something, she assumed eggs. Adam showed no surprise at all at seeing her. He was playing with toy cars, enacting a police chase on the tabletop.

'Hello, Dr Bancroft.'

'Elizabeth, Adam, please,' she said.

'Hello, Elizabeth.'

'Good morning,' Mark said, without turning round. Then, 'Young man, I'm ready to take your order.'

Adam parallel parked his cars on the table. 'I'd like a Red Bull to drink. Don't worry about pouring it. The can will be fine.'

'So that's a glass of apple juice.'

'And a jam doughnut, please, with lots of icing sugar.'

'So that's scrambled egg. Toast on the side?'

'And for dessert, I'll have chocolate ice cream.'

'You don't have dessert at breakfast.'

'Please? Can't I have it just this once, Dad?'

'I'm afraid not.'

Adam looked up at Elizabeth. 'It's child cruelty. My father is a man without a heart.'

'How did you sleep?'

'Well. I think.'

'Did you dream?'

'Did I! Yes. Liverpool won the title. They beat us in injury time at home in the last game of the season. It was a complete nightmare.'

She smiled. The resilience of children never ceased to amaze her. It was wonderful of itself, of course. And it was wonderful, she knew from her professional dealings with the bleaker sort of family, because it was so often necessary. But Adam really did look untroubled.

'Are you going to stick around today, Elizabeth? Can you do stuff today with Dad and me?'

'What do you guys do at weekends?'

'Canoeing, walking, sometimes climbing and abseiling,' Mark said, joining them at the table with plates of toast and bacon and scrambled egg. 'A bit of exploring, castles and grand houses, places of historic interest.'

'Car boots, when Dad feels like putting his hand in his pocket,' Adam said. 'Does any of that sound like it might be fun?'

'All of it. But I can't today. I have obligations, Adam.'

'That's a shame,' he said. He looked like he meant it.

Ruth Campbell had been hanged, convicted of witchcraft in the autumn of 1656. The officials of Cromwell's Protectorate had been zealous in their eradication of the black arts. Nowhere in the Commonwealth was spared the commissions, the trials, the ordeals and the executions. It was probably worst in Ireland and England's West Country. But it had been bad too in the Highlands of Scotland, where envy and spite sparked the deadly rumours that spread until they eventually brought the witch finders thundering up from Whitehall on the iron hooves of their great horses, with their Model Army outriders and their instruments of interrogation dragged behind them in rattling carts.

Ruth had been Elizabeth's grandmother, with so many 'greats' positioned before the 'grand' that Elizabeth had never been able really to properly remember their exact number. It did not matter. The bloodline was pure and the genetic link undeniable. Then there was the legacy. Ruth had been a healer. That was what had got her into trouble. She had not been the lonely crone of witch stereotype. She had been the wife of a prosperous beef cattle farmer and the young mother of two infant sons. She had been, by reliable account, a popular, pretty woman, characterised by vitality and good humour. But she had possessed a healing gift. And when someone in the community, envious of her other attributes, decided to bring her down, it was this that they used, to cruel effect, to do so.

After her bloody trial by ordeal she was made to watch, broken, as they burned the farm buildings and cast out her husband and sons from their home. Then they dragged her, bound behind a horse, through a jeering throng to the place of execution. The executioner placed a rope around her neck and she was hoisted on to the gallows. It was the slower sort of hanging. There was no merciful drop to snap her neck and deliver an instant death. Instead she was strangled, kicking, as the rope tightened with the burden of her weight. The contemporary account said it took her two or three minutes to die. During that time, someone emerged from the watching crowd and stole the shoes from her feet. She died eventually. But even then, her ordeal was not at an end. She had shown insufficient shame and remorse, the commissioner said. Picked at by carrion crows, putrefying, her body was left suspended for a month before her father was allowed to take it down.

By the time Ruth's father performed this pitiable task, the witch finder who had condemned her was dead himself. Judge Josiah Jerusalem Smith had suffered his fatal stroke in the house on the hill Mark Hunter now owned. His body had been taken back to London and buried with some ceremony in consecrated ground. Ruth's remains had been burned on a pyre, her ashes scattered to the winds, no man of the cloth to be found with the courage or compassion to preside over a Christian burial.

The house owned by Elizabeth's own mother was a walk of only a couple of miles from the scene of the burning and the subsequent execution of her ancestor. Staying in the locality had been an act of defiance for Ruth Campbell's husband John and her boys and their descendents. To go would have damned them, confirmed their collective guilt in the eyes of everyone who had known them. So they had stayed and borne the stigma down the generations with a bloody-minded sort of defiance. And the Campbell women had carried on with their custom of healing

The thing she wanted to look at was kept in the stable. It was an object both of veneration and mystery. It was the one relic rescued from the fire that destroyed his home by Ruth's widower, John Campbell. The scorch marks were still there to see at its top edge, three hundred and fifty years on from the blaze. The stable of course was no longer used as such. It was no longer used for anything. It had been the repository for her tools and sometimes a potting shed when Elizabeth's mother had possessed the energetic strength for her large garden. But she was old now and frail. She did not garden any more. Elizabeth paid for a man to come and tend to the garden. In the summer months, he came twice a week. In the autumn and winter, he came for just a few hours every Wednesday. In the summer, her mother would walk in the garden on her frame or on Elizabeth's arm. In the winter she was pretty much housebound. But she was old, her home was comfortable and warm and her daughter visited pretty frequently. The hired hand worked out of the back of his van. The stable door was locked with the sort of large padlock bought to discourage the depressing recent rise in rural theft.

Elizabeth waited until her mother was soundly asleep in her armchair after a large and cheerful lunch before going and fetching the padlock key from its hook in the kitchen. Dusk was an hour away. She was anxious to see the object stored in the stable in daylight. This was partly because she wanted to scrutinise it in detail. It was equally because, if she was honest with herself, the thing had always unnerved her. From her first, childhood glimpses exploring the stable in games, it had not seemed to her quite right. There was a furtive energy to it, a quality not wholesome. If you looked at it out of the corner of your eye, you could swear you sensed a sly movement. And that was not possible.

The stable was about eighty yards from the house. Elizabeth put her coat over her head against driving rain and ran the distance with the big brass key held in one fist. She did not feel in any great hurry to get to her destination. But she wanted to get this over with. The tightness in her stomach she had controlled earlier was a swarm of beating butterflies now. She released the padlock and it tumbled heavily through her hands and dropped to the ground. The stable door opened outwards. Inside, she could smell the ghosts of old plants, compost, mildewed hessian from a pile of slowly rotting sacks. And it was cold. She could see her breath. Her object rested on the shelf against the rear wall; a heavy cloth, secured by its top edge, was covering it. She walked over and released the cloth to reveal the object.

It was a carved oak relief. It showed a scene from a banquet. The diners were seated at a long table in a sumptuous chamber. A chandelier hung above them. Florid candelabra graced the table. The windows in the wall to the rear of the chamber were set in high Gothic arches and tapestries hung between them. It was night in this depiction of a feast. There were stars visible through the windows. But though they possessed some anthropomorphic character and handled their cutlery with apparent ease, the guests at the table were more beast than human being. The constellations through the windows were alien to any Elizabeth had learned to recognise by looking at the night sky. And the tapestries hanging between the arches depicted shapes that seemed unstill in their shifty mockery of geometric proportion and truth. Holding the heavy relief firmly between both hands, Elizabeth looked away from it, to her left. Then she risked a sideways glance at it. And in the swiftness of a glance the figures seemed to shift and leer and wink outward from the wood. She almost dropped it. She put the relief back on the shelf and picked the cloth up from the floor to cover it again.

'You should not play with that,' a voice behind her said.

Elizabeth turned. It was her mother. She was at the open stable doorway on her frame and her expression was one Elizabeth could not remember having seen since childhood, when mischief had sometimes crossed the line into wilful disobedience.

'I was curious to see it.'

'Cover it,' her mother said.

Elizabeth did so. As she did, she smelled distinctly the

charred scent of the wood and felt the heat of recent scorching through her fingertips. But she knew both sensations had to be imaginary.

'Come here. Bring the key. Do it quickly, girl.'

Her mother had not used this tone with her since Elizabeth's adolescence. She had been a very loving mother. But her mother had needed to be the disciplinarian in the house because her father had died when she was young and was not present to restrain her.

The door locked, her mother turned to her. She looked very old in the light. The rain had been a heavy shower but had given way now to bright autumn sunshine slanting from the low corner of a sky about to surrender the day to darkness. It was a harsh light on her mother's blue-veined cheeks and papery skin. But her eyes looked fierce in its orange cast.

'Some things are best left undisturbed,' she said.

'Do you mean artefacts, or do you mean secrets, Mum?'

'I mean what I say. You meddle with the past at your peril, Elizabeth. Please promise me not to visit that object again.'

The sternness had gone from her mother's expression, replaced by a look deep with concern. Elizabeth wanted to offer her mother reassurance. And she had seen what she had needed to. 'I promise, Mum,' she said. 'I promise.'

Her mother smiled. 'Good. Now be kind enough to come and make an old lady a cup of tea.'

She sat over tea with her mother, in her mother's familiar house. She could not have been more at home, nor felt further away from it. She looked around. And it was as though she saw the mirror image of everything. She trusted none of it. Everything, every feature, seemed out of kilter. She had to ask.

'Are we a family with a secret, Mum?'

Her mother smiled. The tea seemed to have revived her. She looked composed and alert. 'All families have secrets, Lizzie. Your vocation must have taught you that.'

She nodded. It had. But her inquiry of her mother had been in the singular. The reply had been plural. She wondered how many secrets there were. She wondered whether she wanted any of them revealed.

'There is a transcript of your unfortunate ancestor's trial, Lizzie.'

She was your ancestor before she was mine, Elizabeth thought. 'Have you read it?'

'I have not. I have always believed what I said to you outside, that some things are best left alone. You must keep your promise to me about that artefact.'

'I will.'

'But I cannot stop you reading the transcript if you choose to do so. If you really want to find out more, I mean.'

'Where is it?'

'Judge Smith left an archive of papers. They survived the Restoration. They are at the British Library, I think. I doubt they are available for general public view. But your name should enable you to see them without academic credentials if you wish. Access to such resources is much easier now than it was when I was a young woman.'

Elizabeth thought about this possibility for a moment. It would mean a trip to London. That was impractical just now. She wondered was there any real point. She looked at her mother. 'Don't you wish to know what's made me curious?'

'No, Lizzie. I don't. I have your promise concerning the thing in the stable and I know my daughter is a woman of her word.'

Elizabeth nodded. She did not quite know what to say. The conversation seemed to be over.

'Leave that awful relic to itself,' her mother said. 'Read the transcript of Ruth Campbell's trial.'

As the aeroplane achieved its cruising altitude on the flight to Switzerland, Mark Hunter thought about the feeling of revulsion that had overcome him at Elizabeth Bancroft's physical touch. He hoped with all his heart he had not allowed it to show in his expression or body language. He had done everything but recoil. He knew very well what had provoked the reaction. It was the same consideration that had made her such an immediate success with his son. She had meant well of course in reaching out to him, sensing the depth of his emotions and his struggle to control them in the moment. And there was no question that she was a compellingly attractive woman. The problem was that she reminded him so very strongly of another woman he had not only found attractive but come to love very deeply. Elizabeth reminded him so forcefully of Lillian that at one moment on the Friday evening, tired after a couple of whiskies, he had almost slipped and called her by his dead wife's name.

She was a fine person, intelligent and caring. She was helping not only Adam, but him. She was a generous and compassionate soul and she was even blessed with a sense of humour. But he knew that he was attracted to her for reasons that were anything but healthy. Would courting Elizabeth Bancroft raise the ghost of his wife? Or would she instead be a replacement so perfect he would eventually come never again to feel the pain of Lillian's loss? He would not find out. He had more urgent priorities on his mind than a romantic dalliance with the good doctor. He was very tempted but knew that giving in to the temptation was something he would come to regret.

He smiled to himself, looking at the approach of the coastline, blue and hazy through his window. He thought about the arrogance and vanity he knew had always undermined his character. He had postulated all this of course on the assumption that the attraction would be mutual. But why should Elizabeth Bancroft have the remotest romantic interest in him? Should she do so because she resembled Lillian, who had loved him? The idea was nonsensical. He was merely her patient's father. That was all he was to her. She had been intrigued by his background. But its clandestine nature and relevance to the case had prompted a curiosity there that was only natural. No. Where he was concerned, Dr Bancroft was courteous, professionally sympathetic but personally, profoundly indifferent. And that was just as well.

He thought about the specifics of how she looked. Her hair was cut into a shorter style than Lillian had worn, but the colouring was the same and he knew if he stroked it with his hand, the texture would be too. The eyes were the same shade of green and had the same feline upward slant. She had the same generous mouth. He knew how her lips would feel against his in a kiss. And she had the same appraising expression, with the eyebrows subtly arched, that he had never learned to read in his wife. She was an inch or two taller than Lillian had been and shared his dead wife's slender figure. It was as natural he felt attracted to her as it would be unnatural to try to do anything about it.

If he was honest with himself, it was not revulsion he had really felt when Elizabeth had briefly held his head and then taken his hands in hers. He had become a very lonely man. The intimacy he had enjoyed with Lillian had been taken from him suddenly and for ever. He had missed it too much either to try to reconcile himself, or to attempt to replace it. He was worried to distraction about his son. He was greatly afraid for Adam and, though fear was not a new emotion to him, helplessness in the face of fear was something he had never felt before. When Elizabeth had held him, he had actually felt a surge of pleasure and relief so strong it was as though for a moment his heart had slipped unbreakable chains. The revulsion had swiftly followed. And it had all been felt not for her, but for him. He had felt it for his own self-deluding weakness. And he had torn himself away and climbed the stairs to his bed shackling his heart again in harsh confinement as he took the ascending steps.

He had endured nights of cold solitude in remote and sometimes hazardous places throughout his entire professional life. He had done so willingly and without ever entertaining a single self-pitying thought. At whatever distant and hostile spot he found himself in the world, there had always been, after all, the prospect of Lillian and home, of warmth and welcome and the love of his wife and the intimacy of their sleeping embrace on his return. That was gone now and its absence was a thing he knew a part of him had always dreaded the prospect of confronting. It was his solitary fate and there was no relief or escape from it.

Walking through Geneva airport it felt strange to Hunter not to have a strategy. This was a mission more important to him than any he had undertaken in his long and some-times distinguished military career. But there was nothing he could do, beyond turning up on time, to prepare for it. He had not really thought about the woman who called herself Miss Hall between his last, sinister sighting of her at the window of the house in Magdalena and his recounting of the story of the Bolivian incursion on the previous Friday evening. Before Friday, he had not spoken about what happened in Bolivia for better than a decade. In that time he had occasionally thought about Mrs Mallory. She had faded in some of the more disquieting particulars, over the passing interlude, like a bad dream. But her more prosaic partner, or protagonist or whatever she had been, had slipped from memory completely. It was odd, he thought now, because he was still very wary of Rottweiler dogs. Hunter always gave the breed a cautious distance on the pavement. And he was always very aware of precisely where Adam was in relation to the dog if he saw one in a park or on a beach or common. He was on his guard in the presence of the breed of canine that had almost cost him his arm. But he had never reminisced for a single moment about the woman whose strange and querulous intervention had certainly saved it.

He did not have a plan. Her self-styled emissary had been very clear on the urgency of the meeting but very opaque about its purpose. Without knowing precisely what it was Miss Hall wanted from him, he could not decide how he was going to react. A long time ago she had said she was more good than bad. As the aircraft taxied and the seatbelt sign went off, he unfastened his and he looked at his watch. It was just after noon. Their meeting was scheduled for eight. In slightly less than eight hours, he suspected he was destined to discover whether hers had been an honest boast or not.

He had boarded the flight with nothing but a single item of hand luggage. He would be through the formalities and into Switzerland quickly. He sighed, despite himself. Geneva was not an easy place to come to. Most of the places he had travelled to in the world reminded him of missions he had undertaken. But this one reminded him above all else of family holidays. His family had skied as often as they had been able to. He walked past the baggage carousels and saw his own ghost with his dead wife and Adam and his much-missed daughter, Kate, waiting excitedly for their bags and skis and boots to appear through the rubber curtain and approach them, Kate in her dungarees with her blonde hair in ballet dancer's braids. He sighed again and dragged his eyes away. God, he missed his wife and precious daughter.

He missed them so. There were just two of them now. He wondered whether Adam would ever ski with him again.

He had no plan. But Hunter did have his instinct. His hotel was outside the city, on the southern shore of Lake Geneva, a few miles from the address the emissary had given him for the rendezvous. And he was sure that he was not followed from the airport in the taxi he took there. But he was equally certain that he was seen as he emerged through the gate into the arrivals area. The terminal building did not seem especially busy and one man in particular caught his attention. He was about fifty yards away and seated, apparently engrossed in a magazine. Even seated, Hunter could see that he would stand about six-three and run to maybe three hundred pounds. He wore wrap-around sunglasses with pale yellow lenses. His shaven head was bare. As Hunter passed him, just beyond the point of closest observation, he glanced back casually, just a momentary flicker of study. And he saw that the man wore make-up. Thick panstick or foundation covered his face and scalp. He remembered Abel Gaul then, with his tobacco discoloured teeth and the gentle, North Carolina lilt of his country dialect. Hunter did not think it fanciful to suppose the make-up on the man watching him might conceal a facial tattoo. He sniffed the air. But it carried no trailing taint of corruption. It smelled of nothing at all.

The window of his hotel room enjoyed a pretty view of the lake. The room itself was as characterless and antiseptic as they always were. Switzerland was no longer the pristine country of his own youth. They had litter and graffiti now. But there was still an underlying precision and order about the place that seemed a bit joyless and defeating to Hunter. The mountains were the mountains. But the country that lay beneath them, he had always found slightly clinical and depressing.

He kicked off his shoes, discarded his coat and jacket and

unbuckled his belt, then lay on his back on the bed. He still had hours to kill. He thought of Abel Gaul again, with his open face and the feral alertness that had failed to save him in Bolivia. They had all died. He was the only one left alive. Of course he was. What was the point of Mrs Mallory's curse, if he was not still around to witness his son's torment and destruction?

He thought about Bolivia, about the specifics of the mission and its aftermath. He had told Elizabeth every detail he had been able to recall. But now he searched his memory for anything important he might have missed. It was not pleasant to do this. And it was exhausting. But it was necessary, he knew. He pictured every scene as the mystery and horror of it unfolded and he heard in his head afresh every spoken word. When he had done this and knew that his mind offered nothing further to discover in the past, he slept where he lay for two oblivious hours.

Elizabeth's home was a small cottage overlooking a stream about four miles south of the village where she rented the two room breeze-block building that housed her surgery. The surgery was functional, utilitarian. Her cottage was stone with ivy clinging to it and leaded windows, and a heather descent that grew quite steeply down to the run of the water. The cottage had been vacant for a long time before she had bought it, on her return to Scotland and home after her disastrous period with the Red Cross. It had been somewhere between badly run-down and completely derelict. Restoring it had been a full-time job for the six months after Grozny. And the distraction of that had been exactly what she needed.

Then, after she moved into her new home and acquired her surgery and started to practise as a GP, the sound of the stream had been just what she needed. When she got into bed at night, she discovered its watery trickle had a narcotic rhythm that lulled her gently to sleep. Her mother had lent her the money for the cottage deposit. And her mother had lent her the money to buy the lease on the building that became her surgery. Both sums had long been repaid. But the total loan had not been without risk. Not everyone in the vicinity responded positively to their family. There were those who would rather endure illness than have someone with her bloodline treat them. Highland memories were long and sometimes unforgiving. That was something Elizabeth was reminded of as she approached her door at dusk on the Monday evening, a few hours after Mark Hunter passed on his way out of Geneva airport.

A cross had been crudely daubed upon her front door. The door was original, as old as the cottage, gnarled and knotted and weathered by time. The cross was about three feet high and had congealed and was turning a brown colour in those thinner stretches where it had dried. Elsewhere it was still red and sticky and, up close, carried the odour of the abattoir. It was relatively recent, this work. She looked at her watch. She had returned home for a change of clothes for tomorrow. She was on her way to the Hunter house to take care of Adam overnight. The nanny finished at six. Elizabeth could spare the ten minutes or so it would take hot water and a hard bristled brush to scrub off the offending symbol. Not that the symbol itself was offensive, of course. But the sentiment that had inspired this piece of spiteful mischief was very offensive. Oh, well. She had lived in rural Scotland for too many years to be traumatised any longer by its prejudices. A cross daubed in animal blood was still some way off an arson attack carried out while she slept inside. She had taken her keys out of the ignition on parking her car. They were looped by their key ring over her thumb. She resisted the temptation to look behind her like someone spooked and afraid. A strong breeze gathered at her back and she felt its force push her towards the wood and its new sign, glistening where it had been painted thickest in the last of the twilight. It was recent and cowardly work. Everyone knew the hours she was away from home. Everyone knew that she lived in the cottage alone. She found the key to the door and let herself in to get her change of clothes.

The timing of the attack left little room in her mind for doubt. But she wanted whatever reassuring corroboration she could get. So Elizabeth drove well beyond the speed limit on her journey to the Hunter house, making time for a quick diversion to the Black Boar, the pub to which she had sent Mark on Friday evening for his less than jolly night out. The landlord, Andy McCloud, was behind the bar as he always was, polishing a glass, his cheeks red in the glow of his generous fire and with a plaid lumberjack shirt rolled to his elbows. Behind him, arcane and curious whisky brands were lined up on a shelf ready for the tourists who never came. He saw her and approached the spot she chose at the bar cautiously. There were only two other customers present this early in the evening, both regulars, and they were out of earshot. He knew something. He knew everyone and everything, she thought.

'What's your pleasure, Doctor?'

She would get to the point. 'Someone left a message for me at my home. It was unwelcome. A serious insult totally uncalled for.'

'Unless it was a warning,' he said.

'Meaning what?'

He hesitated. When he spoke, his voice was a murmur. 'Not everyone thinks a woman with your ancestry a fitting antidote to the troubles of the family on the hill.'

'What's the word, McCloud?'

He leaned forward. He had been a policeman before he had been a publican. He was honest and fair to a point, but he was local to his core. He would betray no names, she knew.

'You are treating our war hero, Colonel Hunter, for depression, yes?'

'No. I am not.'

McCloud blinked at this contradiction of what someone had told him and he had clearly believed to be the truth. 'That's the story. He is depressed as a consequence of losing his wife and his little girl. What man would not be? He cannot reconcile himself. It has made a recluse of him. You are treating him. And ever since you've been doing so, the boy has been having nightmares so bad he's too disturbed to attend to his lessons at school.'

'That's the rumour?'

'It's what I've heard.'

'And spread?'

He put his towel down, placed his polished glass carefully on the bar. 'I would have hoped you knew me better.'

Elizabeth stood straight. She blew a stray strand of hair away from her face. Her voice was not discreet, now. It was loud. 'If that nonsense is what people really believe, wouldn't calling ChildLine be more effective than painting my door in fucking pig gore?'

McCloud just looked at her. But she was fairly sure she had got her message across. Her response would reach the perpetrators. She did not think it would halt their campaign. Her mother had once endured something similar and she knew how the story unfolded. Poison pen letters would come next. Excrement would arrive through the post. Her car might be vandalised. They might nail the head of their slaughtered pig to her door or daub a pentagram. Windows would be smashed in the depths of the night. A bit of shouting and sarcasm would not stop it. Mark Hunter might help her do that, though, when he got back from Switzerland. He was the sort of man who would repay a favour. And she thought him truly formidable. Most important, though, his son was her patient. And no amount of bigotry and physical interference would prevent her doing all she could to enable Adam's recovery.

Despite her resolve, Elizabeth pulled to a halt outside the Hunter house feeling shaken as well as indignant. Her home had been violated. And by extension she had too. She pulled down her sunshade to look in the small mirror backing it and switched on the interior light to examine her reflection. She was still struggling with the implications of what she had revealed to herself at the stable at her mother's house on Saturday. The cross on her own front door was not as troubling as that. But it was particular to her, intimate in its scorn and distaste. She composed herself in the mirror. She looked all right. Children could be extremely sensitive to stress and anxiety in adults. Adam needed her to be carefree and calm. She did not think she looked very much like a witch. There could be a hint of hauteur about her appearance when she pulled back her hair and made herself up. It was the shape and colour of her eyes, she supposed. But despite her bloodline she did not think she looked blackly magical or even malicious. Outside the car it was fully dark, the night moonless. She looked towards the warm illumination of the house. There would be the smells of cooking and a roaring fire within. She hoped to God there would be no nightmares, no ancient, rusty voices emanating from the sleeping boy in Mark's absence. She hoped the crone whose call he'd answered was a woman of her word. She smiled in the mirror. And her reflection smiled back at her, unconvincingly. She snapped back the sunshade, switched off the light and got out on to the gravel. It was five minutes to six.

* * *

The phone rang in Hunter's hotel room at 7 p.m. and it was reception to tell him that a visitor awaited him in the lobby. He knew it would be one of two people. It would be Miss Hall's emissary or it would be the man from the airport whose face wore a masked tattoo. He stood up from the bed, from where he had taken the call using the phone on the bedside table. He had showered and was dressed in a lounge suit for his audience with the fat sorceress. He had been tying his tie knot when the phone rang. He had no weapon. He had no uniform inside which to feel confidently clad for combat. But he felt secure enough in himself. He was skilled at half a dozen sorts of unarmed combat and had used them all his professional life, distilling what he considered most practical and lethal from each. A man weighing three hundred pounds would try to grapple him to the floor and kill him with a choke hold. But a man weighing that much lacked mobility and Hunter would knock him cold and break his neck before he got the chance to take him down.

He took the stairs because emerging from the lift gave him no perspective on what its doors would open to reveal. He pushed through the fire door. It was not the airport sentinel. Only one man waited, seated in the lobby. He was attired formally, in evening wear. Over it he wore an astrakhan coat and hat in a matching grey. He was tall, but he was very thin and was scrabbling absently at a set of worry beads. Hunter approached him. The man saw him and stood up. He was quite pale and his face cadaverously gaunt. He blinked and looked around. He seemed afraid. But there was no one else present, no one lurking. Hunter was combat alert now. And he would have sensed the danger.

'I am the Comte de Flurey,' the man said. He made no offer to shake hands.

'Sir,' Hunter said. He did not know the protocol for a

French count. He considered France a republic and French aristocratic titles a silly affectation. But then Miss Hall's emissary had already signalled an inclination towards pomp over the phone.

'May I say how very sorry I am about your son's ordeal, Colonel.'

'Why are you here? I have the address.'

'I am to drive you, if you will permit me.' The Comte gave a short bow. Hunter pondered the offer. It deprived him of the security of a taxi driver as solid witness to the journey he was about to take and its destination should he fail to return. But the hotel staff had anyway seen the Comte. He was not an inconspicuous man.

'The house is high above the lake, remote,' he said. 'The route is not straightforward.'

'All right,' Hunter said. He walked across to the reception desk to cancel his cab. He slipped the key to his room into his pocket. The hotel would have others. But it was still a precaution, of sorts. He turned back to the Comte. 'Let's go.'

Chapter Five

The car was not her glossy Palmetto bug of a limousine. It was a mundane Mercedes people carrier in the metallic silver ubiquitous on Europe's roads. Hunter hesitated for a moment over whether to get in beside Miss Hall's emissary or behind him. But practicality was more important than etiquette, and so he got into the front passenger seat. He did not particularly want a conversation with this man. But he did want all the information he could amass before they reached their destination.

'How is Miss Hall's demeanour?'

'Her demeanour? She is very sick, Colonel.'

'What's her mood?'

The Comte shrugged. 'Resigned,' he said. 'She knows she has little time.'

Hunter remembered Mrs Mallory's boast about comforting Rupert Brooke in Berlin, a full eighty or so years before the Magdalena confrontation. Mrs Mallory had looked decades younger than Miss Hall had done. She might well have little time. But the thought of how much time she might already have enjoyed made him shiver in the chill of the car's interior.

'Would you like the heater on?'

The Comte was very observant. It was interesting that the cold did not afflict him, despite his being so thin. There was not much flesh on him to insulate his bones. It was getting colder because they were ascending well above the level of the lake into thinner air.

'Have you been with her for long?'

The Comte smiled. 'Always.'

'You were not there at Magdalena.'

'That was a private encounter, Colonel. Nobody should have been there but the two protagonists. As I understand your comrades learned to their cost.'

'It's why I asked about her mood,' Hunter said. 'I have seen what these people are like when they are angry.'

The Comte drove for a while in silence. 'I will offer you two pieces of advice,' he said. 'Never make the mistake of thinking of them merely as people. And do not compare Mrs Mallory, in her wrath, with my employer and benefactress. Miss Hall is far more good than bad.'

Hunter nodded. It was a claim he had heard before from the horse's mouth. He asked no more questions because he sensed that what the Comte had said was a sort of summing-up of their conversation. The people carrier twisted along the steep incline of the road in first gear. The Comte smelled vaguely of some antique cologne. It was very faint, as though he put it on and then showered afterwards to avoid the vulgarity of being scented to excess. Hunter recognised it and knew he would remember the name. It was the women's perfume Shalimar. There were rings on the third fingers of each of the Comte's hands. His hands were pale and bony on the wheel and the stones set in the rings glittered blackly. After a few more minutes, they were there.

The house occupied by Miss Hall was tall and narrow and shuttered. It stood in isolation, flanked by ascending pines on the steep slope that rose behind it. The Comte had to get out of the car to open the locked gate between the walls that guarded the house. The walls were high and constructed from old stone but, despite their age, were smooth and sheer. Hunter was no authority on domestic architecture. But as they passed through the large ornamental iron gate, he judged the house to be an eighteenth-century construction. There was that classical coldness about it, that essential formality. There was no garden at the front of the house. There was just a generous rectangle of gravel deep enough to crunch audibly under the wheels of the Mercedes. There was a sundial directly in the centre of the route from the gate to the front door. The Comte got back in when he had closed the gate behind them and steered carefully round this object and parked. He was nimble enough to get out and round the front of the vehicle to open the passenger door before Hunter had quite freed himself from his seat-belt. He was not just nimble, Hunter thought, as the Comte treated him to the death's head leer of what he supposed was intended to be a smile of welcome. He was preternaturally fast.

The Comte approached the large front door and let them into the house. Beyond the door, a spacious entrance hall led to other rooms on the right. To the left, against the wall, rose a broad flight of wooden stairs behind a carved balustrade. The whole space was lit, somewhat dimly, by a single chandelier. The chandelier was huge. But it depended from a short chain and was remote from where they stood.

'Wait here,' the Comte said. Hunter nodded, aware that he had no choice. The Comte took the stairs. Once more his movement was so fleet that his ascent seemed like some cinematic trick, a jump-cut rush rather than a natural progression to whatever awaited on the upper floor. The thin aristocrat had the knack of devouring space. Outside a door, he knocked and waited before he opened it. He went through and then closed the door softly behind him.

Hunter looked around. He was aware of his heart beating in his chest. But the rhythm was steady and his pulse rate deliberate. He was reconciled to being here, resolved to do whatever was necessary to help his ailing son. He was less afraid in truth than he had been before the call purporting to be from Mrs Mallory. Then he had been entirely without a direction to go in, beyond trying to follow a trail allowed to go cold for more than a decade. Now, however sinister the circumstances, he felt that a measure of hope had been extended to him. Looking around, he saw that there were carved reliefs in oak lining the walls. There were tapestries, reaching almost to the high ceiling, above them. The floor was a design of red and white diamonds. He thought the bold pattern on the floor engaged the eye in the dim light in a restless way when he examined it. It created the illusion in his peripheral vision that the figures in the oak reliefs on the walls twitched and shifted slyly. His gaze kept returning directly to the figures depicted there. But whenever he looked at them properly, they were cunning and bestial, clothed in human apparel and entirely still. He had seen them before. He had liked their effect no better then.

The Comte appeared at the top of the stairs and invited him up with a curled forefinger. The door behind him was open. But from the bottom of the staircase, Hunter could see no light beyond it. He climbed the stairs. They were carpeted in some rich, soft stuff that sank luxuriously under the weight of his tread. It was not a pleasant sensation. The pile of the carpeting was so deep it seemed to stick under the soles of his shoes and cling in the manner of something viscous and sticky. Approaching the landing, he heard faint music from the room beyond the Comte. And he knew it. He was almost entirely ignorant of classical music, but Lillian had possessed an ardent love for a number of romantic and choral works. He recognised the Ninth Symphony by Mahler. It was the Berliner Philharmoniker version recorded under the baton of Herbert von Karajan. Lillian had owned the CD. She had played it constantly, laid up in the late stages of her pregnancy in the weeks before Adam's birth. It was the second time he had been reminded of his dead wife in half an hour. For Lillian had worn Shalimar perfume, also.

'Enter, Colonel Hunter,' a voice said. He would not have recognised it. It was not the deep, querulous contralto he remembered, or thought he did. Her voice had not lost its relish for command. But the body had gone from it. And when he entered the room and sensed the discreet withdrawal of the Comte behind him to another part of the house, he was immediately able to see why.

He had expected Miss Hall's domain of sorcery to be lit by candles, or at least oil lamps, something suitably Gothic and antique. But the large room was illuminated by electric globes that each offered a yellowy seepage of light too feeble to cast shadows. They hung from the ceiling on chains and were evenly spaced. She sat upright on a plumply uphol-stered leather sofa and looked like some gaunt, living ghost. A velvet skullcap covered her bald head. He could not keep the shock from his face on seeing her. She drew shrunken lips back from her too large teeth and he saw that they had developed a tortoiseshell pattern of decay. She was dying, all right. He would have known it blindfolded. He would have known it from the odour in the room. She clapped her hands together. The impact was harsh, the skin stretched over her palms brittle sounding. He would have bet she had no more than a few days left in her. She cocked her head to the side and laughed.

'You are no sort of actor, Colonel. But you never were. You could not disguise your revulsion for me a dozen years ago. And that was when I was well, before you took the action that condemned me.'

'I did not condemn you, Miss Hall. You saved my arm and probably my life and I was properly grateful to you. I killed Mrs Mallory. I regret I pointed my gun at you. But I meant you no harm.'

Her eyes were large in her shrunken face and they gleamed. 'You were a fool then. You are a fool now. Why should I have supposed you would be any different from how you were? Perhaps I am as big a fool as you are.' Her hands had dropped to her lap. Now she lifted one of them and brushed away something imaginary. She looked up at him again. The glint in her eyes was still present. She was angry, perhaps even furious. Her demeanour did not seem resigned to him. 'What do you think happened, Colonel, all those years ago in Bolivia? Have you ever allowed your mind to consider that?'

'We blundered into something we did not understand,' he said. 'We had no mechanism for dealing with it. It was beyond our remit and experience. We were motivated by damage limitation and the instinct for survival, when it all went wrong. And when we discovered the mutilation suffered by Major Rodriguez, I am ashamed to say I was driven entirely by the impulse for revenge.'

Miss Hall seemed to consider this. 'What do you think we were about, at Magdalena?'

'I don't know. It was beyond my scope, beyond my comprehension.'

'Do you believe in magic?'

'Not really. But that's not really the point. You do. That's wholly the point.'

Miss Hall nodded. She coughed. Affliction soughed through her like a stiff breeze through autumn leaves about to fall. 'Look around you.'

He did. There were more of the sly carvings on the walls that cavorted on the edge of vision. There was a sculpture on a tabletop; an expression of solid geometry featuring spheres that would not stay circular and squares undermined by their own odd angularity. Studying this piece provoked a queasiness that could easily have risen to nausea.

Miss Hall said, 'Are you really so arrogant as to think that your species has this world to yourselves? Perhaps you are innocent enough to believe, Colonel, that the meek will inherit the earth? I do not believe you are. And I assure you, they will not.'

He thought it was odd that he had not been invited to sit. He did not truthfully want to be anywhere closer to her than he was. But he had assumed he had been summoned to provide some sort of service for her. As it was, he was the naughty schoolboy being carpeted for long-ago acts of stupidity and disobedience. Hunter felt he ought to move matters along. 'Here's what I think. You are a powerful hypnotist. Your rival and adversary Mrs Mallory was a powerful hypnotist. You might have thought yourselves witches or black magicians and you might think that still, Miss Hall. But the power of auto-suggestion is what you actually possess.'

'And your son's dreams?'

'Triggered by something programmed in me, I think. I don't believe I remember everything that happened to Captain Peterson or me in the canvas labyrinth.'

'How did auto-suggestion heal your arm?'

He shrugged. 'Positive thinking can be very beneficial.'

'The dog was rabid and the limb already gangrenous. Either infection would have killed you.'

Hunter smiled. 'Perhaps you are mistaken,' he said.

'No. But you, Sir, are very much mistaken,' said Miss Hall. She rose frailly to her feet.

He saw how loose on her the clothing she wore had become. It had been cut to accommodate her obesity. It resembled sacking more than items of dress. She had not possessed the optimism or the energy, apparently, to replace it with something literally more fitting. She did something with her hands. She folded them in some complex choreography. It looked like origami without the use of paper. That hard glitter had not left her eyes since his entry into the room.

He was unaware of his feet leaving the floor. The process was too rapid. He was aware of the smack of his skull against the bare stone of the wall and the way his brain juddered and the fact that his nose had begun to bleed with the physical shock. He thought too a tooth might have chipped. He knew that his heels trailed the floor by a couple of feet when he hit the wall. And there was a band of iron around his chest that prevented him filling his lungs.

'Is this auto-suggestion,' he heard the sick sorceress say in her brittle, autumnal voice. 'Do you die at the mercy of illusion?'

His backside and shoulders scraped stone. He was shunted sideways. He felt the breath of the night from a window towards which his body was edging. He managed to turn his head to look at it. The effort was immense. The window was arched and as tall as he was. He shunted further with a scrape of good cloth towards the carved ornamental edging, an inch or so proud of the wall. It rippled under his shoulder blade.

'I could put you outside. You might survive the drop. It's about seventy feet. And you are not wearing your parachute now, Colonel.'

He could not breathe in the iron corset encasing his lungs. She knew. Perhaps she wanted to prolong his agony. He felt a fractional space of relief and gasped into it. And his heels juddered and rocked on stone. He was a strung puppet.

'Look at the arm I healed. Better, look for it.'

The limb was no longer there. His suit coat was pinned at the elbow of his left arm with the neat, tailored habit of amputation.

'What shall I do with you?' Miss Hall asked, approaching him.

He knew this was not hypnosis. Hypnosis could not kill you. And the sorceress was intent on his destruction.

She had come up very close to him. Shallow as his breathing was, he could smell the stink of her approaching death. In an effort to avoid the sight of her, he managed to twist his head and look at the wall to his right. The beasts in the carvings mounted there were an audience now, all pretence of innocent stillness gone. They watched the spectacle and did not hide their wolfish grins of appreciation. Miss Hall grinned too. Her voice rattled out of her. 'Is this still hypnotism, Colonel Hunter? Perhaps this is telekinesis, or some other fashionable phenomenon. Before the conclusion of the Cold War, the Russians experimented with telekinesis. I believe they once moved a domino on a tabletop a distance of two inches. Extraordinary.'

He thought it wiser to say nothing. He had antagonised her enough. Anyway, the iron corset of her spell did not allow him sufficient breath to speak.

'I could put you somewhere, Colonel,' she said. 'I could put you anywhere. I know you have a fondness for the mountains. There is a storm on the Eiger just now. Here all is calm. But up there, in the high Alps, the storm rages. I could put you there, above the second ice field, clinging to scant handholds with the void below you in the shrieking gale. All I have to do is will it. You are prodigiously fit and strong. But even if I returned your arm to you, how long do you think you would last before you lost your grip and plunged the vertical mile in darkness to the meadow at the foot of the face?'

'A minute,' Hunter managed to say.

'Less,' Miss Hall said. 'Less than half that. Trust me. I know.'

There was a phantom itch in his missing limb. The press of the stone against his back was suddenly profoundly cold.

It caused the muscles in his back to spasm. It was the black chill of the Eiger's north face. It was the merest hint of what she could accomplish.

'But I have in mind something much more mundane,' she said. 'I think I shall simply put you under the ground beneath the gravel outside. Eight feet down you will discover a dark, dense berth of clay and rocks. It is very inhospitable. For a few moments, you will suffer unendurably. But after a short struggle you will suffocate and die. Then you will discover rest in your grave. The burden of grief you carry for your wife and daughter will be lifted. And your son's predicament will no longer be of any concern to you.'

There was a knock at the door.

'Enter.'

Hunter slipped down from the wall and fell to the floor and broke his fall with both hands, made aware by doing so that the missing limb had been restored to him. He was trembling and sweating, his suit was torn and his shirt streaked and stained from his nosebleed. There was a cut to the back of his head. He could feel blood sticky in his hair. The Comte entered wheeling a silver trolley piled with dishes under polished metal domes. To Hunter, the smell of food was impossibly rich. What breath had been allowed him in the last few moments, he knew, had come from up there on the remote reaches of the Eigerwand. The trolley rattled towards the centre of the room. Swallowing blood, with his cheek against the waxed floor of Miss Hall's dining room, he said, 'I thought you were more good than bad?'

'I am, Colonel Hunter. Were I not, I would have killed you at Magdalena.'

Getting to his feet would take a moment. He managed to get to his knees.

'Let us eat,' Miss Hall said. 'I trust you are not a vegetarian?'

'No.' He was overwhelmed now by a feeling remembered from then, from Bolivia, the feeling that nothing was mundane or innocuous or really solid in the world. Certainties were built on shifting sand. Malice lurked wherever the light did not burn brightly. It was overwhelming and depressing and it was frightening. Worst of all, this feeling, this suspicion, was defeating. He had not felt it even at Adam's bedside, listening to the sleeping child speak in forgotten languages. But he had felt it very strongly in the cathedral of black canvas outside Magdalena. And he recognised it again in himself here, in Miss Hall's grand house above the shores of Lake Geneva.

'You may wish to clean up. You are a mess. The Comte will show you to a bathroom where you can restore and compose yourself. Then we shall eat. And I shall tell you what it is that you must accomplish if your son is to live and recover.'

Hunter could not yet gain his feet. Strength and balance were returning to him. But it would be another minute. He smelled the rich aroma of the food. He heard the discreet clatter of the Comte laying plates and cutlery in the background.

'Goodness,' Miss Hall said. 'I am forgetting my manners. You have been my guest here for nigh on fifteen minutes. And I have not yet offered you anything to drink.'

On that first full night of his being under her care, Elizabeth let Adam stay up later than his regular bedtime. He had enjoyed two good nights since the phone call in the early hours of Saturday. There had been little debate about returning him to school on the Monday morning. School would seem much more familiar to him than spending the day with a nanny he had never met, regardless of her competence or professional qualifications. His father had been anxious to try to return him to normality as soon as possible. Normality meant routine and that meant school. And Adam wanted to see his schoolfriends. He was buoyant, excited by the prospect, rested, the dark confusion of the dreams already receding from a life where Man United topped the Premiership and he'd just downloaded Girls Aloud's killer new single on to his iPod.

But his dad was away. And Adam had never been away from his dad since the day of his mother's and sister's deaths. Mark had told her that himself. There was every chance that Mark would feel the separation more acutely than his son. It was Elizabeth's experience that children were much less sentimental than adults tended to be. But she thought it best to keep him occupied and entertained and then pack him off to bed when he was tired enough to fall asleep without pondering his father's sudden absence. He had been told his dad had needed to go off on business.

'Business?' he had said. 'What business? Your business used to be jumping out of aeroplanes with a big gun. You're a bit old for that these days, Dad. And you've given your army clothes back. Plus, I don't see any big gun.'

But he had not questioned further. He trusted his father. He had never in his life been given any reason not to do so.

The woman Mark had employed on her own recommendation had prepared a dinner of roast chicken and put it in the oven half an hour before Elizabeth's arrival at the house. She washed up and changed in the spare room and Adam chatted to her as she boiled the potatoes and steamed the broccoli and peas and made gravy. Her mother had taught her to cook. It was her mother's recipe she followed almost without conscious thought as she made the gravy for their roast dinner. She felt ambivalent about her mother, she realised. She had always taken Mum for granted, as she imagined most grown-up daughters did. But now she wondered how well she actually knew her. Certainly she now thought there was more to her than the sweet, elderly, forgetful caricature recent years had allowed her mother to become in her mind prior to Saturday afternoon.

'Elizabeth?'

'Adam.'

He was seated at the kitchen table taking the tyres off a toy car. 'Can I have a Diet Coke?'

'No.'

'Please?'

'Your dad told me your regular tipple is apple juice. Nothing carbonated. No caffeine.'

'My dad's a monster when it comes to nutrition.'

'He's responsible for your health, Adam.'

'He knows no mercy.'

'I wouldn't go quite that far. There's apple crumble and ice cream for pudding.'

'I see you've got some greens on the go.'

At the sink, Elizabeth drained the broccoli. 'Is that a bad thing?'

'I suppose it could be worse,' Adam said. 'It could be Brussels sprouts.'

'And we all know what they do, don't we?'

He grinned at her. 'They make you blow off,' he said. 'Like a wizard.'

She peered through the oven's glass door. The chicken looked ready. She thought that Adam Hunter was definitely on the mend.

After dinner they played a couple of games of chess. Adam won both, Elizabeth sensed with something to spare. She was reminded that this was a boy who could read fluently at the age of three. Things came very easily to him. He was extremely bright and, physically, nothing short of beautiful. He should not have had a care in the world. After the chess, he asked if he could watch a DVD. Elizabeth would have baulked at one of the spookier *Dr Who* episodes; but his choice was a Jeremy Clarkson programme in which Clarkson made fun of some easy automotive targets and then destroyed examples of these sad vehicles from the dark days of British engineering and design by dropping them from a crane. There was a popcorn maker in the kitchen. Elizabeth made Adam popcorn with hot maple syrup and butter and he ate it lounging on the sofa, laughing at Clarkson's grown-up schoolboy antics, yawning when the programme finished, definitely ready for bed.

He stood up and stretched. 'Goodnight,' he said.

'Don't forget to brush your teeth.'

'I won't. Will you come and check on me in ten minutes?'

'Yes, of course.'

He just stood there. She realised that he expected a good-night kiss. Of course he did, his father never failed to provide him with one. Elizabeth pecked him on the cheek and ruffled his hair and he reached around her waist and hugged her.

'Goodnight, Adam.'

He smiled. 'Your popcorn is epic,' he said.

When she checked on him ten minutes later he was deeply and restfully asleep. On her return to the sofa in the sitting room, she picked up her phone and saw that someone had texted her. Mobile reception was patchy in the area at best and the text could have been sent hours earlier and only just reached her. Anything urgent and it would be the message light flashing, not the text icon showing on the display. But she opened and read the text anyway. To Elizabeth's great surprise, it was from her mother. She had not even known her mother could text. She smiled to herself, but the smile was grim. She was learning more about her mother all the time.

The text was a question. Her mother wanted to know

whether Elizabeth had made any inquiries about the Campbell witch trial archive left among his papers by Judge Jerusalem Smith. She scrolled down and saw that the text had been sent at 6.05 p.m. Her mother had allowed her one working day in which to contact the British Library. But given that she was in no position to plan an imminent trip to London, she had not even thought to do so. In her mother's mind, there was clearly urgency here. It was as though her mother was in a hurry for her to discover something. Elizabeth wondered why. She did not think the reason for her mother's anxiety likely to be a very happy one. She did not think any truth she might uncover likely to be innocent. There was nothing good or wholesome about the one relic of Ruth Campbell carved in singed oak in the stable at her family home, was there?

She took the Clarkson DVD out of the machine and put it back in its case with the others, stored in a neat row under the player. Most of the DVDs were feature films and it was very much a boys' collection: *Gladiator*, *Casino Royale*, *Men in Black* and *The Bourne Ultimatum*. There was a discerning section Mark must have hand-picked for Adam; vintage action films such as *The Vikings* and *Jason and the Argonauts* and Eighties children's classics including *The Goonies*, *Ghostbusters*, *Back to the Future* and *Flight of the Navigator*. There were *Torchwood* and *Doctor Who* of course. And there was Clarkson. And there was a narrow section of cases with hand-written titles on their spines. *Klosters, 2007*, one of these said. Elizabeth took it out and slipped the disc into the player. Maybe it was morbid to watch a Hunter family home movie. Certainly it was an invasion of privacy. But she also thought it might justifiably be called background on her patient.

Klosters was cold. The light was flat, the sky overcast. The snow had that fluffy, powdery consistency it only has when the air is so far below freezing point that there is no moisture in it at all. The family were well wrapped up against the elements in ski suits and gloves. They wore hats and hoods and masks. Their features were completely concealed. Mark, presumably, was behind the camera as his lost daughter skied towards him down a long, steep slope followed by her brother and then, lastly, by her mother. They were all obviously expert skiers. But Kate had a particular grace and lightness, a distinctive poise. She skied very fast but was totally in control of her neat, rapid turns as she descended and then stopped with a slewed flourish inches from the lens. Her breath came through the scarf covering the lower half of her face and clouded on the frozen air. She lifted her mask and her eyes smiled. And Elizabeth remembered that she had been on the way to a ballet class at the time of her death and wondered how Mark ever found the strength to watch what she was watching now. Probably, she thought, he did not.

Adam came next. He hurtled down the slope, taking moguls straight on as jumps, skiing on the edge of control, almost achieving with strength and athleticism the speed his sister had reached with her pure and effortless talent.

Lastly, Lillian came down. Even in her ski clothes, Elizabeth could see that she was slender. She wore her hair long. It switched against her shoulders in a light-brown ponytail when she executed her turns on the steep slope. Like her daughter, she skied very gracefully. Adam made a crack to his father about how slow she was and Mark chuckled and the camera trembled slightly in his hand but it did not shift from its subject or lose focus. She was not slow at all; she was rhythmic until she checked at the bottom of the slope and planted her poles. The rhythm stopped and she bowed her head and regained her breath after the effort of the long descent. She said something. She made a joke about how unfit she was. She had the cut-glass enunciation of a privileged English birth and upbringing. She shed her gloves, took off her hair tie and shook out her ponytail. She lifted her head and slipped her mask up to her forehead and unwound the scarf concealing the lower half of her face. She looked into the camera lens, grinned and shaped a kiss, and Elizabeth found herself staring back into her own laughing eyes as they looked out at her from the Hunters' plasma television screen.

She had been eating the remnants of Adam's popcorn. She only became aware of that now as the bowl fumbled through her fingers on to the rug.

'Jesus. Jesus Christ.'

There was a cry from upstairs. Elizabeth stood and turned off the DVD player and went to see what the matter was with Adam. No wonder, she thought, he had felt entitled to a goodnight kiss.

Hunter suspected that the food was delicious. Dying, he thought that Miss Hall probably lived very well. There was, no doubt, an excellent chef somewhere in the depths of her house above the lake every bit as much in thrall to his mistress as was the Comte. But he could not taste anything as the wine was served, as the bread was torn, as the courses came and went. His hostess ate prodigiously. But her rate of consumption of food was nowhere equal to the hunger of the thing eating her from within. She did not have long. It was the only certainty, Hunter felt. And it gave him no comfort.

'You have the skill of scrutinising without appearing to do so, Colonel. Your training, I suppose. Eat something. You will need the nourishment to sustain you.'

'In Bolivia, how did you know our names?'

She sipped wine and grimaced, as though the question was unworthy of reply.

'How could we surprise you if you knew our names?'

'I was wholly preoccupied with my struggle with Mrs Mallory. I had only that moment achieved victory in the encounter when your dashing Major blundered in and complicated things. Ordinarily, your approach would have been something to which both of us would have been alert long before you breached the perimeter fence. But we were engaged with one another. It distracted us.'

'How old was Mrs Mallory?'

'It is of no importance.'

'Indulge me.'

'She was young when the century was young.'

'She claimed she comforted the poet Rupert Brooke.'

Miss Hall sawed at the meat on her plate. It was very rare and glistened under the yellow electric light. 'Not that century, you fool. She was young when the French dragoons trampled her father's harvest and looted his harvested crops on their route through her family's land on their way to Moscow. They laughed, under their plumes, in their bright, braided tunics from their saddles. They were not laughing when the winter came and inflicted the long agony of their retreat.'

'She cursed them?'

Miss Hall rested her knife and fork to either side of her plate. 'Russia cursed them. The weather gods cursed them. Perhaps Mrs Mallory cursed them too. She was not Mrs Mallory then, of course, that conceit came much later. And whatever comfort she offered Brooke would have been cold indeed. Consolation is not among her skills.'

Hunter nodded.

'Or instincts.' Miss Hall shuddered. 'But you are making me digress. What is important is that your intervention with the gun enabled her escape from the fate I had planned for her. She had gambled against me and lost and had accepted the consequence. She is nothing, if not a woman of her word.

So she was reconciled. Then you released her. That's history, though. What matters is what she intends to do now her power is almost restored to her.'

'What will she do?'

'Listen to your son. He will tell you. Before he loses his mind and perishes, he will indulge the affliction of prophesy. She will brag through him, her instrument. That is your curse.'

Hunter shifted in his chair. The chair was wooden and ornate and the high carved back painful against his bruised spine and shoulders. He was being asked to believe in the spite of a sorceress who had witnessed the marauding arrival of the horsemen of Napoleon's invading army as a young girl. He had put two bullets squarely into a woman's brain and was being told that a decade on she lived unscathed, gaining power. He had heard the voices emanate from his son's mouth while the boy slept. He could feel the throb of impact still, under the blood congealing in his hair from when the dying creature opposite had earlier toyed with him. And he remembered what had happened in Bolivia. He had spent the better part of twelve years attempting to forget it. But he had brought it all back in his lakeside hotel room and he knew he would never now forget the oppression of the canvas labyrinth or the smell of the Major's mutilation or the sight of his wife's features worn on the face of the witch in Magdalena. He sighed. In the chamber where he sat, the wooden walls were furtive with movement. Behind him, the Comte waited, silent and obsequious. Across the table, Miss Hall ate methodically, the scrabble of silver cutlery on the bone china of her plate like dancing insect limbs.

'Why was she so angry? It seems to me that the intervention of the Major was her reprieve. How did he incur this wrath? Why did she punish him in so vile and brutal a manner?'

Miss Hall smiled. 'How well did you know the Major?'

'He was brave and intelligent. He was learned. I had known him only for a few hours. I knew him hardly at all.'

'He was a devout Catholic. He was one of three brothers. There was the Franciscan, the Jesuit and the soldier. It was our misfortune, and his, to encounter the soldier. He approached us with his carbine trained on us and a rosary wound around the barrel of the weapon. He was incanting some prayer to his Catholic God. It was this that enraged Mrs Mallory.'

'How do I stop her, Miss Hall? Do I burn her at the stake? Put a pointed wooden stake through her heart? Do I buy some silver bullets for my gun?'

'Sarcasm is not helpful.'

'It is when it's all I've got.'

'First, you must find her. I cannot even help you in that. I do not have the time left for the pursuit.'

'I'm sorry.'

'Whether you are or you are not is immaterial. You are here because I am more good than bad, despite what you might think evidential to the contrary. Even if I had the time to help you find Mrs Mallory, I am too debilitated by illness to confront her as I once did. And she is cunning and a quick learner, so I doubt I would have the wit to trick her again. You must find a way. I will tell you what I know. You must track her like prey and then like prey you must kill her. I will tell you everything I know about your quarry. I can furnish one address where you might learn something.'

Hunter sat forward, alert.

'No, Colonel. I do not think you will find her there. But you will find her spoor. You will pick up her scent.' Miss Hall hesitated over her next words. 'Mrs Mallory likes to live. And that might yet be her downfall.'

'What do you mean, she likes to live?'

Miss Hall exposed her teeth in a decaying smile. 'In life, to use the current idiom, Mrs Mallory likes to party.'

It was very late when the Comte drove Hunter the steep route back down to his hotel. Or it was very early, because it was now Tuesday morning. Despite his nap on the Monday afternoon, he felt tired the way that combat left you feeling, bone weary, his stomach and the back of his throat sour with spent adrenaline. This low feeling usually followed a combat high. On this occasion there had been no high, only the low and the listlessness and inability to think with urgent clarity.

His expedition had been open-ended in the sense that he had not told Elizabeth Bancroft exactly when he would return. He had figured on anything from one night away to a week. The address Miss Hall had given him was a lodge, high and remote in the Austrian Tyrol. It did not sound like the home address of someone who liked to party. Hunter thought something like a Venice palazzo or a Manhattan loft apartment much more likely bets on that score. He had met Mrs Mallory in Magdalena. In life, in the brief time she had revealed her true face to him, she had been nothing if not glamorous. But Miss Hall had been adamant that he would not find his adversary at the lodge perched at the top of the mountain. Perhaps it was a place where she had stored things. If so, he hoped the things she had stored were not trophies.

He had not really been convinced by talk of her spoor. This was because he could not believe in the notion of her as prey. That would surely be a very dangerous conceit. He had no choice but to try to destroy her. What he had learned in the last hours from Miss Hall made her eradication the most important mission of his life. But he had tried before and apparently failed when her powers had been depleted. He did not underestimate the difficulty of the challenge. Even the term adversary, with its implication of a somehow equal match, seemed arrogant. At the start of their evening, Miss Hall had teased and pawed him like a cat with a mouse. And she was weak. Miss Hall was dying.

He would sleep for a couple of hours and then call Elizabeth before her departure for her rounds and explain that he would return after two more nights away. With luck, he would be able to have a chat with Adam and gauge his son's mood. Adam was as reticent with his father on the phone as most children of his age were, answering any question with a cheery monosyllable. But even his tone would tell Hunter what he needed to know, give him the reassurance that Miss Hall was keeping her word about holding the dreams, for the duration, at bay. He thought she would. He considered Miss Hall honourable in her way and honest too. But he did not think she felt such things as pity or compassion. And she would not feel compelled to act out of either urge. Compassion, when all was said and done, whether you regarded it as indulgence or attribute, was a very human impulse.

Someone had been in his room. He knew it straight away. Switzerland was a fastidious country, almost clinical in its neatness and precision. There was an odour in his room, a dead reek at odds with the taut cover on his immaculately made bed and the way that the blades of his window blind cast perfect horizontals of light from the sodium lamps outside on to his spotless carpet. He remembered the tattooed man at the airport. He thought there might be three hundred pounds of malevolence waiting, lurking in the bathroom. But he did not really think the stink strong enough. He remembered Private Gaul's description of the smell. Like something dead left neglected to decay, Gaul had said. He had been very accurate. The smell was faint, hours old. But it was still corrupt enough to gag on after the congealed richness of Miss Hall's extravagant dinner.

Cautiously, Hunter opened his bathroom door. He flattened himself against the wall beside it. He waited and listened. Nothing that breathed lurked in the darkness there. This was Switzerland, so there were no drips from the shower head or taps. And from the bathroom, the taint on the air was even fainter, fought by some lemony disinfectant and apple-scented soap. His intruder had gone.

Hunter took a long shower. He washed the matted blood from his hair and sluiced warm water over his wounds. It wasn't just his back. His whole body was a pattern of contusions and bruises on their painful blossoming from yellow to dark blue. It wasn't just the consequence of the actual assault, he thought. It was as though his body had rebelled at the unnatural way in which the trauma had occurred. Hunter did not feel violated. But he did feel humiliated. And he had felt helpless. Lastly, draped in a towel, he went over to his window and looked out at the trees over the road outside and their gentle descent to the pebbly shore and the still inkiness of the night lake. There was starlight and it dabbed at the rough fur coats of the conifers. And he thought he saw the bald gleam of the scalp of someone watching him from among them. But this sentinel would not resolve itself into convincing shape and Hunter decided eventually that it was nothing more than a trick of the light preying on tired eyes. He could not remember having ever felt more tired.

He lay in his bed. It was quiet and dark and he was warm under the covers, and the steam from his shower had cleansed his room of the last hints of the earlier smell of corruption. Without knowing why, he was reminded of something. It seemed a random recollection and it came to him on the edge of the abyss of deep sleep.

The man with whom Lillian had wasted two years had

been an airline pilot. She had found a prescription for Famciclovir when looking for dental floss in his bathroom cabinet. Confronted, he confessed he had contracted genital herpes having unprotected sex with a Tokyo lap dancer during a one-night stand. Lillian had not been infected. But infection, even the risk of it, was not the point. Deception was the point and the lies it had necessitated. You only needed to lie to Lillian once. Her pilot had spun her a whole web of them.

A fortnight after he met her, Hunter had been having dinner with Lillian at a pavement table outside a Covent Garden restaurant when a man approached them. Lillian grabbed Hunter's wrist. Hunter could tell from the expression on the man's face that he was intent on confrontation. He did not require gilt lapels or a peaked cap for Hunter to guess who he was. And he could tell from the look of contorted fury on the face of the man that he knew exactly what it was in his life he had lost. Lillian had told Hunter his name. It was Albright. He was George Albright.

Lillian later told him that her pilot was an expert at tae kwon do. He attended the dojo twice a week when he wasn't reassuring his passengers in a British Airways purr over the intercom. But his opponent on this evening was a man who had studied every form of unarmed combat in existence. And he practised them with regularity and great seriousness in his working life. The ability to win a fight was life or death for Mark Hunter in the job for which he was paid and possibly born.

He stood up. His attacker aimed a downward kick intended to dislocate his knee. Hunter stepped inside this and put him on the pavement with a leg sweep, hitting him just to subdue him with a short punch to the jaw as he went down. Hunter followed him there. Someone at an adjacent table screamed and Albright tried to backhand Hunter from where he lay.

Hunter blocked the blow. He leaned close and said, 'Get up and walk away. Do not cast a backward glance. Do it, or you will leave here on a stretcher with your back broken.'

He did as he was told. Hunter felt a bit sorry for him as he walked off along Bow Street. He had lost Lillian. And now he had lost whatever myth he had harboured concerning his own invincibility. Lillian had, subsequently, been very critical of how Hunter had dealt with the confrontation. And it was this that he remembered now, as sleep overcame him. She had said that a man possessing Hunter's resources could have handled the situation without escalating the violence. She said that he had hurt and humiliated George Albright in a confrontation someone with his skills could easily have defused. And in this she had been right.

Lillian was a compassionate woman strongly opposed to the gratuitous infliction of violence. She was fastidious about pain, not so much squeamish as merciful and kind by nature. But after they were married, on his return from Magdalena, when he had told her about putting two bullets into her head in the execution of Mrs Mallory, Lillian had neither flinched nor criticised nor even commented. There had been no condemnation, just that enigmatic judgement exonerating him. Was there a paradox there? Was there a contradiction? Hunter was too tired to think it through. He later wished he had. But he was exhausted, and anyway, he was not to know that then.

Chapter Six

Elizabeth emailed the British Library inquiring about the archive left by Cromwell's Scottish witch finder, using Mark Hunter's desktop computer first thing the following morning. He had told her how to operate the machine as a guest user. Adam came down while she was typing her email request to arrange to see the material relevant to her ancestor. His dream the previous evening had been benign, his audible sigh as he slept probably popcorn induced and certainly nothing to do with his recent nocturnal trauma. He looked refreshed and carefree.

'Just going into the kitchen,' he said.

'I'm almost finished,' Elizabeth said. 'Another minute and I'll get you some breakfast.'

'I can help myself,' he said.

'Great.'

'Okay if I help myself to a Red Bull?'

'Fine,' Elizabeth said. 'The day hell freezes over.'

'Not even on medical grounds?'

'Only if you can specify the medical grounds.'

'You're even more heartless than my dad.'

'I'll take that, Adam, as the compliment I know you intend it to be.' She heard the nanny using the key she had been given to open the heavy locks that fortified the front door. She pressed Send and then shut down the computer. She got up and ate a quick breakfast at the kitchen table with Adam, then grabbed her bag, intent on an early start. She wanted to make time, if she could, to pay a surprise call on her mother after her mother's lunchtime nap.

Scotland's first female surgeon famously qualified to practise in 1914. The country had always been at the forefront
of pioneering medicine. But Edinburgh was a long way from
a remote practice in the highlands. Even after the Second
World War, the majority of rural Scots preferred a male to
a female GP. It was perfectly all right for a woman to be
trusted with lives as a district nurse or midwife. But male
GPs were widely considered a safer, steadier, altogether more
knowledgeable bet. This prejudice was particularly
entrenched among older women. And it had made the early
part of Margaret Bancroft's career always challenging and
sometimes worse than that. On occasion it had been callous,
and sometimes it had been downright cruel.

Elizabeth thought about the treatment meted out to her
mother on her way back to her cottage. That was only a
slight detour on the route from the Hunter house to the
surgery. She wanted to see if any further damage had
been inflicted. She thought it more likely a window had been
broken than the place burned to the ground. A rock flung
through a pane with a note tied to it was a favourite tactic
in any campaign of menace aimed at a domestic target. But
she had resolved that if anything beyond the daubing of the
cross had been done, she would involve the police. She was
innocent and angry at the violation already carried out and
would not tolerate its escalation. Her bit of theatre in the
pub the previous evening might have reached the right ears.
She hoped it had done the trick. She did not think painting
a cross in pig's blood on someone's door a crime that would
exact any great punishment in the courts. But any more
abusive nonsense and she would go to the boys in blue. She
had an excellent relationship with the local police. Like most
rural forces, they were under-resourced and the services of
a police doctor were theirs only after formal written requests
and delays that could be inconvenient or catastrophic,

depending upon the seriousness of the crime. Independent and unattached, Elizabeth was a medical expert for whose availability they had often been given cause to be grateful. And they were grateful, and she knew that they thought highly of her professionalism and not just of her willingness to help.

Her cottage sat in the early morning sunshine, untroubled and untouched. She went in only to open the curtains and to put fresh water in the vase of flowers on the kitchen table. She knew why she was thinking about her mother and the daily trials of her professional life and the campaign of hate she had endured in the summer of 1972. It was because she felt hostile and suspicious towards her mother after the stable incident. The text had only increased the feeling of suspicion. And what she wanted to feel towards her mother was warmth and sympathy. That was what she had always felt towards her in the past. Now, Elizabeth felt that her mother had become someone she didn't really know, a stranger to her, almost overnight. She did not want this mother. She wanted back her mum.

Margaret Bancroft was waiting, her face a pale, distorted shape in the lozenge panes of the right-hand window as Elizabeth approached the house. The door was on the latch. Elizabeth had a key in her bag but had known the door would be standing unlocked when she saw her mother waiting for her. As she walked the path to the door she glanced to the right, in the direction of the stable, and shivered. It was not cold. It was bright and unseasonably mild. But she could do nothing about the chill of dread and trepidation as it trammelled through her.

'You were waiting for me.'

Her mother had not risen from her chair. 'Have you read it?'

'Of course I haven't. There has not been time.'

'Then why are you here?'

'Because there are things you have not told me. Were you telling me the truth? When you told me you have never read the trial account?'

'I have never dared.'

Elizabeth sighed and shook her head. This was so odd. She had not embraced her mother as she always did. There had been no invitation to do so. She had not even sat down, and now felt scant invitation to relax.

'I'll tell you what I can, Elizabeth. I'll do that. Then judge me if you must.'

'Then there is something you have kept back.'

'You are my child. I never wanted to frighten or estrange you from me. I felt the same way about your father.' Margaret Bancroft smiled. 'Sit down, Elizabeth. I'll make some tea. And then I'll tell you a story.'

She had first become aware of her ability to heal as a little girl. She thought she had probably been born with the compassion of a healer. When she was five, her own mother asked her if she would like as her pet a kitten from a litter born to a tabby cat owned by their postman. But she said that she would not. She knew that she would love the kitten. And when it became a cat she would love it. And when it grew old and inevitably died, she knew that she would find the loss unbearable.

Then one day out walking close to Christmas, she happened upon a robin caught in a thorn bush. It was snowing and she supposed that the robin had lost its bearings on the wing and landed badly. Or it could have been forced into the refuge of the thorns by a hawk or even an eagle. Over the course of a bad winter the eagles would come inland from their eyries on the coastal cliffs to hunt. Kestrels were common. Whatever, trapped and flapping feebly, the tiny bird seemed to have damaged a wing and broken a leg. It was only half alive as Margaret prised it from between the barbs of the thorn bush and wrapped it in her woollen scarf and put it into her pocket.

Her first thought trudging home through the snow was that her father could provide the injured bird with a quick and painless death. He was a practical man with a strong stomach and would pinch the robin's neck between finger and thumb and break it cleanly and easily. Margaret would scrape a little grave for it in the turf under the snow so that it would not become carrion. All the way home she could feel the tremble of its tenuous life as it beat with its one good wing in the pocket of her coat against her hip. And she could not later have said at what point on her journey through the pretty white landscape this ceased to be her plan. But at some point it did, because she got to the house and stamped the slush from her boots and took them off and hung her coat on the hook, careful to remove her scarf and its precious living cargo from the pocket with only a nod at her father reading in his favourite chair before taking the stairs to her room. Her father did not even look up from his paper. Margaret held the scarf to her chest in both hands and climbed the stairs. It was the first winter she would recall as an adult with singular clarity. She was eleven years old.

The house was warm. Her parents were more prosperous than they were frugal. They did not follow the country custom of heating only the one room. Dusk had descended by now. Her walk had been a long one taken after their main meal at midday on a Saturday and the land vanquished the light early at this time of the year. The sun was an orange smear on the brink of the white moor, reddening through her window, and her walls were blood-coloured. With a hand pressing her scarf to her breast, Margaret opened the window. Then she let the scarf fall to the floor, enclosed the damaged bird in the cradle of her hands and parted her thumbs fractionally. She closed her eyes and blew gently through the gap. And she opened her eyes and hands and the bird gathered itself and flew through the open window strongly into the cold and the twilight. It swooped and thrummed on vibrant wings. And she knew it was healed. And she knew that she had healed it. And she was not, when she considered it, in the least bit surprised.

'I called it bone magic,' she told her daughter. 'I was eleven. Eleven-year-olds need names for things, especially when those things are abstract.'

'You really think the robin lived?'

'I think it may live still.'

'The magic was that strong?'

'I felt it in my bones. Thus the name given it by the child I was. I felt the age and the power of it very deep in me. I felt it in my marrow.'

'Wasn't it frightening, Mum?'

'In the end, it was terrifying. I healed a few injured creatures. I always did so secretly. Then when I was fourteen, I heard a blind shepherd was losing his sheepdog to cancer. I climbed the hill route to the hovel where he lived and held the collie between my hands and used my mind to push the affliction out. It was hard. The disease had flourished in poor Baxter's old bitch and was stubborn. But after that, I came to believe I could do anything. I wondered if I could not bring back something dead.'

Elizabeth swallowed. 'Did you ever try?'

'Of course I didn't.'

'Did you ever use your bone magic on a patient?'

But Elizabeth thought she knew the answer to that question already.

In the late spring of 1972 Margaret Bancroft was a seasoned GP, thirty-five years of age and long beyond the point at which the demise of a pet cat could have left her feeling disconsolate. She had seen her share of compassion and cruelty and caprice. She was not the stranger to death she had been as a little girl. Suffering touched her of course. But it was an occupational hazard, like engine oil ingrained in the pads of a mechanic's fingertips. You could not do the job without encountering pain and grief. You had to endure the bad to effect what good your expertise sometimes enabled.

Such was the balance of her thinking when she was summoned to a medical emergency at the farm owned by Andrew Hector. Andrew stood pale-faced to greet her outside his barn. Andrew's wife Susan was within, cradling their son Max in her arms. A makeshift bandage had been wrapped around the lower half of his left arm.

'Do you think he'll lose the limb, Doctor?' Andrew said.

Margaret Bancroft looked at the quantity of blood under the straw on the cobbles surrounding the unconscious boy. She thought it likelier he would lose his life. She squatted beside Max with her bag and unwound the bandage, which seemed to be a torn bed sheet. It was soaked in blood and useless. She revealed the wound, clean and very deep and gushing blood from the severed artery beneath the flesh with each beat of a fading pulse.

'He was sharpening a scythe on the stone. The steel must have caught. Lincoln was ratting in the barn and he fetched me straight away.'

But not soon enough, Elizabeth thought, binding the upper arm tightly and, she knew, too late. 'How long did they say until the ambulance comes?'

'Forty minutes,' Andrew said. 'Only twenty minutes, now.'

The optimism in the farmer's voice was anguished. Light flooded through gaps in the beams above and bathed everything in a fierce, ethereal light. Max Hector had seen the sunshine for the last time. He was thirteen. His parents had been both in their early forties at the time of his birth. There would be no other children.

'Leave me with my patient,' Margaret Bancroft said. Susan looked up at her and let go of her son reluctantly and stood in her blood-soaked blue pinafore and staggered towards the barn door. Her husband steadied her with an arm across her shoulders. And with a glance back towards where their son lay dying, they closed the door behind them. It was an act of faith in her proficiency that Margaret thought heartbreaking. She gripped Max's wrist but she could no longer feel a pulse at all, so faint was it. She had to staunch the blood. She held the injured arm to her stomach and closed her eyes and willed the wound away. And when she opened her eyes, it was gone. And she raised her gaze to heaven in thanks and her eyes alighted on the face and idiot leer of Lincoln, who had been ratting in the barn. Lincoln, who had seen the accident and raised the alarm. Lincoln, the nineteen-year-old halfwit the Hectors employed because they were kind-hearted people and no one else would. He was up in the hayloft that bordered the building's interior. He had witnessed what she had just accomplished.

'And I lost my nerve,' Margaret Bancroft told her daughter. 'I realised that it was something I would never be able to explain. The miracle would cost me my reputation and career. So I undid what I had just done. I did what I should have. And Max Hector slipped shivering from this life a few minutes later, a full quarter of an hour before the ambulance arrived.'

Elizabeth stared into the china cup cradled in her lap. Her tea was stone cold. She had not touched it. She had not even taken a sip. The milk had separated and formed a shimmering ring around the top of the beverage. 'How did you undo what you had done?'

'I reopened the wound.'

'How did you do that?'

'In the same way I had closed it.'

'Was it hard to?'

'The magic was not hard. I had endowed poor Max with the vigour to replenish the blood he had lost. I could feel it in the strengthening pulse under my thumb. I had to take that strength away from him again. Ebb it out of him. It was easy. But it was the hardest thing I have ever had to do in my life.'

'And you've never used that power again, have you, Mum?'

'Never.'

'And Tom Lincoln told someone and they harassed you as a witch. Do you know who that was?'

'I've no doubt it's the same person harassing you now, Elizabeth. That's one of the reasons I have told you this today.'

'You know about the cross daubed on my cottage door?'

'It may be well spaced, but this is a small locality. I have a telephone. And I have a few friends left alive.'

Elizabeth nodded.

'There is something you should know about what I called bone magic, all those years ago,' her mother said. 'I was a soft-hearted girl and I used my gift of it to heal. But when I undid the good I had done poor Max Hector, when I unravelled that boy's young life with my mind, the magic felt exultant.'

'You said it was the hardest thing you've ever had to do.'

'It was. But it felt like what the power was for, you see. I used my bone magic as a force for good. In that barn, the realisation came to me that its intended purpose is quite the opposite.'

Elizabeth looked around the room. She looked at the upright piano in the corner, its polished walnut glimmering in the fading light. She looked at the pictures on the walls, the land and seascapes she had grown up knowing. Against the wall behind her was the radiogram on which she knew her mother listened to *Woman's Hour* each weekday with the clockwork regularity of orderly retirement. She looked at the wood fire burning before her with its warm scent in the grate and the blue surround of floral-patterned tiles and the mantelpiece with its ticking eight-day clock and family photographs in their wooden frames. It was all profoundly familiar but all of it seemed illusory now, as bogus as a stage set full of cosy period props.

'Was I an only child, Mum?'

Her mother stared at Elizabeth. 'Good heavens, girl. What sort of question is that to ask me?'

'One to which I would like an honest answer.'

Margaret Bancroft smiled. 'You think you and your twin sister were separated at birth?'

'Interesting that you say my twin,' Elizabeth said. She was shaking. She could barely keep the tremor out of her voice. 'Interesting also, that it's to a sister you refer. I could have suspected it was a brother I had, after all.'

'Lizzie. My God. You really are serious.'

Elizabeth nodded. She did not trust herself to speak.

Her mother closed her eyes. She began to weep. Elizabeth put down her cup and saucer on the carpet and slid from her chair and knelt before her mother and held both of her hands.

Her mother's eyes opened. They were filmy with tears and age. 'I've kept one secret from you, Lizzie. It's the one I've just revealed to you. And one was terrible enough. You were an only child.'

'Shush, Mum.'

'You were loved and cherished. You were, you know, as you are loved and cherished still.'

Adam Hunter thought it scary, just how much Elizabeth the cool doctor looked like his mum had. He thought his mum had been cool. She had been lovely too. And he did not like to think about her too much because it made him sad and sorry for his dad when he did. But she really had been cool. He'd even overheard grown-ups saying it. And so was Elizabeth, with her green sports car and her black leather jacket and her sunglasses pushed up to her hair and the pilot's watch she wore with buttons either side of the winder and the relaxed attitude about bedtime and her totally deadly popcorn. And she really did look like his mum. Scary was the word for it. Except that it wasn't really scary. It wasn't scary like the dreams. Elizabeth's resemblance to his mum was one of those freaky coincidences life threw up more often than Adam thought the laws of probability should have allowed. The dreams, though. When it came to scary, the dreams were off the scale.

He had lied to his dad about not remembering their detail. He remembered them very vividly. He remembered every detail exactly. The dreams were so strange, how could he not? But he had not wanted to worry his dad. It was bad enough as things were, his dad being so lonely and sad. Adam wanted to cheer him up, not concern him or depress him even further. He knew his dad had done his best. But he also knew what a strain it was. Before the dreams had started, he had lain awake and heard his dad cry from the bedroom next to his in the night and had wanted to go in to him. But he had not. Dad had to learn to live without Mum and Kate. They both did. It was hard, but they had no choice. Mum and Kate were gone and were never coming back.

Adam had lied about the dreams to the cool doctor because he had lied to his dad. She would have had to tell because adults had their own rules about that kind of stuff. Had he made her promise not to tell, she probably would have done. She'd have done it just to get the truth out of him. And telling Elizabeth the truth would have been a relief. Because she wasn't just cool, she was kind as well. And keeping something so horrible totally private was not exactly easy. But she would have broken her promise and told his dad. She would have seen it as her duty. He did not resent that. He understood the grown-up world abided by its adult rules. He accepted it. But it did mean he had not been able to tell her. He did not want to worry his dad. Neither did he want his dad to feel his son had betrayed him through dishonesty.

It was what was called a dilemma. He knew the word from football. When Sir Alex had three forwards in form at United but only room for two in the team he faced what was called a selection dilemma. Football seemed to be full of dilemmas of every sort. But Adam thought his dilemma over the dreams somewhat more serious. The languages, though, he had told the truth about. He had woken once speaking fluent Russian. He had woken once thinking in German. He had never studied either language. But after a few hours awake, the language skills were gone.

Anyway, right now, he had another problem. And this one was a consequence of something else he had not told Elizabeth. He had come back from his first day after his long absence from school with a homework assignment. You could tell Elizabeth wasn't a mum because a mum would have asked if his homework had been done. Elizabeth didn't and so it hadn't been. He had farted around customising a couple of toy cars, and then obliterating her at chess and watching Clarkson, filling his face with popcorn while his homework assignment wasn't being dealt with.

Adam knew why they had been assigned the particular homework they'd been given. It was because a set of statistics had been collated that proved the school library was being used 8 per cent less every year. Either the school reversed the trend, or the library would be seen as more of a luxury than a resource and dispensed with altogether. It was a small school. It had been built in Victorian times. The library had been endowed by some rich American called Carnegie. It sat separate from the main building and was beautiful, like a little Gothic castle. It was shaped in a hexagon and had stained-glass windows and granite walls covered in ivy. Inside was a coke-burning fire with a brass mantel and stuffed wildlife in glass cases and lots of first editions signed by famous Scottish authors. It wasn't really a resource, he had overheard the maths teacher Mr Cawdor say, it was an anachronism. But Adam thought the school library a very pretty anachronism and thought it would look terrible gutted of books, filled with ugly banks of computer monitors on metal-legged tables with veneered tops.

Their assignment was to choose and learn overnight a new poem by a poet they had not studied. This was a strategy meant to send the whole class flocking to the library in search of something short that rhymed and they could easily memorise. It would help buck that 8 per cent downward lending trend. Adam thought each class had probably been set a similar task. It was a way of tackling the anachronistic library dilemma. But it had not worked on him. He had not borrowed a book from the library that looked as though a fey princess in a pointy hat should live there. His dad had a shelf full of books of poetry and listened to CDs of the stuff. You could download poems from the internet and press the print button. He could do that in his room.

Partly, it was Jeremy Clarkson's fault. If Clarkson and those crap cars had not distracted him so successfully, he would have done his homework without any fuss. He was a quick learner. He only had to read six or eight lines twice, if he really concentrated, to know them by heart. But he had been concentrating on Austin Allegros and Hillman Avengers. Damn Clarkson. It was his turn next. He knew it was. Mrs Davies would ask him next and he had no excuse and what made it worse was that everyone else, the whole class, all eleven of them, had done their homework thoroughly. He did know some poems. He knew quite a lot of *The Wreck of the Deutschland* by Gerard Manley Hopkins. His dad listened to it sometimes on the stereo at home. But Hopkins had been Welsh. He knew that one by Seamus Heaney, the one about digging up peat and the milk bottle with the cardboard stopper. Heaney was his dad's favourite poet of all. And Adam liked that one himself. But Heaney was Irish. That was even worse than Welsh. If he was going to recite poetry by a Celt, in these circumstances it really had to be a Scotsman. There was Robert Burns. Burns was actually the only Scottish poet he could think of. But he did not know a single line of Burns. Adam felt his cheeks begin to prickle and glow.

'Master Hunter,' Mrs Davies said. She was standing at the front of the class, between her desk and the blackboard.

The sun was slanting in low through the row of windows to his right. He got to his feet with a squeal of chair legs against wood.

'Your turn, if you please. Culturally, we're very cosmopolitan at this particular seat of learning. English poetry is quite permissible.'

The class laughed at Mrs Davies's well-meant joke. Well meant, because it was intended, Adam knew, to help relax him. Some children found public speaking of any sort an uncomfortable ordeal. That was particularly true, he thought now, when you did not possess the remotest idea of what it was you were going to say. The autumn sun was warm through the window on the side of his face and through the wool of his school jumper. He tried to think, to remember. His mind was as blank as canvas not yet primed.

He did not know how long it was before he sat down again. He was aware only of silence and a slight dryness in his throat. The angle of the sun through the window was the same. All his classmates were looking at him. Mrs Davies was looking at him and her expression was one he had not seen on her face before. She had removed her glasses and held them dangling by one of their arms from her fingers. He had never seen her face naked, without those wire frames and lenses. She looked younger and a bit perplexed. Two lines resonated in his head. They formed a couplet from the long poem he had just recited:

> *The stream mysterious glides beneath,*
> *Green as a dream and deep as death.*

Mrs Davies coughed and put back on her glasses. 'Adam's splendid recitation was a poem by the English neo-Romantic poet Rupert Brooke. Would anyone like to venture an opinion as to what it was about?'

Alice Cranbourne put up her hand. Adam thought vaguely that Alice was probably the cleverest girl in the class. She had earlier recited something by Burns in Highland dialect. Adam had not understood a single word of it.

'Alice?'

'It seems to be about homesickness, Miss. It's got this sad, pining tone to it.'

'That's very astute, Alice. Brooke wrote it at a café table in Berlin in the spring of 1912. He lived near Cambridge, at the old vicarage of the poem's title in Grantchester. He mentions a lot of place names, Cambridgeshire villages. Geographically and in his mind, he was a young man a long way from home.'

Those two lines rattled and reverberated in Adam Hunter's head. They were not redolent to him of forgotten English summers. They did not sound wistful or mournful or sentimental in the slightest. They spoke of blood and stealth and jungle and hinted at the lurking patience of fate. He listened to what Mrs Davies said. He thought it was all very interesting. It was also entirely new to him. Until he'd sat down after the recitation he could not now remember having given, he had never heard of the Old Vicarage at Grantchester. And he was equally certain he had never heard of Rupert Brooke. There had been no pictures in his mind when he'd stood to recite he knew not what. Except that very briefly, he had been reminded of the glamorous woman with the cruel mouth who sometimes smiled at the edge of the bad dreams he had endured.

Mark Hunter had learned to ski on the Stubai Glacier so the Austrian Tyrol was both well known to him and fondly remembered. He had learned as an officer cadet seconded to a platoon of Gurkhas. They had never really progressed as he had technically. He recalled the experience now with a rueful smile. Self-preservation was the instinct that taught you to turn on skis, to carve precisely with their edges to control your rate of descent. The Gurkhas had not seemed to him in possession of this instinct at all. They would listen to the instructor. Then they would point their skis downwards towards their distant, intended destination below. And they would go. Some of them caught an edge and came a spectacular cropper. Most of them made it and were slowed finally by gravity at the bottom of the run. That was proof to these men of the validity of their technique and they would never change it. The instructor bellowed and gesticulated and turned puce with indignation in the cold. But it was no good. The Gurkhas skied like they fought, in a straight line, with total commitment and entirely without fear. More circumspect, on the sidelines, Hunter practised the rudiments of this new skill for a full fortnight, until he could ski down anything. He knew the Austrian Tyrol. But he wasn't skiing now.

It was dusk when he got to where the road petered out. He had taken trains from Geneva to Innsbruck. At Innsbruck he had hired a car. He was about eight kilometres from the Stubai Valley. The country was very remote. There were no dwellings here, no twinkling house lights at the foot of the rising slope. He had a climb ahead of him, but Miss Hall had said it was a climb that could be accomplished without the use of ropes or crampons. He had to climb a path that wound through the tree line and then the going became steeper and more demanding. He looked up. The darkening sky was spangled by crystals of falling snow increasing all the time in weight and density. He had bought boots and cold weather apparel and a head torch at a store near to where he had hired the car and he wore this clothing and equipment now. And he needed it. All he could hear as night descended under the white, thickening sky was the tick of his hire car's cooling engine in the bitter cold. This did not seem a location suited to the sorceress femme fatale he remembered from Magdalena, to the black magician party animal Miss Hall had insisted he pursue. But he was in the right place. It was exactly as Miss Hall had described it to him and he could see the thin path twisting through the dark rise of conifers ahead. He took a drink from the metal water bottle he had bought with the rest of his kit at Innsbruck and had the wit to fill from the water cooler in the car hire office before setting out. The bottle had travelled there on the back seat of the car but its contents were already icy against his teeth and on his tongue. Hunter wiped his mouth with the heel of his hand, screwed the cap back on to the bottle and set off.

He had bought an ice axe in the shop at Innsbruck. And after some hesitation, he had bought a combat knife. The knife had a knuckle duster guard and a saw edge on what would be the blunt of the blade on a conventional knife.

It was Solingen forged steel and its blade was eight inches long and lethally honed, and Hunter had it now in its sheath on his belt. In the display case in the shop it had looked like the hunting knife from hell. He did not really know why he had bought it. In a way it felt like sixty euros' worth of macho folly after the rag doll an enfeebled Miss Hall had been able to make of him with a few vindictive thoughts. What good was a blade, however keen, against such malevolent power? But instinct had impelled him to buy the knife and he had learned over the years not to ignore his deep, nagging hunches. They had frequently urged precautions that had definitely saved his life.

He climbed. The snow was deepening all the time. There was no moonlight through the cloud cover. Nevertheless, he could see quite well along the rising path by using the head torch, without giving himself away. Miss Hall had been adamant that his destination lay empty. But he had been too thoroughly trained to take unnecessary risks. He ascended. His breathing deepened. He climbed the gradient carefully and with deliberation but at pace. He wanted to get where he was going. He was still stiff from the bruises inflicted during the first, unpromising part of his encounter with Miss Hall. He did not want to dwell on what might confront him now at the top of the mountain. That was pointless. He just wanted to get there. In a sense, he knew he had never felt more resolute in his life. He loved his son more than anything, certainly far more than he loved his own circumscribed life. But he felt pessimistic too. The training that enabled his stealthy ascent, with his heart never climbing above sixty beats a minute, bore sometimes impressive results. But it had failed him in Magdalena. And he feared it might fail him again ranged against the same dark and powerful protagonist now.

The summit of the climb was a sharp ridge, high and

ragged and exposed. He was ascending on the southern slope that rose to it. On the other side, to its north, it descended in a vaunting rampart of ice for thousands of featureless metres, Miss Hall had told him. That too was a slope, technically. But it fell in a gradient so steep that local guides referred to it as a wall. His destination was on this side of the mountain, a building constructed on a small plateau, set against the hewn rock that provided its shelter, about four hundred feet beneath the knife-edge of the summit ridge.

There was a narrowing of the trail as shoulders of ice-covered granite loomed to either side of him. Beyond this gully, he knew, was a field of crevasses. It was these that made the place to which he ascended so inaccessible. It was these that kept Mrs Mallory's keep from the curiosity of climbers and mountain guides.

'You need not fear the crevasses,' Miss Hall had told him.

'Are they deep?'

'Deep? They are as near to bottomless as the Alps can boast.'

'It goes against nature. Not to fear them, I mean.'

She had laughed at that. It was a sandpapery, unpleasant sound. She was defiant, dying. 'I have had nature bow to my will many times, Colonel. Perhaps tomorrow I will do it for the last time. But you will not die in the depths of a crevasse.'

Skiing had been a joy to him, with his family, in his life. But he had known tragedy climbing in the mountains. Once in Norway early in his military career, in training, they had lost a brave American to a crevasse. They had been travelling in haste because the weather had been closing in. They had not secured sufficient lines and were testing the snow with their axes in a thickening blizzard. He had survived the drop and become wedged a long way down. They had not had the length of rope to recover him. He had been stoical, resigned in the end. But he had been the father of two young children and only twenty-eight years old. And the necessity of leaving him, the last of his words rising faintly in a brave farewell from the abyss, had stayed with his English comrade in arms.

Hunter thought that he could see the building, now. He had been travelling for well over an hour above the tree line. The light distorted with the shifting weight of cloud, and the thickening snow on the rising ground seemed to shift with it. The wind had risen from the occasional howl through the conifers below to a withering, banshee shriek up here. He had felt he was being trailed, or stalked, for the past twenty minutes at least. Wading through the high drifts he felt the lumbering self-consciousness of someone being watched. And the hairs on his arms and the backs of his hands under his gloves had a razored tenderness, a raw itch of exposure caused by more than just the deepening chill of increasing altitude.

He tensed. He thought he heard the sough through wet drifts of something large approaching him. And then he made sense of the scale and thunderous weight of the sound and knew what it was. Wet snow in a serac at the top of the ridge towards which he climbed had been wrenched off by its own unstable weight and pulled away. He was hearing the mournful rumble of an avalanche away on the mountain's north face. It must be of monstrous size, he thought, a colossal fall of ice and snow for me to hear it from here. But the wind was blowing from the north. And the sound was a signal of how close he was to approaching the ridge and the summit.

He could see his destination clearly now. And there was nothing charming or Tyrolean about it. It was a tall, rectangular building constructed of stained grey concrete. Its windows were as narrow as the gun-slits of a bunker. There was a massive steel door painted with bitumen or some other stuff to seal the metal from rust. Securing the door were two huge padlocks hanging from great, riveted hasps. The place was totally dark and still. It looked impregnable. It also looked to Mark Hunter like the most forlorn dwelling he had ever seen. Peering up at the gaunt edifice before him, he thought that no creature harbouring a soul could live free of despair in such a bleak and forbidding place.

He reached into his jacket pocket for the keys to the padlocks handed him by the Comte in the moments before his departure from the house above Lake Geneva ready for the drive back to his hotel. They had seemed suitably impressive on their iron ring, large items fashioned from brass pitted by time. But he had hefted them thinking them merely props. Miss Hall's fading magic would open the door for him. Mrs Mallory had not willingly surrendered keys to her mountain domain. He would insert a key into a padlock and the frozen mechanism would spring compliantly under Miss Hall's fading spell. Even dying, she was tenacious, determined. Looking at the keep now brooding blackly over him, Hunter thought he knew the source of her determination. She really was more good than bad. And she was his ally in this enterprise. But her magic was a feeble attribute in the face of that possessed by their adversary. He turned the keys. He put them back into his jacket pocket. He unfastened and dropped the sprung padlocks on to the snow. He felt the bone hilt of the impressive weapon on his hip, in which he had, at that moment, not an ounce of faith. He pushed at the door, which opened of course on darkness.

It was fully dark when Elizabeth completed the drive from her evening surgery to her cottage. She had already called Mrs Anderson, the childcare professional engaged by Mark Hunter, to ask whether she would do an hour's overtime to enable the detour. Mrs Anderson seemed amenable enough. She was an accommodating woman, she was being well paid and she had described Adam as a delightful boy. Another hour would not be any great stretch. Her headlamps illuminated the front of the cottage in a bright sweep as Elizabeth turned off the road to park. And so she knew something else had been done to violate her home before she left the safe confines of her car.

Her mobile phone was equipped with a tiny torch light and she used this to examine the recent handiwork. The skull of a goat had been hung on a flathead nail driven into the wood above the knocker. It depended from one eye socket. It sat at the centre of a crudely fashioned pentagram. Pig's blood had not been used on this occasion. The five-sided star was described in silver paint from an aerosol spray. Whoever had done it had done it in relative haste, shy about being seen. Elizabeth walked the perimeter of her home. It had not been breached. No windows were smashed. No one had broken in. But that would be next. That desecration would certainly come.

She did not enter her cottage. She decided that the clothes she wore would do another day. She could wash her under-wear in the sink in the bathroom adjoining the spare room at the Hunter house. It would dry overnight on the radiator under her window. She scrolled through the numbers stored in her mobile until she came to that of Sergeant Kilbride. He served with a local unit of the Perthshire police force. She had a good relationship with Superintendent Galloway, at regional headquarters. But this was not a job for the brass. It was a job for a tough and resourceful local copper and Kilbride was all of that.

He answered straight away.

'Tony? Elizabeth Bancroft. I need a favour.'

'Dr Lizzie! How lovely it is to hear from you.'

Dr Lizzie. He always called her that. 'You won't think it lovely to hear from me when I tell you the problem I've got,' she said. 'You'll think me an imposition and a pain.'

Perhaps she betrayed some of her shock or distress in her tone. It was a few seconds before Kilbride answered her. 'I'll be the judge of that,' he said. 'So fire away.'

She got to the Hunter house just before seven. Kilbride had promised to go and examine the mischief done to her cottage as soon as their phone conversation was concluded. But by then he knew that she had a commitment of care to Adam. And he did not anyway see the need for her to endure the ordeal of awaiting his arrival in the darkness on her own. She had been unnerved enough. She also got the impression that he was not wholly convinced that the mischief maker had gone. He did not say so, but she knew from her own experience of crime that the perpetrators of this sort of offence sometimes stuck around to watch their victim's reaction. That was part of the fun for them. She was happy to leave the scene. And of course, she left the scene intact.

The landline rang at eight o'clock and Elizabeth answered it. Adam was doing his homework at his father's desk in the sitting room. He did not even raise his head at the sound of the phone, evidently thinking it an adult's job to pick it up. Elizabeth was swiftly reminded by that of how isolated the boy was here. He had no neighbouring kids to mix with – no network of friends, evidently, to call or email and gossip among. It was a shame for him. It was not ideal either for his recovery.

'Hello?'

'Dr Bancroft?'

'Speaking.'

'This is Emma Davies, from the school. I teach Adam Hunter English.'

The school had been told about Mark Hunter's absence

from home. They had been given a sketchy account of the reason for Adam's recent absence from class. Elizabeth herself had provided that.

'I'm sorry to call so late.'

'That's absolutely fine. What can I do for you?'

'It might be more a case of what I can do for you, doctor. Adam's class had to recite verse today learned as last night's homework assignment.'

'I see.' Except that Elizabeth knew bloody well Adam had not completed any homework assignment. Jeremy Clarkson had seen to that.

'Adam recited a poem comprising a hundred and forty-one lines. I counted them myself this afternoon. This was a prodigious feat of memory for a boy of his age and, of itself, would have been unusual.'

Elizabeth's breath felt shallow. 'Go on.'

'Even more unusual was the diction.'

'Well. He is from the Home Counties of England and well spoken. His father, until he retired, was a colonel in the British Army.'

'The poem was by Rupert Brooke. Adam recited it in a tone a full octave lower than his regular speaking voice. Then there was his pronunciation. For want of a more accurate word, it sounded Edwardian.'

Elizabeth closed her eyes. She did not think there was a better word. She thought Emma Davies very astute. She thought Miss Hall and her grasp on matters must be weakening. 'How did the rest of the class react?'

'After a dozen lines, most of them zoned out. We've one very bright girl who stuck with the sense of it all the way through. The poem's a dense affair, thematically, for a ten-year-old. I think she thought it impersonation.'

'But you did not.'

'No,' Emma Davies said. 'To me it did not seem like

impersonation at all. It was very unnerving, you see. To me, for the duration of the recitation, it seemed more like possession.'

Elizabeth still had her eyes closed. Now she opened them and looked across to where Adam sat. He was poring intently over his homework books, oblivious.

'I know that the boy has been troubled in some way. I neither like nor peddle in gossip. I only mention it because I think you ought to know.'

'Thank you,' Elizabeth said. She replaced the receiver.

Later, after Adam had gone to bed, Sergeant Kilbride called and shared more with her about his conclusions regarding her violated home than she knew an officer of the law generally would do with a crime victim. After he had left, she built up the fire and opened a bottle of Cabernet Sauvignon and pondered on the absence from the house of its owner. Mark Hunter had been away for only one full night. This was to be the second. It seemed like more. Adam had been free of the nightmares for three nights. Again, it seemed like more, if only because his recovery had been so abrupt and had seemed so complete. But the poetry episode was a concern. She could not see where it fitted into the pattern of things. It seemed ominous, though. It was indicative of how fragile this respite from the nightmares was, how uncertain the prospects of his full recovery. She wondered at her own fitness to help him. Embroiled in magic from two sides, she was beginning to fear its dark contamination. She would be helplessly overwhelmed by something she did not remotely comprehend. And where would that leave the boy?

She went over to his desk and switched on Mark Hunter's computer and accessed her email account. She had two that were unread. One was from the British Medical Association, to say that they had been asked to confirm her identity and credentials and contact details by someone working at the

British Library that morning. They had done so. The second was from the British Library and had been sent that afternoon. It was a cover note with a long document attachment. The cover note politely explained that she had not been sent a copy of Jerusalem Smith's original transcript. Only a practised scholar would have the skills to decipher that. Instead they had sent her a version faithfully reproduced in modern spelling and idiom by a Professor Edwards of Trinity College in 1927. She did not open the document itself. She had neither the energy nor the inclination to begin to read it just then. She hadn't the heart to face what she might discover there. This was because Edwards had been neither a professor of history nor law. His specialism, it was explained in the cover note, had been the occult.

Kilbride had said the unpleasantness at her cottage was not the work of a single individual. They could rule out the theory of the lone crank straight away. Tracks had been left on the turf around the cottage by two sets of boots. They were different sizes but, interestingly, shared an identical tread.

'Do you know the significance of the shared boot type, Dr Bancroft?' He had dropped his Dr Lizzie jocularity. Clearly, he thought her harassment serious.

'No.'

'It's characteristic of paramilitry organisations. You know the kind of people. I'm talking about the more extreme animal liberationists and radical environmental groups.'

Elizabeth laughed. 'I've never so much as torn the wings off a fly, Tony. I recycle all my rubbish. I don't work in the nuclear power industry. I don't think I even have a patient who does.'

'We need to meet again and have a proper talk about this,' he had said.

Elizabeth heard a thump and looked to see if logs had

fallen in the fire. But the noise had come from upstairs. There was silence, the silence followed by laughter, keening, high and far too knowing for Adam's waking innocence. It had begun again. It could mean only one thing. More precisely, there was one thing of significance it definitely meant. Miss Hall was dead. The protection her emissary had promised on behalf of his mistress had gone. The promise had been rashly made by its ailing guarantor, Elizabeth felt, getting to her feet. But perhaps Miss Hall had been desperate. The darkness of events seemed a deepening maw to her as she gathered her courage and ascended the stairs to do what she could for her tormented charge.

Chapter Seven

The door opened on to a vestibule, cold and narrow and high. From somewhere, there came the sound of a dripping tap or snow melt. Hunter did not think it could be the latter. It was as cold in Mrs Mallory's mountain keep as the grave. And the snow was not melting this high on the mountain. He switched on his head torch. The walls within were the same rough concrete as without. Here and there the concrete was crumbling and rust stained and pocked. This place would stand for another thousand years, he thought. And that had been, he was sure, the intention when it was originally built. But it was corroding. There was seepage and damp and the quiet rust of reinforcing bars no longer invulnerable to the wet of summer thaws. How long had her keep occupied this solitary spot? Hunter's guess was better than seventy years. He was no great student of architecture. But the Imperial eagle carved in deep relief in the lintel above the door had been too stubborn a clue to ignore.

At some point, he would have to seek and find the route to the cellar. Miss Hall had been most emphatic about that. But he would not venture there yet. He would gain his bearings and his nerve before subjecting himself to that necessary ordeal. He would explore the ground and upper floors. Glancing around, he was tempted to look for light. There were wall sconces here, pitch-tipped torches thrust into them and scorch marks behind on the dank concrete as proof of their fierce capacity to burn. He thought that they might burn still. The pitch was thickly daubed on them, viscous in the cold. He could ignite them with the waterproof matches he had bought along with the rest of his equipment at Innsbruck. But he was cautious about providing any extravagance of light. The feeling of being stalked had not left Mark Hunter. He needed to see. He did not wish to advertise himself. He remembered the gnawed wrists of Major Rodriguez very vividly. He remembered the cold, grey-eyed beauty of Mrs Mallory and her chiselled bones, and the velvet urging of her voice as she compelled him irresistibly to approach her and greet her with a kiss.

He pushed at the door to a room off to the left of the vestibule and it opened with a whoosh. It was bronzed and engraved and must have weighed upwards of half a ton, he thought. But it rested on balanced hinges and they were smoothly lubricated. The room was vast and less of a room, really, than a shrine. Its contents were of a piece with the Imperial eagle above the entrance. Blood banners topped with gilt swastikas were heaped, leaning in a corner. Their fabric was dusty with time. But their colours were richly embroidered, deeply redolent of the hatred and pomp of the marches in which they had been paraded.

There was a large painting of the Führer, attired as a medieval knight, bareheaded in silver armour in the saddle of a piebald warhorse. There was another, formal painted portrait of the Nazi high command in their uniforms and leather coats at a conference table in the open air in a forest clearing. They were being served refreshments on silver trays in the picture by blond children in folk costume. The painter had been technically skilled. There was sunlight in the forest. It played, making haloes of their fine and wavy yellow hair. There was the still clutter of weaponry about the room. There was a mounted machine gun and a row of carbines and a case of black, gleaming machine pistols. Hunter could smell the thin oil used to clean and service these weapons.

Mrs Mallory had a retinue of course. That's what Miss Hall had called it at Magdalena. She had a retinue. He had seen one of them at the airport and again down among the trees outside his hotel. He had left his faint stink in Hunter's hotel room. He wondered, were any of them here, lurking in the shadows? It seemed more likely than not. Though Miss Hall had insisted he would find this place deserted.

In the centre of the room was a large wooden table bearing a film projector. At slightly above head height, about ten feet beyond the camera's lens, a long thin metal drum, or more accurately tube, was suspended from the ceiling by chains. It was painted green. And Hunter knew it contained the canvas screen he would unroll should he elect to switch the camera on and watch the film sitting loaded on to its large spool. Actually, there was no decision, just as there was no decision to make about his eventual visit to the cellar. But he would not watch the film yet.

Over against the far corner, on top of a bookcase, were three objects he could not make out. They were domestic items, he thought, short, pale cylinders with some kind of decoration. He walked over to examine them. He held out a hand and then his fingers recoiled. They were the shades of standard lamps. They were mounted on short wooden stands. Their bulbs were dusty. Their decoration was tattoos and they were made of human skin. Next to them, weeping out of waxed paper, was a pile of bars of soap. They had become unstable over time of course. Even in the cold of Mrs Mallory's keep, products rendered from human fat would decay. The leakage from the soap was a dark, tarnished yellow and it glimmered wetly in the light of Hunter's head torch.

The bookcase on top of which these souvenirs sat was filled with gilt-tooled leather volumes. It was some sort of set, like encyclopaedias. But the titles on their spines were not etched in German. They were described in some runic script alien to him. There was an ornamental key locking the glass doors of the case. He twisted this, opened the doors and pulled a volume free. The pages were hand-cut but the book was not ancient. He glanced through it. There were trial scenes and scenes of torture depicted in vivid woodcuts. There were the strange, sly creatures which had shifted on the tapestries in the canvas cathedral at Magdalena. In the woodcuts, this lupine breed played the prosecutors and the torturers. Their victims were all people. The last scene he looked at was a moonlit panorama of mass burning and dismemberment. He closed and replaced the book. Perhaps now was the time for a movie after all.

He assumed the projector was battery powered. He also assumed cold had kept the battery from corroding and leaking and spilling over the rest of the mechanism over time. But what had prevented the film in the spool from perishing? Was that the cold as well? This was a spellbound place. That was the truth of it. It assailed and insulted Mark Hunter's usual logic. But he felt the truth of it in every prickling pore of his body and each corner of his mind. He pulled down the screen and switched on the machine, extinguishing his head torch to watch the film as every cinema purist should, in the blackest of theatres.

The film flickered into life depicting the monochrome warmth of a summer city in Germany pictured long ago. The light suggested that the sun was shining strongly from somewhere near its zenith in the sky. The short shadows cast by trees and street railings and café chairs were very sharply etched. The cobbles were glazed with brightness. But this was not the Berlin of a homesick Rupert Brooke. It was not that far back in time. A war had been fought and lost since then. This was a summer that wore the physical trappings of that defeat and its cruel and solemn consequence. Figures in uniform sat at café tables. Most of the uniforms were black. When the camera panned, swastikas were draped heavily from the ornate frontage of some civic building. Hunter thought that it could have been Hamburg or Cologne he was looking at. There were no architectural landmarks famous enough for him to know for sure. He was not watching a travelogue. The footage was more intimate and less formally structured. But he had the suspicion that the city was Berlin. Mrs Mallory had had a fondness for Berlin, even an affinity with the place.

She sat at a café table and smiled in close-up from under the shade of a wide-brimmed hat. She wore sunglasses but the seductive mouth and sharply sculpted facial bones were unmistakeable. There was a small coffee cup on a saucer in front of her and a slice of coffee or chocolate cake she had left untouched. He did not think she had ever been a woman with a sweet tooth. Perhaps the cake had been ordered for her in jest. A cigarette was balanced on the edge of the ashtray next to her coffee cup. Smoke rose thinly from it and disappeared in the brilliant light above her head. She wore a rope of pearls around her bare throat and a satin shirt tailored with collar and cuffs like a man's. She wore a man's wristwatch on a black leather strap. She looked at once exotic and self-possessed. She did not wilt in the heat and the brightness of the day. She bathed in them and they embellished her.

The camera shooting this scene was on a tripod, Hunter realised. You did not get this level of stability and detail with a hand-held camera. There was an establishing shot, a long shot of the principal scene and then this close-up of the film's undoubted star. And Hunter had begun to suspect he knew whose work this polished home movie was. One of his courses at Hereford had been in the creation and uses of propaganda. They had watched *Triumph of the Will* over and over, analysing the seductive power of Leni Riefenstahl's lighting and editing and her selection and composure of images. Hunter had learned about the lenses and film stock habitually used by Hitler's favourite director. He knew her cinematic style. And he was pretty sure he recognised it now.

It was not possible to see with whom Mrs Mallory shared her table. The camera angle was too high and acute for that. But there were some items laid about it that were easily recognisable. There was a silver cigarette lighter. There was a cigar cutter and a large leather cigar tube. There was a holstered Luger pistol on a coiled belt. And there was a field marshal's baton, a polished bar heavily scrolled and filigreed like some priceless heraldic relic on the pure white of the starched table cloth.

Mrs Mallory had been talking to someone opposite her. Her words had gone unrecorded. The film had so far been silent throughout. Now she looked back up to the camera again and smiled. I move in illustrious company, the look seemed to say. And I do so very comfortably. She plucked her cigarette from the ashtray, took a drag on it and then ground it out exhaling smoke. For a moment her face was pale behind the smoke, insubstantial, like that of a ghost. Then it resolved itself again. There was a small black beauty spot to the left of her perfect mouth. She was the very embodiment of poise and glamour. She stood and someone out of shot opened a parasol over her head. Hunter thought the parasol an unnecessary precaution given the broad brim of her hat. But the Nazi high command had been a courtly lot, heavy on chivalric gesture and extravagant good manners generally. The Führer himself had introduced a fashion for the kissing of women's hands in greetings and farewells.

The sorceress and her unseen party moved slowly in the sunshine. She was still the only figure in the frame. They moved on to an area covered in grass. This lawn appeared scorched and scarred in dark patches. It was why the party moved so slowly, Hunter thought. It was insufferably hot. Berlin, of all German cities, had endured these endless summers of soporific heat between the wars.

The camera was hand-held now of course. And beyond the lithe, sinuous figure of Mrs Mallory, it showed where she was walking to. Her destination was a copse of trees perhaps a hundred feet away. In its shade, Hunter saw a waiting car, its windows and headlamps sparkling in odd shards of light let through the heavy leaf canopy above. The car wore a sleek coat of black coach paint. He whistled to himself, recognising the model. And he now knew that what he was watching had taken place no earlier than 1935. The Nazis had come to power in 1933. There was a gloating certainty about the mood of the film that suggested no martial setbacks had yet taken place. There was no sense of military urgency. It was still peacetime. He thought that he was looking at a Berlin day in the summer of 1936 or 1937. That was the time of their complacency and pomp. But that was over seventy years ago. A decade earlier he had met the woman he was watching on the screen now. And he had put her age in Magdalena at perhaps thirty-five. He had been somewhat wide of the mark. And Miss Hall, as he had always known in his heart, had been telling him the truth.

The car was a Mercedes Benz 540K, the eight-litre-engine Swabian Colossus, and only three hundred of them had ever been made after they first rolled off the production line in 1935. Himmler and Goering had each owned one. Hitler had turned his into a fortress on wheels with bulletproof glass and bodywork capable of surviving a grenade attack. You had to be very rich or very high ranking or both to own one of these coveted cars. Or you had to be a very important guest of the Reich, in which case one would be placed at your service for the duration of your stay in Germany.

Mrs Mallory had arrived at the car. Someone reached across from her left and opened the rear door for her. There was a passenger already awaiting her inside. The parasol, still up, concealed his face. Hunter saw that he was powerfully built and wore the pale-grey uniform and insignia of the Death's Head Corps and that his rank was SS-Gruppenführer. The parasol was collapsed. Mrs Mallory took off her sunglasses and climbed into the car. It was very gloomy under the tree canopy and what light there was spangled through the leaves above uncertainly. And in the moment between Mrs Mallory taking her seat and the door being closed behind her, the face of her fellow passenger was visible only for the fraction of a second in which Hunter saw features lupine and predatory grinning balefully at him from out of the car's dark interior.

The Mercedes was shifted into gear and moved smoothly away. The film flickered and the reel reached its end as a grey blur replaced the image on the screen. The thing in the car had not been human. Hunter tried to make sense of what he had just seen. But he could not. He switched off the projector and the whirr of it stopped and the screen went blank. The Germans had lost the war. The Nazis had been defeated. There was at least one eminent historian who put the allied victory down to the fact that morality had played such a compelling part in the motivation of soldiers risking their lives. Just cause had prevailed. But all Hunter could think of now, as he shivered in the marrow-deep cold of Mrs Mallory's keep, was her refusal to lift her curse and the reason she had given for it a decade ago at her house in Magdalena.

My curse makes the world, to me, a more interesting place, she had said. He thought he was gaining an insight into what Mrs Mallory thought made the world an interesting place. And there was no comfort in the suspicion that her curse

and its repercussions and ambitions went far beyond its
implications for his son.

Adam, who was no longer Adam now, was sitting at the
table with his computer when she opened his bedroom
door.

'It's courtesy to knock,' the voice emanating from his small
frame said. The voice was gruff, adult, the accent Canadian.
Elizabeth thought she knew whose it was. She was more or
less certain when she saw the watercolour Adam was
completing with deft brushstrokes and his tongue curling in
childish concentration over his upper lip. It was a represen-
tation of the sea breaking in great waves against the granite
cone of a lighthouse in a storm. And it was better than merely
good. The venting fury of the storm wrought in a child's
palate of paint was a small work of elemental wonder.

'What a marvellous painter you were,' Elizabeth said.

The thing that was no longer Adam looked up at her and
frowned. 'I was. There's little point in false modesty any
more. I was gifted, right enough. I could paint damn near
anything that meant damn all to me.'

'You've gone back to the sea.'

The painting was almost finished. Adam's childish hand
hovered with the brush over it. He looked up slyly with an
expression that was not his. 'I might as well, Elizabeth. A
man can't die twice over, after all. May I call you Elizabeth?'

'Can you not leave the child alone?'

'Not presently. Had I not died by my own hand, things
would be different. But I did and they are not.'

'Why? Why did you?'

'I defied the curse. I couldn't paint, you see. The impulse
to do so seemed to have deserted me. So I defied the curse.
I went back to Melville for inspiration.'

'*Billy Budd*,' Elizabeth said.

Adam looked at her through Daniel Peterson's squinting expression. 'He's told you everything.'

'I think he may have held some things back.'

'I was homosexual. Queer. Gay. That was my orientaton and choice. And of course I kept it secret. I was deep into the Melville story late one evening. The phone rang. And Mrs Mallory laughed over the line and derided me as a faggot and said she was going to tell.'

'Mark Hunter wouldn't have cared.'

The thing occupying Adam seemed to muse on this. 'Maybe he wouldn't. He was an easy-going kind of a guy, for a Brit. He was cultured and intelligent. Maybe he wouldn't have cared. But it wouldn't have stopped with him. It would have been the end of my military career. It wouldn't have sat well in my trade, with my comrades. It would have been the end of who I was. It would have been the end for me altogether.'

'She offered you the rope. And you took it?'

The Peterson thing occupying Adam cocked its head. 'You've got the hots for Colonel Hunter, haven't you, Elizabeth?'

'Who is that really in there? Is that you, Mrs Mallory?'

'He finds you repellent, you know. The very touch of you repulses him. You remind him far too much of his dead wife. Lillian was always an enigma to poor, dull Mark. But she was a very similar type to you, physically. He tolerates your presence because of the good he mistakenly believes you might be able to do his son. But the sight of you makes him morbid and sorrowful and he detests it.'

'You are not welcome in this house, Mrs Mallory,' Elizabeth said. She could hear the shudder in her own voice. She was frightened and she was hurt. She believed the truth of what had just been said to her. She believed Adam was in danger at this moment from the thing possessing him. Miss Hall was dead and their protection had gone and the guardian of the house was absent from it and far away.

The voice was velvety now when it emerged from Adam's throat. She had been right. It was not the dead Canadian occupying the boy. It was the living sorceress who had persuaded Colonel Peterson to so abruptly take his life. 'We'll meet, Elizabeth. Trust me on that. I am nothing if not a woman of my word. We'll meet in time. But it's an encounter only one of us will relish.'

Adam slumped on to the desk top. When she lifted his head there was a smear of sea green on his cheek from the painting, not yet quite dry. Elizabeth felt that she had to take from what had just occurred anything that was positive. If she did not do this, she thought she might be overcome by misery for Adam and terror for both of them. She had suspected the sorceress of the gift of mimicry and she had been right. She had suspected something of the character of Mrs Mallory and seen that suspicion proven. It was not much. But it was something, she thought, as she hauled Adam's slumbering body from his chair and lifted him into bed. It was something. It was enough to slow her heart and stifle the scream in her throat she thought might waken and frighten the child she carried to his rest. She wet a flannel under the running hot tap in the bathroom and, when it had cooled enough, wiped the paint stain from Adam's cheek as his head lay on the pillow and he slept.

The first floor of Mrs Mallory's keep, like the ground floor, was occupied by a single enormous room. This was a dining room. A long table divided it and the wood-panelled walls were decorated with carvings furtive with movement when they were not directly looked upon. There was an old-fashioned radiogram against one wall and when Hunter raised its hinged lid there was a record on the spindle waiting to play. He switched on the machine and the record began to turn. He lowered the tone arm and static at the edge of the disc surrendered after a moment to music familiar from his own contented past. It was Gustav Mahler. It was the Ninth Symphony. It was the recording by von Karajan with the Berliner Philharmoniker. There were banners in this room too. But they were not the blood banners of cobbled riots in Nuremberg and other strongholds in the years before the Nazis swept to power. They were embroidered instead with the anarchic geometric shapes he remembered from the banners under black canvas in Bolivia a decade ago.

The second floor was occupied by a single room just as spacious but much less stark than those beneath. There were couches here of soft black hide and there were animal skins stretched across the walls. There was, against the far wall from the door, a canopied bed. And there were deep-pile rugs scattered on the floor, he saw, as Hunter approached the bed. The bedspread was ivory but the canopy black gauze and the long bolster covered in black satin. He bowed from the waist and sniffed the bolster in the slight depression where a head had lain. It smelled very faintly of a classic scent. He thought it might be Jicky. It was a Guerlain fragrance, he was pretty sure of that. He knew about perfume because his wife had so loved to wear it. Aimé Guerlain had created Jicky in 1889. It had been a youthful scent when its glamorous wearer in this bed had already been a crone in mortal years.

Other things were more interesting up here. There were carved figures from Africa and the East ranged on stacks of shelves. There were corn dollies and elaborate wreaths of shrivelled mistletoe. There were crude voodoo figures and statuettes Hunter thought might have been fashioned centuries ago by Mayan and Inca priests. There was a door knocker cast from brass depicting the Green Man. He thought it probably English and Georgian. Some items amongst this collection seemed harmless and some merely curious and arcane, the hoarded bric-a-brac of someone with a taste for myth. But two objects seemed possessed of such uneasy and profound malevolence that he could barely bring himself to look at them. One was a dagger with the silver boss atop the hilt of a grinning wolf's head. The other was a chalice set with precious stones cut into those queasy geometric shapes the mind could make no sense of. This vessel looked very old, even ancient. He reached out and grasped the chalice in one fist. Dread engulfed him then and he surrendered his grip on the thing with a shudder. It glimmered dully in the beam of his head torch.

He had not thought that things fashioned from metal and jewels could harbour malice and provoke dismay, until that moment. But this one did.

He could put off the part of the visit Miss Hall had insisted upon no longer.

There was a heavy iron latch but no lock on the oak cellar door. It opened outwards on a narrow flight of descending stone steps. If anything, the suspicion of being watched had increased in Mark Hunter's mind. His instinct was to flee this miserable place, with its sense of impending threat and grisly artefacts. But he could not. Miss Hall had made her instructions plain. He must look and learn if he was to save his son. Besides, he thought smiling grimly to himself, he was surely the ideal candidate for the sort of ordeal he was undergoing now. He had spent his entire professional life overcoming fear to face danger with calmness and some-times lethal composure. It could almost be destiny, when you considered it seriously.

He heard a noise behind him then, coming from the hallway leading to the front entrance. He froze at the top of the cellar steps with the heel of his right hand on the hilt of the knife he had bought at Innsbruck. It had sounded like the scrape of bone on the marble of the tiles that paved the way to the entrance. It had sounded like the skitter of a claw. He had not imagined the sound. Alert to anything that might signal threat, he had really heard it. But though he waited for a full minute, it was not repeated. There was a heavy interior silence and beyond that, very faintly from outside, the scream of the wind from the ridge where the mountain peaked above. He descended the steps by the light of his head torch, closing the door behind him.

The large chamber hewn from the living rock under Mrs Mallory's keep was dominated by two machines devised for the killing of men. Hunter did not know much about the guillotine. But the one on which his torchlight shone looked, relatively, like a recently built device. It was not tall and the frame was not a gaunt wooden thing, like those he had seen in engravings describing the Terror that followed the French Revolution. This guillotine did not have eighteenth-century dimensions. Instead its frame was made of riveted steel and the slanted blade was heavy, to give it deadly momentum over the course of a shorter drop. Two thick straps with heavy buckles were screwed to the board on which the condemned man would be bound. There was something sinisterly elegant and even quaint about the French guillotine. This example did not share those characteristics at all. It looked like something built for the cold efficiency of the abattoir. The blade of the machine gleamed in the light from his torch. You could die facing or with your back to it. He pondered for a moment on which would be the worse fate. Closer to it, he saw that there was a manufacturer's name engraved on the steel of the frame. *Tegel*, it read.

So it was not strictly a guillotine but a Fallbeil or falling axe, the more recent German version of this deadly construction. Hunter remembered that Hitler had wasted no time in having them manufactured and used. He had ordered the first of them in Munich in the year he came to power. During the war, more than 16,000 Germans had met their deaths buckled to the boards under the cold honed edges of their blades. The blade was raised on this one. It was poised there, like a threat. He thought it a gruesome sort of souvenir.

The second device on its podium at the centre of the cellar was an electric chair. It lacked the clinical character of the Fallbeil entirely. There were scorch marks on its wooden back and the screws were loose against the wrist manacles on its arms from the dying seizures of its victims. It harnessed electricity but looked almost medieval in its clumsy dimensions and stark crudeness. The cap with its crown of electrodes still stank, as Hunter approached it, with the scent of fear and singed hair. The Fallbeil was a chilling object down here in the gloom and the silence. But he could imagine no more awful keepsake, really, than the chair.

He was studying it, wondering with what possible insights Miss Hall could have intended this tour to provide him, when behind him he heard the whoosh and clang of the descending Fallbeil blade ring loudly home. He turned. There was no hand on the mechanism. There was no torso buckled to the board or head in the waiting basket. But there was blood on the steel in a fresh, dripping crescent. He could smell as well as see it as the coppery odour stung his nostrils. He licked parched lips with a dry tongue and turned and leapt up the steps, having seen more than enough. He closed the cellar door behind him and heard the skittering sound again from the direction of the front entrance. This time it signalled approach. He heard the snarls of a pack of dogs, clumsy with haste over the marble. He looked around him for some means of escape from them.

He remembered the guns then, in the spacious room with the bookcase and the film projector. They were carbines and machine pistols dating from the Second World War but they had gleamed with the lustre of well-maintained and still-functioning weapons. He had not thought to take one for his own protection earlier because Miss Hall had insisted he would be safe here. He had no time to regret that or to ponder on her broken promise. He had encountered these dogs before and knew that they had the feral power to rip him apart. He ran for the room. He plucked a machine pistol from where a row of them were bracketed and began the frantic search for magazines. He found a box of them and opened it, breaking the protective foil with a fevered hand and slotting home the mag as the dogs erupted snarling and foaming, crimson-eyed through the heavy bronze door.

He triggered a sweeping, lateral burst that caught the three of them head on. The heavy calibre bullets ripped into them. They shuddered and paused and one of them let out a sort of mewling sound. The big room had filled already with the potent stink of them. They bled from ragged wounds on to the floor in viscous, purplish blotches. The smell of this excretion was unbearable. But they did not die. They barely paused. They growled and gathered themselves for another assault. He had to get past them. He had no chance otherwise. He let them approach him, separating, leaving wider gaps between them as they stalked him across the floor. This was a very risky thing to do, depending only on the beam from his head torch for his light, the dogs to right and left seeking the shadows of the room as they measured their approach. But he did not have a choice if he wanted to live. He slotted home another mag. On the table to his right, where the projector was mounted, he saw an object that had not been there earlier. It was at once strange and strangely familiar. It was a human head, cleanly severed. The dead eyes of the Comte de Flurey stared dully from it. It was a small and symbolic act of spite on Mrs Mallory's part. It was proof of her vaunting power. And it was proof to Hunter that Miss Hall was dead.

She had broken her promise only because she was no longer alive to keep it.

He emptied his machine pistol into the dog directly in front of him, then dropped the weapon and ran past it through the door. The burst took away most of the dog's head. But it still managed to snap with the exposed remains of its lower jaw as he skirted by, snagging a long fang on his jacket pocket. The ruined head of the beast seemed to ripple, reconstituting itself, the sockets above the snout deepening and then the eyes blinking open with a glimmer of crimson loathing. He tore himself free and shut the door behind him, feeling the impact of the other two dogs as they turned and hurled their weight against the bronze. Her magic was more potent here than it had been in the environs of the canvas cathedral at Magdalena. The beasts among her retinue were stronger. Of course they were. There, she had been tricked and curtailed by the craft of a clever adversary. Here, she was free.

But she was not here. Not in person, she wasn't. She would have confronted him by now if she was. He thought that she was probably in Geneva, in the house of her dead protagonist, gloating over the corpse of Miss Hall and all the time gaining in strength. He looked around. He could not kill the dogs. He could only elude them. If he tried to go back the way he had come they would pursue and catch and overcome him. He would make it as far as the ice field and be swallowed for ever by the abysmal depths of a crevasse. He had no protection now, no fat and querulous guardian angel to keep death at bay for him. Behind him, the bronze juddered. He bit down on his fear with a resolution that brought blood welling from the roots of his teeth. He spat it on to the floor. It was the only blood of his the owner of this place would have today. He owed Adam the life he had not yet lived. He would not die, not easily. He would not forsake his boy.

He would find a way to live through this. He would live to confront and defeat the bitch and he would save his son.

There were stairs. He took them four at a time until they ran out three floors up against the hoar-frosted obstacle of an iron door he thought must lead to the roof. The door was locked. He could hear the dogs panting as they climbed the steps below. He could hear the soft urging of their handler now, could smell his rising odour, the gagging richness of decomposition remembered from Magdalena. And, more recently, from his hotel room at Lake Geneva. He took the keys he had been given by Miss Hall to enter the place. There was no logic to suggest they would work on the exit too. But they did. He was through the door. He locked it behind him and threw the keys away into the darkness. He would not need them again. There was no going back.

Iron ladder rungs ascended above him through hoops screwed to the sheer rock. He thought that perhaps they led to an observation platform at the summit. The Nazis had been fond of eyries. A dog would not be able to climb them. At least, a normal dog would not. The snow was falling heavily. The cold was almost palpable, a thick encroachment that pressed sharp barbs against the exposed skin of his face and filled his lungs with frozen weight. It was hard to breathe. It was almost impossible in the blizzard to see. And he could hear nothing other than the roar of the wind from the north as it shrilled over the razor edge of the ridge a hundred feet above him. He had to consume precious seconds putting on his gloves. The cold would weld the flesh of his hands to the rungs of the ladder if he did not. He pulled them on with his teeth and started to climb as he prayed a dog could not.

Sections of the cage he climbed through were entirely clogged by snow. But it was light and fairly insubstantial, uncompressed in the lee of the wind in the high cold, and he found that he could bull a path through it. He had always been fit and strong. Sometimes fear denuded a man. Sometimes it drained his strength. But he thought if anything the plight of his son made him even stronger than he would have been ordinarily. He looked down, risking the beam of his torch. But he could see nothing through the swirling void beneath him. He raised his head. The journey was upward. There was only the one escape route and he knew he had no option but to take its terrible risk. So he clambered through the cage of iron hoops up the ladder. This old and sturdy construction framed his calm ascent. And then it ended. And it ended in the screaming howl of the ridge a few feet above the snowy concrete platform put there over seventy years ago for preening from on high, above the world created by the Reich.

It had been described to him as a wall. It was covered in ice and whatever snow clung to its steepling gradient. It dropped for a near vertical mile. Shackleton had skidded down a glacier in South Georgia on his escape from shipwreck and the Pole, and had survived along with his entire party. It could be done. Men had done it. The wind might buffet and slow him. The snow that clung to the face might impede his speed in forgiving, clogging drifts if he did not trigger its precarious weight into avalanche. He wore gloves and heavy boots and had the protection of the performance clothing he had kitted himself out with at Innsbruck. Hunter was not a betting man. But asked, he would have put his chances of living through his descent of the north face of the mountain at no better than 10 per cent. If he had any final doubts about trying to survive it, they were dispelled by the thrum through his fingers of vibration on the final ladder rung. They had breached the door. They were coming after him. With a gasp he went up the final few feet, over the ridge and into the void.

*   *   *

Elizabeth opened and printed off the document attached to the email sent by the British Library. With Adam now asleep and apparently restful, she felt like nothing more than succumbing to the refuge of sleep herself. It was a symptom, she knew, of shock. Her conversation with the malevolent character occupying the child had inflicted that on her. It was not so deep as to debilitate her completely but it was genuine enough. She corked the bottle and flushed her untouched glass of wine down the sink. Then she helped herself to a large measure of Mark Hunter's single malt and drank it down in a gulp. It was not the medically accepted remedy for shock but she felt it working almost straight away. She poked at the sitting-room fire and stacked it with a couple of logs. The warmth would be a comfort and the resinous smell of the wood burning a reminder of what was real and demonstrable.

She suspected that Adam Hunter was lying about the dreams he endured. She thought that it was likely he remembered them very vividly. He was reluctant to recall them because in a way that meant they were inflicted upon him a second time. And perhaps he was noble like his father was and wanted to spare them the worry the images and portents of the dreams would provoke in them. She had no proof that he was lying of course. But he was an unusually bright child. Curiosity was a principal characteristic among bright children. They were curious about everything. It was what fuelled their precocious gathering of knowledge. Yet Adam showed no curiosity at all about the dreams that afflicted him. They were not a mystery to the boy. Elizabeth suspected they were anything but.

The logs in the grate caught and flared with brightness and warmth and she adjusted the angle of the lamp on the little table next to her and tried to concentrate on the pages she held in her hand. They had printed in reverse order. She began to sort them sequentially. She blinked and focused on the first words on the title page. Something landed with a wet thump against the front door, startling her. The half-sorted pages slipped from her fingers to the floor. She looked in that direction, but decided against investigating the source of the sound. The door was extremely solid, the house virtually fortified against intrusion. The hazards of his career had apparently made a cautious man of Mark Hunter where his home was concerned. It was approaching midnight now and her curiosity about the source of the noise would wait until the morning and the coming of light to be satisfied. She lifted the telephone receiver from its cradle just to check as a precaution that the line was not dead. Mobile coverage was patchy up here and the phone was a lifeline. She heard the soft burr of the dialling tone and felt grateful for it.

She replaced the receiver and knelt on the floor to retrieve the scattered pages there. Words on the first sheet she recovered caught her eye immediately. On her knees, by the firelight, she read what was written there:

The wench was uncommon comely for a woman accused of such vile and pernicious crimes against God. She was less than buxom and had not the fecund quality creatures of lust find irresistible in a maiden. Her figure was slight, but fine rather than frail or wretched thin. There was nothing openly wanton or ripely lustful about her aspect. Instead, about her head, there was a clean firmness of jaw suggestive of strong character. Her nose was short and straight. Her eyes were of an arresting shade of green under finely arched brows and somewhat cat-like in shape. They compelled attention without implying insolence. Her gaze was steady and true seeming and not suggestive in the slightest degree of boldness or insolence or other womanly vices. Her mouth was well made. Her lips were full and her teeth even. She was pale of complexion and her skin unsullied by pox or general blemish. Her hair was wheat coloured and clean and straight. She appeared taller than her height. But this was less a trick of sorcery than the impression given forth by her calmness and what seemed the fortitude of her character. Hers was a winning personage to look upon. At least in the first instance, there was no doubt of it.

'Oh, Christ. She looked like me,' Elizabeth said. 'She looked like Lillian Hunter did.' She shook her head. She gathered the spilled pages. She could not comprehend what any of it meant. Threads drew together in her mind and formed only a tangled and impenetrable web. The fire warmed the side of her face. And then her skin chilled with the overpowering instinct that she was being watched. She looked up sharply. She rose to her feet.

Adam was sitting on the floor by the door that led to the stairs. He must have awoken and descended them without her hearing him. He was very pale and thin-looking in the baggy folds of his cotton fleece pyjamas. He looked as though he had shed ten pounds in the period between breakfast and now – between that morning, his classroom recitation in the afternoon and the possession earlier in the evening. His eyes were wide with fatigue and sorrow. His blond curls were plastered against his forehead with perspiration.

'I remember the dreams,' he said.

'I know you do.'

He began to cry.

'Come here,' she said.

But she went to him. He stood and she picked him up and hugged him tightly to her. He felt frail and the sobs shook him. She felt the salt tears and snot and saliva of his sorrow on the flesh of her neck and shoulder. And she thought him very brave.

'Oh, Adam. Adam,' she said.

He sniffed. 'I know what she wants, Elizabeth. I know

what it is Mrs Mallory wants. She doesn't know I've heard her. She only whispers, on the edge of things. But I've heard her all right. And I know.'

Elizabeth heard logs collapse in the grate on the other side of the room. She heard the wet thump of something again against the stout oak of the front door. This time the impact was heavier, the door actually rattling in its reinforced frame. The boy felt light and insubstantial in the grip of her arms.

'What is it Mrs Mallory wants?'

'She nearly did it before. She wants to try to do it again. This time she is confident she will succeed. Mrs Mallory wants to put a tilt upon the world.'

Chapter Eight

At just after 10 a.m. the following morning the blood wagon from a ski run a few kilometres away recovered the unconscious body of Mark Hunter near the foot of the northern slope he had tumbled and skidded down. He had been very lucky. A rescue helicopter flying a routine training patrol had spotted his jacket and the vivid frozen bloodstain that leaked from his friction-burned shoulder half an hour before he was located and stretchered down by a rescue team. He was suffering from hypothermia and concussion. He awoke in the one-bed casualty unit of a clinic in Stubai to be told that he had dislocated his left knee and smashed his right elbow.

'Recuperation will take several weeks,' his doctor said, sitting on the bed. To the concussed Mark Hunter, he looked a kindly, middle-aged man of some professional competence. He had reassuring white hair and wire-framed spectacles. 'Your back is another matter. That will require skin grafts. I hope your holiday insurance is of the more comprehensive sort.' The doctor smiled and patted Hunter on his good knee. 'You probably owe your life to the blow to the head that knocked you unconscious. It enabled a relaxed descent. I am assuming your rope snapped. But you should not have been climbing on that face, in those conditions, alone. In fact, you should not have been there at all. It is suicidal, with the avalanche risk.' He pushed his slipped glasses back up his nose and left the room.

Hunter checked himself out the same afternoon, as soon as he had thawed sufficiently and his concussion had receded to the point where he could stand without vomiting. There was no time to languish, with the accelerating speed of events. He stilled the clinic's protests with credit card details and bought a crutch from reception on the spot. Skiing mishaps made them indispensable in such surroundings. And he could not walk without the aid of one. He took a taxi to where he had left his hire car and for a fat tip had the taxi driver help him clear the car of the snow its body had accumulated since he had parked it there. All his stuff, his passport and regular clothes, were in the boot. He looked up at the trail he had taken the previous evening with some regret. He wished ardently that he had torched the evil place on the mountain above before his departure from it. He wished he had burned it to smouldering ruins but had possessed neither the wit nor, in the end, the time to achieve that satisfaction.

Somehow, he drove to the airport at Innsbruck. He bought a single ticket to Edinburgh. The tiny pharmacy at the clinic had provided him with prescription painkillers but he thought the nausea from the concussion would make him throw up if he took them. Anyway, he needed to be alert. There had been clues at Mrs Mallory's keep but he had not yet pondered on them enough to provide himself with the answers Miss Hall had insisted he would find. Maybe she had been right and he was stupid. The hour he endured waiting for his flight he thought perhaps the most uncomfortable of his entire life. He kept an eye out for the bald man with the dark glasses but did not see him. He was no physical match for anyone in the damaged state he was in. The raw agony of his burned shoulder throbbed through him and he could feel the wound weeping tackily through the bandage that covered it. But mostly he just worried, as he waited for his flight, on Adam's behalf. The protection his son had been given had gone. His respite had been very brief. Elizabeth Bancroft was a resourceful and compassionate woman. Healing was her

profession and he did not think she wanted for courage. But
Mrs Mallory was formidable and she was merciless. He
thought he might have a chance against her if he knew what
it was she wanted. If he knew that, he might be able to locate
her and predict her movements.

'Have you spent a decade thinking your presence at
Magdalena an occurrence of mere chance?' Miss Hall had
asked him over their dinner at her house above the lake.

'It was a blunder,' he had said.

'Your arrival there was more than a simple mistake.'

'It was duty,' he said. 'I was there on a mission. I was
there because I was ordered to go. I tried to get out of it.
The irony is that I went there at all only with the greatest
reluctance.'

'Life is full of ironies,' said Miss Hall.

He did not know what she had meant then and he did
not know now. And he thought his visit to her keep had
provided him with more questions about Mrs Mallory than
answers. He sat in a modular plastic chair and sipped Evian
water from a plastic bottle and watched the bustle of
normality around him and heard the indifferent world
through the public address and it all seemed an elaborate
statement of sardonic mockery. He had seen the grinning
thing awaiting Mrs Mallory seated on the plush of her
Mercedes under the false twilight of the trees. And he had
known it was not human. Magic was real. Evil was mani-
fest. He was twenty yards from the metal detector before
reluctantly abandoning the protection of his sheath knife to
the depths of an airport litter bin. If he was being watched,
he thought he probably looked a sorry sight as he hobbled
on his crutch towards the departure gate.

It was not until the early hours of Wednesday morning that
Elizabeth was able to coax and reassure Adam Hunter into

restful sleep. And she did not wake him in time to get ready for school. She considered her patient was in no state, physically or mentally, to go anywhere. She got a sedative from her medical bag and injected a measured dose of it into him shortly after she awoke herself. He did not flinch at the prick of the needle. He did not feel it. He was exhausted. She calculated that it would be the late afternoon before he stirred, by which time she would be back. She would have to abbreviate her workload for the day. She would have to see about finding a locum too. Adam's care was the priority. She would find someone to fill in for her at least until his father returned.

When Mrs Anderson arrived, she briefed her on what she termed Adam's relapse. The carer reacted with concern more than alarm. Elizabeth told her only what she considered she needed to know. There was every likelihood the boy would not rouse himself until her return. But he did not need to rouse himself, if provoked into wakefulness by the intrusion of something malevolent. She told Mrs Anderson only that Adam suffered waking dreams sometimes of being other people. They were a kind of hallucination. They posed no physical danger either to himself or to anyone else.

'The poor bairn,' Mrs Anderson said, when she had been up to his room to see him. 'I'll make some broth. If he does wake, he needs to eat. He looks half starved.'

Outside the front door there was snow on the gravel. But there was no sign of whatever had thumped against the wood late the previous evening. And there were no tracks except those that Elizabeth left herself on the walk across the carpet of snow to her car. She took with her the Jerusalem Smith document, intending to read it over the break she planned to take for lunch. But her mobile rang on the way to her surgery and when she picked it off the passenger seat to see who the caller was, it was Sergeant Kilbride. She called him back as soon as she had parked outside her building.

'There has been a development,' he said. 'Your postman called us first thing. He found the door to your cottage ajar and did not think it a morning suited to that quantity of ventilation. After ringing the bell and getting no response, he entered and had a look around. Pig entrails have been left on your kitchen table.'

'Charming. Did Robert touch anything?'

'Robert?'

'My postman.'

'No. The lad possesses instincts wasted delivering letters. He left the scene intact and called us straight away. There's a message too, written in pig gore on your kitchen wall.'

'Are you there now?'

'Yes.'

'What does it say?'

'It says: "Witch. Leave the boy be or you'll burn." I'd construe that as a death threat. Mr Galloway will have to be told, Elizabeth. This is a significant escalation.'

Elizabeth laughed. 'Is there any good news?'

'Actually, there might be,' Kilbride said. 'Our SOCOs have just arrived. We think there were two intruders and we think we have traces from the DNA of one of them. They got careless.'

'Or they were drunk,' Elizabeth said.

Kilbride was silent on the line. Then he said, 'Care to put anyone in the frame, Lizzie?'

But she could not think of any likely suspects. 'Do I need to come over?'

'I can spare you that. We'll clean the place up once the photographer has finished and I'll arrange for a locksmith.'

'Be sure to send me the bill, Tony.'

'Och, buy me a beer. I'll have the keys dropped round to you there this afternoon. I'll be in touch. And take care.'

The keys were delivered to the surgery by a patrol car at

noon. Elizabeth spent her lunch break on a brief visit to her cottage. She did not feel as brave about the break-in as she knew she had sounded to Tony Kilbride. She would have felt better if she had been able to name a suspect. The fact that she could not freed her imagination to make the culprits more formidable than they probably were. She did not think it was Tom Lincoln, despite her mother's story concerning the fate of poor Max Hector. Tom could be malicious, especially when he'd had a drink. But he did not possess the wit or wherewithal for a concerted campaign like this. He would break a window at most and probably trip over his bootlaces trying to scarper from the scene. The idea that she had enemies was horrible. The thought that they intended her harm was frightening.

The big new mortise lock was incongruous on her old front door but she could live with it, and with the shiny brass Yale lock fitted above it. Inside, her home was immaculate. The only sign that anything had been amiss was the strong smell of disinfectant from the scrubbing of the table and the wall. And when she opened her curtains fully a patch of kitchen wall was subtly paler than the rest of it. It signalled the dimensions of what they had written there. It had been a bold scrawl. They had been lavish with their gore. She put a couple of changes of clothing into a bag. Outside, it was snowing again. The snow earlier had covered the intruders' tracks by the time the break-in had been discovered. But Tony Kilbride already knew what their footwear looked like. And maybe now he had DNA from one of them as well.

She got back to the Hunter house at just after 5 p.m. Adam awoke at six and she coaxed him into eating a bowl of Mrs Anderson's excellent broth. His usual jokes about Red Bull and cola were nowhere to be heard. He was very subdued, almost monosyllabic. He had come down in his pyjamas and dressing gown and showed no inclination to get dressed. She propped him on cushions in front of one of Clarkson's puerile efforts and hoped it would have the desired effect of lifting his spirits and distracting him while she was in the kitchen. He ate most of the bowl of popcorn she made there for him. He smiled at the schoolboy antics on the screen but laughter was absent.

'Did you dream last night?'

'Yes. I was aboard a naval vessel in the Aegean Sea. I was in the sick bay and I had blood poisoning and knew I was dying.'

'You were Rupert Brooke.'

'Yes. I was. Do you know when my dad is coming home, Elizabeth?'

'Soon,' she said. It sounded inadequate and evasive. But she could not be precise and did not wish to raise his hopes in vain.

'I hope so,' he said. 'I hope it's soon.'

At a quarter to ten he started to doze and she took him up to his bedroom. He could not hide the look of fear on his face. She gave him something to guarantee his sleep. She was generally against drugging children, reluctant normally to prescribe antibiotics, let alone opiates. But there was nothing normal about this case and, whether he dreamed or he didn't, he needed the healing balm of deep and uninterrupted sleep.

Fifteen minutes after she had put Adam to bed, the landline on the little table in the sitting room rang. She felt that she had to answer it. She did not think the sound of the ringing would awaken her charge, but the caller might be his father and the call important. She picked up the receiver.

'This is the Comte de Flurey,' a male voice said. 'I wish to speak with Colonel Hunter.'

'He isn't here.'

'To whom am I speaking?'

'My name is Elizabeth Bancroft.'

'Bancroft,' the voice said. 'Such a fine Scottish name.'

'Is there a message?' The Comte's background was not entirely silent. She could hear music playing softly through the receiver. It was one of her own favourites. It was Mahler and it was the Ninth.

'Please be so good as to tell the colonel I called.'

'I will,' Elizabeth said.

She settled down to read what Josiah Jerusalem Smith had penned in the autumn of 1656. He had dated the document October 17. *There is no Kingdom recognised on earth but the Kingdom of Almighty God*, he began. Thus were his Cromwellian credentials established right at the outset. Elizabeth sighed and sipped wine from the glass she had poured herself. She would restrict herself to one because there was a patient lying upstairs and he was in her sole care. But she felt that the one glass would be welcome. She did not expect Judge Smith to provide her with prose to raise her spirits or put very much of a smile on her face this evening.

I am compelled to commit a formal account of this case to the written word as warning to any of my honest fellows called upon to fight the vile evil of witchcraft. Such is done in the conviction that even the most expert and complete of witch finders will judge the particulars set down here more than passing strange. But every word written has been weighed in my mind at length and found to be true. Shocking as the particulars no doubt are, they occurred and were witnessed by sober and Godly men. Like all stories worthy of the telling, this one teaches a lesson. We must be brave and vigilant facing the forces of darkness. We must employ the same great cunning used against us by our adversary.

Mere gossip did not inspire my trip last month to Scotland. Nor was prejudice against the Scots generally a spur. The Lord

Protector admires the industry of the Scottish. He knows their cities are fair and their commercial instincts honourable and sound. Their country might be the best mapped in the whole of Europe and their engineers are the envy of advanced nations. But the reports reaching Whitehall from an area of the Highlands to the north-east of Perth could not in all good conscience be ignored.

Their source was a Church elder residing near the village of Balloch. He was a man of high literacy and sound learning unlikely to be tempted into exaggeration and lies by the wild rumours of farmers' wives and village shrews. In the main his reports were bald and unembroidered. But their claims were astonishing and, if they were true, an affront to nature and therefore to God. Life and death is the province of the creator. Man accepts the fate of himself and the creatures of the earth humbly and without complaint. We live, we die and we grieve. We bear the mortal loss of that which we own with equanimity. To do otherwise is arrogant, mischievous and sinful.

It was said that the woman Ruth Campbell brought sick beasts back to health and even dead beasts back to life. It was claimed she did this for the profit of her husband's farm and the wealth therein accrued her family. Jealousy might have provoked a neighbour into making such a claim. The land about had been sorely afflicted in recent years with the ailments and diseases that claim livestock. But the observation came from a man of the Church with no tie or connection to the land or the profit or loss to be made from its exploitation. The beasts came back but the stink of death lay about them, he said. The milk was sour and the meat spoiled to the taste. But the animals could still breed. And their offspring were healthy and well. And brought back sheep still grew wool and the resurrected horses and oxen could still strongly pull a plough despite their stench of corruption. Something was lost but something was salvaged in this reversal of nature. And if the story was true it was witchcraft of the worst sort.

The Church man was named Daniel Cawdor. I made appointment with him during correspondence. I undertook the arduous journey to *the far north of the Commonwealth with my retinue. When I arrived at Cawdor's house, he would not entertain me. His grown-up son appeared at the door and said his father was indisposed.*

My first instinct upon hearing this was that Cawdor was indeed a crank or gossip, a mischief maker nervous of the consequences now his tale had outgrown its foolish intentions. I had my sergeant draw his sword. My men were formidable, veterans of the recent victorious war. But the boy did not budge.

My father is blinded, he said. He confronted the witch Campbell overcome by indignation at her blasphemous crimes and she obliged him to blind himself by the gouging of his own eyes with his own thumbs. He lies in misery and shame, a tormented encumbrance now to his family.

I dismounted from my horse. The boy was about sixteen. I had my sergeant sheath his steel and spoke to the lad as kindly as my temper would allow.

What nonsense is this? I said.

It's true, Sir, he said.

The Campbell woman blinded him?

He blinded himself, the boy asserted. But the witch compelled him to inflict this awful mutilation on his person.

I strode past the boy and on into the house. Daniel Cawdor, my correspondent, lay on an upstairs couch with his eye sockets bloodily bandaged and an expression of such abject misery about his remaining features as I will never forget. Practically, I had lost my witness to the Campbell woman's occult mischief. But of the two of us, there was no question of who had lost more. The will to live is sometimes spoken of. That afternoon I looked upon the visage of a man in whom that will was entirely and completely expunged.

Low in spirits with fatigue and the grotesque proof of this setback, I had the best forager in my party seek out a place for us to quarter. He returned to the lonely road where we waited within half an hour and we repaired to a tavern called the Black Boar

which possessed both passable rooms and palatable food. I confess
we were almost cheery after a meal of meat stew and fresh baked
bread and the landlord's good brew of small beer. Then something
curious and unexpected occurred. The brave Cawdor boy, the very
lad who had defied my fearsome sergeant, appeared and sought an
audience with me I felt I could do no other than grant him.

The story he told was most strange. But first he brought forth a
warning I would have considered outlandish insolent were it not
for the plain sincerity worn on the boy's young and sorrowful face.

You have no chance against her, Sir, he said. You travel too
lightly. You have but the six horsemen.

All proven veterans of the war, I said. I felt sorry for the lad.
But I was not disposed at all well to disrespect of my valiant
outriders delivered in a Scots brogue by an insolent pup.

You do not travel in sufficient strength, the lad insisted.

God Almighty himself requires only four horsemen for His
Apocalypse, I said. I have six. The joke was poor and even
blasphemous and I was sorry for it even as the last phrase left
my lips. I was tired and the small beer at the Boar surpassing
potent compared to that brewed in my own locality.

She has a familiar, the lad said. I followed her. I am skilled at
stalking and I followed the witch out of concern only for my
father's predicament in damning her publicly. She met with this
creature in the forest where its deepest thickets lie.

Was it a cat? I inquired of the lad. Am I to be wary of some
exotic reptile or venomous serpent? Does the Campbell woman keep
a toad, the warts of which to kiss before casting spells?

My levity was an abuse of the boy of which I have been ever
since ashamed and for which I have paid much penance.

A wolf, he said. A wolf clothed as a man and standing upright
in the abject mockery of a man, he said. She converses with it. It
offers her counsel. Kill that creature and I believe you have her, Sir.
Do not and I believe your enterprise entirely damned.

What is your name?

Matthew Cawdor, he said.

And do you know, Matthew Cawdor, where we will find this abomination?

I do, Sir, he said.

Guide my men to it, I said. Do this without delay. Tomorrow I confront the accused. Have my men bring back the head of the abomination you describe. Accomplish this with all necessary urgency. Go now.

They saddled up their tired horses and off my men went. I have pondered often since on the bloodlust that made me dispatch the party with such haste. Perhaps it was the excitement of the drink. Since, as a consequence, I have forsworn all drink entirely other than for plain water. But I do not in true conscience know what made me bid them go so unprepared for what they were to face. Perhaps it was simply that I believed the boy. I thought to deprive the witch of the power that had blinded his father.

I never saw Matthew Cawdor again. He perished in the encounter with the fiend he led them to. Only two of my men returned, one mortally wounded, the other bearing their gruesome proof in his bloodstained saddlebag. The thing was fast decomposing by the time it was revealed to me, brought from the bag and placed on a plain deal table at the Boar in lantern light. Carrick, the only one of my men left whole, put it there with grim distaste etched on his honest features. A veteran of Edge Hill and Marston Moor and Naseby, I knew he had killed a score or more of men in battle in the recent war. But he looked at me with trepidation as he asked me did I intend soon to confront the woman served by the abomination whose remains lay rotting on the tabletop.

I confess I looked with appalled fascination at this grim relic. The head was neither wolf nor man but both in some horrid collusion of breed. It looked savage, with its great jaw of coarse hair and bristling fangs. But with its sly grin and the cunning slant of its eyes it also looked intelligent. The remains of a linen shirt were bloodily present in a collar still about its neck. And a *jewelled chain hung from a ring piercing the lobe of one of its human ears.*

Did it speak? I asked Carrick.

Aye, he said. It damned us.

How did it sound?

Carrick thought about this. He drank from the mug of ale I had ordered him brought. There was a tremor, I noticed, in his hand as he raised the mug. Refined, he said, like a gentleman, but fierce unpleasant in tone. Hollow voiced, he said. Not a sound I would wish to hear in my life again.

How did it kill the men who perished?

It tore out their throats, Carrick said. It fought with unearthly quickness.

How tall did it stand?

It stood an inch or so above six foot, Carrick said.

Fleas were leaving the horrible trophy on the table with hops and jumps, red and larger than any species I'd seen before and brazen in the lantern light. Burn it, I said to Carrick. Burn it without delay. Break the skull and bury the shards and the teeth in lime. Bury them deep, Carrick.

Gladly, Sir, he said to me. And tomorrow it's the witch we should burn.

I countenanced the insolence of this remark without comment. Men should not speak to their officers so freely. But Carrick was a brave man who had endured a dreadful ordeal. And there might be more and worse to follow before we could return south to goodness and piety, away from the corruption and perversity amid which we had found ourselves cast.

Elizabeth put the pages, half of them still unread, on the table next to where she sat. For the present, she did not want to read any more about her ancestor. She was too tired. She was too shocked by what she had learned already. Either Jerusalem Smith was deluded, the victim of some sort of hysteria, or he was a decent man out of his depth in dealing with something utterly diabolical. The problem was that sanity as well as decency hallmarked his every phrase. He might be ardent in his Protestant faith and Puritanism. But he was telling the truth. She rubbed her eyes. No wonder her mother had baulked at reading this stuff. It was much easier to believe the convenient myth of the brutal witch finder and his summary and indiscriminate punishments in the Highlands than to face the reality of corrupt magic coursing through your own bloodline. She had taken only a single sip from her glass of wine. She poured what remained into the kitchen sink, then showered and brushed her teeth and checked on her charge. Whatever dreams tormented Adam, he looked peaceful enough in sleep. Sleep was what she needed too. She went to bed.

She was awoken at 4 a.m., having heard or sensed something not right. The room was dark. But she could see a figure standing at the end of her bed, the mass of this shape darker than the murk surrounding it, and solid.

'Elizabeth?'

'Mark!'

'Shh,' he said. His voice was a low murmur. 'I don't want to wake Adam.'

'Adam won't wake. I've given him something.'

Hunter seemed to limp forward. He sat heavily on the bed. He smelled of blood and sweat and antiseptic ointment. There was something wrong with him. His posture was wrong, as her eyes adjusted and gathered more of the detail of him.

'So the dreams have begun again?'

'What happened to you? Did you find her?'

He laughed. There was no mirth in the sound. 'It was more a case of her finding me.'

She switched on the bedside light and sat up and looked at him. There was blood seeping through the shoulder and back of his rumpled suit coat. His right arm was pinned to his chest by a sling. There was a crutch lying on the carpet she had not noticed in the darkness. His face was very pale and one leg was thrust out before him as though he could not bear to bend it. Elizabeth pushed off the duvet and climbed out of bed. She slept naked, but this was not a time to be coy. She opened the drawer into which she had folded her underwear.

'Why are you dressing?'

'I'm taking you to my mother's house.'

'What on earth for?'

'You'll see. I've made some discoveries while you've been away, Mark. I've learned some quite useful things.'

'What about Adam?'

'We'll take your Land Rover. I'll drive. I'll wrap Adam in his bedspread and carry him down and lay him on the back seat.'

'Are you strong enough to carry him?'

Elizabeth zipped up her jeans and reached for her bra. 'I'll have to be. You can't do it. I won't drop him, if that's what you mean.'

'Is this really necessary?'

Elizabeth brushed the hair off her face with her fingers. 'It's necessary for you to be well,' she said. 'You're no good to any of us in the state you've got yourself into.'

On icy roads, even with the four-wheel drive, it was a journey of thirty-five minutes to Margaret Bancroft's house. On the route, Hunter gave Elizabeth a brief account of what had taken place during his time away. She listened without comment. Then when he had finished, she said, 'How well did you get to know Lillian's family?'

'Depends,' he said.

'What does that mean?'

'Lillian was adopted. She never knew her real family. I got the impression that she had made strenuous efforts to find out who they were before we met, but that those efforts had been unsuccessful. She was sensitive on the subject. Why do you ask?'

'There is a very strong physical resemblance between your late wife and myself. It's almost uncanny. Why did you not comment on it?'

'Should I have? The resemblance is coincidental. Drawing your attention to it would have been outré and macabre.'

'You must have realised Adam would pick up on it.'

'We're not exactly spoiled for choice when it comes to medical help in this part of the world, Dr Bancroft.'

'Come off it, Mark. You've just seen me naked.'

'Look, Elizabeth. You have an outstanding reputation. I had bigger concerns for Adam than his noticing you share some superficial similarities with his mum.'

Hunter tried to turn round to look at his son asleep on the rear seat. But the congealed blood was tight across his skinned shoulder and, constrained by the wound, he could not do so.

'What were Lillian's books about, Mark? Could you tell me something about their subject matter?'

'They were children's stories. I'll show you some of them. When we get back from this pointless trip to your mother's house, you can see for yourself.'

Things were different between them, Elizabeth realised. They were no longer speaking to one another with the prim formality that had always marked their verbal exchanges in the past. She wondered if he had noticed and thought, probably not. He was in too much pain for such subtle considerations. She peered out through the windscreen at the snowy road, looking for landmarks in the featureless darkness. She saw that they were almost there.

Like many elderly people Margaret Bancroft was a light sleeper. She answered her door almost immediately. She opened it on a wounded man accompanying her daughter, who was carrying a sleeping boy in a blanket. 'What a beautiful child,' she said. She looked up at Mark Hunter. 'You must be very proud of him.'

'I am,' he said.

'We need your help, Mum,' Elizabeth said.

'I can see you do.'

'I know you thought you had finished with the bone magic.'

Margaret Bancroft smiled at her daughter. 'Yes. But I never quite believed it had finished with me. Come in. Put the boy on the sofa. Find somewhere comfortable to sit, Colonel Hunter. See if you can't revive the fire, Elizabeth. The ashes haven't quite gone out. I'll make some tea.'

'Tea isn't the priority, Mum.'

'It is for me. It's nearly forty years since I last did what I am about to attempt to do. Before I do it, I need the fortification tea provides.'

A short while later Hunter limped stiffly after Margaret Bancroft into her parlour. She came back alone after only a few minutes. Her fingers absently stroked the curls on the head of the sleeping child as she walked past the sofa. She sat opposite where Elizabeth sat, waiting by the window with the snow falling through the pane on the white world outside.

'Was it hard?'

'No. I'm old now, but it was never hard. The Colonel sleeps. He'll sleep for a little while longer. When he revives, he will do so quite restored.'

'I've been reading about our illustrious ancestor.'

'Oh?'

'Judge Smith seems to have had a pretty bad press.'

'Really?'

'Ruth Campbell was not exactly the blameless martyr to religious ignorance of our cherished little family myth.'

'I never thought she was, Elizabeth. But I've never had the courage to find out the truth for myself. And I still don't have it. Please don't tell me any more.'

'She looked like me, Mum. Why don't you? I've sometimes wondered where my looks came from. It wasn't Dad.'

Margaret Bancroft bowed her head. 'I used to look like you, Lizzie. Nature blessed me with green eyes and a pretty mouth just like yours. I used the magic to change my appearance.'

'Why?'

'The honest answer is out of shame that I possessed it. I did not want to look like Ruth Campbell's descendant. I had a suspicion she had been bad. I did it subtly and over time. Your father was dying by then. I don't know that anyone else really noticed. The change was gradual and you were an infant and people hereabouts had no adult resemblance to compare to mine.'

'I want to thank you, Mum. I know you broke a solemn oath to do what you did just now. I know you are ashamed of the magic. But Mark Hunter is a good man and you have done a good thing and I am very grateful – and he will be too.'

Her mother looked up at her and smiled. 'You could have done it yourself, Lizzie. Sometimes I believe it skips a generation. Sometimes it might skip several. But it is very powerful in you, much more so than in me. I have known that from when you were a young child.'

Her mother's eyes were hazel under straight brows. And her upper lip was long. It really was quite a subtle change. But it was everything too. 'You wanted me to read the judge's account as a warning,' Elizabeth said, understanding.

'You want me to know what it is I should never attempt to do.'

It was almost seven o'clock by the time they returned to the Hunter house. Adam still slept his narcotic sleep. This time his father carried him from the car to his bed. Elizabeth made breakfast for Mark and herself at the kitchen table and told him about the events that had taken place in his absence. He covered his face in his hands when she told him about the teacher's call and the Brooke recital. She thought he might start to weep. He could endure much, as his life had proven. But if it went on, Adam's suffering would undo him. She left no significant detail out, and he managed to retain his composure until she had finished.

'Is there anything else, Elizabeth?'

'There is just one thing. Late last night the Comte de Flurey telephoned. He left no message other than to tell you he had called.'

'The Comte is as dead as the creature he served. As you said just now, Mrs Mallory possesses a gift for mimicry. It was her calling and she did leave a message, which is that she knows I am alive and where to find me.'

As gently as she could, Elizabeth asked to see the books written by Lillian that he had promised to show her on their return. He went away and returned to the kitchen with a dozen slim volumes. He sorted five of these into a separate pile, explaining that they were a series. She picked up the first book in the series and opened it, saw an illustration and almost screamed. A foppish two-legged figure in a brocade waistcoat and a lupine leer stared out at her from the page.

'Walter the Wolf,' Hunter said. 'He's scary to look at, but sadly misunderstood. Children like a frisson of terror in their fiction. They must do. This was her most successful series by far. It still sells strongly all over Europe. They banned these books in the States, though. They were accused there of peddling moral turpitude.'

Elizabeth flicked through the five volumes.

'I can kind of see their point,' Hunter said. 'Wolves are not camp, kindly anthropomorphic characters with the clothes sense of a dandy. They are the coldest predatory killers of anything warm-blooded on the planet. I never much cared for these books, to be honest. I never saw their worth.'

'This isn't a coincidence, Mark. Neither is the way that Lillian looked. But Mrs Mallory doesn't have green eyes, according to you. And you've described Miss Hall as fat and grotesque. I can't make sense of it, there's no pattern, no continuity. Or there is a pattern, but there are contradictions.'

Hunter got to his feet and went and put fresh coffee in the machine on the counter by the window. 'There isn't really any contradiction,' he said. 'Mrs Mallory showed me her true face and it was Lillian's, just as yours is Ruth Campbell's. She had changed her appearance, as your mother did hers. But she has had more pragmatic reasons for doing so. A woman cannot go on living and not ageing without attracting comment. She has enjoyed any number of guises. And she has enjoyed the lives that went with them.'

'What about Miss Hall?'

'Your mother believes bone magic fundamentally malevolent. It can be used for good, but that is not its purpose. She realised that, flooded with exultation after killing Max Hector. Miss Hall gave me two clues about herself. The first was in calling me arrogant in the canvas cathedral for assuming we don't share the world with a species the equal of our own. The second was her repeated insistence that she was more good than bad. Miss Hall was not a bone magician, Elizabeth. She was never the same as you or your mum or Lillian or Ruth or Mrs Mallory. She was something else entirely.'

Elizabeth heard Adam's feet on the stairs and assumed the boy would join them for their council of war. They had got by on popcorn and hope for the time of Mark Hunter's absence and then on a potent opiate when those other things had proved to be insufficient. He would be refreshed, she thought. He would tell them both about what he had over-heard concerning Mrs Mallory's ambitions in his dreams. Except that it did not happen like that at all. He came down and saw his father sitting at the kitchen table and his father saw him. Adam shrieked with pure joy and they closed the distance to embrace one another. And Elizabeth remembered that since the tragedy of the death of the women in their family, these two had never before been apart.

It was most certainly a special occasion. Adam was allowed to chug down a Diet Coke with his breakfast. Elizabeth thought the narcotic she had administered the day before would have made him dehydrated and felt a stab of guilt at the raw strength of his thirst. But he definitely looked better for the rest. And of course, he looked infinitely better for the presence of his dad. He had come down in his pyjamas and was sent back up to dress warmly in layers of clothes before putting on gloves and a scarf and a hat and water-proof boots. They were going outside to play in the snow. The snow was still a novelty to them of course, she remem-bered. They were newcomers, not long settled here from the south of England.

They went outside. She watched them through the kitchen window as they pelted one another with snowballs. Elizabeth glanced at her watch. On a normal day she would have been on her way to work by now, but she had managed to find a well-qualified locum at shorter notice than she had expected. He had filled in for her before, was good and knew the territory. Watching Mark Hunter in the snow, in his agility and exuberance, she had a moment when she felt crestfallen. He had limped home from Austria gravely injured. Her own healing skills had been scrupulously acquired. It took a long time and a lot of single-minded dedication and financial cost to train and qualify for a degree in medicine. But her abilities were scant and impoverished, nothing to the miracles her aged mother was able to work in a moment in restoring a damaged man to health and strength.

They came back in for Adam's sled. They dragged her outside with them. In the house, in their absence from it, the telephone rang, but of course none of them heard it. They played and skidded and frolicked in the snow. They helped Adam build a snowman. In the proximity of the mouthpiece of the telephone's receiver on the table in the Hunter sitting room, the faint scent of the Comte's cologne went undetected, unappreciated too. It rose and dissipated as the line rang and rang, ignored. Finally, the ringing stopped. The scent faded, reluctantly. And with the dissipating fragrance, faint notes of music faded, unheard. It was not on this occasion Gustav Mahler. It was not symphonic, or sedate. It was the Duke Ellington recording of Billy Strayhorn's 'Take the "A" Train'. It was jazz that Mrs Mallory was listening to. As Miss Hall had observed, she liked to party.

Eventually, they came back inside. They were red-nosed and frozen-fingered and they sought the warmth of the stove. Hunter kindled the sitting-room fire. Elizabeth made hot chocolate. Despite everything, life seemed very normal. Love and joy might be human failings, Elizabeth thought, but they were strong and persistent and wonderful failings. She served up the hot chocolate on a tray. Adam was on Mark's lap in the sitting room, being warmed and cherished in the strength and affection of his father. She sat with them and felt very much a part of things.

When they had drunk their drinks Adam stood and looked at them both. 'I have to tell you about Mrs Mallory,' he said. 'You need to know about what she intends to try to do. She's very confident of putting her tilt on the world. She's tried and failed in the past. She's only very narrowly failed. On occasion, the world has survived by fluke, by the skin of its teeth. But this time, she's confident. She's very certain, she says, of the ground.'

Chapter Nine

Mark Hunter thought there was a profound difference between the magic of Miss Hall and that endowed by the Campbell bloodline. When Margaret Bancroft healed him there was no bit of business with a scarf or show of paper-less origami from dextrous hands. She just closed her eyes and it was done. Miss Hall had been begrudging in her healing of his mauled arm. And his emotional state had been fragile, badly affected by what had happened to Major Rodriguez. The arm had quickly become better but there had been no sense of energy or exuberance about the process. 'I cannot work miracles,' had been her cantankerous complaint. In medical terms, this was not true. She had worked one on a limb so badly infected he would otherwise have lost it. But it was an unspectacular miracle. At least, it was compared to the one he had experienced earlier that day. Elizabeth's mother was elderly, even frail. But she had left him feeling years younger and full of strength and vitality. He suspected it was the difference between magic learned and practised scrupulously and magic yours by birthright. Mrs Mallory enjoyed the latter. He was certain of it. After the way Miss Hall had toyed with him in her house above Lake Geneva it made the prospect of confronting Mrs Mallory a daunting one.

He thought the notion of Elizabeth Bancroft as a witch almost amusing. His attitude towards her had entirely changed. He no longer thought of her as some morbid mirror image of his lost wife. Repellent was the last word he would use to describe her now. He thought this might simply be a case of having recently seen her naked. After all, he was a man. With no clothes on, pained and damaged as he'd been, he could not help noticing just how beautifully put together a woman she was. But it wasn't just that, was it? It was her confidence and lack of self-consciousness as she stood there calmly dressing. It was the way she had taken charge of the situation. It was the way she had made the decisions, carrying Adam down to the Land Rover, putting it firmly into gear in darkness on a freezing road, meeting a dire emergency by cajoling her mother into using skills she'd kept a secret even from herself for forty years. Before she had been almost deferential, someone on to whose wan character it had been tempting to superimpose Lillian because of the resemblance and probably, also, because he missed his wife so painfully. But in the short time since his return, Elizabeth had emerged as so much her own woman he was barely aware of the resemblance any more. She was a stunning individual. She was sexy and clever and strong. The idea that she could be a sorceress like Mrs Mallory seemed almost absurd to him.

And they were communicating. Before his departure for Switzerland, their conversations had held all the emotional nuance of a pair of speak-your-weight machines placed side by side. Circumstances had obliged them to grow closer, become friends. The circumstances were awful. So Hunter was doubly grateful for Elizabeth's friendship.

This was his thinking as he waited for Adam to thaw himself out under a hot shower before telling them about the substance of his dreams. He was sitting alone in front of the fire in the sitting room. He had built up the fire and the room was encouragingly warm. Elizabeth was in the spare room upstairs, reading the rest of Judge Smith's account of his Scottish experience. Hunter would read the whole of it when she had finished. She would come down when Adam did, no doubt having first made sure his hair was properly dried so he wouldn't catch a chill. It was amazing how close the two of them had grown in the short time he had been away. Their body language in the snow had betrayed their closeness. There was no distance between them at all. It was good for Adam and he felt grateful for that as well. He needed answers to occur to him from his time in Mrs Mallory's keep. Without them, his son's ordeal would continue and worsen. He needed some clue, some insight. Without that he could do nothing. He had been a man of action all his professional life. Thanks to sorcery, he was healthy and whole again. He was capable. But he had no idea at all about what to do next. He wished Miss Hall had not left it so late to try to help him lift the Magdalena curse. He wished that she had not died quite so soon. It came to him then that five people had been cursed at Magdalena and not the four he had always supposed. There was Rodriguez first of course and poor dead Peterson after him. There was him and there was his son. And finally there was Mrs Mallory's adversary, wasn't there? Miss Hall had been cursed, or she would not be dead. She had beaten Mrs Mallory and when their blundering mission had voided the victory, an affronted Mrs Mallory had exacted her revenge. It was why Miss Hall had hurt him, despite her wish to help. He had not understood that contradiction. He thought he understood it now.

The phone on the table beside him rang. He picked up the receiver and said hello. Sergeant Kilbride introduced himself and asked would Elizabeth get back to him. She had told Hunter about the harassment campaign and he explained this to Kilbride, who said there had been a significant development in the case. He wanted to discuss it with Dr Bancroft personally. He suggested the Black Boar at four that afternoon and Hunter promised to pass the message on.

When he replaced the receiver and the phone rang again

straight away he assumed it was the sergeant ringing again because there was something important he had omitted to say. But it was not.

'Colonel Hunter?'

He recognised the voice. He said nothing.

'This is the Comte de Flurey.'

'No, it isn't, Mrs Mallory. The Comte is dead. You killed him.'

There was a pause. 'And you killed me. Death isn't everything it's reputed to be.' After better than a decade, the velvet purr of her voice was familiar enough to chill his spine. She laughed her throaty laugh. There was music in the background. It was jazz. It was Bix Beiderbecke playing the cornet. His imagination told him he could detect her scent over the line; strong tobacco and pink gin and Jicky perfume. 'The Comte is alive and well,' she said. 'If you don't believe me, look out of your window.'

Hunter picked up the phone, cradling the receiver in the crook of his neck, and did as she had suggested. The snow was falling in a heavy flurry and the sky was almost as white as the ground in the mid-morning luminescence. A headless figure stood poised in evening wear about forty feet from the house.

'It's a good trick,' Hunter said.

'Colonel, there are plenty I can better it with.'

The figure in the snow shuffled forward a step. Under the sophistication of its dapper attire, Hunter saw that it was shivering. He heard Adam and Elizabeth talking as they descended the stairs, away across the room from the doorway behind him.

'If my son is confronted by that abomination you will burn, Mrs Mallory. I swear to Christ I will hunt you down and build the pyre myself. And you will burn and perish screaming.'

She laughed again. In the snow outside, the apparition disappeared. 'Hunter. You are well named,' she said. 'But your bravado is pathetic. Still, I wouldn't want to frighten the child unduly, Colonel. Not at this stage. Not yet.' The connection was broken.

Firstly Adam tried to explain the misguided good intentions that had caused him to lie about remembering what he dreamed. Hunter tried to picture his son as he thought Elizabeth would be doing. He was a beautiful and articulate boy wrestling with a dilemma no child should have to confront. The dimensions of the chair he sat in made him look small and even younger than he was. His feet did not reach the floor. His unbroken voice wavered as he steeled himself to recall the detail of the nightmares haunting him. He would bring tears to the eyes of a stranger, Hunter thought. He stole a glance at Elizabeth. She was not a stranger, was she? She was biting her lip and blinking too often, struggling to retain her composure as Hunter was himself.

There are the big dreams and the domestic dreams, Adam said. The domestic dreams were the worst because they were all about Mrs Mallory and he did not think Mrs Mallory knew he was having them and he was scared of what she would do to him if she found out. He eavesdropped in the domestic dreams and he thought that would make her very angry and when she was angry she did cruel things. She got pleasure from cruelty, he said. She was a very bad person. Except that she wasn't really a person like other, normal people. And she thought that cruelty was a lot of fun.

'Where do the domestic dreams take place, Adam?' Elizabeth asked.

'At her house,' he said. The look on his face was terrible. Adam was a reluctant visitor to Mrs Mallory's house.

'We'll get to the domestic dreams in a bit,' his father said, gently. 'Tell us about the big dreams.'

Often these took place on battlefields, Adam said. They were a bit like movies except for the frozen corpses and the mutilations. They were much scarier and more gruesome than anything in the movies he had been allowed to see. They were sometimes very noisy with the screams of diving aeroplanes and barrages of artillery fire. Sometimes the battles were from a long time ago and had cavalry with swords and bright uniforms. But they weren't quaint or picturesque. The soldiers were cold and frightened and brutal. You saw more men dead in those dreams than alive.

It wasn't all battlefields. Sometimes it was marching men with flaming torches in what Adam thought was a football stadium. They listened to speeches by night and roared out responses and the worst thing about those dreams was just the general noise and the hot stink of body odour.

And sometimes it was conference rooms. Men in single-breasted suits and thin ties sat around a large table with a big chart on the wall like something from a really dated low-budget science fiction film. There were outlines of countries and dots of red light in strings and clusters on the chart. The men around the table wore old-fashioned headphones and spoke in whispers to one another and seemed to be waiting for something. They drank coffee from a machine out of disposable cups and all smoked cigarettes. The conference room dreams were creepy but boring, Adam thought. But the men in them were not bored. To him, they seemed pale and terrified.

He thought the worst of the big dreams were the executions. These were shootings or hangings and they weren't like the movies at all. It was almost always cold and very early, the victims dragged from a cot in a freezing cell and still stiff from sleep when they were blindfolded and taken to an icy courtyard and killed. He could not believe the speed with which human life vacated the body when it was shot in the head. It happened all at once. It was like watching the strings severed on a puppet, he said. Except of course, the blood told you it wasn't a puppet at all. And he could not believe how slowly life left the body when it was raised on the end of the rope. The hangings were worse than the shootings. The kicking of the corpse just went on and on.

Adam got off his chair and said he needed to pee. He was sorry, but the Diet Coke was to blame. It had gone right through him. He had to use the loo before he got to the domestic dreams.

Hunter and Elizabeth sat in silence for a moment after his departure from the room. Then Elizabeth said, 'I'm no great student of history. But if Mrs Mallory succeeds in putting her tilt on the world, I think we're in for a grim period.'

'That's the prophesy.' Hunter thought about the apparition he'd witnessed earlier through the window. 'Do you think my son can ever recover from what he's been forced to witness?'

'If it stops now, yes, I'm confident he will. He's very aware that these are dreams, however graphic and awful. He's very clear on that. Children are extremely resilient. But if it goes on much longer, it is bound to damage him.'

'I wonder if your mother might not be able to protect him. I mean, just for a while.'

'You want me to abandon my patient?'

He turned to her. 'I want you to help me find and destroy the monster doing this.'

Adam came back into the room. 'I'd better tell you about the domestic dreams,' he said, 'the dreams where I'm in her house. They're worse.'

Mrs Mallory lived in a large house in a spacious tree-lined square. The square was covered by gravel rather than grass. The house had four big rectangular windows and a pillared entrance at the centre framing a huge black painted front door. The stonework was painted cream. A set of steps led up to the door. It had an ornamental knocker. It was a bearded man's head and the bit you knocked with was held between the teeth in his grinning mouth. The curtains at the windows were always closed and Adam never used the knocker to try to enter the house. He could barely have reached it. But he did not need to. These were dreams, after all. They followed a dream's weird logic.

She lived alone in the house. There was someone in there with her but it was not human and Adam did not think that it was any longer alive. It sat in a book-lined room he thought might be her study or library. There were books on the walls in glass-fronted cases, with a globe and astronomical charts and a telescope on a stand and a polished desk. And there was the thing she lived with. It sat on a sort of throne. It was dressed as a man but it was bigger than a man and very frightening to look at. Mrs Mallory spoke to it as though it was alive but it never moved or replied to what she said. Adam did not think he could have endured it if it had. The library was gloomy and so was the rest of her house. She had electricity but the lights were always turned down very low. He thought that she held parties because sometimes some of the rooms were messy and smelled very strongly of tobacco smoke and drink spilled on the soft furnishings or the carpets. But he never dreamed of those. He just saw their aftermath, the overflowing ashtrays and half-empty champagne bottles and discarded items of jewellery and clothing and the litter of sequins and feathers and the bits of foil and smears on tabletops and the syringes left about.

She liked to play cards. Her opponents were always women. If she entertained men, he never saw them. The thing on the throne in the library was male, though. It wore a man's uniform and black, polished boots over its enormous feet. The boots looked deformed on the feet. He did not like to look at them but they were fascinating in their size and ugliness and he thought they must have been specially made.

She did not play cards in the library. None of her guests was invited in there. She had a special room with a roulette wheel and a chessboard with pieces made from marble and some other games in polished wooden cases Adam did not recognise or know. He did not like this room. It had no windows. But he did not like the house. And he did not like the library in particular, where Mrs Mallory spoke gleefully to the grotesque and unresponsive thing on the throne about putting her tilt on the world.

When Adam had finished his story concerning the dreams the three of them went for a walk in the snow together. Hunter was concerned the evening-suited apparition might return to stalk them in its clumsy, headless way through the drifts. But surely she had played out her little joke at the Comte's expense. She had killed and then further humiliated that pompous servant in death. He did not really think her fury at Miss Hall could be sustained now that she was gone for ever. She had more important things to focus her energies on. She had ambitious plans. So they walked in the snow and Hunter hoped that the white purity of the wilderness at the edge of their home and the cold of the freezing air they breathed would expunge the dreams that contaminated Adam's precious soul, at least for a little while. After their walk he drove them in the Land Rover down to the Black Boar and they ate a hearty pub lunch. When they got back Adam curled up on the sofa in the sitting room before the fire and went to sleep.

'A sleep will do him good,' Hunter said. 'He's worn out, poor little fellow, after recounting what he did this morning. I wouldn't mind a siesta myself.'

'You can't afford the time,' Elizabeth said. 'You've got some reading to do.'

'And what are you going to do, while I'm catching up on Cromwell's judge?'

'I'm going to call my mum. I think there might be some merit in your suggestion that she could look after Adam. If push came to shove, I mean.'

'Then you've got your meeting with the policeman.'

'No rest for the wicked.'

'I'm sorry I've not been around to help you with that.'

'You've got enough to deal with, Mark,' Elizabeth said, looking towards the sofa and the sleeping boy.

The curious claim made by Matthew Cawdor wants repeating here. He said the mischief of the witch was not confined to her ungodly interference with the life and death of beasts. He said that his father had complained to him of this: that the Campbell woman had brought a sort of pestilence to afflict their locality. This contamination made women lascivious and men quarrelsome and violent. It was as though the natural order of things was reversed and people hereabouts descended into a pagan brutality without grace or refinement or any vestige of decorum or morality. People had become governed by lewdness and greed. Cawdor used his blind father's phrase to describe this unnatural state of affairs. He called it a plague of the soul.

Their encounter with the beast in the forest had left me without men but for Carrick and the wounded cavalryman dying in a straw-filled cot in the stable of the Black Boar. I had the Lord Protector's authority. But I had also urgent need of willing men. On the morning of my first full day in the region I was obliged to seek out the district sheriff and request of him his assistance. He gave it willingly. He was a man I suspect dubious if not entirely cynical generally on the matter of witchcraft. But he knew which side had won the war and Cromwell's seal, even so far from the seat of his authority, proved a powerful imperative. He had five armed men saddled on sturdy mounts for me within the hour and I took my leave of him with the promise that the fact of his assistance would be strongly noted in my report. This was a pledge duly kept.

It was late in the afternoon and not far from full dark when we reached the Campbell farm and the accused woman was obliged to answer there our summons. She showed no surprise at our appearance on her land. Of her husband and children there was no sign to be seen. She was bound without struggle and put in a cart drawn by one of the mules from her own stable. A smell like spoiled meat drifted like clinging mist in the proximity of this ramshackle wooden structure. But there was no scent of death about the honest animal obliged to draw her the distance to the Black Boar in the cart.

Our route took us of necessity back through the village and, no longer travelling at the gallop, I was able to gain a true impression of the settlement, intrigued to see whether the evidence of my eyes bore out the claim Cawdor had made. It did. It was full dark now but the night lay brightly about under a full moon. Men gathered drunk and quarrelsome at the crossroads while others slept insensible in roadside feed troughs or merely in doorways. The women were of furtive and slovenly appearance and an infant howled unattended, its cries most pitiful through the broken window of a hovel that appeared to me abandoned. That village was not a place of industry or rectitude. It looked dismal, as though God had abandoned it.

Our destination reached, Ruth Campbell spent her first words to me on a complaint with which I could not in conscience quarrel. She said that it was wrong to try a woman of position, the wife of a respected landowner, in a low and common tavern she would never by choice frequent. I would not come here except in chains, she said. I would not bring the scandal and shame on my family name. Toil and endeavour are our bywords, she said. I wish no offence, Sir, she said. But should an innocent woman be judged in a place where men come to squander money on getting drunk?

There is nowhere else suitable, I said, and no one will oblige you to sup wine, madam. And no ale or wine will be taken under this roof either, by anyone, until this business is concluded and you are gone from here to whatever fate your trial has determined before God. And she smiled. And despite her protestations, I could not avoid the suspicion that she had wished offence, or at least some sly measure of mockery. I looked at her in the bright lantern light of the parlour of the inn, made even brighter now by flames from the generous hearth, in which Carrick was setting the large fire needed should we require the hot iron. And there was not the hint of fear or even trepidation about her.

The wench was uncommon comely for a woman accused of such vile and pernicious crimes against God. She was less than buxom and had not the fecund quality creatures of lust find irresistible in a maiden. Her figure was slight, but fine rather than frail or wretched thin. There was nothing openly wanton or ripely lustful about her aspect. Instead, about her head, there was a clean firmness of jaw suggestive of strong character. Her nose was short and straight. Her eyes were of an arresting shade of green under finely arched brows and somewhat cat-like in shape. They compelled attention without implying insolence. Her gaze was steady and true seeming and not suggestive in the slightest degree of boldness or insolence or other womanly vices. Her mouth was well made. Her lips were full and her teeth even. She was pale of complexion and her skin unsullied by pox or general blemish. Her hair was wheat coloured and clean and straight. She appeared taller than her height. But this was less a trick of sorcery than the impression given forth by her calmness and what seemed the fortitude of her character. Hers was a winning personage to look upon. At least in the first instance, there was no doubt of it. She wore a fustian dress or smock over a plain white blouse of good linen. Her feet were shod in stout leather boots, a reminder of the prosperity her husband's farm enjoyed.

I began to question her. She answered with deliberation. She denied every accusation. Her responses had the emphatic weight of honesty about them. I started to consider in my mind the difficulty of proving animals were risen from the dead. It was hardly practical to interrogate the beasts themselves. Rumour was all we had without our dead witness, Matthew Cawdor. I supposed we would have to drag his blind father from his bed and have the poor wretch corroborate. I was loath to resort to torture with Ruth Campbell. I am not a squeamish man. But I am a man and would not easily see a woman's beauty defiled without some sureness of her guilt.

Then something happened. Carrick had not burned everything of our gruesome forest relic. He had taken the jewelled chain from the ear of the beast's head. He had done this to show me the curious stones with which it was set. These gems had been oddly cut. It was not possible to discern their true shape and the study of them provoked nausea in the body and made the brain swim. I had put this evil bauble on the mantel of the fire and forgotten it. Now Ruth Campbell's eyes alighted upon it and I saw from the change in her expression that its significance was immediate to her.

The lanterns all went out. What happened next, we witnessed by the fierce, flickering illumination of the fire. A scream was wrenched forth from her I would not have believed possible in someone of so slight a frame. She shook her manacled hands at me in fists. She pulled back her head and let out a shriek of laughter and then her body rose off the floor and ascended until her head was only a foot or so beneath the beams of the ceiling. Nothing held her there. But there she was. It was not trickery and it was not illusion either. It was impossible and achieved only by vile magic. None of my men moved, as petrified as I was, I confess. The witch held open her arms and the chain binding them sundered with a snap of iron. She flung out her hands and crossed her feet and writhed in a blasphemous mockery of Christ nailed to the cross at Calvary. Blood trickled from her palms and dribbled to the floor from her booted feet in satanic parody of the papist stigmata. She laughed again and lowered herself slowly to the floor and contorted her mouth in a drooling grin.

Do as you will with me, she said. I am entirely finished with this life.

She was supine when bound once more and lifeless when we locked her under guard of two men in a stable stall for the night. The landlord of the inn was summoned and provided me with the name and address of a village carpenter but the man was too dead drunk when Carrick tried to rouse him to be of use to our purpose. My sequestered men were granted little sleep that night. We hammered together a gibbet from what materials we could find about the inn and its outbuildings. In the morning Ruth Campbell was brought bound in her own cart into the village, the gibbet borne by two horsemen, trailing the lanes between their mounts like some ghastly plough, the riders pale still from the ordeal of the previous evening.

I read the verdict and the proclamation and we hanged her before an indifferent crowd of onlookers, dirty and dishevelled and still suffering from their sordid revelries of the night. Her face looked not gross and empurpled by the choking insult of the rope, but serene above the noose as her body swayed gently with the strength of the northerly autumn wind. And I had never been sorrier to see a woman die as a consequence of my own judgement and verdict. Was this because she was so very fair and amenable at the outset? I'll allow in part it was. But it was also because I believed Ruth Campbell more seduced and corrupted than sinner. The beast had groomed her for the evil she did. I was convinced of it.

I did not return forthwith to London. I took a commanding house the sheriff leased me on a nearby hill for a peppercorn. I wrote and despatched my report to Whitehall. I released the sheriff's men and, aye, Carrick too for the suffering and distinction of his loyal service. Fresh men were sent me. And I requested the wolfhounds too be brought from their kennels at Hampton Court.

The Magdalena Curse

And they came, eager on the leash, and I had the forests hereabout combed with them for others of the corrupting breed that now occupied the dreams I suffered at night. But we discovered none.

Stories have been spread in malice concerning these recent events. It is said a confession was tortured out of Ruth Campbell and that she did condemn herself in her innocence when the torment of mutilation grew too great for an honest soul to bear. 'Tis said also that we burned her husband and her children out of their home and, thus doing, gleefully watched their livelihood perish in the flames. These spiteful lies are inspired, I think, by the Lord Protector's many Scottish enemies. There are allies here not just of the English crown but the Scots pretender too. My Lord Cromwell has few friends in this region. If any burning was done at the Campbell farm, it was accomplished by someone else. Perhaps her husband was complicit. The truth is, I care not.

Most curious about the case was the condition of the corpse. I decreed that Ruth Campbell should swing until she dropped from the decomposition of her flesh and separation of her bones as a lesson to others tempted to follow the same dark path. Autumn is not kind to carrion in a country so bleak and cold as Scotland is. Yet the corpse remained untouched. The eyes, the juiciest morsel of all to any scavenging bird, were not pecked at and eaten by the crows. They remained intact under their smooth lids in her pretty head. A fortnight after she was strung up, the witch looked as fresh as she had the day we hanged her. Thus the effect of leaving her on public display became the very opposite of that intended. Unsullied by mortification, she defied God's justice and mocked the honest retribution of the Commonwealth. In the small hours on a moonless night, I had her cut down. We bore her corpse away and I examined it. She was cold. But her flesh was entirely uncorrupted, as if she could snap her eyes open at any moment and leer at me in full defiance of God and all He represents.

My loyal and erstwhile lieutenant Carrick is by birth a man of *the fens. Before cutting down the corpse of Ruth Campbell I had received a curious note inspired by him. He had returned home and told his story. It had eventually reached the ears of the witch finder General Bullock, sent to the low and desolate Fenland of Anglia on a mission not dissimilar from my own. Bullock in his letter to me did confide of an encounter with a beast horribly familiar to me in his description of it. I confess far more learned in the lore of witchcraft than I, he informed me there was one necessary ritual in performing the execution of their sorceress acolytes. This was neither hanging nor even burning. The general was most zealous in his insistence of the need to see this effected. It was the only guarantee of a safe and satisfactory outcome, he said.*

Ruth Campbell was duly buried with this service done her body and, in consequence, her soul. I believe her mortal remains at least now lie in the ground in peace.

Josiah Jerusalem Smith,

Written in truth and most humbly in the service of Our Lord Protector and in the mercy of Almighty God, 29 November 1656.

By the time Hunter had finished reading this account, Elizabeth had set off back to the Black Boar for her appointment with Sergeant Kilbride. Adam was just stirring on the sofa. Hunter got up and put the pages in his desk drawer and went into the kitchen to make tea for himself and his son. He thought in reading the account he had learned something of what Miss Hall had sent him to the keep in the Austrian Tyrol to discover. Then the kettle boiled and switched itself off. His mind returned for a moment to Magdalena, and he had the rest of it in a sudden revelation. He was sure of these conclusions. He was less certain of how they could help him. But it was a start, he thought, stirring milk into Adam's tea.

'Dad?'

In that single syllable, uttered from the sitting room, the fear was palpable. He would have to find a way. He would have to. Elizabeth was right. Adam could not endure much more of this without it inflicting permanent harm.

What had once been the stable at the Black Boar was now a dining room. The Boar had gastropub pretensions. The parlour in which Ruth Campbell had been tried, in which her sacrilegious act of levitation had been performed, was now the lounge bar. The fire still burned the same pine logs from the same forest in the same generous grate. Sergeant Kilbride was seated at a table close to its warmth when Elizabeth walked into the pub. The lunchtime trade had thinned. McCloud stood behind the bar polishing glasses, his bald pate gleaming under the optic lights, his small brown eyes missing nothing.

Meeting Tony Kilbride like this would do nothing for her reputation, Elizabeth thought. He was tall and blond and good-looking and, in common with very few Scottish police officers, spent a lot of off-duty time in the gym. And it showed. He stood and greeted her with a kiss. There had never been anything between them other than professional respect and a strong personal rapport. But McCloud did not know that. Oh, well. She took off her gloves and unbuttoned her coat. She had been here only a couple of hours ago with the Hunters. She had returned just now at the wheel of Mark Hunter's Land Rover. Should McCloud venture into his pub car park, he would be apoplectic with the potential for gossip she was providing him with. And all of it was coming over the course of a single day.

Tony Kilbride was nursing a Diet Coke in a half-pint glass. He did not look like he was staying long. Elizabeth said, 'Are we going somewhere?'

'That depends on how you react to what I've got to say.'

She sat down. He did too. She owed him a drink at the very least for the favour of the new locks on her cottage door. But she needed to hear what it was he had to say before going to the bar. 'You got your DNA match?'

He nodded. 'Aye, we did. Does the name Cawdor mean anything to you?'

'One of my ancestors had some dealings with a man named Cawdor. It ended badly for him. Actually, it ended badly for both of them. But it was three hundred and fifty years ago. Nobody revives a feud after that length of time. Do they?'

'I don't know,' Kilbride said. 'I do know we got a DNA match from the material at your cottage with a maths teacher called Andrew Cawdor. And I do know he teaches at the school attended by the Hunter boy.'

Elizabeth stood. 'Let's go,' she said.

'You want to confront him now?'

'No time like the present,' she said. 'Leave it another night and I might find myself homeless. They might escalate things and burn my cottage to the ground.'

They travelled in the Land Rover to the school. It was much better on the snow and ice of the roads than Kilbride's patrol car. It was less ostentatious and with the four-wheel drive engaged, it was quicker. They would arrive by about 4.30 p.m. There was every chance that the man they were looking for would be there. The teachers did not finish their working day for another hour after that. The children got out at 4 p.m. The timing was ideal. Kilbride said he did not wish yet to caution Cawdor formerly. He just wanted to talk to him. They had no clue as to the identity of the man's accomplice. He might be panicked into providing that, but would likely say nothing if formerly charged with a serious offence. But the evidence was irrefutable. They had one of the culprits for sure. It would come to court. The police would prosecute, even if Elizabeth chose not to press charges.

'From where did you extract the DNA?'

'Do you really want to know?'

'Yes.'

'You have some snapshots tacked to a pinboard in your kitchen. One of you and your mother had been spat upon. It was a spontaneous gesture of contempt or loathing and it will convict him. His emotions got the better of him. The obvious question is why does he feel so hostile towards you?'

'I don't know,' Elizabeth said. 'But something else bothers me. Schools do criminal record checks on their staff. They're generally very scrupulous about it. But you had Andrew Cawdor's DNA on your database. So he must be a known offender.'

'He was arrested once for being drunk but never charged. He was with that silly arse troublemaker Tom Lincoln; they're drinking buddies. They both did swabs voluntarily in the police cell we locked them in to sober up. We were after a sex offender at the time, knew it was someone local, they fitted the age profile and we wanted to eliminate anyone we could from suspicion to identify the right guy quickly.'

'Did you catch him?'

'Yes.'

'But you kept the sample Cawdor provided on your database?'

'Aye, we did.' He turned to her. 'And we could have an impromptu debate about civil liberties. But aren't you glad we did?'

They were at the school. The headmistress, Mrs Blyth, was a patient of Elizabeth's. So were two or three other members of staff there. But that number did not include Andrew Cawdor. They went first to Mrs Blyth's office to ask for permission to speak to him. She didn't ask them why it was they wanted to do so. Discretion was one of her professional requirements. If the matter was serious, the details would be disclosed over time. She took them to a classroom where he was supervising a detention. He grew pale when he saw Elizabeth. But he agreed to talk to them privately. Mrs Blyth took the key to the library from a ring on the belt of her skirt and said it was an ideal location for a confidential chat. Elizabeth liked Mrs Blyth. But taking the library key from its heavy ring, she reminded her of a gaoler.

Cawdor clutched his briefcase to his chest, wrapped in his arms. He was dark-haired, pallid and thin, and Elizabeth judged him to be in his mid-forties. There was a tiny spot of blood on the collar of his shirt from a morning shaving nick. He was a hopeless bachelor type. He wore designer glasses, the heavily framed sort shaped as narrow rectangles. The effect was somewhat spoiled by the thickness of the lenses he required. The cloth of his charcoal grey suit was too light for the weather. His leather-soled shoes slipped on the packed snow of the path to the library and she found herself fighting not to feel sorry for him. She reminded herself that the worst violation had been cleaned up by Tony Kilbride and his team. She had not been obliged to face it. And, symbolically at least, this man had spat in her face.

Elizabeth had not been in the library at the school before and thought it beautiful. The circumstances of her visit to it were not ideal. But she thought she might ask Mrs Blyth if she could come back another time. The stained glass in the windows alone was worthy of proper study. In summer light, this little hexagon of carved masonry and polished wood with its shelves of old books would be an enchanting place.

They sat at the librarian's desk, which was at the centre of the single room the building housed. Elizabeth looked at Cawdor, looking back at her through his trendy spectacles. There was nothing opaque about the look. There was fear there, she thought, or wariness. But mostly there was hatred.

It turned his thin mouth into a grimace. He could not have concealed so strongly felt an emotion. But he didn't attempt to. He must have worked out what had led them to him and realised the futility of denying it.

'Someone has orchestrated a campaign of terror against Dr Bancroft,' Kilbride said. 'I want to ask you if you can tell us anything about it or about the motives for it.'

Cawdor picked his briefcase up from the floor where he had placed it next to him and rested it on his knees. He undid its brass catch with a click, opened it and took out a transparent plastic folder containing photocopied classroom worksheets. He spread the worksheets on the desk and fanned them out. 'Adam Hunter is studying "A" level maths,' he said.

'The boy is ten years old,' Kilbride said.

'This is not a hothouse school. And his father would not sanction the sitting of any formal examinations until Adam reaches the appropriate age. But this is the level of work we have to set him to retain his interest and enthusiasm. That's across the board, by the way. Not just in the one subject.'

'I'm a patient man,' Kilbride said. 'But this seems somewhat tangential to the point.'

And that was an excellent pun, Elizabeth thought. Tangents were a feature of geometry. The calculation on the worksheets described geometric formulas, co-ordinate geometry and curve-sketching.

Cawdor addressed his words to her. 'You're called Bancroft. But it is Campbell blood that runs through your veins. In this locality the Campbell name is remembered for its proven association with macabre and sinister practices,' he said. 'Colonel Hunter was not aware of your ancestry when he had Adam put on your patient list. But I was.' He reached into his briefcase again. This time he took out a single sheet. On it had been drawn a shape in three dimensions. It had been described in what Elizabeth judged was probably HB2 pencil lead. And when she looked at it, it would not stay still on the page and provoked a feeling of dizziness so similar to vertigo that she was forced to look away.

'What is that?' Kilbride said. He had gone pale. One of his blue eyes had become bloodshot. There was sweat beading at his hairline.

'Something Adam concocted, shortly after he became Dr Bancroft's patient,' Cawdor said. With his eyes on Kilbride, he turned the sheet over on the desk. 'Motifs such as that have been symbols of black magic going back centuries. They subvert reason. They undermine rationality. That is their evil function. One of my own ancestors made a study of witch-craft, before an ancestor of the doctor here destroyed his life.'

'Hang on,' Kilbride said. 'You think Dr Bancroft is somehow corrupting Adam Hunter? You think she is an evil influence on a little boy in her professional care?' His voice was incredulous.

'He isn't just a little boy,' Cawdor said. 'He is a phenom-enon. And he is profoundly good. I'm talking about his ethical sensibilities, Sergeant. There is greatness in Adam Hunter. He will grow up to be a significant force for good in the world. That is his destiny. That is what I am trying to protect.' He pointed a shaking finger at Elizabeth. 'That is what she is trying to destroy.'

'You are deranged,' Kilbride said. He massaged his right temple as he spoke and winced. He was a dogged copper and he had looked at Adam's drawing for far too long.

'Ask her mother about what she did to poor Max Hector all those years ago in the barn on the Hector farm,' Cawdor said. 'Better still, ask Tom Lincoln. Tom was there and witnessed the whole bloody, murderous event. He still has nightmares about it.'

They left the library a few minutes later. Darkness had descended. Andrew Cawdor walked rapidly away along the snowbound path, insufficiently clothed for the severity of the weather, slipping and sliding now and then, his working life left behind him in ruins, his briefcase clutched tightly under his arm. Kilbride turned and leaned heavily against one of the library's stone window surrounds and puked on to a border beneath it of frozen thorns. He was sick a second time. The sourness of the hot vomit stung Elizabeth's nostrils. He gasped and apologised. She would have to drive them back to the pub. The policeman was in no fit state to do it. She was glad they were in the Land Rover and not the patrol car. If McCloud saw them return to his car park with her at the wheel of a police vehicle, he would probably explode. There was aspirin and paracetamol in her handbag. There was a water cooler outside the headmistress's office. They walked slowly back towards the main building.

'He's put Tom Lincoln in the frame with him,' Kilbride said.

'I'd just as soon forget the whole business,' Elizabeth said.

'You can, now. You won't be required as a witness. And your home is safe.'

'Yes. My home is safe. And it's you I have to thank, Tony.' She stopped and hugged him. His breath smelled sourly of sick, but she had a strong stomach. He deserved a hug and, she thought, at that moment he needed one.

They walked in silence for a while. The library was a fair distance from the main part of the school and the children had turned patches of the path into skid runs. 'He believes every word of what he said, you know. He's very seriously deluded. Though I must say that picture he showed us was not something I would want on my wall.'

Elizabeth nodded. She looked ahead of her at the lights in the school building. She would not share this with Tony

Kilbride because there would be no point. But some of what Cawdor had said had helped her make sense of Miss Hall's enigmatic claim during their dinner that Hunter had not been in Magdalena just by chance.

Chapter Ten

By the time Elizabeth dropped Kilbride at the pub he was fine to drive. The aspirin had done its job. They did not stay for the drink she owed him for the work done to her front door by the police locksmith. Neither of them felt a celebration was in order as the case of her harassment progressed towards its now inevitable resolution in the criminal court. Neither of them was inclined to drink and drive. And as Kilbride confessed to her, the very thought of a drink of any sort other than water was enough to make him heave again, dryly this time. There was nothing left in his stomach.

Elizabeth felt sad driving back to the Hunter house. She would have to leave it, now. His father was back and Adam no longer required her full-time care. Mark had enlisted her potential help in some future confrontation with Mrs Mallory. But though she had her own suspicions, they had no real idea where Mrs Mallory was. She had no justification for staying at the house. Her cottage had just been made a safe refuge once more for her. She would miss putting Adam to bed. She would miss their kitchen banter and their popcorn ritual. It had only been a few days and nights and some of it had been extremely disturbing. But most of it had been wonderful. Her feelings of impending loss on the drive back made her realise just how lonely and starved of emotion she had allowed her life to become. It was shocking. Surely she deserved better? But you got out only what you put in, she knew. She shifted into a lower gear as the incline towards the house began and she felt the shudder of the snow under her in the torque-heavy grip of the wheels. Bloody hell, she thought, I'm thinking exactly like Jeremy Clarkson would. She laughed out loud, but there were tears in her eyes. When all this was over, she was going to live differently, she decided.

Adam was watching sodding Clarkson when she let herself back into the house. She asked where his father was and he gestured vaguely in the direction of upstairs. Perhaps Mark was having that siesta he had coveted earlier. It was after six now and late for a siesta, but in the army you napped whenever you could and probably the habit had become ingrained in him. She would shower before she packed. Her encounter with Andrew Cawdor had left her feeling soiled. She walked into the bathroom and Hunter turned from the sink to face her. She realised that of course he never locked the door, because why would he? He occupied the bathroom with only his family there to surprise him; he was not used to the protocol of house guests.

'I'm so sorry,' she said. His bare torso had scars and weals across the plates and ridges of sculpted muscle. She could not help looking.

'Not so much a body as a campaign map,' he said. He smiled.

She nodded. It was a good line. She wondered whether he had used it before. But she decided not. He had been anything but a philanderer in his life. She thought his body, as bodies went, went very well indeed.

She had caught him shaving. It was something he could not have done with his injuries and this was the first chance she supposed he had really had since her mother had healed him. His jaw was partially covered in shaving foam. Then his expression changed and she knew he had realised why she was there.

'Oh, God. Please don't leave us, Elizabeth,' he said. 'Please stay?'

He dropped his razor into the water in the sink with a plop and wiped the foam from his jaw with a towel and walked across the bathroom to her and she took his face in her hands and kissed him hard on the mouth and then held him.

That night Adam dreamed of a visit to the pub. He had very much enjoyed his lunch with Elizabeth and his dad. It had made him feel sophisticated and adult and the real joy was that he was supposed to be at school. It was a school day. And there he was, in the dining room of the pub with his dad and cool Elizabeth who was lovely on top of being so utterly cool. It was all perfect really, except for his failure to persuade his dad that two Diet Cokes in one day did not exactly make him the Anti-Christ of proper nutrition. Still, he had been allowed to drink lemonade. And Nosy McCloud (as Elizabeth called him) had put both ice and a slice of lemon in his glass of lemonade. A straw was the ultimate insult. Ice was pretty much to be expected. But, generally speaking, you had to be at least a teenager to qualify for a slice of lemon in your drink.

The pub in his dream was not the Black Boar. It was the Red Bull. And it was not constructed from stone and ancient beams of oak. It was pressed from metal in shades of silver and blue that had an odd, somehow queasy geometry about their shape. And the sign was red of course. The sign was a bright, bloody crimson swinging in the windy night under a pale curve of anaemic moon. Adam knew that he should not be there. He knew that it was way past his proper bedtime in the dream. He did not have any money and his mobile phone, the one his dad insisted he carry, had long run out of credit. But he pushed open the door anyway. He felt reckless in the dream, like one of those characters in a cowboy film or a country and western song on the radio who keeps saying they have nothing left to lose.

Nosy McCloud was not polishing glasses behind the bar. But why would he be? This was the Red Bull. Mrs Mallory ran the Red Bull and she was there, with her glossy black hair playing over the shoulders of her white shirt and a smile on her mouth the same crimson as the sign in the moonlight outside.

'What will be your pleasure, Master Hunter?' she asked.

But Adam was distracted. There were TV monitors suspended all over the pub, he saw. They would not have had that in the Black Boar. The Black Boar was all quaintness and tradition. They did not want MTV in there, spoiling the authentic Highland atmosphere with videos by Kylie and Girls Aloud. Except that these videos were all in black and white. And they had a grainy look. And they were of marching uniformed men in harsh spotlights, with torches that flamed and flickered held on high. And there were roared tributes and songs and staunch salutes. These had become familiar scenes to him in other dreams. He knew their smell, the hot stink of cigar breath and sweat-stained armpits on cruel summer nights.

Adam swallowed. He was afraid. Despite the knowledge that this was a dream he was having, he had remembered everything about who Mrs Mallory was and the things he had heard her say and seen her do. He did not like her just standing there and staring at him, the way someone hungry might look at something appetising on their plate. It seemed best just now to fill the conversational silence somehow, to distract and maybe flatter her. 'You've witnessed a lot of history,' he said.

She laughed. It was not a pleasant sound. It was the scrape of talons dragging at reluctant cloth. 'History is not a spectator sport, Adam,' she said. 'It is not there to be watched like a football game. It is there to be influenced and affected. Sometimes, it is there to be determined.' She laughed again.

He did not know what she meant. He would in time, he knew. It was not the vocabulary. He seldom came across an English word he did not intuitively understand the meaning of. It was the adult way of using language as a code. It took him a little time, sometimes, to decipher it. But he always did in the end.

He did not feel like bothering with a drink. Even if she offered him the speciality of the house, he did not want to stay to drink it. He wanted to go home. It was the yearning impulse he felt always in his recent dreams. He wanted to wake up. He wanted his mother. He wanted the strength and comfort of his father's embrace.

The following morning, Adam again slept late. Elizabeth and Hunter discussed over breakfast what they thought they ought to do next. Outside the kitchen window, the snow fell and muffled the features of the landscape in subtly varied shades of white under a matt grey sky. It was very still and silent out there through the falling petals of snow. In the warmth and light of the kitchen, it was easy to believe that the world was empty and they were the only people left, just the two of them, and the boy sleeping peacefully upstairs. It was a seductive temptation, but of course it was not true.

'She could be anywhere,' Hunter said. 'She could be in Cape Town or Havana or Boston or Madrid.'

'So your journey to that place in the Tyrol was a waste of time.'

'As a means of locating her, yes it was. But I think I found out what Miss Hall intended me to. I told you the last words Rodriguez said. Do you remember them?'

Elizabeth frowned, trying to remember. 'Something about being safe when the current was strong.'

'I thought it was a metaphysical remark, or some Conradian metaphor to do with a river or something. Major

Rodriguez had this poetic side to his character. But I now think he was speaking literally. Miss Hall had ambushed Mrs Mallory. As a magician, she was nothing like a match for her. But she had stacked the odds. Electricity robs Mrs Mallory of her power. I'm sure of it. I think there was a charge running through the chair she sat in and Rodriguez only saw the distress or pain she was suffering and switched it off.'

'Then why did she do what she did to him?'

'He had a gun trained on her. And she took exception to the rosary he had draped across its barrel.'

Elizabeth pondered on what she had just been told. 'That's why she has the electric chair. I think I can work out for myself why she has the guillotine.'

'That was the information provided in Bullock's letter from the fens to Jerusalem Smith. To kill them you need to cut off their heads.'

Elizabeth frowned. 'My own mother is a bone magician and she will die in her bed. Or, God forbid, in a row of her runner beans. I strongly suspect that Lillian could have been one too. And forgive me for reminding you, but she died in a car crash.'

'Your mother has only ever used her powers for good,' Hunter said. 'Lillian lived her life oblivious of hers. The thing we call Mrs Mallory has confounded nature and consorted with God knows what dismal creatures. She is greedy and cruel and self-serving and has used her gift to make herself into something other than merely human.'

'Why would she keep the things that can make her weak and kill her so close to home?'

'In tribute to them, perhaps,' Hunter said. 'Or maybe she had those instruments put there in defiance of them. The place I went to is a sort of repository of her life. She has stayed there. But I sensed only ever briefly. The bed was barely slept in. She doesn't live there. There will be nothing so hazardous to her in the Georgian house my son dreams about.'

'There are no Georgian houses in Havana or Cape Town. And in Aberdeen and Edinburgh our Georgian houses are granite and we do not paint them cream,' Elizabeth said.

Hunter shrugged. 'She's in Boston, then, like I said a moment ago. Or she's in Philadelphia.'

'She's much closer to home, Mark. Miss Hall gave you the biggest clue of all when she told you Mrs Mallory likes to party. What is the party capital of the world?'

Hunter sipped coffee and grimaced. 'London,' he said.

'London is where we will find her.'

He did not comment on this last remark. But he thought it more likely than not. And the plural was not lost on him.

When Adam got up and had eaten his breakfast, his father took him out to walk in the snow. The boy had dreamed again and wanted to unburden himself. Before they left, after lacing on his boots, Hunter took the sled from where it hung on a hook in its cupboard near the door. He never forgot that Adam was a boy and that boys like to play, Elizabeth thought. He was a good father and he loved his son. She realised then how much he must miss the daughter he had lost and never talked about. Not for the first time, she was aware that Adam was all that Mark Hunter had. If Adam died, she knew then with certainty that his father would not survive the loss. They would both perish.

It was Friday morning. She called the locum to make sure that everything was alright at the surgery and with her patients. The snow would be keeping most of them out of harm's way but someone might have had a fall and the winter killer, flu, was always a possibility in so cold an autumn as this was proving to be. He responded to the call cheerfully. There were no tragedies or catastrophes she need concern herself about. Curious after her initial shock, she then went to the shelf in his study where Hunter kept Lillian's collection of children's books. She wanted to take a closer look at Walter the Wolf. She had been dismayed and horrified by Judge Smith's account of the beast with which her ancestor had consorted. And her mother had said she possessed occult powers of her own. And of course, there was her appearance. But she had never knowingly entertained a lupine thought in her life. She didn't think she had even seen a real-life specimen at the zoo.

Lillian could not blame an illustrator for the appearance of her fictional creature. She had done the illustrations in this series herself. Walter was ugly and scary. His insecurity made him a liability in social situations. His anxiety to pass as human was a theme running through the stories. It was intended to be humorous. But Elizabeth did not think it was funny at all. Children invested the characters they read about with their own generous instincts. Elizabeth thought Barney the dinosaur a total wuss but children adored him. The Thomas the Tank Engine stories were enduringly popular despite the catty, spiteful and peevish natures of most of the trains involved in them. Children were forgiving of the fiction they read.

With Walter, there was a lot to forgive. His teeth were a jumble of fangs that meant that he dribbled when he tried to drink from a cup and drooled, struggling to grip a knife and fork between clumsy paws when he ate. Because his coat of coarse hair was more than adequate to keep him warm, he sweated excessively when he assumed the conceit of human clothing. Despite his desire to pass, Walter was not keen on personal hygiene and this was the bit that the children probably loved, Elizabeth thought. He would go to comic lengths to avoid a bath or shower and used cologne to cover the resulting stink. He lived grandly on an inherited hoard of gold coins he would retrieve from a chest buried in his back garden when he needed money to spend. He resided in a grand Georgian house in Cleaver Square in Kennington on the south side of the Thames in London. There was a pub in the north-west corner of the square but Walter was banned from that. Lillian did not bother to say for what. It was probably just expedient to ban her character from the pub, Elizabeth thought. Pubs were an environment young children knew little and cared less about. Their interiors were a slog to draw, with all that detail.

Walter's big secret was cannibalism. He was partial to eating other wolves. It was inferred that he had eaten his parents prior to leaving home. He maintained the pretence that his favourite meal was mozzarella pizza. But what he really liked was wolf. Dog would do at a stretch and, from time to time, he made do with strays. These were never drawn by Lillian. Elizabeth thought her too shrewd to run the risk that the victims might look cute, thus upsetting her young readers and alienating them from horrible, creepy Walter.

His saviour was Miss Kutznetsov, his vampy Russian housekeeper. Lillian had written these stories a full decade before the Eastern Europeans began to come in numbers to Britain to work and live. So Miss Kutznetsov's nationality was a novelty rather than a cliché. She kept Walter calm and civilised when his lupine instincts threatened to overwhelm him (and her). She did it by playing the piano for him. More than any other music, Walter's anxieties were eased by listening to her play Mahler in the drawing room of his grand and spacious home.

Elizabeth replaced the books. She was pretty sure that Cleaver Square was a real place. She had read an article once she vaguely remembered about someone famous who lived there. The similarities between Lillian's books and Adam's dreams were too striking for them to be coincidental. Adam must surely have read the books. Either he had stored these stories somewhere in his subconscious mind and they were inspiring and influencing the dreams he had. Or they were Lillian's clue from the grave as to where they would find the sorceress tormenting her son. Mallory as a name was a long way from Kuznetsov. But Napoleon's invasion of Russia was a long way from the present day. Elizabeth would have bet there and then that Mallory had been Kuznetsov once.

She switched on Hunter's computer and did a Google search. Cleaver Square's famous resident was the actress Greta Scacchi, who had lived there for a time in the 1980s. The pub on its north-west corner was called the Prince of Wales. The Richardson gang had used it as their local when they were the south of the river rivals to the Kray brothers' gang on its northern side in London in the 1960s. Despite this dubious distinction, the Prince of Wales looked very picturesque in the picture she found. The square itself neighboured a couple of Kennington's more notorious sink estates. But it was early Victorian and quite grand and architecturally intact. There was no grass on the tree-lined square itself. Perhaps unusually for London, it was surfaced with gravel.

Hunter and Adam returned. Hunter made them all lunch. The substance of Adam's latest dream did not seem to have troubled him as much as some of the others had; he did not look so pale and tired at having endured it. The tobogganing would have put some of the colour back in his cheeks. But he had not dreamed, Elizabeth did not think, of the house in Cleaver Square. She did not want to ask him and thereby force him to relive the dream for the second time in a day. She would wait to ask his father about its detail later, when Adam had gone to bed. Then too, she would tell Mark Hunter what she thought she had learned from Lillian's books. She felt very comfortable in the Hunter house.

She had thought she might feel embarrassed in the morning after the passion of the previous night. But passion was understandable when two people were attracted to one another. It was human nature. Some of it had been sexual and some of it seeking comfort, and wasn't that always the way? She did not feel embarrassed about it at all. She was glad it had happened.

It was about four o'clock in the afternoon and a powdery dusk was putting its blush on the snow outside. Adam was hunched over the chessboard with his father. Elizabeth was making coffee, having mastered the complex machine men of a certain type always seemed to think essential if you wanted to brew it properly. She was thinking about Cleaver Square. She thought the name itself quite sinister. It was the Cleaver part of course. A cleaver was what a butcher used to chop his meat. And a memory hit her with such force and vividness that she gasped aloud and dropped the glass coffee jug to explode on the stone floor. 'Oh, God,' she said. 'Oh, God.' She brought her hand up to her mouth to stifle the sounds of her own mounting panic and horror. Hunter rushed into the kitchen and skidded on shards of shattered glass. Her hand was trembling, the fingers shaking where she held them over her face. She had to get a hold of herself. She did not want her obvious distress to frighten the child. She closed her eyes and opened them again and focused on the darkening snowfield through the window. Hunter put his hands on her shoulders from behind her and she grasped for them.

'I've remembered something, from Grozny,' she said.

Adam walked into the kitchen, a bewildered look on his face at the crunching sound his shoes were making under him.

'I'll tell you later,' Elizabeth whispered.

She cleaned up the mess with Hunter's help and made more coffee. Gradually, her composure returned to her. Later they went to the Black Boar for dinner. It was Elizabeth's suggestion, an attempt to break the monotony of the white world that had surrounded Adam. He was not yet fit for school in her estimation, but he needed social stimulation and the large dining area of the child-friendly pub early on a Friday evening was a lot better than nothing. She didn't want him to feel trapped by his nightmares. She didn't want him to think he was somehow under siege, she thought, reminded with a shiver of dread of the memory dredged up from Grozny again.

Hunter had looked uncomfortably at his son when she had suggested dinner at the pub. She saw the tightness of anxiety in his expression. But Adam was enthusiastic enough. He rode shotgun in the Land Rover on the way there by special request. His father barrelled and churned through the snow at the wheel and Elizabeth saw the chance to break the somewhat sombre mood that seemed to have settled on the adults, if not the boy.

'Do you think your dad a better driver than Jeremy Clarkson, Adam?'

'Of course I am,' Hunter said, getting it straight away. 'He's not a driver at all. He's light entertainment. Apparently, he's only got a provisional licence.'

'He's a brilliant driver,' Adam said, outraged.

'And your dad?'

'Good,' Adam said. 'But to be perfectly honest with you, he is a bit of a show-off.'

The atmosphere had lightened immediately and it stayed that way unforced throughout their meal. Adam was exhausted, though. Elizabeth assumed that had probably been Hunter's intention in taking him out for their long adventure earlier in the day in the snow. He fell asleep across the back seat on the drive home. Hunter looked at him in the cabin mirror and turned the heater down as soon as he went off. The heat was soporific. There was a definite plan here, Elizabeth thought. It was why Mark had insisted Adam have a pee, whether he needed one or not, before they set off back to the house.

'You're good at fatherhood.'

'Thanks.' He glanced at her. 'Do you mean that?'

'Yes. Why?'

'Because I don't think you could pay me any greater compliment.'

She thought about his medals. She thought about the line from Eliot he had quoted to her back when they had been strangers. She did not speak again until they had returned to the house and he had carried Adam upstairs to bed and they were sitting in opposing armchairs with the large whisky he had poured for each of them.

'Why doesn't Mrs Mallory just kill you, if she thinks you are a threat to her?'

'You have to remember what she said about her curse. When I begged her to lift it at Magdalena? She said her curse makes the world a more interesting place.' He sipped whisky. 'She's enjoying herself, toying with us. She doesn't think me a threat at all.'

'She tried to kill you in Austria.'

Hunter shook his head. 'A member of her retinue tried to kill an intruder using the dogs that guard the place. It wasn't personal. If it had been, she'd have succeeded.'

'I think I know where to find her.'

'You told me, Elizabeth. You think she's in London.'

'I think I know specifically. The clue is in Lillian's books.'

Hunter seemed to ponder this. He reached forward to the grate and poked at the fire until the logs flared and crackled, burning with fresh vigour. 'Tell me about what you remembered today from Grozny,' he said.

*   *   *

The Russians had got her out. A platoon of terrified conscripts commanded by a grizzled veteran of the First Afghan War had braved the bombardment to reach her in the cellar where the shocked remnants of her Red Cross unit had taken refuge. The others had opted to stay. Two were Russian nationals and the third an Italian burns specialist in his early thirties. Staying seemed the safer option than going. But Major Oblensky's platoon did not give her the choice. Her fiancé's death was terrible publicity. She did not think they had any particular regard for her life. But they did not want her to lose it now, in this savage battle on Russian soil with the world watching so intently.

The only aircraft flying in Chechnya were fighters and fighter bombers and helicopter gunships. Their first object-ive seemed to be to get her away from the danger posed by snipers, by stray shells and rocket salvos and friendly fire and minefields. They took her in a flatbed truck to the dense forest region in the low hills to the south-east of the besieged city. She was too stunned by the fact and manner of Peter's death to have much curiosity about what they intended to do with her eventually. Grief-stricken as she was, it was a relief to get away from the pulverising violence of the bombardment. In the forest the sound of whimpering civil-ians trapped in their subterranean shelters was replaced by birdsong and only the wind moaned, through the snow-laden branches of the fir trees.

It was December and bitterly cold. They sheltered in a cabin made from logs with an iron stove at the centre of its single room. The wooden walls were soot-blackened and the window smeared with filth, and in the fuggy warmth of this retreat the men of the platoon would smoke and drink inces-santly in the evenings, playing cards or swaying cross-legged on the floor as they sang their lachrymose marching songs by the light of hurricane lamps. And Elizabeth would drink with them. They had risked their lives for her, however unwillingly. She needed the company and she craved the anaesthetic of potent drink.

Modesty obliged that she dig a latrine for herself a fair distance from the cabin. She tried to use it only during the day. There were the sounds of predatory beasts in the forest at night and she naturally feared them. Wolves she feared the most, because their numbers had grown so exponentially since the end of the culls that had controlled them in the old Soviet days. It was a hungry winter. The bears were safely asleep in hibernation. But the wolves of the forests were emboldened. She had gone to use her latrine early one morning when the event her memory had so successfully and for so long repressed took place.

She was careful about her route. The forest was not only thick but featureless in the sense that every aspect of it looked the same. There were no fallen trees, or streams to act as landmarks or guide her. There was snow on the ground and there were the trunks of trees. Around two of these on the way to her latrine she had tied narrow lengths of surgical tape. Their pale pink was vivid in a hoop against the dark tree bark and signalled her path. Except on this particular day, the second loop of tape was missing. It was alright, because it had not snowed in the night and she was able to follow the impressions left on the ground the previous day by her own feet.

She had just finished when she sensed that she was not alone. She felt cold, even colder, as though she crouched in the cast of a malevolent shadow. She stood erect and turned and saw it. It stood hugely on a small rise a few feet behind her. It wore a long leather greatcoat above scuffed and enormous Cossack boots. A piece of surgical tape ran taut in the grip of its black gauntlets. Under its peaked cap, it wore the snout and jaw of a wolf and it leered at her and the bright yellow pupils of its eyes gleamed as if with glee. And it let out a low grunt of feral appreciation, cloudy and stinking, expelled into the frozen air. And then it grinned at her.

Elizabeth fled this impossible vision. They found her two hours later in the snow hole she had scraped from the frozen ground in her terror. Panicked, she had become lost. She was no longer conscious when they recovered her. Later, before she expunged this experience entirely from her mind, she was grateful it was Russian soldiers she had been among. They knew better than any army in the world about the treatment of hypothermia.

Oblensky had her stripped and her skin rubbed with candle tallow and then zipped into his own goose feather sleeping bag. The trick was not to warm the body too fast, not to let the brain know quite how profoundly cold the body had become. If that happened, the brain would simply switch the body off and the exposure victim would die. Avoiding that and encouraging recovery was an art and it was a science. They put her on a cot. Oblensky himself dripped vodka into her mouth from a forefinger dipped in the glass. The cot was drawn incrementally closer to the heat of the stove in their cabin. Occasionally they turned her. The heat of the stove was kept constant and they were patient as they coaxed her back to life. Oblensky sent out a combat patrol to discover what had frightened the woman. It returned empty handed. After twenty hours she regained consciousness. The men were asleep now but for their vigilant commander, a glass in his hand and a cigarette burning in the ashtray beside him. Her eyes opened and he leaned forward.

'Wölfe?'

German. She had no Russian. German was the language in which she conducted what brief communication she enjoyed with the major. 'Ja,' she said. 'Wölfe.'

He nodded. They never discussed the matter again. Two

days later she was airlifted out. Her mind persuaded her, she assumed aboard the flight, that she would have a better chance of staying sane in her grief-stricken condition if she forgot the matter of the beast in the forest entirely.

'Why did Cleaver Square bring it back?' Hunter asked.

'There was a weapon,' she said. 'It was embedded in the woody flesh of the tree next to which it stood. It had been recently used, was bloody. Blood had frozen in dripping icicles from the spine of the blade. It looked like a cleaver. Though the butcher wielding this tool would have needed to be a giant to have done so, such were its monstrous dimensions.'

'How can a wolf hold a cleaver when it doesn't have a thumb?'

'Wolves don't stand upright either. You remember Judge Smith's description?'

'Neither wolf nor man but both in some horrid collusion of breed,' Hunter quoted.

'It wore leather gauntlets. The fingers were very long. It possessed hands, alright.'

'How tall was the creature?'

Elizabeth shivered. 'It was perhaps seven feet. Perspective is difficult when you are as terrified as I was. But it was bigger than a man. Its mannishness was a masquerade, Mark. It was just its conceit. It was a monster. And it was feasting its eyes on me.' Elizabeth put down her whisky glass emphatically on the table between them. 'You know what we should do? We should see if we can find her on the internet. Party animals are not shy. And if she does not fear you—'

'She doesn't.'

'She won't be hiding, will she?'

They did a Google search using the words Mallory, Cleaver, Square, Brooke, Berlin, Guerlain, Mahler and Magdalena.

The first five pages to come up were a disparate waste of time. But then on page six there was a taster for a profile piece in an obscure style magazine of the sort generally more concerned with paper quality and page layout than journalistic accuracy. Hunter paid the online subscription with his credit card in order to access the entire piece. The words unfurled on the screen before them. He printed two copies out and they sat and read it in their opposing chairs.

Style is not so much an aspiration to Lavinia Mallory as a prerequisite of existence. She is graceful by instinct, beautiful by genetic blessing and witty by gift of intellect. Her sense of humour inclines towards the sardonic and, meeting her, she seems far too frosty and detached for so purple an emotion as passion. But Lavinia is passionate; about poetry, history, symphonic music and even politics.

'Christ,' Hunter said aloud. 'It's her.'

Elizabeth did not reply. She thought the tone of the piece nauseating. But she was engrossed just the same.

The Mallory parties are affairs sufficiently exclusive for common gossip about them to be almost non-existent. Her guest lists include the glamorous, the privileged, the famous and, it must be confessed, the famously louche. Nothing of substance about what goes on at them emerges from the lips of those lucky enough to be granted one of her coveted invitations. That's the deal when you reach those heights of social exclusivity and everyone who is anyone is aware of the fact. So there are no details in the public domain about what makes these long and extravagant celebrations so compulsively enjoyable. But everyone I spoke to about them agreed that Lavinia has achieved a social feat known to be scientifically impossible. She is both the hottest and the coolest hostess in town.

Her soirées, by contrast, are as sober as her parties are bacchanalian. Here, the great and the good gather to discuss the themes and topics that the rest of us will find ourselves talking about eighteen months or so down the line. Here, some of our most influential thinkers, social strategists, industrialists and policy decision makers discuss and debate the tone and tenor of our challenging and sometimes turbulent times.

Yet when I put it to Lavinia Mallory that she is one of the most influential women in London, she merely laughed her delicious, throaty laugh and dismissed the suggestion modestly. 'I am here to enjoy myself,' she said. 'But I have never understood the threat implicit in the old Chinese curse. Personally, I have always preferred to live in interesting times.' I asked why a woman of such obvious means had chosen to buy a house on the south side of the river. Her grey eyes seemed to grow slightly in her lovely head and I had the intuition for a moment that this would be a formidable woman to cross. Then she smiled her seductive smile at me and said, 'I've always seen myself as a Left Bank sort of person. There is a lot of the bohemian in me.'

And a fair bit of the nomad too. She has graced cities from New York to Barcelona with her intoxicating glamour. She was born in Salzburg thirty-seven years ago and grew up in Argentina. Her education was finished, in the traditional sense, in Switzerland. She speaks five languages fluently and still keeps an apartment in Berlin. She has made her mark since her arrival in London eighteen months ago. In that time she has become the Cleaver Square siren, irresistible to the people who matter, as they beat a willing path to her imposing door.

The piece was bylined. Its writer was credited as Lucien Hope.

'Lucien Hopeless,' Hunter said, dropping the piece on to the floor in disgust. 'I wonder if he thought to verify a single fact.'

'I'll bet there are pictures with the original piece,' Elizabeth said. 'We've got all the words here, but not the piece as it would have appeared in the magazine. This is not the actual layout. You can tell from the vacuous tone the sort of magazine it is. Pictures are going to be far more important to its star-struck readership than the written drivel accompanying them.'

'This was published six weeks ago. But the magazine is quarterly and so it has a three-month shelf life. At least, in theory it does. It's too esoteric to be the sort of thing that sells out. I'll locate and buy a copy in Edinburgh,' Hunter said.

'You'll do what?'

'I'm going to take the train to London tomorrow and have a look for myself. It's just reconnaissance, Elizabeth. I'm not going to try to take her on just yet. I'll get the magazine and study the original piece on the way. We have to have a plan for dealing with Mrs Mallory. We'll only get one opportunity and the plan cannot fail.'

'I'll come with you,' she said. 'My mother is fine about taking Adam. Or she could come here and keep an eye on him.'

'No. It's too dangerous.'

'I thought you wanted my help.'

'To be perfectly honest, I don't think I am going to be able to do it without you,' he said. 'But we don't move against her until we have a plan.'

Elizabeth looked deep in thought.

'What is it?'

'Something Miss Hall said to you about your presence in Magdalena being nothing to do with chance. Something Andrew Cawdor said about the potential for the good of the world in Adam. What Mrs Mallory said to you about her curse and what Adam said about her wanting to put a tilt on the world.' She looked at him. 'Be very careful, Mark.'

'I will be.'

'My mother can only patch you up so often.'

'There won't be any dogs. She couldn't run the risk of them mauling her guests. And her guests would object to their stink.'

'There's the wolf thing.'

'Adam said it was inanimate, in his dream. What about the thing you saw in Grozny? What do you think it wanted?'

'At the time, I thought it wanted to hurt me. Now I think quite the opposite. And that's a much scarier proposition.'

Elizabeth got up and went over to the computer. She did a search for Lucien Hope. She found an obituary written for him. It was four weeks old. He had been a photographer, a fashion stylist and a writer. He had been a terrible journalist, but his intuition had been sound in fearing he had antagonised Mrs Mallory with his careless slight concerning her south London address. She would have been doubly irked, because he had repeated the insult in print. A further search revealed a short news story offering more specific and grisly detail. He certainly would have regretted his misjudgement, she thought, bleeding to death in the bathtub of his council flat after slitting his wrists. Perhaps he'd had a chip on his shoulder about his own postcode. His flat had been in Brixton. She switched off the computer. This was one sombre footnote she felt she could spare Mark Hunter. He had more than enough as it was to be concerned and depressed about.

Adam took it very badly when his father broke it to him the following morning that he was going away again. He started to cry. He stood there in his pyjamas and his dressing gown and slippers in the kitchen and bawled, sobbing so hard that his shoulders shook. Elizabeth felt she ought to spare him the embarrassment of her witnessing this. But far from being embarrassed, it was to her he went for comfort, putting his arms around her, his hot little face burying itself in her stomach, reminding her that for all his precocious intelligence and the worldly confidence he affected he was at a very young and tender age. She slid down, kneeling so their heads were on a level, and hugged him. Hunter stood awkwardly with the table between himself and his son.

'Tell him not to go,' Adam said. 'Tell him he can't go. Please tell him, Elizabeth, he takes notice of you.' He started sobbing again through the tears and snot. 'Please,' he said.

Elizabeth reached for a paper napkin from the table and dabbed at his face, looking over his head towards his father.

'Order him,' Adam said. He sniffed. 'You can do it, you're a doctor.'

Elizabeth smiled despite herself. 'And your dad is a colonel.'

'No. He's a retired colonel.'

'Elizabeth will stay with you,' Hunter said.

Adam turned to look at his father. 'And I love Elizabeth. I do. But when you're here, Dad, I feel safe.'

Hunter walked round the table and took his son by the hand. 'It's only for a single night,' he said. He ruffled Adam's hair. He led him away into the sitting room and from the kitchen door Elizabeth saw him sit them both by the cold ashes of last night's fire to comfort and reassure him and bring him round. In this, he was unsuccessful. She could see that by the abject look on Adam's face at the window when his father drove the Land Rover away from the house through the snow an hour later at the start of his journey.

Hunter found a copy of the magazine at a place in the Old Town that sold esoteric books and arts and fashion-based periodicals. He took it out of his bag to read it as the train left the station. There was a picture of Lucien Hope on the contributors' page. He had styled the main fashion feature, as well as writing the sycophantic little assemblage of clichés and myths about Mrs Mallory. There was a fey look about his bleached blond hair and the hint of black eyeliner he wore. And there was an eagerness to please in his too-wide smile.

The piece had been laid out across four pages. The opening spread comprised a single full-bleed picture with a slab of intro copy reversed out on the right side of the right-hand page. The title of the feature, described in an italicised font across the top of the opening spread, was the terrible pun, 'Meet Cleaver'. Elizabeth had been right, though. Inept with words, the magazine knew what it was doing when it came to picture quality. The black and white portrait photograph of Mrs Mallory was back-lit using natural light filtered through two rectangular windows. Its subject sat, or more accurately lounged, on a large leather sofa. She was wearing a black dress made of some clingy fabric with a sheen that showed off her long legs and slim, supple curves. Her shoulders and arms were bare, smooth and firmly contoured. Smoke from a cigarette held poised in the fingers of her right hand rose in a languid spiral upward. She was bare-headed, looking straight at the camera. A choker of black pearls emphasised the elegant length of her neck; it was not there to disguise wrinkles. Mrs Mallory did not do wrinkles, Hunter knew. Just as she did not do frugality or exercise classes or social networking internet sites or coffee at Starbucks or supermarket shopping or political correctness in being mindful of not being photographed smoking. She was disdainful and apart. The practicalities of life did not afflict her and neither did its mundane and pedestrian values. I don't care, the picture said. I really do not give a shit.

She was very beautiful. Hunter had been trained to be objective and there was no other word adequate. She was sexy and she was glamorous and she was beautiful. She wore her hair longer now than she had at Magdalena. The added length should logically have aged her. But it had the effect of making her appear more youthful and feminine. It fell unconfined from a casual centre parting and its waves rippled blackly down to the top of her cleavage. Her eyes were grey and sparkling and sardonically amused. Her facial bones were coldly sculpted. But their perfection was offset subtly by the hint of warmth in the half-smile playing on Mrs Mallory's succulent lips.

'Kiss me,' she had commanded Mark Hunter a dozen years ago. Those lips had parted as she spoke the words. And if you judged her only on this picture, it would seem an invitation wholly irresistible. He smiled to himself. He was almost alone in his carriage. It was the West Coast service and he had paid the ticket collector the upgrade to Weekend First. It was odd to think that the woman in this photograph had once looked like Lillian had, like Elizabeth Bancroft did. They were beautiful too. But she was self-invented. She had been long toiled over. And it was fair to say that Mrs Mallory had created, in herself, something of a masterpiece.

Kate Hunter's ballet tutor had been Miss Dupree. And Miss Dupree had been a piece of work. She had a light physique and pulled-back hair, and splayed feet when she stood on one hip in the repose of the stereotypical ballerina. But she had retired from performance at the end of the 1980s. The odd thing about her was that she seemed to be ageing in reverse. 'She's a work in progress,' Lillian had said, laughing at what she considered her husband's ludicrous naivety when he'd pointed this out. 'There's more Botox in her face than face, Mark. She's had more lifts than most skyscrapers are equipped with.'

Hunter asked his wife what Botox was and was given his reply. She told him about collagen and the other cosmetic alchemies that kept affluent women forever young-looking.

And he looked at his wife, who had not visibly aged one

single day since the one on which they had met. 'Do you use this stuff, Lillian?' he had asked.

And she had laughed again. 'There are easier ways,' she said.

'Easier?'

'More natural, you might say.'

Rosaline Dupree had not looked natural. But Mrs Mallory did. There was this tautness about everything above the jaw on the ballet teacher's face that made it impossible for her features to register emotion. All the facial muscles need to do so had been frozen by the cosmetic toxin, Botox. But when Mark studied the magazine portrait of Mrs Mallory in pale November sunshine through the train window, she did not even look airbrushed. He smiled despite himself. No wonder poor, fat, cantankerous Miss Hall had always been so crabby about her.

He turned the page. The second spread comprised a full-page ad for Shalimar perfume on the left and a full-page-bleed editorial photo on the right with more reversed-out copy. It was another interior shot and again it was black and white. Black predominated. But then, this was Mrs Mallory's world.

Nevertheless, Hunter thought the photographer had composed the image. She stood resting her right hand on the top of a Steinway concert grand piano. In the grip of her left fist were a bunch of white roses with their blooms pointed at the floor. Her eyes were downcast and petals lay in a pale cluster on the floorboards beneath the bouquet. She was smiling at some secret amusement and her lower lip had snagged slightly on her teeth. This imperfection made her look human and gorgeous. Lucien Hope, he assumed, had styled her for this shot. She wore a man's three-piece evening suit. The trousers showed off the length of her legs and the tightly buttoned waistcoat how slender she was at the waist.

It struck Hunter as a picture that could have been taken at any time over the last eighty years or so. A bronze bust rested on the piano and he recognised the florid handsomeness of its subject, Rupert Brooke. He remembered the opening lines from Brooke's famous, prophetic poem.

> *If I should die, think only this of me:*
> *That there's some corner of a foreign field*
> *That is forever England.*

By way of the Russian Steppes and Berlin and Magdalena and who knew how many other places on her dark odyssey, Mrs Mallory had come to England. She was not English, though. And she had certainly not come to England to die. But Hunter was an Englishman and he had chosen to live in the white, winter wilderness of the Scottish Highlands. The lines of the poem filled him as he recalled them with a cold blossoming of dread. For reasons he could not have articulated, they made him think of Adam, his son.

He could see the profiling of Lavinia Mallory in a current magazine piece, however esoteric the magazine, as a fortuitous break that would aid him in his quest, Hunter thought. He could interpret it as nothing other than a happy coincidence. But it was a part of a pattern that had begun at Magdalena and accelerated alarmingly with the dreams inflicted on his son. She was featured in the magazine because she had a public face now. She enjoyed stature and acclaim. She was influential where it mattered most. The time was coming when she would attempt to put her tilt upon the world. It would be her time and it was surely imminent. And its arrival would be swift and terrible and, when it came, there would be no escape from it.

Chapter Eleven

As soon as Hunter left, Elizabeth started to mobilise Adam for a little excursion. She wanted to take him into the village to buy him something. She knew it was considered low and shallow and ultimately self-defeating to try to bribe a child into a more positive frame of mind. She'd done the reading on child psychology as part of her job training. But in the days when she had had a life, she personally had loved to get unexpected gifts. It was human nature. And just this once she thought that it would benefit the boy without necessarily critically undermining the rest of his life. The fact was she had recently become a bit cynical about orthodox psychology. She had found herself in circumstances that had forced her to reappraise its value. It was nowhere near the catch-all she had once complacently believed it to be.

Firstly, though, she wanted to stop off at her mother's house. They had met before, but Adam had slept through the encounter, thanks to the medication Elizabeth had given him. It was likely that Adam would be left at some point in her mother's care and therefore important that they met prior to that and got on okay. Adam did not appear particularly thrilled about meeting an elderly woman. Why would he be? But he was excited at the prospect of sharing Elizabeth's two-seater car on the journey. She thought of her MG as a runabout. He thought of it as a sports car because it had a soft top and was painted green. To him his dad's Land Rover was staid and boring. Elizabeth's car was cool. She was more alarmed than excited as it skidded and slid along the snow-packed roads and grateful there was no other weekend traffic. She drove dreading the slow but inevitable drift into a drystone wall that would wreck the bodywork and rob her of her dignity. He visibly brightened, enjoying the ride.

Her mother was bright-eyed and seemed energised when she opened the door. She looked, Elizabeth thought, a full decade younger than she had a week ago. She wondered whether this was to do with unburdening herself of the truth about Ruth Campbell's malevolent nature. More likely she had been energised by summoning her magic after all those dormant years. She had restored Mark Hunter. In doing so, she seemed to have replenished herself. She made tea. Then she said, 'Do you like bonfires, Adam?'

'Is the Pope a Catholic?' Adam said.

'Yes, well, I expect he is. And I have my answer.' She walked him over to the window. She pointed to a rough circle of stones about eight feet across and about twenty yards from the house. 'Kindling first,' she said. 'Then twigs and finally, fallen branches.'

'I know how to construct a fire,' he said. 'Before we came to live here, I was in the Cubs.'

'Good. There are three copses of trees around this house. They will provide you with everything you need. Don't venture beyond them. Do not cross the road. Do not cheat and take any of the logs from the pile chopped and stacked outside my door. They are for my grate and I will know. I have counted them.' She looked stern and then winked at him and he grinned. 'Now put your coat back on and off you go.'

He opened the door and skipped out into the snow. 'Plenty of wood, mind,' she called after him. 'We want a proper blaze.' She closed the door.

'So, Mum. How long have you been a pyromaniac?' Elizabeth said.

Margaret Bancroft turned to face her daughter. 'I'm going to destroy something I should have dispensed with a long time ago,' she said. 'I want the flames high and the seat of that fire white with heat and fury. When I watch that devilish object burn, I want none of the vile things depicted in it looking back out at me with anything but the pain of their destruction.'

'How much do you know, Mum?'

'I know that the child and his father face grave danger. And you do too because you've come to love the father and you're devoted to the son. And you are loyal and have always been much braver than I am, God forgive me.'

Adam had been gone only for a moment. He would be out for at least half an hour, Elizabeth reckoned, probably longer. He could endure the cold. He had inherited his father's physical toughness and, for all she knew, his mother's too. He would want to build his bonfire well. 'Teach me to do it, Mum. If I have it in me, you can tell me what it is I need to do to bring it out.'

Her mother looked at her levelly. 'There's no trick to it. There's nothing you need to learn. It was stronger in you than it's ever been in me before you could walk or talk.'

'There must be some technique to it.'

Margaret Bancroft glowered. She looked angry, indignant. 'Some knack, you mean?' She walked over to the kitchen counter and took a boning knife from a magnetic strip of knives below the row of kitchen cupboards. She placed her left hand palm up on her chopping board.

'Mum—'

She drew the blade across the open palm of her hand. She kept her knives sharp and her stroke was sure. The cut was deep. Elizabeth glimpsed white bone and the blue of cartilage before the parted flesh became aware of the insult to it and blood welled out over her hand and on to the chopping board. 'You can start with that,' Margaret Bancroft said, nodding towards the wound. Her voice was calm, devoid of inflection. 'Since you think you need one, that can be your apprenticeship.'

He did not go straight to Cleaver Square. He had phoned ahead and arranged to meet first with an old comrade in arms. James Preston was one of the finest soldiers Hunter had ever had the distinction to serve with. But he had been cashiered out of the army after failing a random drugs test a few years earlier. He had been one of the fittest men ever to pass selection into the Parachute Regiment. Now he put his knowledge of exercise to profitable use as a personal trainer. He operated out of the ground floor of an old light-industrial building converted into fashionable apartments in a mews in Bermondsey. His own living quarters occupied one panelled-off corner of the apartment he had bought. The rest was taken up with Cybex machines and clusters of free weights in iron piles and punching bags. He trained some very high-profile clients, many from the film industry. Because he knew what he was doing, he got noticeable results very quickly.

The door was not locked. Hunter had walked in on a training session. Jimmy just nodded to him from over a clipboard, a client in front of him on a running machine. The air in the gym was hot and slightly fetid. He hoped the client, someone he thought he vaguely recognised, was warming down rather than warming up. He liked Jimmy very much. But he did not have time to hang about today. He went and sat on a workout bench to wait. The place was impressively sized and equipped. It had been bought, he knew, with a family legacy. Jimmy's background was privileged. There was income from endowments, stocks and shares. Hunter suspected most of the money he made himself still went up his nose.

The client was warming down. Ten minutes later he left

and Jimmy took the precaution of locking the door behind him. He sauntered back to Hunter and the two men shook hands. 'That thing over there in the corner, Jimmy,' Hunter said, gesturing.

'No problem. It's decommissioned.'

'It's a Milan, for Christ's sake. It's an anti-tank weapon.'

'It's a souvenir,' Jimmy said.

'Doesn't it frighten the clients?'

'Most of them think it's a prop.'

Hunter had to smile. Some people came out of the regiment totally immune to the standards demanded by civilian life. Captain James Preston was one of them. But then he had not left the army by choice. 'Did you order the item I asked you to?'

'Why don't we call a spade a spade?'

'You did order it?'

'You could have ordered it yourself on eBay.'

'Jesus, Jimmy.'

'It's on its way, Mark. Calm down. It's the most powerful you can get, fucking lethal. It's on its way to Scotland as we speak.'

Hunter looked at his old friend. He was wearing combats and a green ribbed singlet and jungle-issue boots. He looked very fit. But the fitness was cosmetic, the taut musculature flattered to deceive. The nose candy took its invisible, inward toll. 'You seeing anyone?'

'I go on the odd date. Nothing serious, though. I wouldn't want to risk the prospect of domestic bliss.'

'Domestic bliss isn't called that for nothing,' Hunter said.

'Whoever sang that song got it right, for me, mate. When you've got nothing, you've got nothing to lose.'

'Well, I'm grateful for the favour. Thanks. Thanks, Jimmy.'

'No problem.' Jimmy seemed to hesitate. 'You got time for a coffee?'

'Another day,' Hunter said. 'I'd best be on my way.' He turned to go.

'Would you like to borrow a gun?'

He stopped. 'You've got a gun?'

'Course I've got a gun. Jesus. What do you take me for, Mark, a fucking pacifist?'

'Why would I want a gun, Jimmy?'

'Because wherever you're going, mate, that look on your face tells me you'll very likely need one.'

But guns were of no use, were they? He thought about this on the Underground on his short journey to Kennington. He thought about the double-tap execution he had performed, or believed he had, on Mrs Mallory. He had stood outside in the rain in Magdalena and watched Miss Hall sway in the window and thought she was performing some ritual of grief for her dead adversary. But Mrs Mallory had not died. She had slithered to her feet off the tiles in her drawing room and cursed Miss Hall, inflicting the disease that would eat away at her from the inside until her death a dozen years on. What he had seen from the street in the rain had been Miss Hall grieving for herself.

It was raining when he exited the station at Kennington. It was six o'clock in the evening and dark and raining hard. Big drops were bouncing off the bodies and through the windscreen grilles of the two police riot vans parked at the station entrance. In the bath of yellow light from the station Hunter could plainly see the rows of seated officers within, grim-faced and staring straight ahead from behind their visors in full riot gear. There were officers with dogs on the pavement, the leashes straining and the pelts of the powerful animals drenched.

He took a short cut through an estate to get to his destination and was sorry he had done so almost straight away. Clusters of hooded youths lurked in communal doorways and at the bottom of stairwells eyeing him with hostile looks, emboldened by the pit-bulls providing their back-up, snuffling around their masters and tethered to chain leads. Most of these kids, he suspected, would be armed with knives. They were innately hostile to alien species and that was exactly what his age and dress and bearing made him. He knew he was not a natural target for assault. He looked far too strong and knowledgeable for that. He recognised the unease in himself he had sometimes felt on the streets of Northern Ireland, first on foot patrol and later, when he joined the regiment, operating clandestinely. He had never felt this sort of urban trepidation before in England. He read the papers. But he'd had no idea that things had got anywhere near this bad. He was about a hundred yards or so from Kennington Lane and the last bit of the route that would take him to the square when he was confronted.

The youth in front of him was white and febrile, rain-drenched and with the spasmodic mannerisms inflicted by chronic crack addiction. He had a blade gripped in his right fist. 'Put the knife away, sonny,' Hunter said. His voice was even. 'You're dealing with a grown-up.' He held out his hands, the palms flat, the fingers splayed and rock steady. 'These are all I need. They can put you in a very dark place.'

'It's dark where you're going,' this apparition said, grinning before skulking damply back into the shadows.

Adam's industry was very impressive. It was a full hour before he returned from building his bonfire. Margaret Bancroft made him hot chocolate to thaw him out after his freezing toil in the snow. She grilled crumpets to go with the beverage. There was nothing at all wrong now with her hand.

'Crumpets, Mum?' Elizabeth said. 'Have you gone soft? Where's your patriotic pride?'

'I can't inflict oatcakes on the poor wee lamb,' her mother

said. 'I just can't do it. We're approaching the season of goodwill to all men. That includes boys.' The mood between the two women had improved.

The pyre was about eight feet high. Otherwise occupied, they had not watched through the window as he had constructed it. Elizabeth could not understand how he had erected something so substantial without the use of a stepladder. There was a stepladder, but it was under lock and key in the stable.

'Same principle as pyramid construction,' Adam said. 'You start with a broad base to give your structure stability. Course, you don't want too much density, because fires feed off oxygen. Fortunately, branches have one architectural advantage over bricks. They interlock. They meld. Get your base right and you're away. It's construction work until it exceeds the height you can securely reach. After that, you're basically lobbing the branches on and hoping they won't slide back down and land on you.'

'Is branch avalanche a risk?' Margaret Bancroft asked.

He turned to her. 'That's got to be your worst nightmare with a bonfire, Mrs Bancroft, construction-wise.'

'Call me Margaret,' she said. And then more quietly to her daughter, 'He's as bright as a button.'

They let Adam light the bonfire. It was his creation to ignite, after all. When it was burning so fiercely the heat bathed their faces in its furious glow, Margaret Bancroft slipped away to the stable, fishing the key to the padlock that secured its door from the pocket of her cardigan. Adam stood before Elizabeth and leaned against her. She linked her arms across his chest and he grasped her hands for a full minute before realising she had even done it. They stared into the cracking red-white furnace of the bonfire's seat. And then they saw a large flat object cartwheel into the centre of the fire, sending ashes sparking and hissing into the cold air with the impact. The panel caught immediately. The cloth in which it was wrapped shrivelled and seemed to evaporate. Shapes appeared to shift in turmoil on the surface of the object as the flames licked at and the heat devoured it in a sudden audible roar. It rippled, the wood buckling and blistering like something alive. And then the animation left it and it was engulfed and turned to ash, betrayed by its age and the dryness of the centuries-old wood from which it had once been mischievously carved.

Margaret Bancroft dusted her hands together with a sound not unlike applause. Elizabeth turned to her mother. She had recently hefted that object herself and would have put its weight at upwards of forty pounds. Her mother had hurled it into the flames as someone might toss a pillow. She did not wonder from where the strength had come, though. She knew that she herself had provided it, earlier in the kitchen, as Adam constructed the meticulous pyre warming the three of them now.

Elizabeth had been a practical sort of a child. She had enjoyed building things. After the bonfire and lunch, her mother located a boxed hoard of her old Meccano in the loft and brought it down to an intrigued and, after a short while, gleeful Adam. They cleared a space on the sitting-room floor and he settled down to build something while the women talked in the kitchen.

Elizabeth thought her mother would be honest with her now. 'Have you ever seen a wolf, Mum?'

'No. But I think I know what it is that you're talking about. They're not really wolves and they're not really men either, are they? They're the creatures depicted in that carved panel I burned. They're like some evolutionary step that might have been taken had the world taken a darker turn than it has. I dreamed of them. I thought it was a Freudian thing. But there was nothing wrong with my sex life and my marriage to your dad was truly happy. I used the strength to stop them.'

'You used the magic to stop the dreams?'

'Yes.'

'What were they like?'

'They were so disturbing and frightening that I had to put a stop to them. The creatures in them walked on two legs. They affected the conceit of human dress. And they possessed the mannerisms of people and the power of speech. And they tried to communicate with me.'

'What did they say?'

'I don't know, Lizzie. They didn't speak English. I don't speak any language other than a smattering of Gaelic and a bit of French. But I recognise other tongues. They spoke Russian and German, and on the most terrifying occasion I dreamed that one spoke Latin to me. It seemed quite blasphemous, somehow.'

'It sounds grotesque.'

'You haven't heard it?'

'I've been spared it, thank God,' Elizabeth said.

The gift for Adam was never bought in the village because his mood was so successfully lifted by the building of the bonfire and the discovery of the Meccano. He took the giant box of it away with him when they left. He was halfway through some complex construction and delighted with the discovery of this old-tech model building kit. He played with it intently when they got back to the house. Then just before dusk they went for a walk in the snow and then Elizabeth made dinner and they ate popcorn together and watched the first and second movies in the *Back to the Future* trilogy and speculated afterwards on the practicalities of time travel. Then it was time for Adam to go to bed.

He showed no trepidation climbing up the stairs. Elizabeth

supposed he had inherited his father's courage as well as his physical endurance. But perhaps that was actually doing the boy an injustice. His demons might not be his own, but the fortitude he had shown in dealing with them surely was. She tucked him in and kissed him on the cheek. He turned his head and closed his eyes and she looked above where he lay at the shelf of books there.

He had almost the complete set of the Eye Witness series. She saw the one about the *Titanic*, which had photographs of the vessel taken by a submersible, quiet and still and gravely enormous in the fathomless depths to which it had sunk. She saw the one about the Apollo space missions, which had a picture of a cold and pitted moon on its cover. She looked at his other bits and pieces; the toy cars and discarded batteries and the Swiss Army knife and a set of fake joke-shop teeth and a tarnished leather cup with a pair of antique ivory dice he must have bought with his pocket money at a car boot sale. A sudden and intense feeling of anger overcame her then. This boy had been robbed of the right to dream with the happy freedom other children did. A vital part of him had been stolen. She shivered, though it was warm in the Hunter house. And she turned and left as Adam descended into what she hoped would be a deep and untroubled night of sleep.

She switched on the computer downstairs just to catch up on her email. She was pretty tired and thought she would not be long in following Adam up to bed. She had been sent something by the British Library late the previous afternoon. It was an addendum to the document they had dispatched her already. She opened it. It wasn't very long. She printed it off and took it into the sitting room to read.

I write this only because I fear my time is short and wish to die with my conscience clear and no secret unrevealed and festering to trouble my immortal soul. I have said that the witch Ruth Campbell was removed from the scaffold and dealt with according to the protocols laid down by Bullock in his urgent missive from the Fens. And this was eventually so. But I was guilty of perjuring myself in my previous account of the event. I told the truth. But I did not tell the whole truth about what did occur.

The corpse of the Campbell woman had been taken from the gibbet and buried a full week by the time Bullock's letter came to me. It was plain from the contents that we were obliged to carry out the distasteful ritual of disinterment. It was done on my part with a heavy heart. My instinct was to leave the dead to lie in peace. But Bullock's instructions were most emphatic and precise and I dared not fail in their execution.

We were compelled to sever the head from the body. An axe had been procured with which to carry out this grisly necessity. A stout veteran by the name of Jones had volunteered to deliver the blow. He had never used so cruel an instrument on flesh. But clearance had been his civil occupation and left him facile with an axe between his hands. She looked like sleep when we removed the winding sheet. Jones touched the blade to the spot to true his aim before raising the axe. The keen edge of the blade pricked the skin of her neck and her eyes opened with a start. She snarled as Jones dropped the axe in shock and she sat upright and naked pale. She spoke my name. I drew my own sword and cut off her head with a single clean stroke. And the head did speak then from the floor, cursing me. And only after did the witch perish and with the two parts of her bloody and at peace in their final mutilation.

I believe that in the time of her trial, grief for the creature with which she had cavorted made her indifferent to her own fate. But it would have come to what remained of her mind in time that she had not died on the gallows. She would have crawled from her grave and resumed her mischief. What we did was fully justified by need. But the cost to me has been a heavy one. I am visited by the black visions that precede a seizure of the brain. That was her

*curse. I pray only it is fatal when it comes. I would not be left a
dribbling fool enduring only as a burden to my wife.*

*My affairs are settled and my widow will not want for comfort.
My children are grown and fair. I am content I did my duty to the
Commonwealth, the Lord Protector and my God. I do not indulge
the sin of feeling pity for myself. I have lived through a great and
eventful moment. I would have been spared the revelations of these
last few weeks, but cannot in truth complain about my lot.
Nothing matters more than I face my Maker with my conscience
unsullied and the last of the words committed here are written now
in the belief I do.*

In God and in His truth,

Josiah Jerusalem Smith.

Cleaver Square was suddenly more salubrious than the
streets he had just risked. No one haunted the pavements.
He made for the Prince of Wales pub. There was music
playing inside. It was Duke Ellington, 'Take the "A" Train'.
The pub was very hot and crowded and it was a jostle to
get to the bar. When he did get there and had been served
a pint of beer, he looked around. He thought that maybe
he had stumbled into a stag party or a themed night. But
there were too many women present for a stag do. Most
of the men were wearing black tie. The women, for the
most part, had on cocktail frocks and more make-up than
he could remember having seen slapped on since the early
1980s, when he had been a callow youth. There were pillbox
hats and hats with veils and elbow-length gloves. People were
smoking in the pub and they were not doing it furtively.
The air was bitter with smoke. Almost everyone seemed to
be drunk.

'What's your story, pilgrim?' the man next to him at the
bar said.

Hunter didn't like conversations casually struck up in pubs with strangers. He didn't particularly like being called pilgrim, either. But he decided on the path of least resistance. He could not afford to be conspicuous.

'Just fancied a pint,' he said. 'And I wanted to get out of the rain.'

The man smiled. His teeth were discoloured. Hunter noticed that the collar of his dress shirt was rimed with dirt and the satin lapels of his jacket greasy in the light from the bar. 'You're telling me you came in here on the off-chance?'

Hunter took a sip of his beer. It tasted brackish. 'What's wrong with that?'

But the fellow seemed momentarily to have forgotten him. Two men over by the entrance to the Gents had begun to fight. They were clumsy and inept and it went straight away to the floor where they bit and gouged in a tangle of limbs. Hunter's new acquaintance pushed his forefinger and thumb into his mouth and let out a piercing, celebratory whistle. But the combatants were becoming exhausted and feeble, already spent. One of them started to vomit copiously, and the other tried to escape his grip and scramble out of range of the bucketing puke.

The whistler at the bar remembered Hunter. And he remembered what Hunter had just said to him and frowned. 'No one comes in here on the off-chance, pilgrim,' he said.

'Are you telling me this place is a private club?'

The man opened his mouth to reply and then hesitated because a woman behind him was now tapping him on the back. Hunter looked around him at her. She wore thick foundation that failed to conceal acne scars and eye shadow so deep it made the sockets they shaded into blue caverns. And blue was the wrong colour. Her eyes were brown. 'He says it's fifty,' she said.

'It's forty,' the man said back to her.

'He says it's fifty now.'

'Forty's my limit. Offer him a hand job to make up the difference. A blow job, if he says no.'

She pouted and turned and walked unsteadily away. Hunter had time only to see that the stockings were laddered above her red stilettos before she disappeared in the throng. He put down his glass.

'Leaving already, pilgrim?' his new friend said.

'Out of my league,' Hunter said. 'This place is far too sophisticated for me.'

If anything it was raining harder when he got outside. He looked around. Cleaver Square wasn't square at all. It was a quite narrow rectangle. Most of its houses occupied two long Georgian terraces that faced one another on either side of the strip of gravel between them and the trees surrounding it. The square was dark as well as wet, the gravel puddled, the trees tall and dripping gloomily. But it was not difficult as he walked to identify Mrs Mallory's address. He had Adam's detailed description of its façade and Green Man door knocker. When he saw that, he saw also that the houses to either side of hers were both for sale. He was not surprised at this. She had been in London for a while. It must be tough to be a next-door neighbour of the hottest, coolest party hostess in town.

Her house was dark. His instinct told him that she was not at home. He had known she was there at her home a dozen years ago at Magdalena. He felt her absence from this place now as surely as he had felt her presence then. Of course it was possible she could be at one of the darkened windows, receded just far enough into the shadows around her to be invisible. She could be watching him. But he did not think she was. He felt afraid of what he was going to find in the house. But Mrs Mallory tonight was doing her own fearful business somewhere else.

Hunter made his observations without pausing or even appearing to look towards the address he intended to enter. The garrulous loser who had spoken to him in the pub could be outside it now, just as curious as to what he was doing in the neighbourhood as he'd been about his presence in the Prince. There could be alert eyes on the other side of the square. These handsome houses were obvious targets for burglary, given the sink estate poverty that pervaded elsewhere in Kennington. He did not have a convenient set of keys conjured into existence by his erstwhile ally Miss Hall. He would have to scale the wall at the far corner of the terrace and steal through a series of gardens to reach the point where he could get through a back door or window. He was well qualified for this sort of work. But you were only ever successful at it if you were extremely careful. The weather was on his side. The rain meant thick cloud cover and that meant no moon. He had gained the end of the terrace. He looked around once more and prepared to climb.

Because the house was dark it would have to stay that way. His eyes would have to adjust and a meagre pen light was all he could risk beyond his night vision. He doubted Mrs Mallory subscribed to the local Neighbourhood Watch scheme. She wasn't really the type. But he would have bet the people living on the other side of the square in the houses facing hers did. He stood in her kitchen and waited for the darkness around him to clarify into something more detailed and paler. When it did, he looked at a room that never properly functioned. The glass-fronted cupboards were empty of provisions. There was a light sheen of dust on the hotplates. The sink too wore a patina of dry neglect. He did not open the fridge because he could not risk the brightness of its interior bulb. But his hunch was that it would contain ice cubes, champagne, white wine and possibly vodka. There would be no food. What Mrs Mallory's guests consumed came from an outside caterer. Just as she wasn't much of a neighbour, he did not suppose she was much of a homemaker either.

Her drawing room wore the chill of a mausoleum. There was a waxy smell of polished furniture and the bulk of the concert grand with the bronze bust of Brooke on top of it. He thought there were poets whose themes were far better suited to her character and inclinations. Eliot and Yeats were much more her style. In the pale cast of streetlight through the window he could see the spot where she had stood for her Dietrich moment. Or perhaps it had been her Garbo moment. That would surely have been what Lucien Hope had in mind. Fashion stylists thought in visual clichés. They referenced everything. But the effect of the photograph had been to out-glitter either star, in truth. There was still a single rose petal curled and atrophied like a withered fingernail on the floor.

Her library was his real destination. That was the focus of the house in the dreams that tormented his son. And he was intent upon it. But curiosity took him firstly up the stairs. He knew from her keep in the Tyrol that she did sometimes sleep. He climbed the uncarpeted steps with practised stealth. He was beginning to appreciate the incredible power of seduction she possessed. The house was dismal with menace in her absence. Her willing presence was all that must make it tolerable for her guests. More than tolerable, they found it thrilling. She dazzled and toyed with them. He climbed. When he reached the landing he sniffed the chilly air. Perfume betrayed her. He followed the scent of Jicky cologne into the open-doored maw of a spacious room. Her spoor was here. Her cold intimacy lay about the place in strewn underwear and rumpled sheets. The curtains were closed in heavy velvet folds and he thought he could risk his pen light. Its thin beam fingered gossamer negligees and brassieres filigreed with lace. She wore only black or ivory against her skin and favoured silk and satin. He went over to the bed and pulled off the wrinkled counterpane. There was no odour of sex. Yet she attired herself at night in a manner bound to stir arousal. Did she have lovers? Perhaps she lived in the night-time on the memory of sex. There was a bedside cabinet from the top of which rose the acrid odour of a heaped ashtray. He squatted down and opened the cabinet door. Ampoules of some clear liquid sat in a neat row in a wooden rack beside an old-style steel and glass syringe. There was no blood on the needle.

There was a high double-fronted wardrobe against the wall opposite the bedroom window. Its doors wore a lavish walnut burr. When he opened it, the space within was hung only with dresses. She must keep her coats elsewhere, he thought. And her accessories, her shoes and gloves and bags and scarves. All of her dresses were black and when he stretched with his pen light to look at their labels many of them rustled with sewn beads and brocade. There were no real surprises. She favoured Chanel and Dior and Schiaparelli. He sniffed at the fabrics, but they were not musty and old. And there were some of the newer couture names Lillian had liked to spoil herself buying when the money from the books had started coming in. Mrs Mallory sometimes wore Katharine Hamnett and Bill Blass. It was just the colour, or lack of it, that never varied.

He walked into her bathroom. Here the smell of perfume was stronger. What looked at first in the darkness like an open door leading off somewhere else was in fact a full-length mirror. The mirror was disconcerting. Hunter did not want to dwell on what its depths might reflect. He took in soft white towels folded over a chrome rail and a large bathtub veined in purple marble. From the sink, there was the rhythmic lisp of a dripping tap. On a shelf above the sink there were nail clippers, tweezers and an uncapped

Chanel lipstick with a waxy peak that looked black in the absence of light. It would be red of course. Mrs Mallory habitually wore red on her lips.

It was time to face his demon. It took him about ten minutes to pick the lock securing the library door. It was a complex mechanism and it did not help that he was rushing things. Where calm deliberation was called for, he was now edgy. She could always come home. He looked at his watch but his watch had stopped. He remembered his grope through the canvas labyrinth in Magdalena, where his watch had also stopped. Then, Mrs Mallory had distorted time, Miss Hall had told them. While he blundered in that dark limbo with Peterson, Rodriguez had been given the leisure to gnaw his hands to the wrists. Hunter's own hands were not so steady now as they had been when he'd held them out to discourage the crack addict from the thought of attacking him in the street earlier in the evening. And the palms were sweating. He wiped them on his thighs, crouched before the lock and heard its final click of release and rose and opened the library door.

The seated creature of Adam's dreams was enormous. Its stillness on its wooden throne added to the impression of its size. It looked somehow poised and alert. It was clothed in the same grey uniform it had worn when he glimpsed it in the staff car in the film of Mrs Mallory in that summer in Berlin. He closed the library door softly behind himself and studied it. He approached it. And then it shifted and moved and he was not in the least surprised. He would hear the strain of the leather that shod its huge feet as it rose and the stiff boots took its weight and it strode forward, covering the distance between them. Dread engulfed him and he tensed and reached for the weapon he did not possess. But the impression of movement had been caused by the beam of a car headlamp on the street outside, travelling through the square and sweeping through the closed drapes over the library window. It was no more than a trick of the light. Hunter swallowed and came closer to the beast. Adam was right. Its boots were of grotesque size. So were its hands, sheathed in leather gauntlets and maintaining a firm grip in death on the carved arms of its throne.

And it was dead, wasn't it? 'Mr Mallory, I presume,' Hunter said. But the bravado felt entirely hollow and he dreaded the reply his crass jibe might just have provoked. None came. The yellow eyes in the creature's great head stared glassily at nothing. Its long jaw was set in a mocking leer. Instinct told him not to turn his back on it. But he would have to, if the library was to reveal its secrets to him.

Her desk was an antique item of the roll-top sort and it was locked. But unpicking this lock was the work of only a moment. He revealed a clutter of papers and books. The books had been written by hand rather than printed. Scribes had done the work. Two of them were bound in what he strongly suspected was human skin, dried and cured for the purpose. He sighed to himself and opened one of them. Its pages were filled with runic symbols, some antique language he did not understand but suspected he had heard spoken by the vessel she had made his son when her curse was inflicted and he dreamed on her behalf.

The papers were sketches of colossal public buildings. There were figures in them drawn to show their oppressive, monumental scale. Hunter recognised none of them. There were sketched symbols too, motifs that were subtly reminiscent of the swastika and SS lightning strikes, of the brutal iconography of a time she no doubt remembered with nostalgic fondness. And he knew why it was he did not recognise the buildings. None was from the past. He thought of what Lucien Hope had said about Mrs Mallory's soirées. He was looking at the blueprints for the future she planned.

He thought about the riot police outside the station entrance not half a mile away and the vacuous look behind the blue mascara on the face of the woman with the laddered stockings in the pub. He looked at the monster slouched in the shadows of the room he was in and repeated Adam's warning out loud to himself, 'She wants to put a tilt on the world.'

He wanted her to know he had been here. That was his real purpose in coming. He had told Elizabeth it was just reconnaissance. But that had been a lie. He had been hoping she would be absent so that he could violate her home. He wanted to provoke her into making a mistake, goad her into hasty retaliation. He was sick and tired of her tormenting his son. He wanted her to come for him. Then he would defeat and kill her. Miss Hall had all but out-manoeuvred her at Magdalena. There was a precedent. It could be done.

He walked back over to the seated creature. It was not a comfortable companion, he didn't think. For all its apparent lifelessness, it possessed the sly insistence of a threat. In death it was disconcerting. In life he sensed it would have been a force of pure malevolence, only ever a bringer of dread and pain. Had the leer worn on its hungry jaw grown wider since he had entered the library and encountered it? He could have sworn it had. He fought the urge to flee, and studied it. He saw that it was armed. It wore a pistol belt and a leather holster shaped to house a Luger. It wore an SS dagger in a scabbard on the belt. Both weapons must have been hand-fashioned, their scale slightly greater than normal, individually tooled to suit the dimensions of their owner. The beast had evidently been held in high esteem. Hunter took the dagger. He unbuckled the belt and took the scabbard off it, put the belt back on and then slipped the dagger in the scabbard down his boot.

The taking of trophies was a long-established military custom. It was only ever done of course in victory. There was a fine line always fiercely argued between what were legitimate souvenirs and what could be condemned outright as looting on the field of conflict. Hunter did not trouble himself over the finer points of military ethics in this situation. Neither greed nor profit had prompted the theft. The dagger would go through the grid over a gutter drain as soon as he regained the street. He figured that she would notice its absence straight away. That was the significant thing. Adam said she spoke to this unresponsive confidant all the time. She would not respond well to the insult his petty act of thievery represented. She did not like to be disrespected. That was the point.

Up this close, the clothed creature stank. Its odour was an unhappy mingling of ancient sweat and feral decay. Hunter glanced at his watch out of habit, but the luminous dial did not tell the time because of course the movement had stopped and the hands were still. It did not matter greatly. Whatever time it was, he thought it was high time he left. The leer had diminished, his training for detail insisted, on the face of the beast. It now wore something closer to a snarl. Was it his heightened imagination? He could not have said. He had a night train to catch, back to the snowbound Highlands of Scotland, back to that foreign field to which he had taken, in the indulgence of his private grief, his precious son in their shared exile.

The streets surrounding Cleaver Square sounded like a war zone. There were angry cries and screams, the barking of dogs, sirens wailing, the sound of glass shattering and the unmistakeable, staccato crack of small arms fire. When he reached Kennington Tube station, it looked more like a stockade than a place where you accessed Underground trains. Police officers armed with machine pistols stood in a grim-faced cordon at the entrance.

'Nothing in or out of here tonight, mate,' one of them said to him. 'I'd scarper if I were you.'

'Is it always like this around here?'

'We have it under control,' the officer said. Then he grinned to signal his personal contempt for the official line, the lie he was obliged to recite contradicted by the violent chaos around them.

They seemed short of manpower, unless they were just short of willpower. Hunter walked along Kennington Park Road towards the Oval. He thought he might be able to hail a taxi back to Euston Station if he turned right on to Kennington Road. There were usually plenty going north along that route after dropping fares in Clapham and Wandsworth. When he passed the Cost-cutter branch at the T junction, its windows were smashed and a fire seemed just to be taking hold inside. Looters were fighting on the pavement over bottles of liquor and cases of beer. There were no taxis. There seemed little point in heading for Oval Station because, like Kennington, it was on the Northern Line and that line was closed.

He stuck to his original plan and walked down Kennington Road. The sound of violence faded after the junction with Black Prince Road. But he was past the Imperial War Museum and on Westminster Bridge Road and able to smell the chill and damp of the approaching river before he was able to hail a black cab.

'Where to, pilgrim?'

Hunter almost did not get in. Twice in a couple of hours he had been called that now by strangers. Maybe it was a London fashion, an idiomatic craze of the sort that came and went in a month. In the back of the cab he thought about the appellation itself. It was a curious one. Where he was concerned it was ironic. He had not come to Cleaver Square on any kind of pilgrimage. Quite the opposite was true. He had carried out what Mrs Mallory would see as an act of desecration. Not that the wolf creatures were deities.

They were mortal. The one he had just seen had died of disease or some other natural cause. Perhaps it had just been old age. The one Ruth Campbell consorted with had died very hard. Against odds of six to one, it had killed five veterans of the English Civil War, men who'd done their fighting hand to hand with the cold and bloody iron and steel of pikes and swords. But they had subdued and slaughtered it. They bled and they perished, these creatures, whatever they were. They were not God-like in that they were not supernatural. But Mrs Mallory would still see as desecration his taking of a relic from the body of the beast. It occupied pride of place in the most secret part of her home. She held its memory and remains in high regard.

'Lively in Kennington tonight,' Hunter said to his cabbie.

'It's kicked off good and proper in Holland Park too, according to the radio. And there's aggro in Whitechapel. There's no pattern to it, but it's night after night. And it's killing our trade.'

The radio was on, Hunter realised. Someone was singing the Kurt Weill lyric to 'Alabama Song'.

Oh, show me the way to the next whiskey bar . . .

It sounded like Jim Morrison's mournful baritone. That would make sense. The Doors had covered it, hadn't they?

'It's not been the same since the crisis,' the cabbie was saying. 'I mean, a coalition government? What's that all about? People are being lynched in the streets, hung from lampposts. You can't have that. You need decisiveness. The country needs leadership.'

Hunter realised with a vague pang of guilt that the crisis had rather passed him by. He had an army pension, the income from Lillian's books. In the aftermath of the crisis he'd had his grief to contend with. Anyway, soldiers were able to wash their hands of politics with a clean conscience. He had always willingly exercised that right.

'Where you headed?'

'Scotland. I live there with my family.'

The cabbie didn't comment for a moment. If anything, the rain had become heavier since Hunter had left Cleaver Square. He'd been okay in his waterproof jacket and boots. His performance clothing insulated him from the climate as surely as his guaranteed income had from the broader repercussions of the crisis. But urban violence of the sort he'd seen was the stuff of stifling summer nights in the city, not drenched and dark Novembers. The single wiper on the windscreen was batting furiously back and forth against the water streaming down the glass.

'You're facing a fair old journey home. But I envy you, pilgrim, I honestly do. London's become a right dump. Half the town's a no-go area. England's going to the dogs.'

Chapter Twelve

He was back at home just after 5 a.m. Elizabeth was not in the spare room. She was on the sitting-room sofa under a blanket with the fire built up, alternately dozing and listening out for his return. He let himself in and they embraced. Elizabeth felt a strong surge of pure relief. She had grown anxious in the hours since putting Adam to bed. She thought it might have been partly seeing the things cavort on the wooden carving as it burned on the bonfire in her mother's garden. It might partly have been reading the ghastly account of the details of her ancestor's death. But mostly she thought it was just concern for Mark, braving the lair of the sorceress tormenting them, braving God knew what retribution her caprice and cruelty could determine as fitting punishment for breaching her privacy should she catch him in her house.

Hunter poured himself a whisky and Elizabeth made herself some tea. They sat down and she studied him. He looked drained.

'What day is it?'

'Sunday,' she said.

He nodded. Of course it was. He had travelled Weekend First down to London. He had travelled the same way back on an almost empty train. He opened his bag and handed Elizabeth his copy of the magazine containing the feature on Lavinia Mallory. She studied the pictures without comment. She got up and fetched the printed addendum to Jerusalem Smith's grim account of Cromwellian justice meted out to a Scottish witch.

'Jesus,' Hunter said when he had read it. 'It's like dealing with a contagion. No offence to your Campbell ancestry.'

'No offence taken. In my professional opinion, though, you need to go to bed.'

He knew that was true. The visit to the house in Cleaver Square had enervated him. He felt as emptied by the ordeal as he had when he'd lost a lot of blood in combat, wounded and with the adrenaline of the moment spent. 'I'll go as soon as I've had a look in at Adam,' he said. 'Has he been okay?'

'He's been a dream. A good dream, that is. My mother introduced him to Meccano. I think you might have an engineer on your hands.'

'I don't think there's much he couldn't accomplish. Aren't you going to turn in?'

She nodded at the discarded pages of the judge's account where Hunter had left them on the little table before the fire. 'I'll be up as soon as I've bid for a sword on eBay,' she said.

Despite everything, Hunter laughed. He pulled her to her feet and hugged and then kissed her. 'No need,' he said. 'They gave me a sword when I retired from the regiment.' He looked thoughtful then.

'You really own a sword?'

'Probably my second most valuable possession,' he said. 'After an original Daniel Patrick watercolour someone was kind enough to send me.'

The magazine Hunter had bought in Edinburgh was also on the table, open at the picture of Mrs Mallory androgynous in men's evening wear, leaning on her piano and clutching her fistful of rose stems. Except that she wasn't really androgynous, was she? She was too vampy altogether to be convincing as a boy. Elizabeth cocked her head to look at the image upright. 'They must have removed the thorns. Otherwise they would have pierced her flesh, so tight is her grip on that bouquet.'

'They wouldn't have needed to bother,' Hunter said. 'I don't think she bleeds.'

She cuts, though, Elizabeth thought. If she doesn't, we haven't a hope. 'She's quite a piece of work, isn't she?'

'Oh, she's that.'

'I mean, she's extraordinary. She's so beautiful.'

'She is,' Hunter said, after a hesitation. The lie would have been absurd in the face of the graphic physical evidence. And in the hesitation, he had resolved never to lie to Elizabeth Bancroft, just as he had never lied to Lillian. And he found himself making this silent promise to himself for precisely the same reason as he had then. He kissed her goodnight, a long and tender kiss, and he went up the stairs to check on Adam and then take to his weary bed.

Adam woke early. It was not yet light. The lines of that infuriating poem would not stop going around and around in his head. It simpered in his mind. It had begun the day before, just after he had watched that strange piece of wood burn on the bonfire. Mrs Bancroft, who had told him to call her Margaret, had thrown it into the fiercest part of the blaze. She was old. She was so old he did not feel comfortable calling her anything other than what he had. Margaret just wasn't plausible. You did not call people that ancient by their Christian names. It didn't seem right. Her name provoked a dilemma. Should he be sent to stay with her he would be confronted by a selection dilemma over what name to use to address her by, which of course he would from time to time be obliged to do.

She hadn't seemed old throwing that weird carved board into the bonfire. She had hurled it so that the sparks spat and scattered with the impact. And he had watched it cartwheel and land and settle and take, and the creatures it depicted seem to try to flee as though the subjects of some creepy, ghoulish cartoon chase. But they had not been able to. He knew that before his view of the carving was obscured by the smoke it provoked. And when the smoke cleared there was just ash, red and white and making the air distort with heat ripple when you stared at it for too long.

At first, after the burning of Mrs Bancroft's board, he thought about that odd doodle Mr Cawdor had been so angry at him for drawing. He could hardly remember it. He had drawn it in a daydream and Mr Cawdor had confiscated it almost straight away. It had felt as if he hadn't really had a great deal to do with it, except for Mr Cawdor's irritation. He remembered its impossible shape after the burning of the board. He saw it as though it hung from a chain and was suspended in three dimensions in a room he knew. Then he knew with dread that it was Mrs Mallory's library he was in. And he knew from the familiar objects around him that the thing he most feared in the world sat on its throne behind him. But then that vision faded and the queasy geometric object with it. And he was stuck with this poem.

If I should die, think only this of me:
That there's some corner of a foreign field . . .

And without checking with the encyclopaedic mind of Mrs Davies or clever Alice Cranbourne, he knew that it was verse by the person Mrs Davies termed the English neo-Romantic poet Rupert Brooke. It was very odd, remembering something you were sure you had never learned in the first place. In certain circumstances, it was a knack that could make the whole experience of acquiring knowledge, and particularly of exams, quite painless. The trouble was, Adam did not think it exactly a happy knack. He had the suspicion it was anything but. It was of the same province as the dreams he had finally confessed to having remembered. It was in the same domain as the headless man he had seen walking outside in the snow and kept entirely to himself.

He had seen the headless man only periodically. And he had not been particularly frightened at the spectacle. It was nothing like so disconcerting as the execution of the tall bearded man he dreamed of sometimes, who would not die. The black-bearded man roared with defiance as the men killing him stabbed and shot him and finally forced his still-living head under the ice they broke on the frozen river to which they dragged him. His blood trailed over the ice, a gleaming smear left in the moonlight. And then the turbid, freezing water in the ice hole bubbled with the man's breath and fury and reluctance to die as he sank into its depths and the sluggish current took him. Adam hated that dream. It was a dream close to Mrs Mallory. It was a dream he had been obliged to live, in a sense. He had felt the knife and bullet wounds freeze with the stupor of the cold and stop hurting the man. He did not wish to live in the head of a murdered, murderous stranger in his dreams. But Mrs Mallory had obliged him to.

If I should die, think only this of me . . .

By comparison, the sight of the headless man was what a man he had dreamed of named Rodriguez would have called a walk in the park. He was nice, Rodriguez. He was scary at first because he had these gristly stubs where his hands should have been and he had this melancholy demeanour. But he was nice and he had said nice things in the dreams about Adam's dad. And he talked about fear and courage, and how some things were a trawl through the valley of death and some things were a walk in the park. The headless man was very much in the latter category. He could not hurt you. By contrast Mrs Mallory, Rodriguez cautioned gravely, was worse than a trawl through the valley of death. Mrs Mallory was Death itself.

He hauled himself out of bed. He looked out of the window. His window looked out upon the view from the back of the house, the slope on which they tobogganed, the slope at the top of which they had built his snowman. It was snowing again. His snowman had lost its features in the white blur of the fresh fall. There was no sign of the headless man. But the headless man was not some kind of sentinel. He came and he went and Adam had only ever seen him through the window. And he moved slowly. His progress was a blind trudge in the wrong sort of shoes through an unseen landscape. Maybe he had been gracious and agile once. His bearing and his clothes suggested that. But he was no longer so with his pitiful and gruesome handicap.

He dressed warmly in his thermal underwear and put his clothing over that, as his dad had drilled him in the current severe weather to do. And he brushed his teeth and descended the stairs. He wanted to wake Elizabeth. He wanted company and it didn't come much better in an adult than hers. But it was a Sunday. Some people liked a lie-in on a Sunday. She was a doctor and she worked very hard. He did not think it would be at all polite to wake her. He would have to be on his own for a while. Sometimes you had to be stoical. It was one of the words Rodriguez used in the dreams. Adam had needed to look that one up, a rare thing for him. And he did try to be stoical. But he wished his dad was back at home. His dad had said he would return after one night away and his dad always kept his promises. But with Brooke's overblown verses echoing through his head, he wished with all his heart his dad had not gone away again and left him.

Adam saw the picture in the open magazine on his drowsy path from the stairs through the sitting room to the kitchen and his date with a slice of Marmite toast and a glass of cloudy apple juice. Such was the shock of recognition, he dropped the Meccano construction he had toiled over the previous afternoon and evening and brought down with him for comfort and security. It hit the floor. No damage was done to it by the impact. Meccano was made of tensile steel and his construction robust, tethered by nuts and bolts. The thing he had so painstakingly built remained intact where it lay.

Mrs Mallory looked up at him in man's clothes from a room he recognised in black and white. Her tooth snagged and done something kind in the photograph to her mouth. Or, more accurately, it had done something to her smile. She looked amused and human in the photograph. In life, Adam knew she was never really either of these things. He wished with all his heart his dad was home. He progressed through to the kitchen. And through the window he saw that there was a figure standing in the snow. It was not the headless man. It was not the bearded giant who was killed in his dreams so stubbornly. It was not sad, stoical Rodriguez and it was not the flowery poet, Rupert Brooke. Of all people, it was his maths teacher, Mr Cawdor. Mr Cawdor smiled and waved to him through the window, through the white, descending snow crystals. And Adam was very happy and relieved to see him there. Mr Cawdor was an enemy of the lovely school library, which he considered a wasted resource. And on his worst days, he could grump for Scotland. But the picture of Mrs Mallory in the magazine on the sitting-room table had frightened Adam. And Mr Cawdor was a familiar figure from a world he trusted and understood.

Adam went and fetched his boots and pulled them on and opened the kitchen door and walked outside. There was no wind and, though it was early and snowing hard, it felt quite warm. He looked around for Mr Cawdor's crappy car. He wasn't supposed to say crappy, but there was no other word for the two-door automotive travesty Mr Cawdor drove. It looked like a Trabant. Mr Cawdor claimed it was a Fiat. Jeremy Clarkson would have taken it to a disused quarry and shot it with a bazooka. But there was no sign of Mr Cawdor's crappy car. Adam wondered, was he dreaming?

'You have to come with me, Adam,' Mr Cawdor said. He spoke very quietly, as though someone might overhear him. But there was no one around to do so. 'It's your father, you see. He's in trouble and he needs your help very urgently. He sent me.'

Adam hesitated. He had noticed Mr Cawdor was not really dressed for the weather. He was wearing the clothes he wore to teach in under a long thin overcoat. And the narrow lenses of his rectangular glasses had steamed up with the condensation from his breath. 'My dad said I'm never to go anywhere with strangers,' he said.

Mr Cawdor put his head to one side and smiled. 'Come, I'm hardly that, laddie,' he said. 'Your dad needs you.'

Adam looked back to the house and then at Mr Cawdor again. It was a dilemma, wasn't it? It was a genuine dilemma. He wasn't dreaming it. Should he waken Elizabeth? He was supposed to be respectful to teachers. 'I'm sorry,' he said. 'I'm not sure I believe you.'

Mr Cawdor nodded. 'You've every right to caution, Adam.' He put his hand into his overcoat pocket. 'I've no idea why, but your dad said to show you this.' His hand emerged holding a Red Bull can. The normally bright blue and silver livery was dull in the matt, sunless light. This reference to a private joke between them could only have come from his father. It was a confidential signal and he trusted it. 'Okay,' he said. He would help his dad. He would show courage and resourcefulness. He would make his father proud of him. 'Do I need to bring anything?'

'No,' Mr Cawdor said. 'And we need to leave immediately.'

He pocketed the drink can. He began to labour down the hill through the snow. Adam went after him as he'd been taught to do, in his footsteps.

Margaret Bancroft stared at the ashes of the bonfire they had lit. A whole night had passed and it was snowing but the earth still retained its heat and no snow would settle yet inside the circle of stones in which Adam Hunter had built their fierce wooden inferno. She looked at the ground. She studied it. A superstitious person might read some symbolism, some runic significance, into the pattern of ashes heaped and lying there. But she did not consider herself a superstitious person in the slightest. She smiled to herself and looked at her healed hand in the early light.

It looked the same. Her self-inflicted wound had left no scar. But it was better than before. The strength she had surprised Adam with in hurling that heavy carved obscenity into the flames had not been the only side effect of the healing done by her daughter. There was much more. For one thing, her arthritis had gone. She had never mentioned her arthritis to Elizabeth. What would have been the point? It was a consequence of old age. She had been lucky to live so long. It was a price paid for her general good fortune and, if it was sometimes uncomfortable and painful, then so what? She endured it without complaint, thinking it a minor inconvenience in the scheme of things. She had never mentioned it to Elizabeth. And now it had gone. It would return of course. Nature had been only temporarily reversed. In time she would retain of what her daughter had achieved for her only the deliberate magic of her healed hand. But that morning she had climbed out of bed without pain and stiffness in her ankles and wrists and fingers for what had felt like the first time she could remember.

The magic was very powerful in Elizabeth and she had

told her daughter truthfully that she had known this since Elizabeth had been a young child. But she had not told her how she knew. She had spared Elizabeth that. Elizabeth did not remember and that was a blessing. The things she had accomplished when she had not long been walking and talking had frightened and disturbed her mother. She thought it was comparable to one of those cases where an infant stumbles upon a powerful handgun in the home of one of those American families indulging their constitutional right to turn their house into a garrison. And the child starts waving this lethal weapon around and discovers the trigger. Except that it had been much scarier than that, hadn't it? And the potential for death and tragedy had been far greater.

Elizabeth had been three. Their nearest neighbours were a couple, Gavin and Lucy Jackson. The Jacksons were desperately upwardly mobile, Gavin a grammar school boy with a chip on his shoulder who worked for Martins Bank. His wife, Lucy, ran a children's clothes shop in the village. The Ladybird logo decorated its picture window in a bright display of colourful woollens. It was a charming shop. But there was nothing charming about Lucy Jackson. She was taciturn in her dealings with Margaret Bancroft to the point of rudeness. Neither of the Jacksons was neighbourly. The Bancrofts made overtures, but these were ignored. Margaret privately suspected that Lucy at least was jealous of her university education and professional status. She heard second-hand remarks about who wore the trousers in her house and these were attributed to the Jacksons. But she ignored them.

What the Bancrofts could not ignore, though, was the Jacksons' dog. They owned a large German Shepherd bitch called Sheba. Sheba was very territorial. And the Jacksons let Sheba roam rather than exercising the dog properly. She thought her territory extended far and wide. There were complaints from local sheep owners that Sheba worried their flocks. But unless they caught her in the act, they could do nothing. And Sheba was not the sort of dog it was safe to approach, much less hang on to over a mauled sheep carcass until the constable arrived. The only people she did not seem to intimidate were Gavin and Lucy. But though she never seemed to growl at or go for them, nor did she appear inclined to obey their commands.

She barked incessantly. In those days, a cart track led off the road proper to where the Bancrofts and the Jacksons lived, in homes built about a quarter of a mile apart. This track was lined by drystone walls. And Sheba sometimes guarded it. And when she did, it was just the sensible thing if you were on foot and a Bancroft to clamber over the wall and approach the house through the fields.

In those days, Margaret Bancroft drove a Morris Minor. Her job made a professional necessity of the car. But she suspected that Lucy Jackson was jealous of that, as well. Her husband used their car to commute to the town and the bank. She rode a moped and the sight of her in foul weather, buffeted along in her yellow oilskin and sou'wester astride this puny machine, was a grim one. But if she was jealous of Margaret's car, Sheba saw it as a goading challenge. Her furious barks would greet the vehicle until Margaret could safely pass the dog and accelerate away from her.

It happened one Sunday afternoon when the family were returning from a bike ride. Elizabeth sat on a saddle screwed to the crossbar of her father's bike and his arms sheltered her and made her stable. When they rode slowly she held on to the handlebars. When they rode fast she screwed her little fists into her father's sleeves and held tightly on to him. Her mother rode alongside on her own bike. And they were returning from their picnic on a bright afternoon and Sheba had been lying in wait. She must have been. They had heard no bark to warn them and would have braked and stopped a safe distance away if they had.

Her assault was furious. They were all three spilled into the road. But it was Margaret the dog targeted, tearing her calf with a deep and savage bite before her husband could drive her away with blows from the heavy brass buckle after removing his belt. John Bancroft was obliged to carry his wife the remaining distance home in his arms with their daughter following forlornly behind, their bikes in a tangle, the breeze blowing their spilled picnic detritus behind them all over the track.

Margaret cleaned the wound and gave herself a tetanus jab. She would be better by morning of course. But she would not carry out the healing on herself until after her daughter had gone to bed. Until then she would do what other less fortunate people were obliged to do and endure the pain of the wound and the inconvenience of not being able to walk. Her husband seethed. He was a mild-mannered man but did not trust himself to confront their neighbours until his anger had subsided. Elizabeth seemed unusually subdued. When her father went to retrieve their bikes, she asked could she go with him. He told her it wasn't safe, with the dog. And she said something that struck Margaret even then as curious. She said, don't worry about the dog, Daddy. The dog's been put away. It's been put away, for ever and ever in a far distant place.

Gavin Jackson hammered on their door at eight o'clock that evening and accused them of stealing his family's beloved pet and John Bancroft, a patient man pushed beyond what he could endure, floored him with a punch that caught him squarely on the chin. And after that, no member of either family ever spoke to their nearest neighbours again. Over the following days, Margaret noticed a real brightening in the mood and demeanour of her little girl. She skipped and sang to herself. She glowed.

Sheba was eventually found. Six weeks later, a man using a metal detector on the shingle beach at Buckhaven thought he'd struck lucky. But the thing buried four feet down was the badly decomposed carcass of a large dog. The metal identification disc on its collar had triggered the bleep heard through his headphones. Indignant about this time-wasting find, he reported it to the Perthshire police. Margaret heard that they questioned the dog's owners. She heard this from McCloud, a retired policeman like the son and later landlord of the Black Boar. Her daughter would come in time to know him as an even more accomplished gossip than his father.

She had told her father not to worry about the dog when they went to retrieve their bikes because Elizabeth had put it away. She had put it away cleanly and neatly four feet under a beach thirty miles from where they lived. She had achieved what she had with a thought. Fear had prevented Margaret from confronting her daughter about this feat. She had long acknowledged that. She knew she was a coward. She had been afraid of her daughter's powers. She had been even more afraid of the uses to which a grown-up Elizabeth would be inclined to put them.

The cancer which killed John Bancroft claimed him very quickly. It was not diagnosed late. Margaret might have been a coward, but she was a good doctor. The diagnosis was rapidly confirmed. But the disease was swift and ruthless. Elizabeth was four. There was no hospice within a practical distance and Margaret could not bear for the husband she had faithfully loved to die alone. He lay in the house, skeletal, his pain subdued by morphine, his life ebbing.

But he did not die. Weeks passed. He was fed through a drip. He was barely conscious, but he stayed alive. It made no sense because a disease as rapacious as the one afflicting him did not pause in its progress.

Margaret looked at her daughter. They were seated by the fire, Elizabeth on the floor, playing with the kitten Margaret had bought her, teasing it gently with a ball of crimson wool. And suddenly she knew.

'How long are you going to keep Daddy alive?'

'I don't know. I don't know, Mummy. If he dies I will miss him and you will cry.'

'He'll find peace, dead. His suffering will be over, Lizzie.'

Elizabeth raised her face to her mother. In the firelight, tears scalded her cheeks. 'It's only till I work out how to think him well. There's more of the disease than there is of him now. I don't know how to do it yet.'

'Let him die, Lizzie.'

Elizabeth sniffed and smeared her tears with the back of her hand. 'And bring him back, when the disease is dead, you mean? Is that the best way? I know how to think that, Mummy.'

It was shortly after this conversation that Margaret made the first subtle changes to her own physical appearance.

She stood in her garden and looked at the circle of stones the boy had filled with his industrious pyre. And she remembered the exultant gleam in her four-year-old daughter's eyes when she had suggested summoning John back from the grave. The truth was she had always loved Elizabeth. And she had always been afraid of her. Elizabeth had grown up good. She had forgotten the bone magic, had seemingly forgotten how to be bad. But it was very powerful in her and Margaret had prayed daily that she would never rediscover it and succumb to the seductive temptation of using it in the malevolent manner for which her own instinct told her it existed.

She felt the warmth of the heat rising from the stone circle and she winced. She had been afflicted by a sudden ache. It had been twenty years. She smiled, marvelling at her daughter's potency. It had been twenty years, but she did not have to be a doctor, only a woman. Margaret Bancroft knew a period pain when she felt one.

He'd been drowning his sorrows in the lounge bar of the Thistle in the village when the woman had approached his corner table. She had stood and appraised him for a moment and his first thought was that she could not be a police-woman because the expenses budget wouldn't run to the wardrobe she wore and the salary wouldn't get there either, whatever her rank. Andrew Cawdor mostly wore Paul Smith himself. Clothes and accessories were his indulgence and he knew them. And because he did, he knew she could not be a social worker either, for the same reason she wasn't with the Perthshire force. The suit under the black cashmere of her unbuttoned coat was a couture item, he was sure of it. Perhaps she was from the General Medical Council. Maybe she was a barrister. She looked too prosperous even for the higher echelons of the teaching profession. But he was certain her appearance here had something to do with the business over Adam Hunter. He stood. His chair legs scraped in their retreat on the boarded floor.

'Mr Cawdor?'

'Yes.'

She was prising off a pair of leather gloves. 'I'm Dr Lavinia Mallory,' she said. Her voice had a velvety coarseness. It was very seductive. All of her was. 'May I join you?'

'Of course you may.' They sat, simultaneously. 'Can I get you something to drink?'

'In a moment,' she said. She matched the fingers and thumbs of her gloves and smoothed out their wrinkles on the tabletop with the flat of her palm. 'Have you any idea why I'm here?'

Her eyes were grey, like crystal shot through with sea fog,

and they glittered when she spoke. He found it difficult to meet them. He found it a struggle to look at her. She was the most glamorous woman he had ever seen and he felt intimidated and even slightly overwhelmed by her. He did not reply. He shook his head and curled protective fingers around his pint glass.

She reached across the table and stroked the back of his hand with her fingertips. Her touch was soft and warm. 'I am here because Adam Hunter is in danger,' she said. 'I know you feel a duty of care towards your star pupil. His father is away. He is not a bad man, but he is misguided. He believes his son safe in the care of Elizabeth Bancroft. But she is corrupt and intent on corrupting the child. She has done a great deal of damage already. Without swift and decisive intervention, she will succeed in achieving her immoral and degenerate objective.'

'She's a witch, is what she is,' Cawdor said.

Opposite him, he saw Dr Mallory throw back her head and laugh out loud. Her neck was long and white and exquisitely framed by the glossy tresses of her hair.

'I assume you're a doctor of psychology.'

'Psychiatry,' she said. She took a pack of Gauloises from the breast pocket of her suit and turned it in her hand the way a cardsharp might a wrapped deck. 'Uncivilised,' she said.

'Elizabeth Bancroft?'

'The smoking ban,' she said. She smiled at him. 'You can help the child, which I know has been your unselfish motivation all along. You could play a vital role in saving him. In a sense, you have nothing to lose. Your career is damaged, probably irretrievably. But helping Adam could be more than consolation, Andrew. It could be your salvation.'

'I would not quarrel with a single word of what you've said, Doctor. But I do need to ask how you know so much about the circumstances.'

She seemed to ponder the question. Then she said, 'In absolute confidence?'

'I swear not to tell.'

'Elizabeth Bancroft is being monitored. I'm a member of the monitoring panel. We do not believe this is the first instance of its kind.'

'Jesus.'

'Indeed.'

Cawdor sipped beer. It was tepid from the grip of his hand and the warm taste of it made him wince. 'He's a very special boy, you know. He's destined for great things, for noble achievements.'

Mrs Mallory smiled again. 'He is unless he's stopped,' she said. She leaned forward. He found that he could look her in the eye now. He had never been remotely this close to a woman so beautiful. But they had a shared purpose, they were allies and if they were not quite equals, she nevertheless needed and had asked for his help. 'Buy me that drink, Andrew, and I'll tell you what it is I would like you to do for me in the morning,' she said.

Later, on the walk home, it occurred to him that he had not asked to see her professional credentials or even proof of her identity. He should have done, of course. His own professional caution should have prompted the request. But he wasn't a professional any more, was he? His professional life lay in ruins thanks to the Bancroft sorceress and her dark ability to influence the police into pursuing inquiries that were really none of their concern. Anyway, he did not doubt Dr Mallory was who she said she was. She knew too much about the circumstances of the case to be anything else. She knew too much about the character of Adam and the specifics of the relationship the boy enjoyed with his father. And her words had throughout possessed the authentic ring of truth.

He had taken the wrong approach with the Bancroft

woman. His efforts at intimidation had been crude and in-effective, largely the brainchild of that witless drunk Tom Lincoln. Tom blamed his drunkenness on an incident involving Margaret Bancroft that he'd witnessed when little more than a child himself. And Dr Mallory was mistaken. The Bancroft women were witches. But you could not blame a trained psychiatrist for her scepticism. And his own approach had involved too much beer and mischief and been too much influenced by an ancient grudge. Dr Mallory's forensic approach was a much cleaner and more effective way of getting Adam out of Elizabeth Bancroft's clutches. The only slightly weird bit about it was how exact her predic-tion was of when the boy would awaken the following morning. She gauged it to the minute and announced it with the flat emphasis of fact.

Oh, well. She was part of that monitoring panel and perhaps they monitored Adam Hunter's sleeping patterns. He was glad he was going to play such a crucial role in rescuing such a singular child. Dr Mallory was right, there was something redemptive about it. He slithered home along the packed, snowy pavements of the village, thinking about this. His car was laughed at by the more macho staff members at the school. He drank much more than was good for his liver. He lived in a modest home and the gossips at the Black Boar thought it was amusing to raise questions about his sexuality. But he was about to do something significant and worthwhile.

When it was done, he would think of some way to take his revenge on Elizabeth Bancroft. He owed it to his ancestry. Once he was sacked, he would have the leisure time to dream up something hurtful and foolproof. It was true what they said. Every cloud had a silver lining. He was off to try to get a good night's sleep in his little rented flat. Once upon a time the Cawdor name had been one of prosperity and standing in this part of Perthshire. But the family had been cursed and traduced by the Campbell sorceress as he was being now by her descendant. Lavinia Mallory had laughed at the notion of witches and would no doubt laugh at the idea of curses too. Analysis and rationality were the bywords of her discipline, and psychiatry provided her with a very decent livelihood if her wardrobe was anything to go by. Of course she would dismiss the notion of malignant magic. He knew better. He would help her, nevertheless.

Chapter Thirteen

Mark Hunter knew his son was missing when he saw Adam's Meccano construction lying abandoned on the sitting-room floor. Adam never neglected any novelty and the Meccano was certainly that. Hunter had never known him play with the stuff before. He picked it up too stunned in the moment to imagine doing otherwise. He carried it in the cradle of his hands back up the stairs. And he opened the door on an empty bed, still warm, in an empty room.

The grief in the roar that left his lungs woke Elizabeth like the prod of a tender wound. She rose and flung the covers back and ran out to the source of the sound. He turned to her. He had the complex thing Adam had built the day before held tightly to his chest. She was vaguely aware that she was naked. But she had the feeling that beyond the tears filming his eyes, Mark was seeing only Adam's absence from their visible world.

She needed to take charge. He was strong in other circumstances. He knew only one fear in his life, one loss. And it had happened now and he was unmanned by it. She walked across to him. She wrenched the childish object out of his grip. She slapped him hard across the face, again and again, until the glaze of shock left his features. She could not afterwards have counted the blows. She gripped a fistful of his hair and pulled at his head until his eyes met hers. Eventually they did so. And the pain in them was a torment to her and her heart was cleaved for him. But she had to be strong for both of them until he discovered again the will to act.

'You have a sword.'

'What? What are you talking about?'

'You own a sword. You were given it.'

'Yes.'

'Fetch it now and sharpen it, Mark. Hone the blade. Make it keen. We're going after her and we're going to save your precious son and she is going to die.'

The words had their effect. His posture was suddenly less abject and his focus clarified. He let out a shuddering breath and breathed in again normally. Strength and resolution returned to the set of his jaw. She did not think she had ever seen so much guilt and fear in a man's expression. He held Adam's duvet in bunches in his clenched fists. But he had regained a sort of composure.

'Did anything arrive for me yesterday?'

'A parcel did,' she said. 'I had to sign for it. There was some tax I had to pay on it too.'

'Good. I'll need that as well as the sword. We need to go now, right away. The snow is falling and covering any tracks.' He finally noticed her. She was shivering, it was cold in Adam's room. 'You'd better get dressed,' he said. He lost the focus again momentarily. He looked at the bits and bobs of Adam's life on the window sill, the books and toys and models there. The grief hitched and hovered, poised like some breaking tidal wave of emotion in his chest. But she knew that there wasn't time for this. There just wasn't. She untangled his hands from the bedding and hauled him with all the naked strength she possessed away from the empty room.

He sharpened the edge of the sword with a whetstone as they walked. She thought that in his greatcoat and boots, he looked like someone might on their way to Moscow in Bonaparte's misguided winter of invasion. The breath plumed out of him in the white and grey world and the metal glittered in his hands with malice as they followed a set of fading tracks through the downward-leading wilderness. The tracks petered out to nothing on a lane a mile and a half from the house. Hunter continued to look around. The sword was in his belt. He examined the ground with his eyes in the steadily falling snow, absently tearing tape and brown wrapping paper from the thing the FedEx truck had delivered the previous morning. Elizabeth could see no point in this examination of the terrain. There was nothing to look at, the snow blanketed the world and made it featureless.

'Are you learning anything?'

'The stride of the man who took my son puts his height at about five-ten. He doesn't weigh above eleven stone. He was wearing street shoes and they had leather soles. It was not one of her retinue.'

'It was definitely a man?'

Hunter nodded. The object he had been sent was revealed now in his hand. He looked at it and then put it and the litter that had wrapped it into separate coat pockets. 'His car was parked here. It was a small vehicle with a short narrow wheelbase and tyres ill suited to the ground. Know anyone who drives anything like that?'

'My mother does.'

'Your mother didn't take him.'

'You're sure it was a man?'

He smiled at her. It was an expression without mirth or very much hope. 'Mrs Mallory doesn't do treks through winter country. It's been a long time since she was an outdoor girl. And she doesn't have size nine feet. Adam followed those feet, stepped into their impressions as I'd taught him to, to save on the effort of pulling his feet free of snow still fresh and unpacked. There's a kind of intimacy about the practice, if you think about it. He went with someone he trusted.'

Elizabeth nodded. Of course he had. He would not have

gone otherwise, or there would have been a struggle, which would have alerted them. The trail went cold here. They would have been moving again, had it not.

'We should go back for the Land Rover,' Hunter said. 'Now we know which road they took, we need a vehicle.'

'We don't have a clue as to which way to go.'

Hunter pointed south along the road. 'They went that way. If we knew who he'd gone with, we'd have some clue as to their destination.'

Elizabeth did not think this necessarily followed. She did not wish to erode any hope he held. But if this was Mrs Mallory's work, and it was, the abductor would be following her instructions rather than acting according to habit or character. 'Should we call the police?'

'Of course we should. We'll do it the minute we get back to the house.'

The climb back was hard. The hill was steep and the snow heavy. Elizabeth had never known a fall like it in November. She expected that the coming winter would be long and severe. For Mark Hunter, she feared it might become unbearably cold and desolate. But the arduous test of the climb back to the house was at least a good thing. It would dissipate Hunter's physical energy. Whether he knew it or not, he needed that. And she did too. The only way of enduring a crisis like this was incrementally, measuring what you did moment by moment, avoiding speculation and fighting the onset of panic and despair with calm deliberation. It was her ordeal as well as his, she thought, as she climbed in Hunter's wake, in his steadily ascending footsteps. She did not need the tears pricking her eyes to tell her that. As she had come to love the father, so she had come to love the son. Adam was remarkably gifted, as his sad and obnoxious maths teacher had pointed out. But he was also sweet-natured and funny and astonishingly brave.

'Mark?'

He stopped and turned. She stood up to her knees in snow on the steep incline, her breath panted out in plumes of frozen air, her eyes an intense green against the white landscape, staring out at him from the scarf wrapping her face against the cold. 'I think I know who took him. I think it was Andrew Cawdor.'

They increased the pace of their climb. Hunter started to rush. Elizabeth could keep up, just. She had been born here. If Cawdor had taken Adam there was hope. However misguidedly, he had his best interests at heart. They would be on their way to a ferry terminal somewhere. The possibilities were pretty varied. They could be on their way to Germany or Holland or somewhere in Scandinavia. They could be headed to Ireland or the Isle of Man. But their progress on the initial section of their journey, by road, would be slow in such hazardous conditions. And whatever tale Adam had been spun to part him from his father could not be sustained once a port came into sight. He could not be abducted unwillingly. He was too big and strong to be easily subdued by Cawdor and far too conspicuous.

The phone was ringing when they got back to the house. It was Sergeant Kilbride and his tone was sombre when he asked Hunter could he please speak to Dr Bancroft.

'We have found a body,' he said.

Her eyes were on the dead hearth, the unlit fire, its cold ashes flat against the grate. She closed them. It could not be Adam. Kilbride would have broken the news face to face to his father. There would have been a patrol car outside the house. He would have been told in person, that was the protocol and it never altered. 'Go on.'

'It's Andrew Cawdor,' Kilbride said. 'We're still awaiting formal identification. Mrs Blyth has agreed to come from her weekend place in Buckhaven for that. She hasn't arrived yet. But it's him.'

'Where did you find him?'

'The driver of a gritting lorry saw his car in a drift on the Fort William road and thought to do the Good Samaritan routine. Poor man got the shock of his life.'

'Was Cawdor alone?'

'Aye, he was very alone and very dead.'

'Was there any sign of anyone having left the scene on foot?'

Kilbride let out a sigh. 'There was no sign of anything like that. There were no footprints and there was no physical sign of a disturbance of any sort. And some very experienced men attended the scene. It was bizarre, but it wasn't murder, Elizabeth. It was suicide.'

'Carbon monoxide?'

'No. He didn't gas himself. I misjudged the man. When we met him, I thought he had quite a lot of self-regard. His choice of clothes and general demeanour with us certainly suggested as much. But he must have loathed himself.'

'How did he choose to die?'

'He bled to death,' Kilbride said. 'He bit out his own wrists and bled to death.'

She put Hunter on to Kilbride to report Adam's abduction. Kilbride accepted that it was a case of kidnapping without any reservation. Like any good copper he knew the territory and the people on it and he was fully aware of the colonel's background and capabilities. He listened without comment to Hunter's account of what they had found that morning and then said, 'The car is still at the scene. I'll have a dog tracker team go back there. The dogs are good over snow, the spoor strong, as you probably know, Sir.'

'Yes,' Hunter said. He knew the policeman was a friend

of Elizabeth's and knew the man was trying to keep the pessimism out of his voice. But he wasn't really succeeding. The signs were ominous and he was too experienced an officer not to see them.

'We'll need something carrying Adam's scent. Probably easier if we get that from the school.'

'It's Sunday, Sergeant.'

'And this is a small community, Sir. We can get keys from the caretaker or there'll be a set at the fire station in the village. Is there anything there?'

Hunter coughed to clear his throat and fought to restrain himself. 'His PE kit,' he said. 'It's in a bag in his locker.'

When the conversation was concluded, Hunter had to go outside for a few minutes. He went out of the kitchen door. He felt properly grateful for the way Elizabeth had brought him back to himself after the discovery that morning, but he needed a moment now. His heart was heavy and his conscience burdened him with a weight he could not carry. He could not escape the conviction that he had condemned his son. His blundering at Magdalena and his arrogant dismissal of the curse in the years that followed had finally robbed his son of his chance at life. It was his fault. He was entirely to blame. Adam's face, under its halo of curls, painted itself on his mind and he sank to his knees and wept as he had not wept even at the graveside on the awful day when his wife and daughter were buried together. He had needed to be strong then. He had needed to be strong for Adam. Now Adam had gone, and with him had gone the source of his strength.

Elizabeth watched Hunter through Adam's bedroom window. She wanted to go to him, but there was no consolation she could offer. Despair would hit and sometimes engulf him in waves. In these awful circumstances, that was inevitable. But he was a strong man with a formidable will and, until confronted with the proof that hope was futile, he would just have to endure periods like this. Whatever he was feeling now and however bad the eventual outcome, he would not give up until he found his son.

She looked around the room. She had come up here not out of any morbid desire to surround herself with Adam's keepsakes, but because her intuition insisted there was some clue, some key she had missed that was important in the resolution of all this. She looked at his posters and his painted Airfix kits and PSP player, at the spare Duracells and the Hot Wheels cars and the boot-sale dice in their leather cup and the general clutter on his shelves. She looked at the spines of his Eye Witness books about Brunel and the *Titanic* and Ancient Rome and the Apollo moon landings. There was something here. She was sure there was. But wherever the clue lay, she had not discovered it yet.

She looked down out of the window. She was relieved to see that Hunter was back on his feet, wearily dusting the snow from his knees, wiping his eyes. She would go out to him now.

'Adam is alive, Mark.'

He smiled at her. She thought the effort terrible. 'Why do you think that? You're familiar with her curse concerning my son. Why would you imagine there are grounds for hope?'

'I'm not blinded by sentiment. I think he's alive only because Adam is the bait. She promised she and I would meet. Why would I risk going otherwise? And she wants revenge on you for the slight of Magdalena. She wants to lure you to her too.'

'Isn't the curse revenge enough?'

'No. Not for her, it isn't.'

'What do you propose we do?'

'We do the hardest thing of all, for a man like you. We wait. We wait for her call. And, believe me, she will call.'

He thought she was scarier in the flesh than in his dreams of her. In his dreams he had only overheard her and seen her from a distance. In the flesh, she was three-dimensional and he could smell her scent. There was the brown stain between two of her fingers. There was the hard glitter of the stones set in her rings and on the necklace around her throat. There was the audible clack of her high heels on the stone of the floor whenever she got up and moved. There was the sculpted thickness of her crimson lipstick. They were sharing a small room and she kept staring at him in a way that made him feel uncomfortable at first and then really frightened.

Adam had never been bullied. He knew this was only the case because he was smart. He knew about Tall Poppy Syndrome, having been the tall poppy all his school life. So when he sensed confrontation, he was always several moves ahead of the biggest, most violent boys. It was a bit like chess. You could outmanoeuvre them. You could confuse their intentions before their intentions were properly resolved in what passed for their minds. You could, through suggestion and diversionary ploys, deflect them and nullify the threat.

One of the first signs that prompted this strategy in Adam was the gleam of spite in a would-be bully's eyes. There was something wild and uncontrolled about it and it always signalled impending violence. When Adam saw it in the school playground, he always knew what to do. Mrs Mallory's eyes had that look. They had it all the time. And they possessed it with an intensity he had never encountered before. There was a word, wasn't there? He would have it in a minute. The word was feral. Mrs Mallory had an expensive haircut and a sophisticated bone structure a bit like a prima ballerina or a catwalk model and she wore a lot of jewellery. But her grey eyes had a feral look when she focused on him. And, even scarier, he had noticed that she did not blink.

'What's going through that bright little brain of yours?'

'I was just wondering when I will get to see my dad again.'

She laughed. 'Liar,' she said. Then, 'Don't worry, Adam. You'll see him soon enough.'

It was very smoky in the room they were in. Mrs Mallory smoked a lot. His dad had a friend from the regiment called James Preston and Adam had met him a few times and hadn't thought it humanly possible to smoke more than James Preston had. But Mrs Mallory did. She smelled strongly of tobacco and some rich perfume and what he thought was the fur collar of her coat. It was real fur and still bore features of the animal that had provided it. It was as though the animal itself lay stretched across her shoulders.

'Sable, Adam,' she said.

He had heard of mink. In the old days people had worn mink and beaver and fox. He had not heard of an animal called a sable. But that was another thing. She seemed able to see into his mind as plainly as he might open a book and read the words printed on the pages there.

'Did you kill it yourself?'

'What?'

'I mean the sable.'

She smiled. It was not the human smile of the snagged tooth that had made her look lovely in the photograph he had seen that morning in the magazine. It was her real smile and, though it was beautiful, it was as cold and deadly as a steel trap. 'You wouldn't be making fun of me, would you?'

Adam swallowed. 'No, I'm not, not at all.'

'Good. Doing so would be most unwise.'

'I wouldn't dream of it.'

'I didn't kill the sable. I coveted it. I killed the cavalryman who owned and wore it first, because I wanted it for myself.'

'Is it very old?'

'You've no idea.'

But he thought he had.

Her car was only slightly less frightening than she was. It had been waiting at the side of the road. Mr Cawdor had pulled up gingerly in the falling snow and Adam had seen the looming shape of this monstrous limousine and known he was betrayed and trapped. The car had black and glossy curves and looked like some great, crouching insect amid the white drifts. He had no choice but to go where they wanted him to. He looked at Mr Cawdor's expression in the cabin mirror of Mr Cawdor's crappy runabout and knew that.

'Get out, Adam.'

Mr Cawdor knew at some level that he had made a terrible miscalculation. Adam could see it in the turmoil on his face. But the petulant set of his mouth told him he would never admit it even to himself and that therefore pleading with him would be hopeless. Nor could he bolt for it. The car door was unlocked. But they were miles from anywhere. He had learned a lot about survival from his dad and he knew that without fuel and food and, crucially, some means of navigation and communication, these conditions could not be survived for very long. He had his mobile phone. His dad made him promise always to carry it. But he had run out of credit and could not remember the last time he had used the charger so the batteries were out. He wouldn't have bet on getting a signal out here anyway. It was useless. Mr Cawdor reached across him and opened the door. Adam got out and slammed it behind him without saying goodbye.

He got into Mrs Mallory's car and slid along the back

seat. The leather was cold against his legs, even through his weatherproof trousers. She had no heater or, if she did, she had not bothered to switch it on. He could see her breath wisp and curl on the air of the gloomy interior when she twisted round and said, 'It's a pleasure finally to meet you, Adam.'

'Likewise,' he said, reflexively, drilled by his dad to respond politely whenever people were polite to him.

'No,' she said, releasing the clutch and easing them away, 'I think you'll find the pleasure is all mine.'

She braked. She put the car into neutral. 'There's one more thing I need to get Mr Cawdor to do,' she said. 'Excuse me for a moment.' She got out and Adam watched her walk away. She was dressed with no concessions to the weather. She should have sunk to the calf at least into the snow. She was wearing high-heeled shoes. But she seemed able to step across the crust. She tapped Mr Cawdor's window and he rolled it down. Whatever she said was said very briefly. She walked back and got in, smiling to herself. There was a squeal and then a crump as the tyres rolled and the limousine moved forward.

'Snow chains,' Mrs Mallory said.

In the small room they were now in, Adam said, 'Where are we?'

'Where do you think you are?'

'I think I'm in some corner of a foreign field,' he said. His voice sounded very young and forlorn.

'You really are every bit as bright as everyone thinks you are,' she said, smiling at him.

At the house, Mark Hunter took his sharpened sword and put it back in the scabbard. The sword they had given him at Hereford was a sabre. It bore the royal warrant, stamped into the blade where it met the hilt. Hundreds of years of tradition and craft had gone into its manufacture. The steel had the pure integrity of the finest it was possible to forge. He had fenced at Sandhurst. He had won a cup. The épée, rather than the sabre, had been his weapon of choice in competition. He had never thought to wield a sword in anger. He smiled to himself.

'Do you think she will have her retinue with her?'

'No,' he said. 'I don't. She's used Adam as a sort of conduit. In his orbit, she's always known what's going on. She had me followed in Switzerland because it was the way to keep track of me when I was out of Adam's orbit, and because she was cautious about Miss Hall. I think part of her feared and maybe even respected Miss Hall. But Miss Hall is dead now and she has no fear of us.'

'What made you smile just now?'

'Oh, I was reminiscing just then about Adam. When he was three I bought him a plastic suit of armour with a sword and shield. I strapped him into his breastplate and he put on his helmet and marched with me to the park. I carried the rest of the stuff because he wanted his hands free to play. When we got to the bottom of the climbing frame a boy a bit older than him at the top looked down at him and sang, *I'm the king of the castle, you're the dirty rascal.* And Adam reached his arm back to me and in his best Arthurian voice said, "Dad, my sword."' He paused. 'There are so many happy memories, Elizabeth.'

'And many more to add to them,' she said. But she did not really believe it.

The phone rang. Hunter picked it up. He listened. Without speaking, after less than a minute, he put it down.

'That was her,' Elizabeth said.

He nodded. 'She's at your cottage. She wants us both to go. We're to arrive just after dusk. She says that if we try to alert anyone else or attempt to bring anyone else along, she will act accordingly. She says that Adam is alive, and I believe her. I know I seemed to be despairing of that hope outside, earlier. But I think I would know if my son was dead.'

'Do you have a plan?' They were in the Land Rover. The snow was still falling and even the four-wheel drive struggled on the big, slippery banks and odd ice patches on the treacherous descent of the hill.

'I'll tell you something about plans,' Hunter said, his eyes intent on the cloaked landscape in his headlight beams. 'They are always formulated for situations that have changed by the time you try to put them into practice. It's a truism of military life. You know my old regimental motto?'

'Who dares wins.'

'It sounds like a barroom boast, I know. It's the sort of bluster a braggart might come out with. But it's very largely true. Nerve and momentum usually carry the day.'

He was much better now, with the promise of impending action. The odds did not matter to him. It was black and white, very simple. He would save his son or die. She said, 'Was that just a long-winded way of telling me you don't have any plan at all?'

'Pretty much.'

In her pocket, in their leather cup, Elizabeth rattled the dice she had taken from the shelf in Adam's room just prior to their departure. 'Do you remember, Mark, Miss Hall telling you once that Mrs Mallory was nothing if not a woman of her word?'

'She isn't a woman at all.'

'But you do remember?'

'Yes. She said the same thing to you herself when she predicted the two of you would meet.'

'I think it's meant literally,' Elizabeth said. 'You spoke once about the dismal creatures with which she's consorted in her life, the bargains she's struck in confounding nature for so long. What if she really is nothing if she doesn't honour her word? What if honouring her word is a precondition of her existence?'

Hunter did not answer. He did not really believe all that greatly in plans. But Elizabeth thought that a plan of sorts was forming in her own mind. It was not so much a plan, she knew, as a ploy. She would resort to it only if things became so desperate that she had to.

They were there. Hunter switched off the ignition. He turned to Elizabeth. 'I might be better doing this alone,' he said. 'I've seen up close what she can accomplish. She is powerful and her cruelty is monstrous.'

'She said I was to come.'

'I'm going to go in there and do everything I can to kill her,' he said. 'This is not about etiquette. If we follow her protocol, we're finished.'

Elizabeth opened her door and jumped down to the snow. 'She's in my fucking home,' she said. 'She's sitting on my fucking furniture with your abducted son. What the hell are you waiting for?'

Mrs Mallory was lounging on the sofa in Elizabeth's sitting room with Adam's sleeping head in her lap. She teased the tresses of his hair between long, lacquered nails. There were no lights lit. But the snow outside bathed the cottage interior in a pale luminescence. She looked up as they appeared on the threshold. 'Colonel Hunter,' she said. 'It's been ages. And you've brought the Bancroft spinster too.'

Hunter did not break stride. He hauled his son by a fistful of his jacket on to the floor and took out the taser Jimmy Preston had obtained for him. He jerked the woman to her feet, tearing open the clothing that covered her chest, and shoved the taser into her bared sternum knowing it would put sufficient volts through Mrs Mallory's convulsing body to disable her. The weapon had only two settings. They were stun and kill, and Hunter had chosen the latter. He squeezed the trigger with a grunt. And nothing happened. A slight odour of singed flesh ghosted through the chilly room. The taser crackled, impotently. Mrs Mallory began to laugh. 'Manners, Colonel,' she scolded. The taser was in his left hand. His right had gone to the hilt of the sabre on his belt, behind his back. He had assumed, in his lack of a more subtle idea, that he would use it. She looked at him. And he made the mistake of returning that look.

'Kneel,' she said. And he found he was compelled to do so. He knelt over the sleeping body of his son on the rug and groaned. But he could not look at Adam. His eyes were held rapt by those of the sorceress. 'Take a seat, Dr Bancroft,' she said.

'You're not human,' Elizabeth said.

'That's a value judgement. Sit down.'

Elizabeth slumped into the chair next to her own unlit fire. She saw Hunter drop the taser on the rug next to where he knelt. 'You're supposed to be vulnerable to electricity.'

Mrs Mallory sat back down herself. She adjusted her torn dress to cover her bare chest. She lit a cigarette. But her eyes stayed locked on Hunter's. 'I sometimes speculate on how many hours poor, fat, talentless, self-taught Rachel Hall spent toiling over her spell books to inflict that particular vulnerability. I'd have to concede she did the work craftily and well. It surprised me. And it almost succeeded. But it did not. And after Magdalena I had to take the necessary steps to eradicate the weakness she had imposed upon me. You do not live as long as I have by being idle.'

'And you have your tilt to put upon the world,' Elizabeth said, 'like you did before, in 1933.'

Mrs Mallory smiled. But her eyes stayed locked on Hunter's. 'Only about ten good years,' she said, 'the blink of an eye. This time it will last much longer. Not that you will live to experience it.'

'Brooke puzzles me,' Elizabeth said. 'I would have thought Yeats much more your thing.'

'Slouching towards Bethlehem? You think in clichés, Doctor. Brooke was cute. Berlin was pretty. I was bored. And your efforts to divert me are pathetic.'

'Do you really intend to kill the boy?'

'No. I intend to have his father do that. And I require that you watch.'

Adam slept. The sleep was not free of dreams. But it was free of Mrs Mallory's dreams. He felt restful and secure. He did not mind dreaming. He honestly preferred it when the dreams were his own and this one was not, was it, entirely? But at least it was not a dream imposed upon him by the witch. There was kindness and warmth in this imagined land-scape. There was urgency, but it was a calm and deliberate sort of urgency. The orchestrator of his dream was patient and good. He did not trouble himself in his slumber with their identity. He took what rest and refuge he could simply in being asleep.

Elizabeth watched, unable not to, as the point of Hunter's sword scraped at the stone flags of her cottage floor and he brought it out of his belt and raised it high. It descended slowly. Adam's head and chest were visible to her to Hunter's left, the rest of him concealed by his father's kneeling shape. Mrs Mallory stared and smoked. The sword touched Adam's throat. Beads of blood gathered on the keen blade at the point of contact.

'Cut,' Mrs Mallory said.

Elizabeth heard Hunter groan. She heard the tendons strain and crack in his arm and shoulder with the force of his will and defiance. He was far stronger than Cawdor. Perhaps he was stronger than Rodriguez too. Certainly he was, she realised. She heard muscle tear and something snap that sounded like his wrist and then a loud crack as his shoulder blade broke with the stubbornness of him and he cried out in raw agony.

'Transfer the sword to your other hand,' Mrs Mallory said. Her cigarette was smoked almost down to the touch of her skin. Her voice was growing impatient. The sword skittered between Hunter's trembling fingers on the rug. He clenched its hilt in his left hand. His body was convulsing with resistance and his right arm hung as hopelessly as Elizabeth considered their cause to be by his side. She slipped the cup and its cargo of ivory dice from her pocket and spilled the dice on to the floor in front of the cold hearth where they chinked and shivered and stopped still. Mrs Mallory glanced towards the sound and her eyes switched back to Hunter. 'Rest,' she said. Hunter turned the hilt of the sword in his hand so that the flat of the blade lay on Adam's throat. He shivered and groaned.

Mrs Mallory flicked her cigarette stub into the fireplace. She looked at the dice. Elizabeth thought that her pupils had grown larger in the snowy light. She was someone who liked to gamble. There had been a card table at the centre of the canvas cathedral. Adam had dreamed of her windowless games room at the house in Cleaver Square. 'What's this?' she said. 'Surely you would not wish to play against me?'

'The curse on the boy,' Elizabeth said. 'It's entirely of your making?'

'What concern is that of yours?'

'You serve someone. Or you serve something, don't you, Mrs Mallory?'

'Whether I do or not, the curse you speak of was inflicted entirely for my own entertainment.'

Elizabeth thought there was a bit more to it than

entertainment but did not want to labour the point. 'So you can lift it without repercussion?'

'You are beginning to irritate me,' Mrs Mallory said. 'You can die well or you can die very badly indeed, Doctor. Irritating me is most unwise.'

'Three throws of the dice,' Elizabeth said, nodding at the two pale cubes of ivory on the stone of her cottage floor. 'We play the best of three. If the total scored on the face of the dice is six or below, I win the throw. A score from seven to twelve and you win.'

Mrs Mallory chuckled, her eyes on the ivory cubes. She lit a fresh cigarette. 'I win nothing I don't already have,' she said.

'But can you resist?' Elizabeth raised her arms, widening them at the cottage interior. They felt stiff and the gesture forced. Her stomach was cramped with fear. He voice sounded like that of a stranger to her own ears. 'This is a dull evening in a drab little location. Surely a momentary diversion would be welcome?'

Mrs Mallory smiled. The smile broadened into a grin. Her teeth were very white against lips that looked almost black in the moonlight reflecting off the snow through the cottage windows. 'What if I lose? You want me to lift the curse on the boy? You expect mercy from me?'

'I expect more than that,' Elizabeth said. 'If you lose I want your word you will go into exile.'

Mrs Mallory laughed again. But she was still staring at the ivory cubes on the floor.

'At the location of my choosing,' Elizabeth said. 'For the length of time I dictate.'

'You are close to your mother, are you not?'

'Yes.'

'If I win, her life is forfeit.'

'Done.'

'Do you wish to know the manner of her death?'

'No.'

'I have decided she will burn. Start grieving for her now. You have not much time left to you.'

'You have not yet won.'

Mrs Mallory was silent. The only audible sound in the room was Hunter's ponderous breathing. He was spellbound. She did not need to maintain eye contact with him to keep him so, as she had at Magdalena. She was stronger than she had been then, enfeebled by Miss Hall's craft and cunning. Elizabeth wondered how strong she was now. She thought that Hunter was probably in shock too, the refuge enforced by his brain from the pain inflicted on his body. A refuge too from thinking about the obscene crime he was in the middle of being compelled to commit.

Adam dreamed. And someone familiar appeared in the dream. He was in a house with a ticking clock and a polished sideboard and there were butter-smelling crumpets in front of him and Mrs Bancroft handed him a mug of hot chocolate but he did not know if he would be able to drink it because his throat stung, and then she smiled and leaned forward and whispered to him and said, 'Don't worry, Adam, you will never be obliged to call me by my first name. You are right and I am far too old for that.'

Mrs Mallory uncoiled out of her chair and shook off her coat, shrugging the sable wrap from her shoulders. She dropped and scooped the dice into the leather cup and, on her haunches on the flags before the fireplace, she rattled it. Her hair was loose and it shook blackly in the snowy paleness against the line of her jaw and tumbled glossily down her shoulders and back. Elizabeth saw that her torn clothing had repaired itself. She slid from her own chair and kneeled beside her, close enough to smell her scent, urgent with sex, sweet with the heavy perfume worn over it. Her dress was tight and satiny against the length of her thighs and her taut belly and the blossoming push of her breasts. She was a powerful and immensely seductive presence this close to, and the effect on Elizabeth was defeating as she listened to the hollow rattle of the cup, thinking that she could not possibly succeed against such an adversary.

'You take the first throw,' Mrs Mallory said.

Elizabeth took the cup. Their fingers brushed. She had expected her opponent's touch to be cold. But just now, it seemed there was much more fire in her than ice. She rattled the dice.

'They are old,' Mrs Mallory said. 'But I sense that you are new to this. Some players think it lucky to blow on the dice.'

'You?'

'I've no great faith in luck.'

'You were very lucky at Magdalena.'

'That was fate.'

'Then why play, if you don't believe in luck?'

'Chance and luck are not the same.'

Elizabeth threw. The dice bounced and settled. Face up, they showed two sixes. There could have been no more emphatic result in her opponent's favour. But Elizabeth sensed that the cast dice had settled free of interference. She had lost the throw fairly. On the other side of the room, Hunter was shivering over his sleeping son, the flat steel of the sword blade matt in the ghostly light cast by the snow under a cruel November moon outside.

Mrs Mallory plucked the cup from her hand and scooped the dice into it. She smiled at Elizabeth with a glittery narrowing of eyes and the dice were flung with a snap of her wrist on to the floor. They danced and jittered, as though their facets flirted with destiny. Then they stopped. And Elizabeth saw that a two and a four were studded on their face sides in black against the white.

'Down to the final throw,' Mrs Mallory said, then louder, 'Not long now, Colonel Hunter. I'll be back to attend to you and Adam presently.' She gathered the dice and handed Elizabeth the cup containing them. Elizabeth saw that the grey eyes had widened. Her opponent was appraising her.

'Will you try to determine the outcome?'

'Of course.'

'Then what is the point of playing? If the result is predetermined, chance cannot prevail. It does not exist.'

'I used to look like you do,' Mrs Mallory said. 'I rather enjoyed the way I looked then. I was pretty, as you are, shared those feline features all of us who share the gift enjoy. But it seemed pragmatic to change, over time. And I have turned out rather well, I think.' She nodded at the leather cup in Elizabeth's fingers. 'I will try to determine the outcome. And so will you. That is the point of playing. It amuses me to gamble. And I have not gambled, really, since my win at Magdalena. Are you ready, Miss Bancroft?'

Elizabeth rattled the cup and blew on the dice.

'That's the spirit,' Mrs Mallory said. She laughed.

Elizabeth threw.

And the ivory cubes tumbled downwards as though weightless on a slow-motion descent to the cold, chisel-scarred flags of her cottage floor. The sound was like slow motion too as they collided with the floor and then rebounded and bounced again with smudged, dissonant clacks, mocking time and gravity. One of them settled and Elizabeth's heart thudded with dread in her chest as she saw that it showed a five. She heard a peal of laughter, the sharpness of it blunted by the thickening air that seemed to suspend the second dice a few inches above the flags. It was hard to breathe. And the shape of the unsettled dice seemed unsettled itself, subtly corrupt, its simple geometry deformed and palely repulsive, so that looking at it she winced and felt vomit sour at the back of her throat.

Elizabeth closed her eyes. She hoped that Mrs Mallory had spent too much of herself. A great deal of her must have been lavished just on sustaining the affront to nature her long life represented. But it was Mark Hunter's resistance that might have depleted her now. She had surely not expected the obdurate stubbornness of his love for his precious son. It must have cost her something. By contrast, she herself was young and entirely unspent. She was inexperienced at this, a novice only, but her mother had said she was strong. She summoned the strength that lay in her, almost untapped and, she saw now with a blossoming sense of wonder, quite immense.

'No,' she heard her opponent say.

'I think you might have underestimated me.'

'No,' Mrs Mallory said. Age withered through her voice like a reedy sigh. 'You can't!'

'I can,' Elizabeth said. 'And I have.'

She opened her eyes. The second dice lay, innocently shaped again, a few inches from the first. As she had willed it to, it had fallen showing the one. She had won. Mrs Mallory stood next to where she knelt. She had put on her coat and her sable wrap. She was nothing, if not a woman of her word. She was ready for departure, dressed for exile. And she would need the comfort of the fur across her shoulders. Where she was going, it was very cold indeed. Elizabeth got off her knees. She had no need to play the supplicant in victory.

'Where do you insist I go?'

Elizabeth told her.

'For what length of time do you insist I stay?'

Elizabeth told her.

Mrs Mallory smiled. She was pulling on a pair of leather gloves. 'A merciless exile,' she said.

'You are a creature with no right to speak of mercy.'

Without a glance at Mark Hunter or his son, Mrs Mallory strode towards the cottage door. It closed on her with a cold soughing of breeze through falling snow. Elizabeth had for a moment to hold on to the back of her chair. She felt giddy with her gift, almost exultant in the thrill of her victory. Mrs Mallory had been right. Only one of them had enjoyed their encounter. In the end, and to her own astonishment, Elizabeth had enjoyed it very much. She would heal Hunter now. He was suffering greatly and it would only take a moment.

'Don't,' he said. His voice was thick and sludgy with shock and pain. He had a tender hand on Adam's throat. But the wound there was superficial, little more than a break in the skin. She would mend that in a moment too.

'I could hear your game. I was praying for you. She's gone?'

'She's gone.'

'You beat her.'

'And now I will make you better.'

'There'll be no more magic,' Hunter said.

'What?'

'No more magic. Ever.'

'Then how will you heal?'

He laughed. 'Laboriously. That's my penance for Magdalena, for what I did, for what I've put Adam through.' He looked up at her. 'There can be no more magic. Not if we're to be together, Elizabeth. I very much want us to be together. But the magic has to cease here. It has to stop now. Do you understand why?'

She did understand. Of course she did. Her mother's

caution lived with and within her too. But she also believed there was magic in the world beyond the scope of sorcery. She knelt and smiled and gently held the wounded man she loved.

Epilogue

It was a warm evening in late July and Elizabeth could feel the heat of the pebbles under their picnic blanket as she watched Mark and Adam skim stones at the edge of the sea. The sea was tranquil and the sun was descending and Mark's arm was strong and true and moved smoothly in the execution of the hard, flat throw he used.

The remedial work had been done in Edinburgh. Most of the procedures had been carried out by two eminent surgeons of her mother's acquaintance. Mark was naturally strong and had healed quickly and his high pain threshold had helped with the recovery because he had never shirked what the physiotherapist had asked him to undergo. He pushed and pushed himself and she was looking now at the result. And if her mother thought it an unnecessarily complicated way of returning him to health, she did not say so. In fact, Elizabeth suspected she was relieved and approving. The time for confounding nature, in both of their lives, was gone.

The sun had set by the time they stopped their game and Adam walked back to where they had earlier had their beach barbecue. His father stayed at the water's edge, at the brink of the vast Atlantic, as gentle as a pond under the summer night. Adam sat down on the blanket next to her.

'What do you think he's thinking about?'

'Oh, you know Dad. He'll be reminiscing about jumping out of an aeroplane with a big gun. He's a sentimental man.

He gets nostalgic about wasting enemies of the Crown on secret missions.'

Elizabeth laughed.

'He's probably thinking about a name for the baby.'

'We don't yet know if it's going to be a boy or a girl.'

'So he's got plenty of names to choose from.' Adam laughed himself. 'He'll likely be there all night.'

'He'll need to watch out for the tide if he is.'

'I'll bet he goes for Eve. If it's a girl, I mean.'

'Don't worry. I'll threaten to divorce him if he suggests that.'

Adam was quiet for a moment. Elizabeth knew what was coming next. He had never referred to it before, but she felt certain he was going to do so now. He looked up at the ascending moon, out at the glittering sea beyond the distant silhouette of his father.

'Do you think she will ever come back?'

Elizabeth shivered. Warmth radiated through the blanket under her. It was a balmy evening, but she shivered just the same. 'They do say never say never, Adam. But I think it extremely unlikely.'

'Good.'

'Why do you bring it up now?'

'Brooke is on the curriculum in English at school. It reminded me.' He shrugged. 'I'm okay with it. It seems like a bad dream now, after all this time. Just a bad dream I woke up from and, like a dream, it's fading.'

'That's a good way to think of it.'

He smiled at her and there was mischief in the smile. He glanced again up at the moon and out over the water. 'Where did you send her?'

'What makes you think I sent her anywhere?'

'I just know you did. Where is she?'

'She is somewhere very dark and very cold and very lonely.'

'You're not going to tell me, are you?'

Elizabeth reached for him and ruffled his hair. 'A wicked stepmother needs to keep some things secret, Adam. Otherwise I wouldn't be able to call myself wicked at all.'